Entangled with the Earl

ROGUES OUT OF TIME
BOOK 1

PATRICIA BARLETTA

Published Internationally by
Patricia Barletta
Boston, MA, USA
Copyright © 2025 Patricia Barletta

This is a work of fiction. Names, characters, places, and incidents are either the product of the author's imagination or are used fictitiously. Any resemblance to actual persons, living or dead, or actual events or locales is entirely coincidental.

PRINT ISBN 978-1-7355994-4-1
EBOOK ISBN 978-1-7355994-5-8

Exclusive Cover and Interior Formatting and Design: Joanna D'Angelo

Editor: Joanna D'Angelo

For permissions or inquiries, please contact: patricia@patriciabarletta.com
patriciabarletta.com

PATRICIABARLETTA.COM

This book is dedicated to Joanna D., who has traveled a very bumpy road with me. Thank you.

Entangled with the Earl

ROGUES OUT OF TIME
BOOK ONE

PATRICIA BARLETTA

PATRICIABARLETTA.COM

One

T*HE END.*

Emma Blake sat back and stretched. She'd written the very last word of her historical romance. Her characters' voices were finally silent.

This was her third novel, and with each one, she'd lived through her characters, experiencing their heartaches and loves right along with them. But this story had been special, inspired by the portrait of a woman she had seen in her father's high-end antique shop on Newbury Street in Boston, Massachusetts.

"I'm afraid that is not how it ended."

The voice came out of nowhere. Gasping, she spun around in her chair, goosebumps popping on her arms. "Who's there?" She flung the question into the empty room.

No answer.

Frozen, Emma scanned the space, looking for signs of an intruder — a shadow that shouldn't be there, a billowing curtain where there was no breeze. All she saw was the undisturbed living room in her father's London flat, his *pied-à-terre* when he returned to his birth city on a buying trip for antiques. She'd left Boston to try to escape the grief of her father's sudden death, and had holed up in the flat for the three months she needed to finish her manuscript.

And she was alone.

Of course she was. She must have imagined the voice. Last night, she'd watched the classic movie, *The Ghost and Mrs. Muir*, so materializing spirits and speaking ghosts were probably still bobbing around in her subconscious. But still, that voice sounded very real.

Discombobulated, a bit uneasy, she shook her head at her imagination, rubbed her eyes and turned back to the computer screen. She'd been working nearly non-stop all day after getting the call from her editor that she needed the manuscript *now*, so they could put out ARCs — Advance Reader Copies. On top of that, she'd been writing five to six hours a day for three months straight, and that was bound to make her brain soggy. But she'd been driven to finish the novel, wanting to give the woman in the portrait a happily-ever-after, because the woman's eyes looked sad.

Emma had done some research and learned the subject of the painting was a woman named Elizabeth Sommers, and that she was quite young when she died, only in her early twenties, but that's all she could discover. Emma had decided to write a happy life for the woman, because she wrote romances, and romances had happy endings. Always. So she had given Elizabeth a hero who swept her off her feet and adored her. Emma wasn't going to change a thing in her novel, despite what she'd imagined that voice said, whatever or whoever it was, or where it came from. Because she had fallen in love with her hero right along with Elizabeth.

She scrolled back to the scene where the heroine meets the hero for the first time.

His face was solemn as he reached out to help her stand, but his gray eyes held an amused glint. Placing her hand in his, she felt the restrained power of his hold. With effortless ease, he pulled her to her feet as if she weighed nothing.

Tilting her head back to look up into his face, she saw he was quite handsome, with smoky gray eyes, straight nose, and strong jaw. A curl of black hair had fallen over his forehead and made him look like an impish lad who had just pilfered one of Cook's freshly baked pies. Despite her annoyance at being knocked into the filth of the street, she found she could not deny the smile that curved her lips in answer to the roguish grin that now graced his face.

Yes, she'd created a great "book boyfriend." But that was all he was, a fiction, a made-up man who would never be as handsome or kind or generous or loving as a real-life person. She'd had experience with some of the self-centered ignora-muses on the dating apps, and her last relationship had ended very badly. But her hero was *perfect*. Well, almost. She hoped her readers would fall in love with him like she had.

Just as she was about to save her work, she watched in disbelief as "THE END" disappeared letter by letter. She ground the heels of her hands into her eyes and looked again. The curser flickered with benign menace over the period of her last sentence. She glanced down at the keyboard, then glowered at her fingers. Had she erased those words by mistake? Was she so tired that she couldn't remember? She immediately hit the Undo button, and blew out a breath to see the words reappear.

"No one lives happily ever after," the voice said right next to her.

With a yelp, she shot from her chair. Her heart lurched into overdrive. The voice was definitely male, smooth and deeply melodic. Dreading what she might see, she turned in a full circle and peered around the room.

No one was there.

This was spooky. More than spooky. Weird. Eerie. Maybe even threatening. She grabbed an antique paperweight that sat on her desk. It was a heavy globe of glass the size of her two fists together, with a medallion depicting Venus embedded in the bottom, a knickknack from her father's antique shop, and would make a decent weapon. He had gifted it to her upon the sale of her first book.

Taking two steps forward, she was ready to confront the

intruder. Then she halted, not sure where he might be hiding. Hefting the paperweight, she glared into the room.

"Come out now, or I'll call the police." She edged toward her phone on the table a few feet away.

No one appeared.

No one answered.

Her heart thumped as she swept up the phone. Her hands shook. She took a deep breath as she tried to steady her fingers long enough to punch in the emergency number. But she had a niggling feeling that the police would find that no one had broken into her flat. That idea didn't comfort her at all, because it meant...what? That she was hearing voices that weren't real? That the flat might be haunted?

Both of those options sent chills down her spine. But she'd never heard disembodied voices before, not when her dad would sometimes bring her and her sisters with him on his business trips, and not during the months she'd lived here. Her dad had never spoken of any ghostly manifestation in the flat. Even though she believed in spirits haunting places, nothing like that had ever happened to her. She sent an apprehensive glance around the space, then relief rushed through her when the dispatcher answered.

"This is Emma Blake. I think there's an intruder in my flat." She congratulated herself for sounding so calm. She gave the dispatcher her address and disconnected the call. The police would take care of the intruder.

A soft male chuckle floated to her from the vicinity of the sofa, but no one was there. Of course.

"I must be exhausted," she said aloud, just so she could hear a real voice. "I need a rest, a vacation. That's it. That's all it is. It's just stress. Trying to finish the manuscript. And Dad…"

She swallowed back her grief and took a breath. Her father had been in a catastrophic plane crash nearly six months ago. He'd had his pilot's license and owned a small two-seater plane that he flew to out of state auctions and consulting jobs. The plane had plunged into Cape Cod Bay and his body had never been found. The authorities blamed the crazy currents that ran through the bay. But in a tiny corner of her mind, she always thought of him as alive somewhere, maybe with amnesia, happily living out his life. It was an absurd idea, but it was the only thing that helped her deal with the grief.

He had been a great father, acting as both dad and mom to Emma and her two younger sisters their whole lives, since their mother had died when they were very young. Emma hardly remembered their mother. She had only vague memories of a beautiful, gentle woman who would sing her to sleep. Now she had no father or mother. But she had to move on with her life, and at this moment, she had to deal with whatever was going on in the flat.

With another glance around the empty room, deciding

she was exhausted, she said, "As soon as I send off this manuscript, I'll take a long vacation. Starting tomorrow."

"Not tomorrow," the voice murmured in her ear.

"Yow!" She jumped away. Had she felt his breath? She rubbed her ear and scowled at the air. This was too much. Grabbing her purse and keys, she hurried out into the hall and slammed the apartment door behind her.

Her heart thumped. Her knees turned rubbery. As she leaned against the wall to keep herself upright, she took long deep breaths. The intruder was welcome to whatever he wanted. Except her manuscript. Anything but that. Then she remembered she hadn't saved those last few pages. How could she have been so stupid? The thought of her unguarded computer and the possibility that all her hard work on that unsaved chapter might be erased drew her back. She put her hand on the doorknob.

"Idiot," she mumbled. What if he wasn't after her manuscript or anything else in her flat? What if he was only after her? She released the doorknob, clamped her lips together and rushed downstairs to wait for the police.

A few minutes later, a police car pulled up with lights flashing. The two constables searched the flat, room by room. Of course, they didn't find anything unusual or out of place. Bravely, Emma told them about the voice, and she was grateful that they very politely didn't look at her as if she'd lost her mind. Instead, they suggested that she might have heard voices from the street coming through the window. But all her windows had been shut.

After they left with admonitions to keep her doors and windows locked, she prowled the flat, paperweight in hand. Nothing had changed. Everything was in its proper place. It was the same London flat she'd been living in for the past three months. Her dad's flat.

His bedroom, with a forgotten tie still draped over the closet doorknob.

His chair near the window with the shade of the reading lamp next to it tipped just so.

His favorite brand of tea still in its canister on the kitchen counter.

Maybe it was her dad's ghost who was trying to connect with her. But it didn't sound like her dad and he'd never interfere in her writing. Maybe she was trying to block her grief by staying inside the fictional world she'd created where everything ended happily ever after. Maybe she hadn't really heard a voice. Maybe she was still in writing mode and she was hearing characters in her head.

She drew in a shaky breath, tears stuck in her throat. This was the real world and everything didn't end happily ever after. Her dad had died in a plane crash. One day he was here, and the next he was gone. And she missed him terribly. So yeah, she'd immersed herself in a fictional world that she could control, but the real world wasn't like that. For instance, the voice that had come out of nowhere. Maybe it was some weirdo who had invaded her space.

She couldn't control fate, but she could take control of an intruder in the flat—or whoever had spoken. Gripping the paperweight, she swallowed back her tears, straightened her shoulders, raised her chin, and took three strong steps into the middle of the living room.

"Whoever you are," she announced, "I'm not afraid of you." *Liar.* "And if you touch my computer again, I'll knock you over the head with this." She held up the heavy paperweight.

Right. What if the guy was six-eight and weighed three-fifty? Straightening to her full five-feet-two-and-a-half-inch height, she declared, "And I know karate, too, so don't think I can't defend myself." The self-defense moves she knew could fit on a pinhead, but this guy didn't need to know that.

She glowered at the room, but all she got was silence. A falling feather would have been louder. Either her visitor had left, or he wasn't talking.

She glanced down at the paperweight. What was she thinking? She'd been speaking to thin air. There was no one in the room. She hadn't heard any voice. Her imagination had run wild.

She turned to her computer, re-saved that last chapter, and sent the manuscript off to her editor. "There. Done." As a wave of exhaustion hit her, she headed toward her bedroom. To her fluffy comforter. Soft pillows. And wonderful, glorious sleep. First thing in the morning, she'd make plans for an extended vacation and invite her sisters. And she wouldn't tell a soul about that darn voice.

But she set the paperweight on her nightstand within easy reach. Just to be safe.

EMMA SWAM UP INTO VAGUE AWARENESS FROM A DEEP SLEEP. She rolled over, trying to figure out what woke her. Cracking open her gluey eyelids, she saw the sun peeking through the blinds. With a groan, she burrowed down into the pillow and squeezed her eyes shut.

Her manuscript was done. She'd sent it off yesterday. She could sleep late this morning. And go back to dreaming about her hunky hero.

But a noise from the living room made her eyes pop open. She stayed absolutely still and listened. What was that sound? Was her intruder back? A chill shot down her spine. *Whirr, click-click. Whirr, click-click.* She bolted upright. It was her printer.

She jumped out of bed, dashed into the living room and stopped short. The printer was spitting out page after page. And no one was there.

The voice last night. A man's voice. The intruder. Was he

back? Was he some creepy stalker working remotely? Was he holed up in some empty warehouse and watching her? Had he somehow hacked into every electronic device in her flat?

Black spots swam before her eyes and the room undulated. Collapsing into a chair, she put her head down between her knees before she passed out. After a few deep breaths, after the oxygen and blood reached her brain, she felt better.

While she was upside-down, she gave herself a good scolding. She was being ridiculous. She had forgotten to shut down the computer last night. There'd been a power surge. Or something. There had to be a logical explanation. But the idea of a power surge snapped her head up in panic.

She rushed over to the computer. Not only had she forgotten to shut it down, she hadn't backed up her work. Stupid, stupid, stupid. All those words, sentences, paragraphs, chapters could be dissolved in one flash of an electrical surge. Despite having her manuscript in the Cloud, she worried that she wouldn't be able to retrieve it. And even though she'd sent the manuscript off to her editor, she worried that it hadn't arrived, because she hadn't received a confirmation last night. Maybe the weirdo stalker had wiped it out. Anxiously, she checked her email and saw that her editor had indeed received the story. While the manuscript was printing—it never hurt to have a hard copy—she backed it up again, then puffed out a breath of relief. Her book was safe.

"It's all right," she said aloud.

"I apologize for causing you any difficulty." The voice came from somewhere behind her.

She screeched, shot from her chair, and swung around. Of course, no one was there.

"I wished to see how you made everything end happily ever after," the voice said.

"Who are you?" She was having trouble breathing.

"Him."

"Him?" She squeaked the word.

"Yes, him. The one in your story. Brandon Connaught."

"That's impossible." She felt faint again and grabbed the back of her chair. "You're not really real. You're fiction. I made you up."

"I assure you, I am quite real, or at least, I was at one time." There was a hint of melancholy in his voice.

"So, you're a ghost?" Her question squeaked. Again.

"I prefer spirit," he said.

"But how can that be? I never knew he—you—existed. I made up the story after I saw that portrait of a woman in my father's antique shop." Emma thought she might be having a very realistic dream.

"Ah, yes. The portrait. Elizabeth." He spoke her name in a sorrowful tone.

"Elizabeth?" The question came out in a third squeak. She swallowed and cleared her throat. "You know—knew—the heroine in my story?"

"Of course. Miss Elizabeth Sommers, the woman I was to marry, the subject of the portrait in your father's antique shop in Boston."

"But I made up her character in my story after I saw the painting." Emma was very sure about that.

"Did you?" His tone implied that she was wrong.

"You mean I didn't make it all up?" She was glad she was holding onto the chair. Her stomach felt a bit queasy.

"The mind can do very strange things. Perhaps I'm your muse," he suggested.

She thought about that. Then she straightened as his meaning whammed into her brain. "Are you saying you put thoughts and ideas in my head?"

"In a way."

Okay. Her hero had taken over and written the story for her. Having a conversation with one of her characters was a bit extreme, but when she was writing, they seemed alive. Then reality checked in. What was she thinking? Talking to one of her characters? One of her characters writing the story? Unh-unh. No way. That was just crazy.

But she'd been talking with someone. She was certain of that. Maybe she really was speaking with a ghost. A ghost who claimed to be the hero of her story. Goosebumps popped down her arms and up the back of her neck.

She sank into her chair, her thoughts reeling. Maybe she'd tripped over his name while she'd been doing research and he'd stuck in her subconscious, only to leak out when she was putting words on a page. What if he was the ghost of her hero? What if the character she had created had actually lived during the Regency period in England? The ramifications of speaking with someone who had been alive back then exploded in her brain. She could ask him all sorts of questions.

"This is great!" she enthused. "A historical romance that actually took place! Knowing that the Earl of Cranleigh had a great love in his life and was a *hero* is so exciting."

"A hero?" His voice was rich with amusement. "No. I was most certainly *not* a hero."

"What do you mean?" If he hadn't been a hero, then what had he been? A cad? A blackguard? A villain? Warily, she stood and put the chair between her and the spot where the voice came from. She'd left the paperweight on the nightstand in the bedroom. Damn.

"Miss Sommers and I did not live happily ever after, unlike your story. She was forced to marry my half-brother, that scheming wretch. I was never the Earl of Cranleigh."

If he hadn't been Cranleigh, how had she written him in her book? "Then who were—are— you?"

"I'm afraid you'll have to decide that for yourself."

"How am I supposed to do that?" She started to edge toward her bedroom where the paperweight was. If he was a villain, she needed a weapon to defend herself if he attacked, and the bedroom was closer than the kitchen where the knives were.

"Going after that paperweight?" he asked, amusement rippling beneath his words.

"Ah..." Damn, how did he know that?

"It used to be mine."

Her mouth dropped open and she froze.

"I'm glad you like it," he said. "Miss Sommers gifted it to me. Just before her parents locked her away in her bedchamber and forced her to wed my half-brother."

Sympathy for the woman shut her mouth and she swallowed. "That's awful. It's barbaric."

Before he could respond, a knock sounded at the door to the flat. From the other side, a voice announced, "Flower delivery."

"From an admirer?" The ghost's words held cool curiosity.

"I have no idea who they're from," she said, wondering who could have sent them.

"It's not proper for ladies to receive flowers from strangers," he said. "I shall send the delivery boy away."

"No!" She panicked at the thought of what might happen if the voice — or ghost — or whatever — made his presence known to the unsuspecting young man on the other side of the door. "Don't say a word," she warned as she walked to the door.

"I will be as silent as the grave," he said from across the room.

Obviously, the grave wasn't so silent, because he'd been

talking to her since she finished her manuscript. Ignoring him, she peered through the spy hole. Seeing a scrawny teenager with a long white box in his hands, she undid the two locks on the door, but left on the safety chain, and peered around its edge. The delivery boy stood grinning at her. She was suspicious and feeling vulnerable, especially with an unknown spirit in her living room, because she hadn't buzzed the delivery boy in past the security door to the building.

"How did you get inside?" she demanded.

He shrugged. "Came in with another tenant, didn't I." He shoved the long box at her. "Here you go, then." With another grin, he was gone, not even waiting for a tip.

Relieved the ghost had remained silent, she closed the door, relocked it, and smiled at the unexpected pleasure of the delivery. Who could the flowers be from? She untied the huge red bow and took off the cover. Inside were a dozen yellow roses with a small white card lying on top.

"Do you get flowers often?" His voice came from the middle of the room and held a note of disapproval.

Emma shook her head as she sniffed one of the roses. "Aren't they gorgeous?"

"A bit ostentatious." His voice was a little nearer. "Who sent them?"

"I don't know." She picked up the card.

"*Pemberton*," he read, next to her ear.

Startled, she twitched away and flattened the card against her chest. "Do you mind? This is private."

"Hardly private to receive such a conspicuous gift," the ghost said as his voice moved away.

Emma glanced down at the card again. She had no idea who Pemberton was or why they would be sending her flowers.

From across the room, the ghost said, "My half-brother held the title of Viscount Pemberton before he became Earl."

The coincidence gave her pause. "The one who stole Elizabeth?"

"The very same." His tone was guardedly neutral.

Tiny hairs on the back of her neck stood up. Taking a breath, she tried to make sense of the bizarre situation. Why would Viscount Pemberton be sending her flowers? She was sure she'd never met anyone with a noble title. Was the ghost telling the truth? But what reason would he have to lie? She wished she could see his face so she could know what he was thinking.

Relying on common sense, she said, "Well, I have no idea who Pemberton is. The delivery boy probably mixed up the orders and delivered the flowers to the wrong address." Except her name and address had been on the box.

"Are you sure?"

She narrowed her eyes at the spot where the voice came from. "Are you saying that I just received flowers from a descendant of your brother?"

"Yes." His single word was indisputable.

She carefully placed the card face-down onto the table and shook her head. "No, that's impossible. He can't be a descendant. Why would a descendant of your brother send me flowers?"

Her phone rang before he could answer. The name that came up on the screen was her father's contact in London, Stephen Thrale. She'd had a crush on him for several years, ever since the first time he flew to Boston to consult with her dad, and she had met him several times when she accompanied her dad to London so she could do research.

Stephen was a handsome man in his mid-thirties, suave and debonair, with perfect manners. And he was quite wealthy. They would flirt whenever they met, just for fun, and she'd fantasized about having a relationship with him.

Just after she had arrived in London three months ago, when she was still deep in her grief, she had met him by chance at the Victoria and Albert Museum. He'd asked her to a late lunch that went on for hours. They talked. He sympathized with her grief. They flirted. He invited her back to his flat. By that point, her better judgement had disappeared out the window. And they wound up in his bed about two minutes after they crossed his threshold.

Their relationship blossomed, and she thought she had found Mr. Right. Stephen was attentive and caring and romantic. For about a month.

Emma blew out a breath. She was trying to avoid

thinking about the last time she'd seen him. In his enormous flat. In his enormous bed. Just after they'd spent the night together. Because the last time she'd seen him was the morning after, still tangled in the sheets, when he was on his cell phone talking to the fiancée she didn't know he had.

Being thirty-two years old, she should have had more sense and been more cautious. She thought he was an honorable man, especially as a business associate of her dad, but she had been blinded by the fantasies of her younger self. Embarrassed, hurt, disillusioned, she had pushed that whole month out of her mind. Or tried to. Now, the only fantasy in her life was in her books.

She let the phone ring several times as she tried to decide if she wanted to answer it.

"Can you stop that infernal noise?" the ghost complained.

Huffing an annoyed breath in his direction, she stared at Stephen's name on her phone's screen. Her curiosity at the reason for his call made her decision.

"Hello?" she said in the most impersonal tone she could muster.

Stephen's smooth baritone curled into her ear. "I wanted to see if you received the flowers."

"They were from you?" Surprise and confusion and anger halted her breath for a moment. "Why did you send me flowers?"

"I'm sorry about how things ended the last time I saw you. I'd like to make it up to you." He sounded contrite.

Emma wanted to lash out at him. The last time they'd seen each other was two months ago, when she'd scrambled from his bed after learning who he was talking to on his cell phone. He'd waited two whole months to apologize. The words he'd spouted as he followed her around while she threw on her clothes didn't count.

She'd been insulted and hurt that he thought he could use her to cheat on his fiancée. She had considered him a friend. Her father had relied on his expertise and had been quite fond of him. She didn't want to make things awkward if Maggie, her middle sister who had taken over the antique shop, wanted to continue her business relationship with him. But he had been a first-rate jerk.

"Does your fiancée know you sent me flowers?" she finally asked.

"We are no longer together." His cool words revealed nothing about how he felt about that, or even if he told the truth.

Emma decided she didn't want to know details. Instead she asked, "Why was the card signed *Pemberton*?"

The hesitation before he answered was minuscule, but Emma heard it.

"Yes, sorry about that. I had my assistant order the flowers and she told the florist what to put on the card."

Of course he had his assistant place the order. He

wouldn't have performed such a menial task himself, not even to apologize for seducing her. She pushed away her anger because she needed to verify the truth of her ghost's information. "Is Pemberton your last name? I always thought it was Thrale. Or is that something else you lied about?"

A quick intake of breath from his end, then, "Thrale is my family name. Pemberton is my title."

"Your title?"

"Viscount Pemberton."

His announcement turned her speechless.

At her silence, he said, "I rang you up to ask you to go out to dinner with me."

She nearly threw the phone across the room at his conceited, self-centered audacity. But after taking a breath, she focused on getting information rather than releasing her anger. "Why didn't I know that you are a viscount? Why didn't you tell me? Did my father know you had a title?"

Another tiny hesitation on his end. "Yes. I asked him not to reveal it to anyone."

She felt a tiny sting that her dad knew and hadn't told her. But if Stephen had made the request of her father, then her dad would have kept the secret because he had principles. Unlike Stephen. But the request sounded strange.

"Why?" she asked.

"For privacy." His short answer held a barely audible sigh of vexation, as if he was constantly hounded by the paparazzi.

Okay. She could understand that. Sort of. But why wouldn't he tell her? She nearly asked him, then decided she didn't want to know because she was done with their relationship.

After a pause, he said, "You didn't answer my question. Dinner? This evening?"

No, she did not want to go to dinner with him. She wanted to slap his handsome face. Why did he extend the invitation now, and what was his reason?

"Do you think I'm that easy, Stephen?" she snapped. "Do you think sending me flowers will make up for what you did? You were engaged. You lied. For a whole month."

She sensed his wince through the phone. "I'm sorry. I wish to explain and make it up to you." He paused, then said, "I can tell you about my ancestors. Aren't you always looking to do research?"

He had dangled the perfect bait. Was Stephen the descendant of the ghost's half-brother? If she went to dinner, maybe she could find out for certain. But could she tamp down her anger in order to spend an evening with him to fish for information?

She had to think this through, so she put him off. "I'm running up against my deadline," she lied, but close enough to the truth. "Can I get back to you in a few days?"

"Of course." His tone turned intimate. "I'll be waiting to hear from you. Please don't disappoint me, Emma."

While his last words sounded like a request, she had the

sense they were more of a command, and that added to her anger. After they disconnected, she stared at the phone as her thoughts whirled in her head and her emotions see-sawed. She really didn't want to spend an evening with him. On the other hand, the ghost's tidbit of information about his half-brother intrigued her, so if she went to dinner with Stephen, she might be able to learn more about his ancestor and about poor Elizabeth.

"Was I correct?" The voice spoke right next to her.

She startled. "Will you please stop sneaking up on me?" she snapped and backed away two steps.

"My apologies," he said, sounding not at all sorry. "Did you discover that your admirer is my brother's descendant?"

Emma tried to process what she'd just learned. Stephen was the Viscount Pemberton. That meant that at least part of what the ghost told her was true.

His voice came from across the room. "Ah, I see that you did."

"All I learned is that Stephen is the Viscount Pemberton," she said. "How do I know that you're not making up this story about an evil half-brother?"

She felt his heavy sigh like a chilly, light breeze through the room.

"I suppose I must tell you the rest of my story." His tone was part reluctance and part exasperation.

"The rest—?" She took a breath. What more could he tell

her? What she had learned from him so far had been tragic. But she was curious. "Yes, I would like to hear it."

He was silent for so long that she thought he might have left, gone to wherever ghosts go when they weren't haunting someone. Finally, his voice came from the vicinity of the couch.

"As I told you, Miss Sommers wed my half-brother, because I was not considered Quality."

"Not Quality? But weren't you the son of an earl?"

"Yes. His bastard son." His answer was nearly a hiss. After a short pause, he continued, "I did not inherit the title. My younger brother, that swiving cur, convinced the authorities that I murdered our father. And I was shot in the back, supposedly while trying to escape to the Continent."

"That's terrible!" she sympathized, then sent a suspicious glance in his voice's direction. "Did you?"

"I beg your pardon?"

"Murder your father?"

"Of course I did not!" He sounded quite insulted. "I may have been considered a rake and a rogue, but I certainly was not a murderer."

Emma thought that over.

"You do not believe me," he said.

She was afraid if she admitted that she had doubts, he might get angry. But what could an angry ghost do?

"Would it help if I showed myself to you?" he asked in an equitable tone.

Emma wasn't sure she wanted to see him. Would he be filmy and floaty and see-through and wearing something like a sheet? Would he be horribly decayed with his flesh dripping from him? Would he be desiccated and shriveled like a mummy?

"You can do that?" she asked.

"Of course, if that's what you wish."

"Um..."

Before she could make up her mind, the air seemed to glitter. The sparkles coalesced and he was there, his hip perched on the back of sofa. Unnerved, in shock, she shot from her chair and stumbled back a few steps to put some distance between them.

He wasn't transparent, but he wasn't solid either. He sort of shimmered. His face and hands glowed oddly, the only parts of his skin she could see, because the rest of him was dressed in perfect Regency era clothing — high white collar, intricate cravat, dark blue coat, pale yellow waistcoat, and soft tan leather breeches. Because of the sofa between them, she couldn't see his legs below the knees, but she'd bet any money he was wearing highly polished Hessian boots.

His hair was dark. It could be black. His eyes were gray. They glinted with humor. Straight nose, strong jaw.

Holy smoke!

He looked exactly the way she had described him in her book!

And he was gorgeous.

Two

Emma collapsed onto a nearby chair and tried to catch her breath. This could not be happening. Why was she seeing a character from her story as a ghost?

Covering her eyes, she flailed around for some explanation. Maybe she was still asleep. But she never would have dreamt that Stephen had called. And the flowers on the table were very real. She could smell them. So that left only one option. Her hero was real and a ghost and he was in her living room.

"I need a drink of water," she croaked and tried to get up, but couldn't summon the strength to move.

"Allow me to get it for you," the ghost volunteered.

Peeking through her fingers, she watched him stand and walk toward the kitchen. Good Lord, he was dazzling. Broad shoulders, narrow hips, moving smoothly like an athlete. And yes, he was wearing Hessians.

As he walked into the kitchen, she saw a bright, shimmering light radiating through a small hole in the middle of his back. It was the bullet hole where he had been shot, his essence shining through.

Stunned, she stared at the door to the kitchen while she tried to process what she had just seen. He was the personification of her hero, whom she'd given a happy ending, but the reality was quite different. Her ghost was telling the truth about his death, or at least his version.

She heard several cabinets open and close, then the sound of running water. Moments later, he appeared carrying a glass of water.

"Don't you have any servants?" He held out the glass.

"No, I'm not wealthy." With suspicion, she eyed the glass of water in his hand. It looked odd, sort of shimmery and glowy. "Could you put the glass down there, please?" She pointed at the table next to her.

He set the glass down and moved back to the sofa, but didn't sit. "Not wealthy?" Clasping his hands behind his back, he looked around. "These are certainly very comfortable rooms."

She followed his gaze, noting the high ceiling with its central medallion, corner cornices, and intricate moldings that were very familiar to her. "The building is an old mansion that was divided up into flats, so I only live in a small part," she explained.

"I seem to remember..." He looked around the room once more. "I believe it belonged to a reclusive widow when I was —" He shook his head. "It is of no consequence." His gaze focused on her again. "You must at least have a lady's maid," he persisted.

"No." She turned to study the water.

The glass and its contents had returned to normal as soon as he had set it down and taken his hand away. Maybe it would be all right to drink. Tentatively, she reached out and touched the rim. Nothing strange happened. Bravely, she wrapped her fingers around the glass. It felt normal, cool and hard. She lifted it and swirled the water about. That seemed okay, too. Deciding she had nothing to lose by taking a sip, she closed her eyes, held her breath, and prayed as she tipped the glass to her lips. Relief blew through her when she tasted normal London water.

He peered at her. "Are you feeling better now?"

Her nod seemed to reassure him.

A corner of his mouth twitched up. "Do you know that your eyes turn the most incredible shade of violet when you're upset?"

"You can see that?" She was intrigued.

"Of course. I can see everything you can see." His voice dropped lower. "Maybe even more."

What could he see? Realizing she wore only her pajamas,

she pulled a throw hanging on the back of her chair around her shoulders.

"A woman in your position should at least have a lady's maid."

"A woman in my position?" She squinted up at him. "What position is that?"

"A woman of quality, well-bred, gently reared."

Heat rose in her cheeks at his high opinion. "This isn't the nineteenth century. There are very few people who can afford full-time servants."

"Back in my time, you would have had several servants to wait on you." His intense gaze made her squirm. "I would have made sure of that," he murmured.

Mesmerized by his tone and those gray eyes, she stared at him a moment. She could have fallen into those eyes with no problem. Nope. Not happening.

She blinked and put the glass down. "In your time, I probably would never have met you. You're the son of an earl —"

"A bastard," he interjected.

"And I'm just a commoner." She shook her head. "Never would have happened."

"Why do you think that? People mingle all the time."

She was surprised that a man from his time should be so broad-minded. She had done her research and knew that classes were clearly defined during the Regency period. "Well, in the first place, I'm American. You're

English. And in the second place, my ancestors were poor who had to work hard for a better life. Or so I've been told."

"Stranger things have happened," he said enigmatically.

She stood, oddly unsettled at his implied assumption that they would have been a hot item back in 1814, because he was supposed to be in love with Elizabeth Sommers. But he did admit to being a rake. Instead of some erotic fantasy of a ghost, she focused on what was happening in the here and now.

"That's right," she said. "There are some pretty strange things happening around here. How are you able to carry a glass of water?"

He shrugged. "It is one of my abilities."

"And how can you materialize just like that?" She snapped her fingers to demonstrate.

"I apologize. That must have been quite unnerving."

"You bet it was." Suspicion narrowed her eyes. He looked much too innocent. "If you're going to be hanging around, like that" —she waved her hand at his very attractive and visible form— "then I'm setting up some rules."

A dark brow arched up. "Rules? My dear Miss Blake, I never followed rules when I was alive. Why should I do so now?"

"Because this is my home and I said so." She set her mouth in a determined line.

"Of course. Please forgive me." Placing his hand over his

heart, he bowed. But when he straightened, a corner of his mouth twitched the tiniest bit upward.

Emma scowled, not trusting that apology in the least. "Why are you haunting me?"

He appeared appalled at the idea. "Haunt? I do not haunt."

"Then why are you here?"

"You wrote a story that is not true. Do you not feel guilty about that?" he challenged.

"Guilty!" she sputtered. "Why should I feel guilty? I didn't even know you were a real person until yesterday, when you started talking to me out of thin air. And I'm not sure you didn't make up the whole thing just so you could haunt—ah —visit me."

"I am here to help you fix things," he said, sounding very sure of himself.

His suggestion that he could help solve her problems aggravated her. "Fix what? Everything was great until you showed up."

And that was a big lie. Her former boyfriend was a cheat and a liar. She was thirty-two years old and still living in the apartment above the antique shop where she had grown up. Her father was dead. Her life was a mess. The only thing that had been great was the story she had created, and now a ghost was telling her she had to change it. So, not so great.

He said nothing, his silence indicating that he knew very well she was bluffing.

She sank back into the chair. Instead of arguing about her life, she deliberately misunderstood what he really meant. "The book is only fiction," she argued. "You know, make-believe. Writers take true stories and twist them around all the time, so they'll have happy endings."

"I did not have a happy ending," he said, sounding quite offended.

She winced at his insulted tone. "I'm sorry about that."

"Thank you." His gaze warmed.

Curiosity mixed with sympathy for him. "Why didn't you and Elizabeth run away to Gretna Green to get married? That is, if you don't mind my asking."

"Are you certain you wish to know?"

"Yes, I do."

He stared at her for a moment, his expression so solemn that she felt a tiny chill chase up the back of her neck.

"It's not a particularly pleasant story," he said. "And I am not especially proud of some of the things I did."

"I promise not to make judgments. I just want to know more about you."

Her words appeared to please him, and a small smile curved his lips. "Elizabeth did not seem to mind that she would be married to someone whose father would not acknowledge him. I was quite well off, for I had made some good investments with my winnings at the gaming tables. Of course, her father was not at all pleased with the match. He didn't approve of my gambling and was looking to marry his daughter to nothing less than an earl. Quite frustrating, since I had been trying to force my father to recognize that I was his son and name me his heir." Becoming solemn, his glance slid away. "He kept my mother as his mistress for years, but couldn't bring himself to honor her enough to wed her."

"I'm so sorry."

His gaze rested on her again. "Thank you."

"In my book I made your mother Irish," she put in.

He nodded. "Yes, that was true. Being Irish, she wasn't good enough to be his wife. Elizabeth didn't mind my unfortunate circumstances. I wished to do right by her, so I thought that by having my father acknowledge me, Elizabeth's father would bless our marriage. Of course, my father would not, and her father refused to give his permission, so we had planned to run to Gretna Green. Then she discovered she was going to have my child. She was ecstatic about it. So was I."

He looked away and a muscle jumped in his jaw. "Somehow, my brother discovered our plan. He had always wanted Elizabeth for himself and decided this was his chance. He went to Elizabeth's father, revealed our intention and offered for her hand."

"I bet he made himself appear like the savior of Elizabeth's reputation." She could almost hear his brother's sly, convincing, sympathetic words.

Her ghost nodded. "Elizabeth's father was so angry with

her that he locked her in her room and forced her to marry Stephen."

"Didn't you get to talk to her? Couldn't you have persuaded her to escape from the house?"

"I saw her once, the day before the wedding. By then, she had convinced herself that she was doing the right thing for her family. She was going to tell Stephen after they wed that the child was his. There was nothing I could do."

"So, she married Stephen," she said sadly.

"Yes." His answer snapped out. He was silent a moment, then he took up his tale again. "I had bribed the physician and the midwife to tell me when she delivered. Her labor lasted for two days. She gave me a beautiful son, with black hair and blue eyes." His expression softened, and his lips curved into a smile of remembrance. Then he sobered and turned away.

"I'm so sorry." Emma empathized with his grief. "I got the story all wrong in my book."

He turned back to her with a sad smile. "Yes."

At least he hadn't said, *I told you so.* "What happened to your son?" she asked.

"I met the midwife at the servant's entrance to the estate and I was able to hold the child. He died in my arms."

He focused on the paperweight she had replaced on her desk. She saw him swallow, then clench his jaw. Sympathy for his loss welled in her chest.

"I'm so sorry. That must have been terrible," she said, blinking back tears, his grief echoing her own.

"Yes," he answered without looking at her.

She wanted to comfort him, but didn't know how. Instead, she asked, "Did you stop trying to get your father to acknowledge you?"

Turning to her, he shook his head. "No, never that, because I had a suspicion that Stephen was involved in something very bad, but I could never prove it. He didn't deserve to be earl. About a year later, I discovered an unsigned document naming me as my father's heir and evidence that my brother was involved in some very illegal activities." His face twisted with contempt.

Emma held her breath.

He continued. "My brother learned that I planned to confront our father when he came to London. On the night before I had planned to do so, a lunar eclipse occurred. I knew it was a bad omen. The following day, Stephen murdered our father and made it appear that I had done it, so he would be assured of gaining the title and I would be arrested and hanged. I was caught in the trap. When the authorities arrived, I knew there was no hope of making them believe I was not guilty. I thought if I could get away, I would have time to prove my innocence. I was shot as I tried to escape. By my brother."

Emma gasped. "That's terrible! What a wicked thing to

do!" She shook her head. "But I can't change the ending of my book. It's a romance. It has to have a happy ending."

He studied her a moment, then wandered across the room, stopped after a few steps, and turned back to her. "You can go back, you know."

"Go back where?"

"Actually, to *when.* To my time."

Wait. What? She gaped at him. Had he just told her that she could time-travel? Impossible. No one could time-travel. That was just something that happened in books and movies.

"And, of course, there is that old oak tree in Hyde Park," he added.

"What about it?" She remembered she had seen an ancient, gnarly oak on one of her jogs through the park.

He shrugged as if what he was about to say held no importance. "The tree was in the park when I was alive, and it was ancient then. There's a legend that says the Druids used it to travel to other worlds and times."

Of course. A legend. So not true. Practical, twenty-first century logic took over. "Time-travel doesn't exist," she scoffed.

He just smiled, and his gaze dropped to her wrist. "That's a lovely bracelet you're wearing."

The sudden change in subject made her think the discussion about time-travel was over. She was happy to let it go because it was only fiction. Raising her arm, she let the sapphire and diamond charm in the shape of a flower bud dangle from the delicate, white gold chain around her wrist. "Thanks. The pendant is from an antique necklace that belonged to my mother. My two sisters each have a charm just like it." Emma heaved a sigh. "My mother died when I was very young. I barely remember her."

"My condolences," the ghost said, glancing once again at the charm. Then he turned that intense, gray gaze on her. "Wouldn't you like to go back in time, Emma?"

His question sounded like more than simple curiosity. He had moved closer, and she gazed up at him — all the way up. She surmised he must have been nearly a head taller than most other men of his time. But his quizzical look had morphed into vulnerability. He wanted her to go back to his time. No, more than that. He needed her to go back.

Why? Did he think that if she went back to his time, she could save him from being murdered? That she would be able to stop the wedding between Miss Sommers and his half-brother? She really didn't want to step into that quagmire.

But she couldn't save him because she couldn't go back in time. No one could. The idea of time-travel was appealing to her author brain, but terrifying to her practical side. What if she went back to his time and then couldn't get back to her own? What if by going back, she changed history — her history — and when she returned, everything about her life was different? What if by changing history, she no longer existed? What if he was tricking her into believing he had been framed by his half-brother when he had actually committed the crimes? What if she was dreaming and this entire conversation was only in her head?

"I don't know," she answered both to him and to herself.

"Well, it would be an adventure, would it not?" he suggested with a crooked little smile.

"I guess so." Definitely an adventure, she decided. But a good one or a disastrous one?

"I know you have begun to believe in my innocence and can fix things," he said with assurance. The air around him glittered as he began to fade.

Anxious to have him stay, she jumped from her chair. "Wait a minute. How do you know I can fix things?"

He grinned. "Because you write happy endings." In a twinkle of shimmering air, he was gone.

She stared at the empty space in front of her. What she had experienced during the last twenty-four hours made her head reel. The implausibility of it all was enough to make her crawl back under the covers and pretend it had never happened. But it had. A ghost—her book's hero!—had appeared and then disappeared before her eyes. He had spoken to her, carried on a conversation as if it were the most normal thing to do. It was like something out of the movies. Unreal. Fantastical.

Shaking her head, she muttered, "I definitely need a vacation."

Three

Later that day, Emma jogged through Hyde Park and mulled over Brandon's story. Her instincts told her he was being truthful. She didn't think he had killed his father. After all, he was the hero of her novel. But going back to his time? Impossible.

Her usual route took her past an ancient oak tree that she never paid much attention except that it was enormous. As she approached it, she slowed and peered at its huge, gnarly limbs that overhung the path. Its trunk looked wide enough to hold a whole village of evil spirits. Spooky. But it couldn't possibly be the one her ghost had mentioned that had been alive during the time of the Druids, because that would mean it was thousands of years old. Trees didn't live that long.

She detoured off the path to jog around the massive

trunk. If it held a portal to the past, where would it be? That swirl in the bark? Or that scar down near the root? What was she thinking? Portals through time were a fantasy, something made up by storytellers. The legend Brandon had told about the Druids was just a myth, not truth at all. And the tree was just an ordinary tree, despite its enormous size and eerie form. But an idea for a new historical time-travel romance began to take shape.

As she absently wandered back onto the path, a gust of wind made the large branches overhead dip, nearly brushing her head, and the bracelet with her mother's charm tingled, as if a mild electric current ran through it. Absently, she shook off the weird sensation. But her charm turned hotter. It sparked, fiery and bright, glowing with unnatural light, so dazzling she was blinded. Hissing in pain from the burn, she slapped a hand over her eyes to protect them.

After a moment, the light faded. Slowly, she dropped her hand and glanced around. She expected to see singed grass and crisped leaves. But everything looked normal. Even her charm didn't glow, didn't burn. But her skin still hurt where the charm had brushed against it. What had just happened?

It must have been the sun glinting off something metal. That was the only logical explanation, except she didn't understand why her charm had burned. That was weird.

With a mental shrug, she started jogging again, but after only one step, the bracelet burned and tingled again, more intensely than before. With a yelp of pain, she stumbled back and stepped in a hole. A very deep hole. Crying out, flailing around to catch herself, she seemed to fall forever. Time slowed to a crawl. Everything around her blurred. The hair on her neck and arms stood up. She was going to twist her ankle—or worse.

She landed on her butt. Hard. Her breath whooshed out. She sucked in air, then embarrassed at her clumsiness, she glanced around to see if anyone had noticed her fall. But no one was near. Relieved at that, she scrambled to her feet, and while she rubbed her sore bottom, she scanned the ground for that hole. But the dirt path was smooth and level. Weird.

Why had she fallen? She wasn't usually so clumsy. Her gaze landed on the oak tree, and she blinked as she tried to figure out why it seemed to look different. Was it a bit smaller around the trunk? Didn't that big limb above her head reach all the way across the path before she fell? And wasn't there a flower garden in the middle of the grass over there? Because no flowers bloomed anywhere nearby.

As she tried to figure out what had happened, galloping hoof beats approached. A pair of black horses pulling a curricle—a curricle?—raced around a curve in the path and bore down on her. Transfixed, she stared. Her brain told her she needed to move, to jump out of the way. But her feet remained glued to the path. She froze.

The curricle was approaching fast. Too fast. She could feel the vibration of the horses' hooves hitting the ground, heard their breath. Holy smoke! She was going to get run over!

"Get out of the way!" the driver yelled.

With a shriek, she jumped. But not fast enough.

One of the horses grazed her and she careened into the side of the curricle as it sped past. She flew through the air and landed with a thud on the grass. The wind was knocked from her lungs and her senses spun. Sprawling face down, she gasped in air and tried to gather her wits. Slowly, she took inventory of all her body parts. Toes, feet, legs, fingers, hands, arms, head, and everything in between. Nothing seemed to be broken. But everything hurt.

A string of profanity interspersed with commands to the horses to stop came from farther down the path. Feet thumped to the earth and running footsteps approached. The driver knelt beside her. She felt a gentle touch to her shoulder.

"Are you all right?" he asked. "Are you alive? Please, don't be dead."

With a groan, she rolled onto her back and opened her eyes. Everything was blurry. A man bent over her.

"I think I'm alive," she said.

"Thank the good Lord," he whispered, then straightened up. "Dammit, woman! Don't you know enough to get out of the way of galloping horses?"

Her sight cleared. She blinked. And gulped. Her lungs stopped working. Because kneeling over her, looking annoyed and concerned all at the same time, was Brandon, her ghost, her historical romance hero, in the flesh.

EMMA CLOSED HER EYES, DREW A DEEP BREATH, COUNTED TO ten, then slowly opened them again, because she was sure she was hallucinating from her fall. But no, her story's hero was still kneeling beside her. Same gray eyes, same strong jaw, and dark hair beneath his top hat. But not shimmery. Was he alive? No, he wasn't. She was merely in a very real dream.

Or was she? She had to find out. She poked him in the chest. He seemed solid. Then she touched his cheek, just to make sure. His skin felt warm. And his eyes narrowed. Okay, he was really irritated. She didn't think he'd be like that in her dream.

"Brandon?" Her question was hesitant. She wasn't sure she wanted to know that this was the flesh and blood version of him. Because the reason for that terrified her.

Confusion creased his forehead. "Have we met? Last night perhaps? I know I was rather foxed, but I did think I spent the night alone."

She noticed his bloodshot eyes then, a sure sign of a hangover. She didn't think ghosts could get hangovers. And he wouldn't have a hangover in her dream. Besides, he'd felt solid when she poked him. He wasn't all shimmery and ghostly. So he was real. Still alive. He hadn't been shot yet.

Her breath halted. She had to be dreaming. Because if she wasn't, that meant she was in the past. Over two hundred years in the past. But that was impossible. Wasn't it?

She fought down the panic that threatened to overwhelm her and concentrated on the immediate present. Brandon looked terrible, pale, with dark smudges beneath his eyes. She surmised he was still mourning the loss of Elizabeth to his brother with drink and gambling. And probably women.

Concerned for his future, she scolded, "You can't keep drinking to drown your heartache, you know."

His eyes narrowed. "What do you know about my heartache?"

"Nothing." She answered quickly before she had to explain something even she didn't understand. "Just a guess. Please, help me up."

He steadied her as she climbed to her feet. A sharp pain shot through her right ankle, and she grabbed his arm to keep from toppling over. Her knees were skinned and bleeding, a large patch had been ripped from her leggings, and she had a bump on her head the size of an egg. But she was alive.

Trying to get her bearings, she glanced around and saw the curricle stopped a little way down the path. The horses were standing patiently, waiting for their driver to return. One of them munched on leaves from a nearby bush. The animals were real. The curricle was real. The pressure of Brandon's hand beneath her elbow was real. That wooziness washed over her again, this time much more strongly than before.

As her knees began to buckle beneath her, she muttered, "Maybe I'd better sit for a minute."

He eased her down onto the grass. With a groan, she let her head fall forward onto her knees. She sucked in deep breaths and tried to decide whether to cry, laugh, or scream hysterically.

"What year is this?" she mumbled, not sure she wanted an answer, but at the same time, needing to know.

Sounding a bit befuddled at her question, he said, "1814, the fifty-fourth year in the reign of King George the Third, in the Regency of George, Prince of Wales."

His answer didn't really shock her. All the same, she was very glad she was sitting down. Some small part of her brain had accepted that, as soon as she recognized him in the flesh, she had traveled through time. How had that happened? It wasn't possible. But Brandon was living proof that she had.

Her heart raced as panic set in. How was she ever going to get back to her own time? What about her sisters? They'd be worried when they didn't hear from her and realized she had disappeared. What would happen to her book? What if she could never return?

She forced air into her lungs. One problem at a time.

Maybe she could figure out what brought her to this time and use it to transport her back to the twenty-first century.

She raised her head. Brandon's expression was a cross between concern and annoyance. Those gray eyes—bloodshot gray eyes—weren't glinting with mischief at the moment.

"Are you feeling better?" His tone held a hint of impatience.

"Yes, thank you."

"Would you care to stand now?" He sounded testy, not at all how she had portrayed him in her book when he had knocked her heroine into the street. She had written him as gracious, and polite, and just a bit mischievous.

"Am I keeping you from an important engagement?" she asked coolly, annoyed at his exasperation and disappointed at his less than gallant manner. He'd just nearly run her over. He could at least be patient.

"Not in the least. I always drive my horses as if I am trying to break my neck." His tone was drily sardonic.

She raised her eyebrows at him.

He sighed, pulled off his hat, and ran his hand through his hair, tousling it out of its carefully arranged style. "Actually, I was on my way to my solicitor's." Shrugging, he said, "I'll send a message that I'll meet with him later." His gaze appraised her thoughtfully. "How do you know my name? I cannot remember being introduced."

Stumped by his question, she floundered around for an

answer. Obviously, she couldn't tell him the truth because he'd think she was deranged. "Um, someone must have told me." As soon as she stopped talking, a flush heated her face. Her answer implied that she'd seen him and been interested enough to ask who he was.

His annoyed manner dropped away, interest sparked in his eyes, and a small, pleased smile curved his lips. "Then allow me to introduce myself properly. I am Brandon Connaught, at your service." He bowed, and when he straightened, his look was expectant.

"Miss Blake," she offered, remembering the proper form for the eldest sister in a family. "Miss Emma Blake," she added, and extended her hand.

He cradled it gently and smiled. "I am very pleased to meet you, Miss Emma Blake."

That smile did something shivery to her insides, not to mention what the touch of his hand did. His physical presence was much more potent than his impression as a ghost. He was hot. Sexy hot. No, no, no. Couldn't think that.

She had to be having some reaction from traveling through time. Her story was still in her head, so naturally, she'd have an intense response to him. But she had to focus. Figure out how to get back to her own time. Learn why she had ended up in the past. With her romance hero. And get some medical attention. Not necessarily in that order. Slipping her hand from his grasp, she tried to stand, but the pain in her ankle made her land back on her butt.

"Allow me to help you," he said, holding out his hand.

Eyeing that large, tanned hand with its long fingers, she hesitated. Accepting his help meant touching him again, and the first time she'd put her hand in his had been a bit unnerving. She decided she was being silly. His touch hadn't really affected her. Just a reaction to traveling through time. And she needed help. She nodded.

He took both her hands and pulled her effortlessly to her feet. Just like in her novel. The similarity to what she had written made her head spin. But no roguish grin graced his face. His smile had faded and he looked quite solemn. What was he thinking? Since he wasn't a character from her book, she couldn't read his mind, which was frustrating.

She ignored the desire to hold onto him and instead hobbled back a step, as she tried to put most of her weight on her uninjured foot. Seeing him in the flesh was unnerving enough. Touching him really messed with her head. This was Real Brandon, not Book Brandon, or even Ghost Brandon.

She was intrigued by meeting her romance novel hero. More than intrigued. Befuddled. Amazed. Stupefied. How had she been able to write such an accurate description of him? Had the ghost been telling the truth when he said he'd helped her write her book?

The answers to those questions would have to wait, because she was terrified at finding herself in a different century. She had to find the portal that sent her here and get back to her own time. Suddenly panicked, she glanced around wildly, trying to orient herself after being sideswiped by his curricle. Where had she been standing when she was dragged through time? There, under the huge oak, that was still enormous, but not quite so big as in the twenty-first century.

On a mission, despite her throbbing ankle, stinging knees, and aching head, she limped to the tree. She remembered stepping in a hole. But where was it? She searched the ground beneath the branches, around the trunk, and out on the dirt path. But there was no hole. And her pendant wasn't tingling or sparking.

She shook it. Maybe it needed a nudge to wake up. Then she rubbed it between her fingers. Nothing happened. It remained just a pendant, beautiful, but normal. After several minutes, she gave up. Her arm dropped to her side.

Dismay draped over her like a wet towel. With a sigh, she accepted the truth. She was stuck in 1814.

Oh, crap.

BRANDON WATCHED AS THE WOMAN—EMMA, MISS BLAKE— hobbled about beneath the tree, and he wondered at her abrupt appearance in the middle of the path. He was sure no one had been in the way when he first rounded that curve. Racing through Hyde Park was frowned upon, but it was the quickest way to his destination. He'd been awakened by his valet who informed him he was quite late for the appointment with his solicitor to investigate another avenue to gain his rightful title. That objective was just about the only impetus to get him out of bed before noon, especially after a long, profitable night at the gaming tables and an over-indulgence in drink.

He felt a trifle guilty about nearly running her over, but what in the world was she doing in the middle of the bridle path? She should have moved out of the way when she saw him. Her clothing was quite scandalous, revealing every lovely curve. He'd never seen the like, not even in Mrs. Tavistock's establishment where the girls were always dressed in the most provocative fashion. Perhaps her clothing had been torn from her when she ran into his curricle and what was left were undergarments, although that seemed highly unlikely. And he'd never seen undergarments like hers in any of his liaisons with women.

He rubbed a hand across his forehead as he tried to ease the throbbing behind his eyes and come to terms with the unusual situation. Perhaps he should look for the rest of her clothes. But the vision of her limping about beneath the huge oak kept him riveted. Who was she and what was she doing alone in Hyde Park? She was well-spoken and mannered, and appeared genteel, so she should have had a companion. But no one else was nearby, so no sign of a companion.

While he was annoyed that he would be forced to postpone the meeting with his solicitor, he couldn't drag his gaze away from the woman. Her hair, a rich, dark brown with reddish hints, was scraped back from her face and tied into something resembling a luxurious horse's tail. Her eyes were a startling blue, about the same color as the sapphire he noticed dangling from her wrist. Her cheekbones were high and her lips were plump, although a bit pale after running into him. She was quite lovely, despite the smudges of dirt all over her.

Something made him want to help her. He wasn't quite sure why she might need help, but she seemed a bit lost, beyond the shock of her tumble. Perhaps she was a demimondaine and had run away from her protector, so she had nowhere to go. He was quite agreeable to stepping into the breach, if she were amenable.

After losing Elizabeth, he was done with love. He had managed to tamp down the pain into a tiny, hard nugget inside his chest and ignore it. When he wanted the companionship of a woman, he visited Mrs. Tavistock's Green Door. Having a mistress would be rather more convenient than visiting the brothel.

As Miss Blake turned back to him, he didn't wish to appear to be staring, so he peered around at the ground as if looking for something. But he was very aware of her interested gaze on him. And that made him smile.

EMMA WAS FLUMMOXED AT NOT FINDING ANY HOLE OR PORTAL that would take her back to her own time. Now what was she going to do? She had no place to live, and she knew no one, except for Brandon. But she didn't really know him, because she'd only met his ghost.

Panic tightened her chest. Supporting herself with a hand on the tree trunk, she fought for breath. She sucked in air and slowly let it out. Then again, and again. In and out. As her breathing calmed, her brain started working. Why was she in the past? In all the time-travel stories she'd read, someone was sent to the past for a reason. Why had she been sent back in time?

Her gaze flicked to Brandon, who stood watching her and no doubt thought she was acting weird. Ghost Brandon had told her that the ending of her story was wrong. What if she had been sent back to fix it? What if she could give him and Elizabeth a happy-ever-after ending?

A nebulous plan began to form in her head. But in order for it to work, she had to stay close to him. Somehow, she had to get Brandon to take her home with him. When she glanced his way again, he appeared to be searching for something.

"What are you looking for?" she asked.

He continued to scan the ground. "Where are the rest of your clothes?"

"The rest?" She checked her tee shirt and leggings. Nothing was missing, except for that piece torn from her leggings. "This is all I've got."

He stopped short in his search and stared at her. "Good God, woman, you cannot wander about London like that no matter what your profession."

Still thinking in twenty-first century mode, she said, "These aren't my professional clothes." She'd never show up to a conference, book signing or reading in running clothes, although the idea tempted. "But when I'm working—"

He held up his hand to silence her. "Please spare me the details. Even though some may have another opinion, I do still think of myself as a gentleman. I do not consider it any of my business to pry into what you wear—or don't wear—as you make your living."

Confusion wrinkled her brow. Then she realized what profession he thought she pursued. Heat rose in her cheeks. "I am not a—a—" She tried to think of the correct word for the time. "I'm not a doxy."

"Of course you are not." His quick agreement implied just the opposite.

She came up with another word. "I'm not a Cyprian. Really, I'm not."

He looked skeptical.

"I'm an author," she explained. "I write books. You know, like Jane Austen."

"Yes?"

He still didn't believe her. Of course. In 1814, Jane Austen was writing anonymously, so he didn't know who she was.

He shook his head. "Whatever you are or whatever you are not, you simply cannot traipse about London like that." His gesture took in her whole running outfit.

She wasn't going to convince him, not dressed as she was in tee shirt and leggings. And since she seemed to be stuck in the nineteenth century, at least for now, she had only one alternative. "Okay. Could you help me get some clothes, please?"

His brows shot up, then slammed together in annoyance. "I am not in the habit of clothing every young woman who happens to run into me in the park."

With a scowl, she said, "Do a lot of young women run into you in Hyde Park? And for the record, *I* did not run into you. *You* ran into me."

Before he had the chance to respond, the sound of hoof beats approached from around the corner. "Brandon! Darling!" He swung around to face the newcomer, and she caught a glimpse of an attractive woman on a horse before he pushed her behind him.

"Arlene," he greeted the woman with a quick bow. "This is a surprise."

"A pleasant one, I hope," Arlene purred as she held out her hand to him.

"Always," he murmured, as he took her hand and kissed it.

Arlene's gaze landed on Emma. The woman's eyes widened as she took in Emma's running clothes. "Oh my," she murmured, then her gaze narrowed slyly. "And who is this creature?"

Emma took offense at the woman's condescending tone, despite knowing that she stepped beyond propriety with her unusual clothing and by being alone with Brandon. The woman seemed to be Brandon's friend, so she decided to be nice.

Limping forward, she smiled brightly. "Hi. I'm Emma Blake. From America."

"My cousin," Brandon added.

Emma bit her lip in pleased surprise at his addition. By claiming her as a relative, he was throwing a protective shield over her.

Arlene's forehead wrinkled, then her mouth pursed in distaste. She turned her lovely dark eyes on Brandon. "Darling, you never told me you had a cousin living in America."

He threw a glance in Emma's direction. "Yes, well, she's just arrived in London." To Emma, he said shortly, "This is Arlene, Lady Farley."

Arlene ran a cool gaze over her. "Women dress very strangely in America. Is this the normal attire for a ride through the park in America? In your—ah—whatever do you call those?"

"No." Brandon answered quickly as he took off his coat and threw it around Emma's shoulders.

"Yes." Emma answered at the same time. "We find this is much more comfortable than frocks and petticoats." She pulled his coat close around her, but the front was a cutaway, so despite its large size, it didn't do much to hide her legs.

"But how immodest!" Arlene's eyes opened wide in practiced surprise.

"Oh, that's no problem." Emma embroidered a story. "You see we have city ordinances that close the parks to men during certain hours of the day so we women can enjoy the freedom of walking about in breeches."

"How extraordinary." Arlene studied her a moment, then with a sniff said, "We have no such ordinances in London. You might wish to dress more modestly here according to our custom." She turned to Brandon. "Darling, the *on-dit* making the rounds this morning is that you destroyed a certain baronet at the tables last night."

He shrugged modestly, but a corner of his mouth tugged upwards. "The cards happened to fall in my favor."

"I heard the stakes included a tin mine up north," she purred. "Bravo."

"My skill at cards far exceeded the baronet's," he said.

"Skillful at so many things," Lady Farley murmured.

Her suggestive comment made Emma wonder how intimately she knew Brandon.

Lady Farley tugged on her horse's reins. "I must be off. So lovely to meet you Miss Bridgeley," she said with a nod to Emma. Then with a warm smile to Brandon, she said, "Delightful to run into you."

"My pleasure," he answered with a charming smile.

Turning her horse, she cantered off.

When she was out of earshot, Brandon asked, "From America?"

"Yes. From Boston, actually." Then she countered, "Your cousin?"

He raised a cool brow. "Would you have preferred her to draw her own conclusions about seeing you alone with me and in those clothes?"

She studied him a moment as the implications of his question ran through her head. Gossip. Bad reputation. Assumed to be a member of the demimonde. "Thank you for protecting me."

With a nod, he mused, "Boston has some very strange customs. I hope you don't mind being my cousin."

Grinning, she said, "Not at all. I couldn't come up with anything to explain why we were alone. I'd just nearly been run over."

He sighed and ran a hand through his hair again. "My

apologies for that. May I drive you someplace? Where are you staying?"

His question posed a problem. The flat where she was living in the twenty-first century belonged to that reclusive, wealthy widow in the nineteenth century, so she couldn't go there. The logical place for her to go was an inn, but she couldn't dredge up the name of a single inn she had read about in her research. Besides, she had no money. And if she was going to give Brandon and Elizabeth a happy ending, she had the feeling that she needed to stay with him. She hadn't worked out the details yet, but her writer instincts told her to stay close. Maybe if she pretended amnesia, he'd take her to his house.

"Ah..." She gave him a blank stare. "I don't remember."

"Your companion must be frantic."

"Companion?" She blinked.

"Don't you remember your companion?" he asked.

Emma shook her head and bit her lip. But she knew that every well-bred lady traveled with a companion. Except those who time-traveled.

"Very well. Perhaps Mistress Dumfey has available space in her rooming house," he said.

The last place she wanted to be was in a rooming house. How would she be able to help him? Besides, she'd be all alone, with no clothes and no money. She had to get him to take her home with him. With a groan, she put her hand to her head. "I don't feel very well." Her ruse had to look good, so she swayed back and forth. And her head really was throbbing.

Brandon put a hand beneath her elbow to steady her. "Perhaps you should sit down."

As he began to guide her to the grass, she let out a yelp. "Ow! My ankle!"

Without warning, he scooped her up into his arms. "You need a physician."

Ignoring the strength of his arms and the hard muscles of his chest and his scent of spicy lime, Emma tried to remember the type of medicine practiced in the nineteenth century. Did doctors still bleed people? Did they still use leeches? Did they still diagnose based on the humors of the body? That was one area of the nineteenth century that she hadn't researched very thoroughly. Few characters got sick or injured in her historical romances.

She squirmed. "No, I'm fine."

"You are not." His blunt rebuttal dared her to disagree.

She argued anyway. "Yes, I am. Really. I don't need to see a doctor."

He sighed as if she had provoked him to the edge of his patience. "Miss Blake, you have nearly fainted and you are barely able to walk. You seem unable to remember where you are staying or who accompanied you on your journey to England. You sustained injuries because you ran into my curricle."

"*You* ran into *me*," she corrected again through gritted teeth.

"Yes, well, however you view it, the point is that you are injured, and it is my responsibility to assure myself that you are safe and well." Without waiting for an answer, he strode to his curricle and plopped her on the seat.

She liked the fact that he wanted to care for her, but she certainly didn't want him leaving her with strangers. Real Brandon seemed much bossier than her Book Brandon. No wonder Ghost Brandon was so pushy about changing her story.

"Where are we going?" she asked, watching him walk around to the other side of the curricle.

"My house," he said shortly. "My housekeeper, Mrs. Porter, can care for you until your memory returns."

"Okay," she agreed meekly. "Thank you."

She had achieved exactly what she wanted. She was going home with him. All she had to do was stay with him until she could figure out how to save Elizabeth and how to get back to the twenty-first century.

He climbed up beside her and snapped the reins to get the horses moving. As they rolled past the ancient oak tree, she peered at the ground and tried to find that elusive hole, but she saw nothing except the dirt of the path below the curricle and the grass. And her pendant remained cool and normal-looking. A surge of anxiety rose up in her chest. How was she ever going to get back to her own time? She'd never see her sisters again. She'd lose her book contract. Worries piled up in her head like a stack of cards.

Emma glanced around as they exited Hyde Park. Carriages, sedan chairs, riders on horses, messengers and delivery boys, shoppers, and people merely out for a stroll clogged the street. The sounds were very different from the traffic noises of her own time. Instead of car engines and honking horns and squealing brakes, she heard the clatter of wheels on cobbles and the neighing of horses and the clip-clop of hooves. The shop fronts were small and quaint, no huge expanses of plate glass. Fascinated and distracted from her dark thoughts, she drank it in. Everything she had researched for her books was here before her.

Maybe the way to help Brandon and Elizabeth was hidden in the book she just wrote. She just had to think about it when her head didn't throb and everything else didn't hurt. Then she'd be able to return to her own time. Her anxiety eased away.

As she glanced from one side of the street to the other, she took surreptitious peeks at Brandon. Intrigued and dumbfounded at finding herself sitting next to her novel's hero, she wondered how closely Real Brandon compared to her fictional version. She'd already discovered that he was more masterful than Book Brandon. His profile was strong and very attractive as he concentrated on driving his horses, this time at a sedate pace. The pull of his magnetic presence was undeniable. He was a handsome, charming, real-life version of one of her heroes. But was he truly the living, breathing Brandon who had become her ghostly Brandon?

Of course, he was. He looked the same. He sounded the same. On the other hand, she was disoriented from her fall and finding herself in a time very different than her own. So maybe he just seemed to be the same. With her throbbing ankle, her stinging knees and her pounding head as distractions, she couldn't concentrate. She would figure it out later.

Then her stomach rumbled, reminding her she hadn't had breakfast. She covered it with her hand, as if that would silence the noise.

His lips curved in a smile. "I might be able to prevail upon my cook to prepare a nuncheon. Perhaps that might aid the return of your memory."

"Oh, that is kind of you. I hope my memory returns soon." She forced optimism into her voice as she wondered how long she could keep up her charade. She'd worry about telling him the truth later.

Four

Brandon concentrated on guiding the horses as they wound between carriages and around pedestrians, but his thoughts kept returning to the woman beside him. She was lovely, with her dark, luxurious hair and deep blue eyes that were nearly violet. He tried not to think about her shapely legs revealed by the form-fitting pantaloons she wore, for he had been raised a gentleman, despite occasionally not acting as such.

Her clothes were strange, especially her shoes, and her mannerisms and speech were odd. Perhaps what she said about being allowed to romp, wearing practically nothing, through the city parks in Boston was true, but he had never heard anyone who had returned from America relate such a thing. That tidbit of scandalous gossip would have definitely made the rounds at his club and in the scandal sheets. Was she lying?

Perhaps she was not someone's cast-off paramour. Perhaps she had just arrived from America and become lost. Certainly running into his curricle and the resultant bump on her head could scatter her thoughts and cause her to forget where she was staying in the city. But even as he came up with possibilities, his thoughts and doubts whirled in his head.

He felt terrible for nearly running her down and causing her injuries. On the other hand, if he had not, then he never would have met her. And that would have been a sad thing, indeed. She intrigued him. Her spirit attracted him. She did not crumple into a helpless heap when she couldn't remember where she was staying or whom she was with.

What was he thinking? He should have driven her to Mrs. Dumfey's and had that woman look after her. Instead, he was taking her to his home, a hare-brained idea if ever there was one, but the urge to care for her had overcome his good sense. After calling in the physician for her, he would send her on her way as soon as she was well enough.

He was still grieving over Elizabeth, his love, and their child who had died. If she hadn't been forced to wed his sneaky half-brother, she might still be alive. Her death had nearly broken him. And her labor to deliver the child that was his had come nearly a month before she was due. A suspicion that Stephen might have laid hands on her and caused the early labor had been nagging at him. When the midwife placed the babe in his arms, she mentioned a dark bruise on Elizabeth's side that might have precipitated the premature birth. His hands tightened on the reins.

The woman beside him gasped, and he realized he had nearly run them off the road and into a couple strolling the walkway. After getting the horses under control, he drew in a breath and concentrated on his surroundings. He had to stop thinking about Elizabeth and focus. His goal now was to get his father to acknowledge him and wrest their father's title from his brother's clutches. And get the woman beside him back to where she belonged with her companions.

He glanced sideways at her. She clutched the edge of the seat with one hand and the side rail with the other, as if she were afraid she would fly off into space at any moment. Had she never ridden in a curricle before? She seemed dazed, but she might still be reeling from running into him. Yet her wide-eyed curiosity about her surroundings seemed to suggest that she had never seen the bustle of London before. Perhaps she was telling the truth about coming from America. Her accents and mannerisms certainly indicated such.

He couldn't stop wondering about her, and imagined she would be striking when she was properly attired. Her pouty lips appeared very kissable, and he had the outrageous desire to kiss them. No, he was not going kiss her or even think about it. She was injured. Why was he having such thoughts about this woman? Mrs. Tavistock's girls served him well enough when he felt the need for release. And he never had any desire to kiss them. He shifted on the seat.

Whoever she was, he decided he would stay away from her and leave her in the care of his housekeeper. He did not want a woman cluttering up his life. The loss of Elizabeth had been too wrenching, and he never wanted to feel that pain again.

With that decision made, he tried to concentrate on guiding the horses, but he was very aware of the woman with her strange attire and quick insight seated next to him.

And he always did have a soft spot for strays.

EMMA KNEW SHE COULDN'T PRETEND AMNESIA FOREVER. SHE had to think of a plausible story about her arrival in London. Maybe she'd be able to get back to her own time before she needed to concoct a story. If she told Brandon the truth, that she was from the future, would he believe her? Or would he think she was a charlatan, or worse, that she was deranged? She would have to decide what to do soon, but despite her conundrum, she drank in the nineteenth century as they rode along.

They had exited Rotten Row in Hyde Park onto Park Lane. Fashionable houses were interspersed with shops along the road. Brandon turned off onto Curzon Street, and Emma gawked at one house after another. Then they turned onto Chesterfield Street. As they passed No. 4, she gasped.

"That's Beau Brummell's house!" She craned her neck to keep the stately black door and entrance in view as they sped past. If she were actually in 1814, then the person who set the fashion for men was still alive. He might walk out his door at any moment.

"Yes," Brandon said with a tinge of distaste. "Are you acquainted with him?"

"No," she said. "I've only heard of him."

"Of course. Everyone has." A corner of his mouth compressed. "A bit high in the instep, if you ask me."

"You know him?" If she could meet Mr. Brummell, she could question him in depth and add all sorts of unknown tidbits to her next book.

"He belongs to my club." Brandon's flat tone indicated he wasn't a fan of the man. He glanced at her. "Your memory seems to be quite clear, except for the name of your companion and where you are staying."

Emma fidgeted. She had to keep him from getting too suspicious about where she came from. No, about *when* she came from.

"Yes, that's very strange, isn't it?" she agreed. "I hope I remember everything soon. I don't want to impose on your hospitality."

"Don't worry about that," he said. "I'm sure your memory

will return once you convalesce from your fall." He threw a smile in her direction.

Emma forced her lips into an upward curve, but she had misgivings about the welcome she'd receive from his house-keeper, Mrs. Porter. After all, she was an unmarried and unchaperoned lady entering an unmarried gentleman's house.

They finally arrived before a large terrace house on Grosvenor Square, a very fashionable address, both in 1814 and Emma's own time. As they rolled to a stop, a footman emerged from the house and held the horses while Brandon jumped down from the curricle. The elegant, black front door with lovely fan light above and a distinctive oak tree doorknocker was held open by a plump, matronly woman in a white mobcap, and a high-necked, long-sleeved dress of dark gray covered by a starched, white apron. A bunch of keys dangled at the end of a chain that was attached to the waistband of her apron. Her expression was a study in neutrality.

"Miss Blake has had an accident and will be staying with us a while, Mrs. Porter," Brandon said, as he walked around the curricle to help Emma down. "Please send for Dr. Beech, and if it's not too much trouble, some light refreshments served in the small drawing room."

"Of course, sir," Mrs. Porter agreed.

"I really don't think I need a doctor," Emma protested, ill at ease being the center of attention. She could feel the woman's gaze on her, and it made her want to twitch uncomfortably. Trying to ignore it, she stepped down from the curricle and a sharp pain shot through her ankle.

"Oh!" Losing her balance, she fell into Brandon's arms. "I'm so sorry. My ankle. I can't seem to walk on it."

"I have you," Brandon said and swept her up into his arms. "You most certainly do need a doctor." He turned those incisive gray eyes on her.

She was caught in that gaze, for some reason unable to look away.

"If you put your arm about my neck, I think you'll be more secure," he murmured.

Realizing she was staring, Emma blinked, pretended he didn't affect her in any way, and did as he suggested. On the one hand, being carried by a handsome man as if she weighed nothing more than a feather made her giddy. On the other hand, she barely knew him, despite conversing with his ghost in her time. But he smelled divine, like spicy lime, and she surreptitiously sniffed it in, secretly wanting to bury her nose in his neck.

He strode to the front door. As they passed Mrs. Porter, the woman's glance strayed to the curricle. "Is there baggage to come, sir?" she asked.

"Not at this time, Mrs. Porter," he said in a tone that warned no more questions should be asked.

Emma ducked her head to avoid the searching gaze of the housekeeper. Mrs. Porter's mouth thinned. Obviously, the woman wasn't thrilled to see Brandon carrying a lady dressed in scandalous attire and with no baggage. Emma reminded herself that she was going to have remember all the rules from her research and follow them.

He carried her up the stairs and into a small drawing room. The walls were covered in grass-green silk damask, and the floor displayed a carpet with a gold floral pattern. Two wing chairs were placed on either side of the coal-burning hearth, and a small round table stacked with books sat near a window. From her experience growing up as the daughter of an antique dealer, she knew the furnishings in the room had been constructed by master craftsmen. In another two hundred years—in her time—they would be valuable antiques.

After setting her down in one of the wing-backed chairs by the hearth, Brandon left for a few moments, then returned with a dark blue, brocade banyan, a man's fancy bathrobe, to put on over her jogging clothes.

"I thought this might protect your modesty," he said as he held it out.

She handed his coat back and slipped on the banyan. The material against her bare arms was heavy, sensuous, rich, not at all like the mundane, raggedy, terry cloth robe she owned back home. And it held his scent. She sniffed it in.

He lifted her injured foot and placed it gently on a footstool. "These shoes are quite unique. I've never seen their like before. Where did you find them?"

Emma glanced at her computer-designed, arch-supported, air-cushioned, aero-dynamically correct, twenty-first century sneakers. "Oh, they sell them all over America." She gave an airy wave of her hand, then quickly changed the subject as she saw a couple of maids scurrying back and forth past the open door. "Is something going on?"

"They are preparing a room for you. I thought you might like to freshen up," he said. "I hope you don't mind."

"Thank you," she said, embarrassed that she probably smelled disgusting after her jog and fall in the dirt.

A knock came at the door, and when he turned to answer, she sniffed her arm pit. Yikes! She needed a bath, and Brandon had been too much of a gentleman to say anything.

A footman entered bearing a tray filled with cold smoked salmon, biscuits, cheese, jellies, and scones. Another footman followed with tea. As the two servants arranged the snacks and tea, Brandon sat in the chair across from her and stretched out his legs.

After the footmen had left, he motioned to the food. "Please, help yourself."

Emma immediately started piling a small plate with food,

and tried not to gobble everything down. After all, she was supposed to be a refined lady, but she was really hungry.

After a moment, he asked, "Why are you visiting London?"

Startled at his abrupt query after being lulled by his courtesy, she blurted, "What?"

"Is that missing from your memory as well?" His words held an edge, as if he didn't believe her loss of memory.

She swallowed the scone with strawberry preserve and clotted cream and decided to ignore his sarcasm. "It's sort of a complicated story."

"Enlighten me with the simple version."

"It's a *long*, complicated story. Are you sure you have the time? Don't you have to dash off to an appointment at your tailor's or at your club? Or that meeting with your solicitor?"

"My calendar is clear for the rest of the day. I am at your service." He crossed his ankles and seemed prepared to listen for hours.

"Uh-huh." She nodded. "Well..." She took another bite of scone. "These are very good. Did your cook bake them?"

"Of course, she baked them." He frowned. "Stop stalling, Miss Blake. The truth, if you don't mind."

"Well, yes, of course the truth," she said, affronted. But maybe just a little lie here and there might keep him from thinking she was completely crazy. "Why would I tell you anything else?"

"I can think of any number of reasons." Dry as the month of August in Arizona, his tone made her wince.

"Well, I am from America, as I've already explained. Boston, actually. But you already know that. I've been in London several months." At least she could tell him that truth. Because she had been in London, just in a different century.

"It is odd that I have never made your acquaintance before this, particularly if it is in your habit to run about Hyde Park in little more than...those." He gestured at her leggings and tee shirt.

Suddenly feeling exposed despite the banyan, she tugged it closer around her. "Perhaps we haven't met before because we are in the park at different times." And that was the truth, too.

"Hm. Go on. I can't wait to hear what other fiction you might invent."

She started to sputter her protest at his skepticism, but a quirked eyebrow and a hard look from those gray eyes made her subside. Time to use her fiction-writing skills. "Everything is still so foggy in my mind, but I think I encountered someone who took advantage of my good nature. This person must have abandoned me in Hyde Park without anything except the clothes I have on."

"You think someone abandoned you?" he asked, his tone loaded with skepticism. "Who might this person be?"

She shrugged. "Well, I really can't remember."

His eyes narrowed. "Just as I suspected. Your protector has turned you out."

"No! I don't have a protector! I don't remember!"

Emma was close to tears. Her ankle was throbbing. She was stuck in 1814, with no money, no place to live, no friends, and dependent on the good nature of a man who — if her ghost had been telling the truth — would be dead very shortly. But if Brandon didn't help her, she had no idea where she could go or how she would live.

He stood and stalked across the room. "This is a beastly situation. I find you without clothes, without means, abandoned in Hyde Park, and with no memory of how you ended in such a state." He ran a hand through his hair. "We must discover where you were staying and who your companion might be. Or your protector."

"Why do you think I have a protector?" she demanded, annoyed at his persistence. "I don't need a protector. I'm perfectly capable of taking care of myself." Except she wasn't. Not in this time period. Anxiety rushed through her like a cold wind.

He paused and studied her, as if trying to come to a decision. "Very well. You will remain my guest until your memory returns, or we find your companion."

Relief, sudden and strong, closed her throat. She ignored his domineering tone and blinked away tears. He wasn't going to toss her out into the street. For that, she was very grateful.

"Oh, blast, I have made you cry." He pulled a large hand-kerchief from a pocket and handed it to her.

"Thank you." She wondered how many men from her time carried handkerchiefs as she dabbed at eyes. "That is very gallant of you."

He smiled. "There are not many who would think that."

Emma elaborated. "Oh, I think you are very gallant and kind." She sniffed and dabbed a bit more. "I don't think there are many who would take in someone who couldn't remember where she lived."

He was silent for a moment, as if mulling over something. "Miss Blake," he said, and took her hand. "I would enjoy being gallant on your behalf, if you would not mind."

His hold was gentle, and she liked his touch very much. Real-Life Brandon was even more charismatic than Ghost Brandon. As she gazed into those smoky gray eyes, a primal response kindled deep inside her, and other places hummed to life.

Dazed at her arousal, she could barely manage to whisper, "I would like that."

He slowly allowed her fingers to slip from his grasp. "Although I find your situation odd, and I believe that there is much that you are not revealing, please know that you have the hospitality of this house for as long as you wish it. But we must find you a companion until we locate the one you lost, for living alone with me will not endear you to society." His lips twisted in a wry smile.

Separated from his touch, she found her brain could work at its normal rate of speed. "Not even if I'm your cousin?" She didn't want a companion who would watch over her every move, despite knowing from her research that she should have one.

"Even my cousin would arrive at my door with a companion."

"I'm not an innocent young woman."

"No?" A single brow rose.

In speculation or disapproval? She didn't like either option, but an unwed woman always had a companion. A widow, on the other hand...

"I'm old enough to be on my own. Tell everyone I'm a widow. If society can't accept me as your cousin from America, then...then...they can go to blazes!"

His eyebrows shot up, then he grinned. "Good show! A woman who doesn't follow the strictures of society. I quite like the way you think, Miss Blake. What an original you are. We will dazzle the bloods and shock the fusty matrons."

Panic shot through her at the thought of having to appear in public and interact with Brandon's friends and acquaintances. Customs and manners were different than what she knew in the twenty-first century. She'd done tons of research, but she was sure there were details that she didn't know. Suppose she made a fool of herself? Suppose Brandon was offended by her behavior? What if she caused a scandal? What if she slipped up and made a mistake with her "story?"

"I'm sorry. I can't." She shook her head.

His brows drew together. "What do you mean you cannot? Are you afraid to go out in public? Do you fear meeting up with your old protector perhaps?"

"I already told you," she snapped. "I don't have a protector." Realizing she shouldn't antagonize him, she indicated her swollen ankle. "I don't think I'll be able to walk."

"Your ankle will be healed in several days," he said.

Helplessly, Emma stared up at him as her mind raced. She couldn't explain the real reason why — that she was from another time and scared to death of shocking his friends, although she was already skipping down that path by refusing a companion. Then she landed upon the most obvious excuse. "I don't have anything to wear."

He smiled. "Is that all? That is no problem. I will summon Madame Fanchon. I'm sure she will be able to find you something suitable."

"Madame Fanchon?" From her research, Emma remembered that she was one of the foremost mantua makers in London. One of her gowns cost a fortune. She shook her head. "No, please don't summon her. I'll remain here while you go about your business."

His brows met above the bridge of his nose. "Miss Blake, you cannot remain here forever, and since you cannot go about London dressed like—like *that* —" He waved a hand at her clothes. "— we must get you proper attire."

He was right. She needed appropriate clothing if she

were going to figure out how to help him and Elizabeth, and then get back to her own time. Besides that, she had insulted his generosity.

"I didn't mean to offend you," she said. "I've just never had anything quite so fashionable."

"Then your last protector must have been a pinch-penny." He glowered.

Before she could argue again that she had no previous protector, a knock came at the door, and Mrs. Porter announced the arrival of Dr. Beech.

He stepped into the room, and Mrs. Porter slipped in behind him.

"I don't think we'll be needing you, Mrs. Porter," Brandon said.

"I'll not be leaving two men with a single lady alone and unchaperoned, Mr. Connaught," the housekeeper said with a sniff, and stayed adamantly near the door.

Emma hid her smile as Brandon silently yielded.

"Bran!" Dr. Beech approached with outstretched hand. "Are you ill?"

"No," Brandon said as he shook the man's hand. "Thank you for coming so quickly. It's Miss Blake. She's had an accident, bumped her head and injured her ankle." He turned to Emma. "This is Jonathan Beech, a schoolmate from Eton."

Dr. Beech bowed. "A pleasure, Miss Blake, although I wish we were meeting under different circumstances. Now, please tell me what pains you."

Emma was surprised that the doctor was young. He was handsome too, with a shock of curly brown hair and light brown eyes. And she was pleased she had learned another tidbit about Brandon's past. She showed Dr. Beech her ankle and the goose egg on the side of her head.

"Miss Blake seems to have suffered some loss of memory," Brandon said.

The doctor gently examined her injuries. "Amnesia, you say?"

"Yes," Emma said. "I can't seem to remember where I am staying or who came to England with me." She hoped she sounded believable.

"Well, a nasty bump on the head will sometimes cause memory loss," Dr. Beech said, "but it should clear up in a few days. Cool compresses and rest will help." He pulled a bandage roll from his bag and went down on a knee beside the footstool. "Now, let's get that ankle wrapped. Keeping it immobile and elevated on a few pillows will help it heal."

"How long should I stay off it?" she asked.

"Two or three days should be enough." He smiled as he tied off the bandage. "We wouldn't want to keep you from too many social engagements."

Emma forced a smile.

Dr. Beech stood. "I'm sure Mrs. Porter will take excellent care of you. I'll check back in a day or two."

Brandon walked him to the door, and Mrs. Porter accompanied him out. From behind her, Emma heard the door close and Brandon's footsteps returning. He stopped before her.

Glancing up at him, she said, "Thank you for calling your doctor. He seems very nice."

"He is a good friend."

His words were short, as if there might be a story behind their friendship, but his manner discouraged any questions. If the doctor was coming back, Emma thought she might be able to get some information from him about Brandon's past. Any tidbit might help her fix the ending of her story, like Ghost Brandon wanted her to do.

A knock sounded at the door and a maid announced that Emma's room was ready.

"We must find you a lady's maid," Brandon mused.

"I really don't need a lady's maid," she said, but when she saw him glower again, she added quickly, "But I do appreciate all that you're doing for me."

She smiled her sweetest smile and stood, then gasped in pain as her throbbing ankle gave out beneath her.

"Miss Blake!" Brandon caught her up in his arms. "The doctor said you should rest that ankle."

Snuggled against him again, she caught another whiff of his spicy lime scent, enhanced by the warmth of his body. She could get used to being in his strong arms. Glancing into those gray eyes, she was drawn towards him, inviting him to...to...to... At the last moment, she caught herself. What was she doing? He was a man of the nineteenth century. She was a woman of the twenty-first. She was not going to kiss the embodiment of a ghost. Besides, he was in love with Elizabeth.

Quickly, she glanced away. "I think I can get to my room by myself. I feel gross and filthy."

"Gross?" he said in confusion. "You are a tiny thing. I do not find you in the least over-sized."

"Um, thanks. But it's an American term that means I need to freshen up."

He grinned. "You look like a woman who has been abandoned in Hyde Park — sweet and vulnerable."

She blushed and shook her head. "I'm not sweet."

"I disagree." With that declaration, he carried her to a bedroom down the hall where a washbowl and pitcher of steaming water waited.

AFTER WASHING OFF THE GRIME OF HER JOG AND THE DIRT OF Hyde Park, Emma sat before the hearth and took in the lovely room, decorated in various shades of blue with yellow accents, but with no personal touches, like trinkets on the dressing table or paintings on the walls. She wondered if Brandon had decorated it in the expectation of Elizabeth living here.

A knock came at the door, and Mrs. Porter asked, "Are you decent, miss?" Without waiting for an answer, she swung the door wide and entered. "This is Madame Fanchon, the modiste Mr. Connaught has engaged to do your wardrobe." She gestured to a petite woman who stood next to her.

Madame Fanchon swept around the imposing Mrs. Porter, and called over her shoulder, "Come, come, *mes petites filles*. We have much to do." Two young women carrying piles of packages and boxes entered behind her. Madame Fanchon turned to Mrs. Porter and said, "*Merci, madame*, if you could ask your footmen to bring up the rest of the things in my carriage, I would most appreciate it. We will let you know if we need anything further."

There was more? Emma wondered as she watched Madame Fanchon direct the two seamstresses to unpack their bundles. The young women, struggling under the weight of their loads, set the packages on every available surface and began to unpack shifts and shawls and bits of lacy and satiny things.

With a sniff at being so bluntly dismissed, Mrs. Porter left, and Madame Fanchon turned to Emma. "*Bon*, you are a pretty one." Then she focused on Emma's tee shirt and leggings. "But these clothes... *Non, non, non*. These will not do."

Uncomfortable under the woman's gaze, Emma crossed her arms across her chest.

Madame Fanchon clicked her tongue. "You must remove

these hideous things. After I have dressed you, Monsieur Connaught will be *infatué!*" She grinned and a twinkle appeared in her bright, dark eyes.

Emma liked the woman immediately, but she realized the modiste assumed she was Brandon's mistress.

"I'm Mr. Connaught's cousin," she said. "From America."

Madame tipped her head and her gaze turned conspiratorial. "*Mais, oui.* His cousin." Then she winked. With a wave of her hand, she indicated Emma's clothes. "Off, off, off." Clapping her hands, she sent her two helpers into a flurry of digging through the piles of clothes.

Emma stripped off her running clothes, and after getting a frown of disapproval from Madame Fanchon, peeled off her underwear. One of the girls slipped a chemise over Emma's head, so she wasn't naked, and another pinned up her hair into a bun. A walking stick was thrust into her hand to help her stand on her injured ankle, and then Emma spent the next several hours being squeezed into corsets, having petticoats dropped over her head and pulled off again, trying on day dresses, afternoon dresses, morning dresses, and evening gowns. Some were too small. Some were too large.

When Madame held up a pair of drawers trimmed in lace and ribbons to show Emma, she whispered conspiratorially, "These are quite *risqué.*"

Emma smiled, for she knew that the usual fashion of women at the time was to wear nothing. The drawers were adorable, and compared to the tiny bits of lacy things sold in the twenty-first century, they certainly weren't scandalous. She wondered what Brandon would think of lingerie from Victoria's Secret.

By the time Madame had gone through all of her bundles and packages, Emma had one afternoon dress of white striped muslin with long sleeves, but it was too short and too loose across her bust. One of the seamstresses had pinned and altered it while Emma had it on. A gown of white lawn with a pale blue silk petticoat had been deemed good enough by Madame Fanchon to be altered and delivered the next day for a dinner frock. The modiste took Emma's measurements and would construct several more frocks for her over the next week.

Emma hoped she would be back in her own time before she needed any of the extra clothes. But dressing up in nine-teenth-century clothing was an adventure. Besides, she could write detailed descriptions of her heroine's clothing in her next novel.

Five

The next day, Emma sat in her room with her injured foot resting on a lovely padded footstool and fidgeted. Not being able to walk around was aggravating. If she was going to help Brandon and Elizabeth get their happy-ever-after ending, then she needed to speak with Brandon to find out where Elizabeth was and convince her to run away with her true love. But she hadn't spoken to Brandon since the evening before, when he had visited just before heading out to his club. He had stayed only to see if she had everything she needed. Of course, she did. Mrs. Porter ran his household like a military operation.

Outside her window, the constant rain made the day dark and dreary. She'd been Brandon's guest for a day and a half, and had been pampered and waited on as if she were made of porcelain, which was very nice at first, but she'd lounged around enough.

After a night spent in the lovely tester bed, she'd been awakened in the morning by a maid with a cup of hot chocolate and a warm roll. Another maid had helped her dress. For the past several hours, she'd huddled close to the coal fire and started a journal, writing down her impressions of what she'd seen so far—the traffic noises of horses and carriages instead of cars, how wearing frocks and stays made her move differently than wearing stretchy clothes of the twenty-first century, the bustle of servants in a house, and every other detail she could remember. But she had finished that.

A nuncheon had been brought to her in the early afternoon, and she had picked at it only because it gave her something to do. After finishing it, she'd hopped to a chair by the window and propped up her sore foot. Now, she stared out at the wet world. The street was nearly deserted. Only an occasional pedestrian hurried past or a hackney carriage drove by. Several hours ago, she'd seen a footman wave down one of the hackneys, watched Brandon step inside and head off. She wondered where he was going. Perhaps to that meeting with his solicitor that she had interrupted the day before.

She still couldn't quite believe she was in the past. While she knew everything around her was real, she felt as if she had really bad jet lag. Although she had decided she'd been sent back in time to help Elizabeth get her happy-ever-after ending, Ghost Brandon had said she could "fix things." Had he meant she could help him gain his title? That she could foil his half-brother's plot to murder their father and then accuse Brandon of the crime? That she could prevent him from being shot? But how could she possibly do all that?

Something to read would keep her mind from going in crazy circles. When Brandon had carried her into the house, she had glimpsed a room with a heavy, carved desk and shelves of books. If she was very careful, maybe she could sneak down to that room for a book or two.

After slipping on her sneakers, not easy with a bandage wrapped around her foot and ankle, she limped painfully out to the hallway and to the top of the stairs. Fortunately, no servants were about. Gripping the banister and keeping her eyes glued on each step, she slowly hobbled down the steps.

"Miss Blake."

Her head snapped up at his voice. "Oh! You're back." She was caught. Damn. But her molecules jumped into excited agitation.

He was standing with one foot on the bottom step. "Yes. Did you think that you could disobey Dr. Beech's orders because I was not here?" One brow rose in sardonic curiosity.

His lordly manner grated. "Yes, actually. That is exactly what I thought," she challenged.

He came two steps closer. "The only way your ankle will heal is if you do not walk on it."

Her chin went up. "I know that. I heard what your friend the doctor said."

"So why do I find you coming down the stairs?" He rose another three steps.

"My ankle is much better." It was, sort of.

"I see." Another step up and he was at eye level with her. "Then it should be completely healed in another few days."

"Oh, I'm sure it will." She smiled with conviction and met that smoky gray gaze.

"I am very glad to hear that," he murmured. "For then I can take you around the city."

The thought of having him as a guide, sitting next to him in his curricle as he pointed out the sights made her insides jump in excitement. "That is very kind of you." She had to fight to keep her words steady.

"May I ask where were you heading?" Wry humor twisted his lips as he indicated the stairway.

"Your library." For some reason, her cheeks heated at the confession.

"Ah." He nodded sagely. "A good book has always helped me pass the time. Allow me to assist you." He stepped up one more step and swept her up into his arms.

"You don't have to carry me," she protested, even as she wrapped her arm around his neck and breathed in his spicy lime scent.

"Of course, I do." His statement left no room for argument.

She lapsed into silence and enjoyed the strength of him as he carried her the rest of the way down the stairs and into the room with the books she had glimpsed before. It was a cozy space with two walls of shelves and a substantial desk situated between a pair of windows that looked out on the street. One of the walls sported a small hearth with a couple of chairs on either side.

Turning his head, he met her eyes. "Will you allow me to choose some books for you?"

When he looked at her like that, she thought she might do anything he asked. "Okay."

His grin grew broader at her slang. "Okay." He deposited her in a chair before the hearth, carefully placed her foot on a stool, and stepped to the shelves.

Emma blew out a breath. What had she gotten herself into? Ghost Brandon was alluring, but Real-Life Brandon was devastating. Sexy. Charming. Hot. And annoyingly masterful.

She watched him peruse the books and pull several from the shelves. Placing them on her lap, he said, "I hope these are to your liking. I found them quite intriguing."

She sorted through the books. Percy Bysshe Shelley. Mary Wollstonecraft. Walter Scott. Lord Byron. And Jane Austen, anonymously. He had given her an overview of British literature of the period. And they were, of course, all first editions. Her father would have drooled over them. She nearly drooled over them.

"These are perfect," she said with a bright smile. "Thank you."

"You are most welcome. Will you promise me now that you'll not walk on that ankle?" He looked very stern.

She chuckled. "Yes, I promise."

"Then I bid you good day, Miss Blake. I have an appointment with my solicitor."

After sketching a small bow, he strolled past her chair. But as he passed, his fingers lightly brushed against her arm. By accident? Or not? Whichever it was, it sent a shiver through her. She drew in a breath.

Maybe she'd be wise to stay put, just so she wouldn't run into him again. She certainly needed to think about something else besides his charming smile, his beguiling eyes, his muscular body...

Opening the Jane Austen with determination, she began to read.

Brandon thoughtfully made his way out to the mews where his horse waited. Miss Blake was an interesting woman. A confounding woman. A beautiful, strong-willed woman. Not anything like his beloved Elizabeth.

Then why did he feel such a compulsion to care for her? More than he normally would as a gentleman helping a lady in distress.

He had returned from his errand to find that lady making her painful way down the stairs. Annoyance at her willfulness and concern over her safety had prompted him to confront her. And then he had made the mistake of approaching. Much too closely. Those sapphire eyes riveted him. Her scent of warm vanilla overcame any decent thought in his head. So he had swept her up, snuggled her softness against his chest, and carried her down to his study. Visions ran through his brain of the two of them locked together in his bed, tangled in the sheets. He didn't want to let her go. Placing her into a chair had required a tremendous amount of will power. Only the offer to retrieve some reading matter for her had kept his sanity intact, because he could have easily kissed her, touched her.... That was insanity.

He had no idea who she was. Before he did anything half-witted, he had to discover something about her. That morning he had hired a Bow Street Runner, whom he had met in one of the more unsavory places he had visited in London, to make inquiries. Who were Miss Blake's companions? Where were they? Where was she staying in the city? How did she arrive in London? Directly from America, or had she traveled from another country? He wanted to know every last detail. Perhaps this need made him a bit touched in the head, but the desire to learn about her overcame his good sense. Or perhaps he still retained a flicker of good sense.

That had not always been the case. Not long after Elizabeth had wed his half-brother, he had met Arlene one night at a gaming hell. In his cups, he had been intrigued by the sultry woman in the mask. Wanting only to dull his pain, he had succumbed to her seduction and had spent an exhaustive night with her, doing things he never would have done with Elizabeth. In the morning, he realized what a mistake he'd made, for she was a married woman and her husband, although only a minor lord, had tremendous influence among a certain faction of the ton. They parted amicably, but Arlene implied she would be happy to repeat the evening. Brandon would not, but understood he should not make an enemy of her, so he played along with her flirting and accepted most of their invitations.

Miss Blake contrasted sharply with Arlene. He enjoyed being with her, despite knowing little about her. She was unlike any woman he had ever met. Beyond trying to unravel those things she appeared to have forgotten, he wanted to learn everything about her. What was her opinion of the books he'd given her to read? Did she prefer tea or hot chocolate in the morning? What was her favorite color? How did she look after a night spent in his bed?

With a shake of his head to rid himself of such thoughts, he strode into the stables behind his house and asked the stableboy to saddle his horse. A ride through the misty city and a conversation with his solicitor would take his mind off all the questions about her. But as he waited for his horse, all he saw were blue eyes surrounded by thick, dark lashes and pouty lips waiting for a kiss.

Not long after Brandon left, Emma heard the doorknocker fall. Absorbed in *Pride and Prejudice*, she barely paid attention to Mrs. Porter answering the knock and the voices in the entry hall, so she was startled when the housekeeper rapped lightly on the door to the study and cleared her throat.

"Lady Farley is here, ma'am," she said.

Reluctantly, Emma dragged her attention away from her book. "Mr. Connaught has gone out, Mrs. Porter."

"Yes, ma'am." The housekeeper bobbed her head. "I told her so. She said she'd like to call on you, if you don't mind."

Emma really didn't want to sit and chat with Lady Farley, but she could see her hovering beyond Mrs. Porter's shoulder. "Of course, Mrs. Porter."

The housekeeper stepped out of the doorway, and Lady Farley breezed in.

"So kind of you to receive me, Miss Bradley," the lady said, then stopped short as she caught sight of Emma's wrapped ankle propped on a footstool. "Oh, you poor dear, whatever happened?"

Emma smiled through clenched teeth at the mangling of her name. "A small mishap in the park."

"That's what comes from exerting oneself beyond the norm. Goodness, running for exercise. What a terrible idea." Lady Farley gave a delicate shiver. "But I am so very relieved to see you attired in the proper fashion, Miss Beakley."

Emma's teeth clenched tighter. "It's *Mrs. Blake*. I'm a widow."

"Oh, of course," Lady Farley said with a dismissive wave of her hand. "How foolish of me. My condolences." Her expression of sympathy for Emma's fictional dead husband was made without the least bit of compassion as she perched on the edge of the opposite chair.

"I'll bring tea," Mrs. Porter announced.

"No, no, that won't be necessary." The lady gave another wave of her hand. "You may go."

Mrs. Porter's face froze at being dismissed by someone who had no authority in the household.

Emma sent the housekeeper a smile. "It's all right, Mrs. Porter. I don't think Lady Farley intends on staying long." She had no idea how long the woman intended to stay, but maybe she'd take the hint and leave. Emma wanted to get back to her book.

When Mrs. Porter left, Lady Farley dug into her reticule and pulled out a sealed note. "I wanted to deliver this personally to Brandon. I'm having a small dinner party, you see. I did not realize his *cousin* was staying with him, but you may join us if you wish." She glanced at Emma's wrapped ankle. "But perhaps your injury will prevent you."

Emma was stunned at the double insult. She didn't miss the innuendo of impropriety that Arlene implied with the word *cousin*, nor the fact that she was being invited as an afterthought. Did the woman expect her to decline?

Emma decided to destroy her expectation as she plucked the invitation from the woman's fingers. "Oh, I'm sure my ankle will be healed soon. I'd be delighted to attend your little gathering."

"Splendid." As she stood to leave, Lady Farley's smile was as fake as the silk flower on her bonnet. "I will look forward to welcoming you to my house. Please extend my felicitations to Brandon and disappointment that I missed him. Good day, Mrs. Benson."

Emma released a breath of relief when she heard a footman open the front door and usher the woman out. Sticking the invitation inside the cover of her book, she returned to the budding romance between Elizabeth Bennett and Mr. Darcy. Later, she would decide whether she actually wanted to attend Lady Farley's dinner party. Perhaps her ankle wouldn't be healed enough. Or perhaps, her "amnesia" was so severe that she forgot to pass along the invitation to Brandon.

THAT EVENING AT DINNER, AFTER BRANDON HAD ONCE AGAIN insisted on carrying Emma down the stairs, she pulled the invitation from beneath her sash and pushed it across the table.

"Lady Farley called on you while you were out this afternoon. She left this." Emma had settled on doing the right thing and let him decide if he wanted to go.

He opened the invitation. "A dinner party."

"I'm sure Lady Farley will be happy to see you," she said.

A tiny line appeared between his brows. "I'm sure she'll be happy to see you, as well."

"No, I don't think she will." She suspected that the woman was jealous, and she was definitely not one of her favorite people. If the woman mangled her name one more time, she might throw something. Remaining in her room and reading instead of attending Lady Farley's dinner party seemed a much more pleasant choice. "I don't know any of your friends, and I think Lady Farley invited me because I happen to be staying here. Besides, I still can't walk on my ankle."

"I remember hearing you say it was better," he challenged. "In fact, Dr. Beech is of the opinion that it will be

98

healed in a short time. The dinner party is not for another two days." Those gray eyes speared her.

"Oh, well, in that case…" Maybe she could pretend it still hurt.

He tapped the invitation. "Lady Farley's dinner party might be a perfect opportunity to gather gossip. Someone might have seen or met other Americans who could be your traveling companions. Don't you wish to find them?"

"Of course, I do." But finding made-up traveling companions could prove to be a bit difficult. "Couldn't you listen to the gossip for me?"

"Someone might say something about them that you would recognize, but I would not."

Since they were fictional, that wouldn't happen. "Oh, yes, of course."

"Then it's settled," he said. "You will attend. I'm sure one of the maids will be able to help you prepare for an evening out. I'll inform Mrs. Porter."

"Thank you," she said weakly, confounded at how easily he had outfoxed her.

His warm smile of satisfaction at her capitulation both annoyed and heated her. Making him happy seemed to have a direct connection to her heart. She told that unruly organ to behave, then she wondered why he was so intent on having her go with him. But that was a mystery to unravel later.

EARLY IN THE AFTERNOON OF LADY FARLEY'S DINNER PARTY, Emma stood at the window and admired Brandon's horsemanship as he cantered off down the road. Because of the rain, she'd spent most of the last two days staying off her ankle and reading, except for an expedition out on a sightseeing tour with him the day before when the weather cleared. He pointed out spots of interest as they traveled around the city, and she tried not to snuggle against him on the curricle's seat.

He had gone out the night before, expressing regret she couldn't accompany him, and because she had been tossing and turning, she heard him arrive home very late from wherever he had gone. His footsteps had stopped before her door. Would he knock? Would he slowly turn the knob and peek in? Would he step across the threshold and approach the bed? She had held her breath, anticipation bubbling through her veins. But after a moment, his footsteps had receded down the hall and then his door closed with a careful, quiet click.

She wondered where he had been. At his club? With a woman? She didn't like that idea. Then she scolded herself for her curiosity. It was none of her business where he spent those hours away from his home. But even though she tried to shut down her speculations, sleep didn't return for quite a while.

Now, she admired his broad back and watched him disappear around a corner. The lack of sleep didn't seem to affect him. His step had been energetic and he had mounted his horse with athletic alacrity.

A knock sounded at her door and Mrs. Porter announced that Dr. Beech had arrived to examine her ankle. Emma had been walking on it all morning and didn't want to incur a chiding from the woman, so she quickly sat and placed her foot on the footstool. Dr. Beech entered, and just as Mrs. Porter was about to follow, she was called away to see to some mishap in the kitchen.

As Dr. Beech stepped into the room, the woman warned, "Since you're a physician, I trust I can leave you."

He smiled. "I assure you I will be on my best behavior. Besides, I have my wife to answer to."

With a sniff and a nod, Mrs. Porter left.

After greeting Emma, Dr. Beech knelt and examined her ankle. His fingers were gentle as he probed the injury, and Emma thought this might be a good time to discover more about her enigmatic host from a man he claimed as a friend.

"I understand you were schoolmates with Brandon," she began.

He glanced up at her, his soft brown eyes surprised. Then with a small smile he focused on her ankle again. "Yes. I saved him from a beating several times."

"A beating?" she asked, appalled. "From whom?"

He ignored her question. "Have you been having any pain?"

Since he had changed the subject, she assumed he didn't want to tell her. "No. I've been walking on it since yesterday."

He stood and held out his hand. "Would you please walk across the room for me?" After she stood and did as he asked, he said, "Neither of us were accepted by the older boys at Eton. One day in the middle of winter, they knocked the hat from my head and threw it onto a frozen pond. When I went to retrieve it, I fell through the ice."

She gasped. "That's terrible!"

"Connaught crawled out onto the ice and used a broken tree limb to pull me to safety," he said with a small smile and indicated she should sit again. "We became fast friends after that and made a formidable team." He unwound the bandage from her ankle. "Your ankle seems to be healed enough that you do not need this any longer."

"Oh, that's wonderful," she said faintly, outraged at the cruelty of the older boys.

He stood. "I understand you have been invited to a dinner party this evening. I see no reason why your injury will keep you from attending."

Emma realized she had made a mistake when she had shown him how well she could walk. She forced a smile.

As Dr. Beech rolled up the bandage, he said, "I am pleased to see Connaught accepting invitations again."

Thinking of the night before, she pretended ignorance. "Oh? Doesn't he usually go out in the evenings?"

"Not since his former fiancée wed another and died in childbirth. He goes only to his club or the gaming hells. Or..." His voice trailed off as he focused on placing the rolled bandage in his bag.

Emma sat up straight. "Excuse me, did you say his former fiancée did in childbirth?"

"Yes." Dr. Beech lifted a surprised brow. "Didn't he tell you?"

She shook her head.

"It was quite tragic," he said. "He was a wreck for months, then he connected with a wild crowd. I feared he might end up in a dreadful situation."

"That is so sad." Emma was so shocked, she could barely speak the words.

The doctor nodded his agreement. "My hope is that he'll regain his good sense. He was quite interested in having you accompany him this evening. Perhaps he will find purpose in helping you regain your memory."

"Yes," she said faintly, as her mind whirled. "Perhaps we can help each other."

"I certainly hope so, Miss Blake. He is a good friend." With a small bow, he bid her good-day.

After he left, Emma sat, stunned, as she tried to re-order her thoughts. She had traveled back in time too late. If Elizabeth was dead, then her plan to help Brandon have his happily-ever-after with his true love wouldn't work. She thought that was the reason why she had been sent back in time. Obviously, not. She would have to come up with another plan.

Ghost Brandon had told her she needed to fix things. But what things?

Before she had time to figure out the answer to that question, a maid knocked and announced that she wanted to prepare Emma's bath and help her get ready for the dinner party.

Six

That evening, Emma stepped down from the carriage and clutched the arm that Brandon held out to her. Her ankle was healed.

So here she was.

At Arlene's dinner party.

Anxiety made her palms sweat. Before her was the imposing entrance to Lord and Lady Farley's London house. In a few moments, she would have to greet Arlene and all of the other guests as if she were a nineteenth-century lady. Arlene would be nasty, recognize her as a fraud, and make her leave. Brandon would get angry and possibly throw her out. She would be abandoned in a city she had only researched and written about — with no money, no friends. With no way to return to her own time.

Her fingers gripped Brandon's arm even tighter. With a reassuring smile, he patted her hand, then led her to the door. She lifted her chin a notch. *Get a grip, girl.*

A gown, different than the one she had tried on, had been delivered early that afternoon and fit her perfectly, a lovely confection of gold silk with three rows of white satin roses embroidered at the hem and around the tiny puff sleeves. Her white silk petticoat and a linen chemise were her only undergarments, for the fashion was to go without any stays, and ladies never wore underwear. Unless they wanted to be racy and wear those pantaloons Madame Fachon had shown her. She had slipped on her panties at the last minute. Despite that twenty-first century addition, she felt very sexy and naughty, for the dress skimmed over her like a nightgown. Madame Fachon had been able to find a pair of dancing shoes, thin-soled with satin uppers, to match the dress.

When she had walked down the stairs, Brandon had been waiting at the bottom. His eyes heated when he saw her. An answering tingle had spread inside her and ended in a throb between her thighs. No man had ever been able to do that to her with just a glance. How would she ever be able to play his cousin for the evening without giving away the electricity between them?

She stole a peek at him, for he looked very dashing in his dark gray trousers, blue silk waistcoat embroidered in red, and black coat. His collar points were perfectly starched and his neckcloth was a complicated, flawless knot. If she were a nineteenth-century woman in the market for a husband, she'd immediately set out to catch him. But she wasn't. And she would most likely get flung back to her own time, never to see him again, so she told her hormones to behave.

A mischievous glint twinkled in his eyes, and Emma knew he was anticipating the stir he would create when he introduced his "cousin from America." He escorted her up the few stairs to the front door and let the doorknocker fall. The door was opened immediately by the butler who greeted Brandon by name, then ushered them up a wide set of stairs to the drawing room, where he announced them. Lady Farley sashayed over.

"Brandon, darling, I'm so glad you've come, and you brought your little cousin from America. How delightful." Arlene bestowed a warm smile on Brandon and a polite one on Emma. "I see your cousin has decided to dress for the occasion."

At Lady Farley's second sly remark about her clothes, Emma forced a saccharine smile. If Lady Farley had lived in the twenty-first century, she would have been one of the mean girls. Emma was not going to let her get away with that.

With an airy wave of her hand, she said, "I always dress appropriately for whatever I'm doing." She let her gaze wander down Lady Farley's translucent gown which hid very little. The woman's nipples and pubic hair were dark smudges beneath her thin, muslin gown. "I see you do as well."

Lady Farley blinked, then her eyes gleamed maliciously, and she glanced beyond Emma's shoulder. "Where is your companion, my dear? Do American women scandalously traipse about unescorted?"

"Her companion was unwell," Brandon answered before Emma could come up with a reply. "I convinced Mrs. Blake she would be perfectly safe with me."

Lady Farley arched her finely plucked eyebrows. "All alone in a coach with a handsome man?" she murmured. "How daring." Then she turned to Brandon. "I have always wondered if the tales of America's wild animals and barbarians were true. I see now that what I've heard doesn't begin to describe the truth."

Emma's temper rose several degrees. She was not going to let the woman belittle or insult her. Glancing around the ornately decorated room with its large gilt vases and statuesque, ornate candelabrum that were taller than she was, she said, "Your house is very interesting." Let Lady Farley decide whether that was a compliment or not.

Doubt flashed through Arlene's eyes, then she smiled coolly. "I had the advice of a wonderful decorator, but I chose most of the furnishings myself."

"How courageous of you," Emma murmured.

Arlene's superior smile faltered, then dismissing Emma,

she turned to Brandon. "Darling, come mingle with the other guests. I think you know them all."

Brandon scanned the group, and stiffened. "Arlene, why did you invite *him?*"

Emma followed Brandon's gaze and gasped. "Stephen." He was there, big as life, dressed in nineteenth-century clothing. Suave and handsome, he chatted with a lovely young woman. How did he get here? Why was he here?

Brandon's gaze sliced around to her. "You know him?" He didn't sound pleased.

Had she said the name out loud? Damn. She blinked and looked again. No, that couldn't possibly be Stephen. She had left Stephen back in the twenty-first century.

"Ah...no." She shook her head. "He just looks like someone I know." She blinked again. But it was Stephen — animated, living, breathing, talking, smiling. Charming. The same blond hair, the same winning smile, the same elegant manner, the same veneer of polish. Anger and resentment at what he had done made the heat rise in her cheeks. Even her ears burned. She wanted to rush over and slap him, but she willed her feet to remain planted solidly where they were. Then she realized this was not the Stephen she knew, but his ancestor, Brandon's half-brother.

This was the man who had killed him.

"How odd that two men who look similar happen to have the same name," Brandon drawled and raised a sardonic brow.

At his tone, Emma shifted from one foot to the other. "Yes, it is very odd." She wished she could dredge up an answer. But this wasn't the time or place to reveal that she was from the future and that she knew what would happen to him. As soon as she had the thought, a vague plan began to form. But she put it aside for now, because she needed to keep her wits about her to navigate the treacherous social currents that were swirling around her.

"What an amazing coincidence!" Arlene's gaze riveted on her as the woman seemed to drink in every word. "I would dearly love to learn about this other Stephen."

Emma sent her a tight smile, refusing to enlighten her.

Stephen glanced around and cold disdain crossed his face when he saw Brandon. Excusing himself from the young woman he was speaking to, he strolled toward them. Beneath Emma's hand, the muscles in Brandon's arm tensed as his half-brother approached.

"Arlene, you invite the most interesting people to your gatherings." Stephen's tone matched Brandon's, and he coolly regarded his half-brother.

"I was just remarking on that very thing." Brandon's expression turned stony.

Giving a light little laugh, Arlene said, "Now, gentlemen, you must behave with civility or I won't invite either of you ever again. Besides, we have a guest from America." She bestowed a superior smile on Emma. "My dear, may I present the Viscount Pemberton?" She turned to Stephen. "And this is Brandon's little cousin from America, Mrs. Emmie Blakely."

Emma offered her hand and smiled through gritted teeth as Arlene mangled her name again. Stephen elegantly bowed and brushed his lips across her fingers. Forcing herself not to pull from his grasp and wipe her fingers on her skirt, she vividly remembered when his descendant had done the same thing. She had been an impressionable eighteen-year-old and had met him for the first time. That time, she had been charmed. This time, not at all. His gaze held a hint of predator as he smiled at her, but with no sign of any recognition. Of course not. This wasn't the Stephen whom she knew. But this one couldn't be trusted either. She jerked her hand away.

With a sly look in her eyes, Arlene said, "Pemberton is Brandon's half-brother, you see, and they still squabble like little boys."

"I daresay fighting over a birthright can hardly be called a squabble, Arlene," Stephen said.

"I plan to get my birthright back." Brandon's words, although spoken in a low tone, seared the air.

Arlene stepped between the men and hooked her arm first through Brandon's, then through Stephen's, claiming possession of both men. Her color was high and her eyes bright with excitement. The woman was enjoying the dissension between the brothers. Emma wondered if she thrived on conflict.

"Now Pemberton, dear, you mustn't bring up such unpleasant subjects at my dinner party. And Brandon, darling, please refrain from losing your temper. You know how I detest having to explain your behavior to Lord Farley. He is so tiresome about allowing me to replace bric-a-bracs that you have tossed at someone in a fit."

"I have only thrown one piece of Delft and that was at this bugger," Brandon muttered.

Emma thought that throwing only one piece of bric-a-brac at Stephen was rather restrained.

A tall, thin man approached. Sparse hair, a large, hooked nose, and pale, cold eyes gave him the appearance of a bird of prey.

He nodded his greeting to Brandon. "Connaught," he said. "Good of you to come to my wife's dinner party." He glanced at Emma, and those pale eyes made her want to take a step back.

As Brandon introduced her to Lord Farley, she decided she'd have as little to do with the man as she could. He made her think of a vulture being offered a succulent feast.

Arlene threw a narrow-eyed, warning glance at her husband, then arranged the couples going in to dinner. "Brandon, you may escort me, and Pemberton, please be a dear and escort Brandon's little cousin."

Lord Farley turned obediently to find his dinner partner, and Emma felt she had suddenly been released from an invisible tether. She was relieved she was unimportant enough that she would not have to endure her host's company through the whole meal. Instead, she had Stephen.

As he offered her his arm, she forced her lips into a smile and tried not to cringe away. She had to act as if she didn't know that he would murder his brother. If she blurted out the truth, everyone would think she was deranged. Taking a quick peek at him, she could see small differences between this Stephen and the one she knew in the twenty-first century. This Stephen was not as fit as the other, and his eyes were hazel, not gray. Would the future Stephen ever be desperate enough to murder?

"So, you are Brandon's cousin from America," Stephen began, interrupting her thoughts. He led her out of the salon and across the hall to the dining room. "That should make you my cousin as well. Isn't it odd that I never knew I had relatives in America?"

"Oh, I don't think you and I are related at all," she said. "I'm related to Brandon through his mother." Too late, Emma remembered she had written in her novel that Stephen thought Brandon and his mother were trash, not only because Brandon's mother and father never married, but because Brandon and his mother had Irish blood. But Brandon had told her the story was wrong, so maybe the truth was different.

"Then it is no wonder that I knew nothing of you. You are Irish." Stephen's tone, although deceptively bland, held a hint of sneer.

Emma gave him her best smile. "No, I'm American. And Brandon and I are very distantly related, barely at all, actually. Third cousins twice removed, I think. Or is it fourth cousins three times removed?"

Looking bemused, Stephen escorted her to the chair the footman held out for her, approximately in the middle of the table, away from both Lord Farley at the head of the table and Arlene at the foot. She saw Arlene had seated Brandon next to her. Of course.

As Emma slipped onto her seat, Stephen said, "Well, perhaps you can explain the connection sometime. I am fascinated by familial relationships. And especially by fourth cousins thrice removed." His tone was warm and suggestive.

"Genealogy is an interesting subject," Emma agreed, ignoring his evocative implication, and couldn't resist a verbal jab. "Just think of all those family branches begun by illegitimate children. And then the scandal when a bastard son inherits a title."

Her barb hit its target. Stephen's eyes narrowed fractionally before he sat next to her. "I don't recall that happening in recent memory."

"Well, perhaps not recently, but I think I read something about that in a history book." Emma smiled innocently.

"A history book? You seem to be quite knowledgeable for a lady," he observed.

Emma wanted to punch him. Instead, she kept her smile

in place. "My father was very forward-thinking and wanted all his daughters to be educated."

"All his daughters?" Stephen asked with a supercilious lift of his brow. "Are there more like you at home?"

Emma was about to tell him that yes, there were two others, and besides that, there were thousands of women back home who knew history and geography, who could run a business or send a man to the moon, because women had brains, just like men. But the gentleman on Emma's other side, a Sir Dotson, distracted Stephen.

"I hear there is quite an unusual beast going up at Tattersall's," the man said. "A galloper. Might be worth a look."

Relieved that another subject had been introduced, Emma said, "Oh, I love horses." She knew nothing about horses except they were pretty to watch, but as soon as she spoke, she realized her mistake. What she had blurted was like saying she loved cars in the twenty-first century, and she didn't know much about cars, either. "I mean I like beautiful horses," she finished lamely.

Annoyance crossed Stephen's face so fast that Emma wondered if she imagined it, but his gaze was warm when he focused on her. "Do you?" he murmured. "Perhaps we could indulge that interest sometime soon."

She wished she had kept quiet. Now she needed to pretend she was flattered at his invitation. She forced a smile. "That would be wonderful."

Stephen turned to Dotson. "A galloper, you say? What makes this beast so special?"

Sir Dotson nonchalantly took a sip of wine before he answered. "It's an Arabian, smuggled out of France, and, I heard, right from under Bonaparte's nose."

The mention of Napoleon Bonaparte and the studied nonchalance in the way he spoke made Emma pay closer attention, because England was at war with France. Was he talking about a horse, or something else, like information? If she hadn't known this Stephen's descendant as a liar and a cheat, if she hadn't known what this Stephen had done to Brandon, she might not have paid attention to the conversation, but her suspicions clamored in her head. She needed to find out more, and so she paid close attention.

"I've heard of that horse," Stephen said. "Quite an amazing feat."

"Oh, my," she said. "From beneath Bonny's nose? How bold!"

Stephen grinned and leaned closer. "Shall I tell you the tale of the adventure? I assure you, it is quite exciting."

"I would very much like to hear it," she encouraged. "I do enjoy exciting stories."

As Stephen began to relate an outrageous story about how the horse came to arrive in England, out of the corner of her eye, she caught Brandon watching her. He didn't look happy. Was he annoyed with her or Stephen?

Emma tried to ignore him, because according to Ghost

Brandon, the man sitting next to her was supposedly his murderer. Was that the truth? Was this Stephen a liar and a cheat and a spy? Was he a murderer? She paid very close attention to his every word, so she could discover the truth.

BRANDON TRIED TO CONCENTRATE ON WHAT ARLENE WAS saying, but his focus was on the woman who sat next to his brother halfway down the table. She seemed quite comfortable in Stephen's company. As if she were thoroughly charmed by him. As if she had known him for some time. A knot tightened in his chest.

She said she had never met Stephen, that she had mistaken him for someone else, but was she telling the truth? The fact that she had blurted his name, that he looked like someone she knew, seemed too much of a coincidence. Something was definitely out of kilter.

Perhaps she did know him and hadn't expected to see him at Arlene's gathering. Perhaps they were plotting something. Perhaps her sudden appearance in Hyde Park had been planned. But why?

She had been injured. By him. Surely that hadn't been planned. And he had taken her in. If she and his brother were plotting something together, then he had fallen into their trap.

No, that was too outrageous. Not even Stephen, his deceitful, lying, self-centered half-brother, would come up with a plan that subtle. But the coincidence of Miss Blake saying Stephen's name bothered him. And the fact that she was smiling and chatting amicably with the cur made his blood run hot through his veins. His fingers curled into a fist, and the urge to land that fist on his brother's nose nearly had him rising from his seat. Only a footman bending near and offering the first course distracted him. Drawing in a breath, he forced down his rage and turned his attention to Arlene, who had made some witty remark and was expecting a response.

EMMA SIGHED INWARDLY AS SHE FELT BRANDON'S GAZE ON HER. She had made a mistake blurting out Stephen's name. Brandon probably thought she was lying about knowing his brother, or worse. How was she going to rectify that? If he didn't trust her, he might throw her out of his house. She couldn't let that happen, so she would have to prove that she supported him. Somehow.

Stephen had finished his tale about the horse and had

turned to converse with the lady on his other side as the footmen began to serve dinner. Watching as the servants passed the head of the table, she found Lord Farley's gaze on her, as if she were an unknown specimen he had discovered under a microscope. His pale eyes gave her the creeps. Not wanting to offend him, she merely offered him a tiny smile and turned quickly away, becoming very interested in the pattern of the empty plate before her.

Something made her look up again in Farley's direction, whose intense gaze was on Stephen. She glanced at Stephen beside her. He was fumbling with his napkin, as if it had begun to slip from his lap, but he was too focused for such a simple task. Emma suspected that he and Farley had just had some sort of silent communication. What was going on?

She added that to the odd conversation about the horse and decided something besides a pleasant dinner party was occurring. Was Stephen really involved in something very, very wrong? In her book, the younger half-brother of her hero had been the villain, a spy. And he had been directed by an older man, the master spy. Was Farley that man? What if she had mirrored real life in her story? What if Ghost Brandon had really helped her write the book?

She glanced at Real Brandon again as he chatted with Arlene, then peeked at Stephen beside her. The coincidence of this Stephen's similar appearance to twenty-first century Stephen boggled her brain. She knew from her own experience that one of them was a cheat and a liar. Ghost Brandon had told her that the other was a murderer. Neither Stephen seemed to be honorable.

Ghost Brandon had told her she could "fix things" if she traveled back in time. But what things? What if she had been sent back to save him from being murdered?

That thought stunned her. As a bowl of soup was placed before her, she decided that was exactly what he meant. Her only problem was how to do that.

Seven

The evening was finally over. Emma had smiled and nodded and chatted, pretending that she had been born in the nineteenth century, pretending that she liked Stephen. He had been charming, but she had to force herself not to cringe away from him. She wondered if he was flirting with her merely because she had arrived on Brandon's arm and he wanted what his brother had. The enmity between the two men seemed to crackle in the air, and she couldn't understand why Arlene would invite them both on the same evening.

She'd felt Brandon's gaze on her during dinner, and then later when the men had finally joined the women in the salon. When Arlene had suggested a game of Whist, Stephen had claimed her as his partner, with Brandon and Arlene making up the foursome at their table. She knew how to play

Whist and was relieved the rules hadn't changed much over time. But as the game went on, the tension between Brandon and his brother grew as Stephen lost trick after trick. By the end of the evening, Brandon had won. Throwing a coolly triumphant glance at his brother, who was looking very bad-tempered, he declared the evening had been delightful and hurried Emma through their goodbyes.

Now, as he escorted her out to the carriage, his lips held a tiny upward tilt. After handing her up and settling beside her on the seat, he turned to gaze out the window.

She suspected he was pleased with himself for outwitting his brother at the card table. In fact, he had trounced his brother, almost as if he knew what card Stephen would play. Had he cheated? But she didn't know how he could have done that.

"Congratulations on your win at Whist," she said.

Her words drew his attention. "I am sorry you lost. My brother is not the best card player."

"But you are very good," she said, hoping he would reveal how he had won.

He shrugged away the compliment. "I've had quite a bit of practice."

She remembered Ghost Brandon had referred to himself as a rake and rogue. Was he a gambler? Is that what he meant?

"Do you go to the gaming hells? I've heard they're quite

exciting." Maybe she could get him to take her, and that would be wonderful research.

"They are not the place for ladies," he said, dashing her hopes. "But perhaps we could have a private game."

His suggestion made heat rise through her. A mischievous plan began to form. Perhaps she could get him to play a game of Vingt-et-un, which she knew very well. "I would like that."

"I could teach you some strategy, something my brother lacks when he plays." Dislike turned down a corner of his mouth.

"I've never met him before, you know," she blurted, then regretted her words as Brandon's good humor fled. His eyes turned cool, but she met that gaze directly. "Really. I've never laid eyes on your brother in my life before this evening."

"Then please explain why you said his name when you saw him."

Good question. "Well, they say everybody has a twin someplace on earth. I guess I must have met your brother's twin." Not really a lie.

"I would say more likely that my brother was your former protector, and he pretended not to know you." He leaned closer and traced his fingers along her jaw. "Tell me," he murmured. "What made him reject you?"

Angry at his assumption about her, she jerked away from his touch and snapped, "Perhaps I rejected him."

"Hm." His narrowed eyes indicated his disbelief. "Perhaps you have forgotten that as well as other things."

"I don't think I would have forgotten something like that," she said drily, even as she realized how ironic her statement was. She vividly remembered the last night she spent in twenty-first-century Stephen's bed, and her anger and sense of betrayal, of being used, the morning after when she learned about his fiancée. "I don't rely on any man to take care of me."

"Yet, here you are, in my care."

Stung, she ducked her head and her teeth clenched in frustration. Then she met his gaze directly. "Yes, I am, and I thank you for that. As soon as I am able, I will leave," she said recklessly. She had no idea where she would go or how she would support herself.

"Yes? Back to your traveling companions?" he challenged. "They must be as forgetful as you, for I've heard of no inquiries regarding a missing American woman."

Emma glanced away out the window as she considered her response. Should she reveal the truth, that she was from the future? No, she decided, he wouldn't believe her, not in the mood he was in. But maybe a partial truth.

She turned back to him. "I don't think I have traveling companions. I think I came here alone."

"Alone?" An ominous crease appeared between his brows. "Then you have regained your memory."

"Well, partly," she hedged.

"Respectable women do not travel alone. Respectable women do not gad about Hyde Park wearing next to nothing. Respectable women do not throw themselves at a passing vehicle and then pretend to lose their memory." With each statement, his tone grew colder and colder.

"I did not throw myself at your curricle. You ran into me," she corrected again in exasperation, but she realized she had to tell him something he might believe. "I know I'm a writer, and I remember I came to London to do research."

"A writer? Of course, you are," he scoffed.

Her chin went up. "Yes, I am, like Maria Edgeworth or Jane Austen."

He waved away her statement. "Even if Miss Austen is a writer, which I sincerely doubt, she lives quietly with her family and does not get abandoned in Hyde Park with hardly any clothes on. I have met the lady. And she is a *lady*."

Emma zapped him a look. "Are you implying I'm not a lady?"

After studying her a moment, in a low murmur, he countered, "Are you?"

His arm rested along the back of the seat and his fingers toyed with the short hairs that had escaped from her upswept hairdo at the back of her neck. The sensation sent a shiver down her spine. But she was not going to let Brandon think he could seduce her, even though he very easily could. She scooted as far away from him as the seat allowed.

"Our customs are different in America," she said, leaving

him to decide if she were lying or not, and turned away to look out the window.

He was silent for a moment. "Yes, quite."

What did he mean by that? Emma turned back to him, but he was staring out his own window. Did he believe her? Would he make her leave? Despite her brave words about being on her own, she wasn't ready to do that. Besides, she sensed she needed to stay close to Brandon if she were to save him. How would she do that if he threw her out?

BRANDON WATCHED THE DARK STREET ROLL PAST, BUT HIS focus was on the woman beside him on the seat. She was an enigma. How did she end up in Hyde Park, alone, and wearing such outlandish clothes? How did she know Stephen's name? Her explanation about being acquainted with someone who looked like him was hardly believable. Was she in league with him? Was she his former mistress? If she was, then she had certainly forgiven him for severing their relationship, for they had seemed quite amicable during dinner.

He glanced over at her. Despite his questions and doubts about her, she intrigued him. She was a puzzle he wanted to solve. The only way to do that was to keep her close. Besides, she was beautiful, and charming, and spirited. Since their accident in Hyde Park, he'd barely thought of Elizabeth, and a tiny twinge of guilt twisted in his chest. But he forgave himself as he reasoned he had to figure out who this woman was and her intention.

Coming to a decision, he said, "I would never throw a beautiful woman out of my house. Please remain as my guest for as long as you wish."

She turned to him and her body seemed to loosen. "Thank you. That's very generous of you."

As he accepted her gratitude with a small nod, he realized something else, something that had been nagging at the back of his mind since he had first laid eyes on her. "I feel like I should know you."

Her lips parted in surprise. "Maybe we've met in another life."

"Another life?"

She paused, as if trying to find an explanation. "Like when we were much younger, only you've forgotten."

"I don't believe I would have forgotten meeting you."

With a wry smile, she said, "I was very forgettable when I was younger."

"I doubt that." He smiled, but even as he did, he began to plan how he would discover this woman's secrets. One way or another.

EMMA SMILED BACK, BUT SHE WAS CONFUSED BY HIS SUDDEN reversal. Was he still suspicious of her apparent acquaintance with Stephen? Or had he accepted her explanation?

"I find you quite refreshing," he said.

Surprised by his admission, she blinked. Was he attempting to seduce her? Despite her suspicion, she blushed.

"I am being quite forward," he said. "Forgive me."

She smiled. "I don't think anyone has ever told me I'm refreshing."

"I have never met anyone quite like you. Are all American women like you?" The tone of his voice dropped.

Although the question was innocent, his low tone made it sound like an intimate invitation. Even in the dark coach, she could see the warmth in his eyes. Relieved that he had stopped questioning her about Stephen, she relaxed.

The romantic atmosphere blanketed her. The seclusion of the coach, the clip-clop of the horses, the dark streets lit only by the occasional gas light. His sexy attraction. The scent of him. She wanted him to kiss her. No. That wasn't happening. She wasn't in the past to have an affair with him. She was there to save him.

Trying desperately not to think about his mouth, or his

broad chest, or anything else about him, she said, "I wanted to thank you for the gown and everything," she said.

"Of course. I couldn't have 'my cousin from America' walking about London in..." He made a vague motion with his hand. "...whatever you were wearing when I found you. You look quite lovely this evening."

"Thank you." She blushed again and ducked her head. She hadn't blushed this much since she was a teenager.

When she looked up, his gaze was on her. Penetrating, deep, passionate. Her breath caught and goosebumps rose on her arms.

He leaned in. The timbre of his voice dropped to a rough burr. "Explain why I shouldn't kiss you."

She was mesmerized by the warm glint in his eyes. Heat curled deep inside her. She felt herself go wet. It would be so easy to lean toward him, to snuggle against him, to raise her mouth and give him her lips...

Unh-unh. That was not going to happen.

Ordering her hormones to behave, she glanced away from him, out the window, and searched for a reason not to kiss him. It was right there, waiting for her.

"Because we're home," she said.

AFTER ENTERING THE HOUSE, BRANDON DOFFED HIS HAT, THEN slipped her shawl from her shoulders. His fingers grazed her skin as he asked, "Would you care for a glass of Madeira before retiring?"

The brush of his fingers made Emma crave more. She was torn between wanting to escape from his alluring pull and wanting to spend more time with him. With an inward sigh, she gave up the fight.

"That would be very nice. Thank you," she said, as she promised herself she'd stay a safe distance away from him.

He opened the door into his study and waved her inside with a smile.

That smile appeared innocent, but Emma had the feeling she was walking into the lion's den. She reminded herself she wasn't going to become involved with him. And she wasn't going to kiss him, although she wondered what it was like to kiss a real romance novel hero.

While he poured a glass of wine for her and a brandy for himself, she wandered about the room and scanned the books lining the walls. Books on science, geography, astronomy, philosophy. Books in Latin and Greek. And books by famous authors, both of the past, like Chaucer, Shakespeare, and Swift, and of his time, like those he had given her to read.

When she came to his desk, she saw the paperweight she had used to threaten him when he first appeared as a ghost in her flat. She ran her finger across its cool, smooth surface. How strange and unnerving to see it here in the past.

On a table near the desk, she noticed a small portrait of a lovely woman with dark hair and lively gray eyes. Next to it was a wooden box of toy soldiers. Several were out of the box and standing guard. Emma indicated the portrait.

"She's beautiful. Who is she?"

Glancing her way as he poured, he answered, "My mother."

Of course. The mistress of Brandon's father. She could see the resemblance to her son — the same dark, luxurious hair, the same mischievous gray eyes.

"Do you see her often?" She wanted to meet the woman who had given up everything for true love.

He shook his head. "She died when I was a lad."

"I'm so sorry." Picking up one of the soldiers, she examined it. It looked well-used, with a bit of paint worn off. Without thinking, she blurted, "Were these for your son?"

His hand jerked as he placed the stopper into the decanter. The ring of crystal against crystal chimed very loudly. She watched him draw a breath.

Without looking at her, he said quietly, "How do you know about my son?"

Damn. She wasn't supposed to know about the boy. "Um, I just assumed..." With a wave of her hand, she indicated the toy soldiers.

He turned to look at her. Those gray eyes were glacial. "He died in my arms."

"I'm so sorry." She wanted to go to him, comfort him, but his icy demeanor warned her to stay back.

"Only a handful of people are aware I had a son." His cool tone underscored his displeasure as he turned back to the glasses on the table. "Only one of them was present this evening. They are all sworn to silence. And Stephen would never talk about the child—unless he has hired you to spy on me." That gray gaze landed on her with cold censure.

She gasped at his accusation. "No! I told you, I don't know your brother. I never met him before this evening."

His silence screamed disbelief.

"You don't believe me." She sank onto a chair.

"You make it very hard for me to believe you. I find you abandoned in Hyde Park, and then I discover you know someone who looks a great deal like Stephen—almost a twin, you say. And oddly, with the same name. I don't believe in such coincidences."

"But what I told you is the truth." Or as much of the truth as she dared tell him.

He stared at her a moment. She could see his mind working behind those incredible eyes. Then he approached and handed her the glass of Madeira. "Of course. My mistake."

His acceptance of her denial was too bland, too quick.

Why did she have the feeling she had just avoided the cow manure in the field only to be confronted by the angry bull?

"I thought we might go riding in Hyde Park tomorrow," he said mildly. "How does that suit you?" He strolled back across the carpet to lean an elbow on the mantle.

The abrupt shift in his demeanor and the innocuous invitation made her uneasy. What was behind it? She wasn't sure she wanted to know, and she certainly didn't want to go riding with him and risk revealing some part of the truth. "Sorry, I don't ride." She took a sip of her Madeira as she tried to decide if he was still angry or not.

"A lady who does not ride?" A brow rose in amazement. "How curious. Then I will teach you, but tomorrow we will ride in my curricle."

"Thank you," she murmured absently, deciding she could come up with an excuse not to go on that ride tomorrow, as she tried to decipher his quick change in attitude. He obviously didn't believe a word she'd said. She had to convince him she had no knowledge about the tragic events that had happened. Rising from her chair, she approached him. "I'm truly very sorry about the child."

Without a word, he turned to poke at the fire. The only sound in the room was the hiss of the coals burning and the tick of a clock on the mantle. He kept his head down and was silent for several heartbeats. Finally, he straightened and carefully replaced the poker in its stand.

"His mother is dead as well." His words were flat and

final. Then he turned to her, his eyes like two lasers. "If I ever hear one word from you about either of them, I will toss you out into the street."

Emma fell back a step. "Of course."

He studied her as if trying to make up his mind whether she was being truthful. Picking up his glass, he swirled its contents, then took a sip. He glanced in the direction of the toy soldiers. "I had planned to give him those. And I had planned to teach him to ride." His gaze swung to her and his eyes darkened. "Just like you, Miss Blake."

"Oh, I don't think..."

Her protest about learning to ride died in her throat as he stepped closer. She had to tip her head back to look at him. The words he spoke were quite innocent, but she had the impression that he was talking about riding more than just horses. In the blink of an eye, his demeanor had changed, from angry to seductive. She was very aware of his hand resting on the mantle beside her.

"You're changing the subject," she said, suspicious of where his thoughts were going.

A tiny smile pulled at the corners of his mouth. His other hand came up and rested on the mantle on the other side of her. She was blocked in.

"I am," he admitted. "We'll go to Hyde Park very early, before anyone is there."

"In your curricle?" She wanted to clarify what he was planning. And keep him talking. Because if he was talking, he couldn't do anything else with his mouth. Like kiss her. And she had the distinct impression that was his intent.

"Perhaps we'll start your riding lessons tomorrow," he murmured.

She swallowed. Again, was he talking about horses? Or something else? His presence blocked out everything. He was attempting to seduce her and she didn't know if she wanted to make him stop. At the same time, she wondered why. What game was he playing?

"I don't have the right clothes," she said, stalling while she tried to make up her mind.

"I'll let you borrow some of mine." He leaned closer.

"But those are man's clothes. People would be scandalized." Her words had nothing to do with the argument going on inside her head. Let him kiss her? Or not?

"You didn't seem to mind scandalizing people when you were running about in next to nothing." While his statement reproached, his seductive murmur implied something else entirely.

"I—" She started to debate about her leggings and tee shirt, then found she had no argument. She *had* been running in next to nothing. Scandalous in his time. Not at all in hers. But her thoughts weren't on her clothes. They were on his intent. If she played his game, would she be able to figure out his motive? Glancing up at him, into his smoky gray eyes, she challenged, "Did you mind?"

He huffed a laugh. "Not in the least." Leaning in, he whispered, "But you appear more respectable now. Are you, Emma?"

"Maybe you need to decide that for yourself." She was treading on dangerous ground with that suggestion. In fact, she had stepped directly from semi-solid ground right into quicksand.

"Ah, a challenge," he murmured and brushed a strand of hair from her cheek. His hand landed on the curve of her shoulder, and his thumb caressed a spot beneath her ear.

Emma nearly melted. She felt as if he were a magnet pulling her closer. And she had no resistance. She swayed toward him. All those arguments about not falling for him dissipated in a puff of filmy mist. He lowered his head. She closed her eyes.

The graze of his lips across her mouth was as light as the touch of a petal. A sigh escaped her. Then she felt another soft kiss. His hand cupped her head and his fingers tangled in her hair. A low growl came from his throat. That kiss of a petal turned into a demand. His other arm dropped to her waist, and he pulled her against him. Emma went willingly. As he took possession of her mouth, all thought fled her brain.

The world collapsed down to him. And his mouth. And the hard body pressing against her. And the insistent bulge in his pants. When his tongue sought entrance, she let him in. Her acceptance was a foregone conclusion. Why wouldn't she soul-kiss with this man who made every one of her nerve endings stand at attention? Just one kiss...

Wait. No. What was she doing?

She pulled back and stared up at him. She couldn't become involved with him. He wasn't alive in her time. He was a ghost! She could get flung back to her own time at any moment, like tomorrow, when he took her on a ride and they passed that ancient oak.

He stared back, his eyes dark and stormy. Passion oozed from him. His arousal pressed against her. Her thin dress and his tight trousers didn't hide anything.

Behind her, the clock on the mantle ticked loudly. The only other sound in the room was her breathing. And his. They sounded as if they had both run a marathon.

He took a step away. Then another. The dark passion in those vivid eyes turned from fiery to cool in a heartbeat.

"My apologies," he said, as if he had merely trod on her toe. "I do not usually ravage women I barely know."

Emma felt as if her brain had been plonked in a jar of marbles and rattled around a bit. First, he accused her of being a spy for his half-brother, then he confided in her about his son, and then he nearly seduced her. Suspicion, trust, and allure. Now, chilly civility.

She edged toward the door. "That's okay. I mean, not a problem."

His eyes crinkled at her slang.

She blinked and took a breath. Her arousal was interfering with her tongue. "It is of no matter," she said, dredging up nineteenth century diction from her addled brain. "We are both tired. I believe I'll retire now."

"Of course."

Emma turned and fled. But she felt his stare between her shoulder blades like an itch.

BRANDON WATCHED HER FLEE, FEELING AS BEFUDDLED AS SHE appeared to be. With her escape, she seemed to take something vibrant with her, turning the room dull and colorless. He never should have kissed her. But for some reason, he couldn't help himself.

She was unlike any other woman he had ever met. And he'd met quite a few. In the year since Elizabeth's death, after his initial period of drowning his sorrow in drink when he'd barely left his house, he'd gone a different route, played the tables and tried to forget his grief by going from one mistress to another. His last had been Arlene, Lady Farley, just for one night. She had cured him of any further desire for a mistress. He had broken off their relationship three months ago, because he had suddenly realized his life was a tawdry waste.

Except for that one night before he ran into the woman in Hyde Park.

Grief had overwhelmed him that night, so he'd indulged in drink to try to forget and wagered heavily at the gaming tables. When he'd set out for his appointment with his solicitor the next morning, his head had been pounding and his eyes were bleary. Lady Luck had certainly been riding next to him, for Miss Blake might have been killed.

He picked up his glass of brandy and stared at the contents. Emma Blake confounded him. Who was she? American, certainly. But what else? The Bow Street Runner he'd hired to visit all the hotels and rooming houses to see if a woman fitting Emma's description had stayed at any of the establishments had found nothing. And no one seemed to be missing her. Had she come to London alone, as she said?

But where had she come from? She hadn't just stepped off a ship when he found her. Where had she been staying? Perhaps his first assumption about her had been correct, that she was someone's jilted mistress. Except she hotly denied that. Was she lying? Was she a respectable young woman or a lightskirt? She'd been kissed before. Of that, he was certain. But she was the one who came to her senses first when he'd kissed her. Was she pretending to be virtuous, or had she truly been saving herself from ruin? Or was her retreat part of a game she played to lure him in?

Her recognition of Stephen bothered him. While she said

she didn't know him, and the two of them didn't act like they knew each other, her explanation sounded untruthful. And then her knowledge of his son deeply bothered him. How did she know about him? The only answer he could form was that Stephen had told her.

He hadn't trusted his half-brother for a very long time. Was Stephen trying to learn how close he was to gaining his birthright? Was the woman a spy for him? Something about Miss Emma Blake did not make sense.

Those clothes, when he found her, were made of cloth that he'd never encountered before, and those ridiculous shoes, that appeared to be heavy as an anvil, but were, in fact, rather lightweight, seemed to come from some magical place. Even her accents and words were strange, unlike anything he had ever heard, not even from other Americans he had met. Was she a fairy?

He scoffed at himself and gulped down the rest of his brandy. His mother had believed in fairies. The little people, she had called them. He had believed, too, once, long ago, when he was young. Not anymore. He wondered what he had done to incur their spite, because bad luck had followed him his whole life. When he'd wanted to wed Elizabeth, she'd been forced to wed his brother instead. She'd bled out while giving birth to his son and they had both died. When his father had gained a legitimate son, he and his mother had been forced out of their cottage and off his father's estate.

No, Emma Blake was no mythical creature. She was a flesh and blood woman. But what sort of woman? Placing his glass on the mantle, he decided he would pursue the answer and gain the truth.

That would be a very intriguing pastime indeed.

Eight

The next morning, Emma entered the dining room to find Brandon already up and sitting at one end of the table. He was hidden behind a newspaper, and for that, she was grateful. She hadn't slept well, having tossed and turned and replayed that kiss over and over in her head. Was he truly interested in her, or was he playing some game?

Hoping to get some caffeine in her before she had to engage in conversation with him, she slipped into a chair at the other end of the table and snagged the teapot. She really wanted coffee, a large latte with a shot of hazelnut, but resigned herself to what was available.

"You don't have to tip-toe about, Miss Blake," he said from behind his paper. "I assure you, I don't bite, not even in the morning."

She stopped pouring at his words. Damn. She was trying to be unobtrusive. And he was back to calling her Miss. So he was ignoring what happened between them the night before. Well, she could, too.

"I appreciate the assurance, Mr. Connaught," she said coolly, "but I am not a morning person. I must have my tea before I can be civil." She topped off her teacup, then added cream before taking a sip.

He sent her a suspicious look over the top of the paper. She smiled innocently.

Folding up the paper and carefully placing it on the pile of other newspapers beside his plate, he said, "I have been perusing the notices for anyone looking for a missing person."

A chill ran through Emma. "Did you find anything?" She hoped she put the proper amount of eagerness in her voice, because she already knew the answer.

Before he had a chance to respond, a commotion erupted in the entry hall, and then a middle-aged woman, fashionably dressed in a traveling frock of maroon and a matching hat dipped rakishly above one eye, swept into the dining room. A white plume curved down the back. Brandon shot to his feet at her entrance.

"Brandon, dear," the woman said as she offered her cheek for a kiss. "I was so happy to receive your message. I came as soon as I could."

He pecked her cheek. "Good morning, Aunt Morrin. Thank you for coming." He turned to Emma. "May I present Lady Selby, my mother's sister." Then he introduced Emma.

Surprised at meeting one of Brandon's relatives, Emma stood, and at the last minute, remembered to curtsy. While his mother had been merely a mistress to an earl, her sister had evidently married a title, quite a difference in station. But the family resemblance was clear. Lady Selby had the same gray eyes as her nephew, but instead of dark hair, hers was a glowing red, although a few gray strands wove through the hair at her temples.

"So," Lady Selby said as her glance took in Emma from head to toe. "This is the foundling you nearly ran over. And she has no memory of her lodgings or companions? Curious."

"That is what she has told me," Brandon said, and sent a warning glance in Emma's direction.

Emma caught that look. Since she'd told him that she might have arrived in London alone only the night before, he hadn't had a chance to tell his aunt. Maybe he didn't want to reveal that to the lady, so she kept quiet.

"But Brandon, dear, she could be anyone, a charlatan." Lady Selby's gaze continued to be fixed on Emma.

"She says she is from America," Brandon said. "I believe her. As I wrote in my note, I have taken her in. We are using the fiction that she is a distant cousin on my mother's side."

Uncomfortable at being discussed as if she weren't there, Emma opened her mouth to say she was standing right in front of them, then closed it again. Manners, she reminded herself. Different century, different mores.

Lady Selby began to strip off her gloves. "Well, we shall learn all there is to learn. In the meantime, I wish to freshen up. Please send a tea tray to my room." She speared a glance at Emma. "You may visit with me when you have finished here." Turning, she swept out.

Feeling as if an elastic had just released her, Emma sank back to her chair. "That was your aunt?"

"Yes."

"You invited her here?"

"Yes." Brandon's gaze challenged her to question his decision.

She questioned anyway. "Why?"

He sat and straightened the fork on his plate, then casually leaned back in his chair. "You need a companion. A chaperone."

"A—?" Emma closed her mouth. Of course, she needed a companion for appearances, despite pretending to be a widow. This wasn't the twenty-first century. She was an unwed woman staying in a bachelor's home. She took a breath and said calmly, "You couldn't find anyone else? She seems rather—um—severe."

His brows shot up. She had criticized his aunt.

"I appreciate your thoughtfulness," she said quickly. "You're right. I do need a companion."

His mouth twitched. "You'll see she's not as she first appears. She can be quite merry, actually."

"Wonderful," she said faintly, and reached for a piece of toast and the pot of marmalade. At least the lady's presence would cut back the opportunities for kissing. And that made her both relieved and disappointed.

EMMA STRAIGHTENED HER SKIRT AND SMOOTHED HER HAIR, then knocked on the door to Lady Selby's room. She had to remember that she wasn't in her own time. At the woman's call to enter, Emma took a breath and walked in.

Lady Selby was seated at a small table before the window and sipping tea. She had removed her hat and spencer, which had been tossed on the bed. Her valises stood in the middle of the room, and Emma stopped when she reached them, leaving them as a barrier between her and the lady.

"Come closer, please," Lady Selby directed. "I want to see you in the light."

Holding back a sigh, Emma stepped forward.

Lady Selby scrutinized her as if she could see into

Emma's mind and uncover all her secrets. Then, all she said was, "Hmm," and took another sip of tea. Thoughtfully, she placed the cup back on its saucer. Indicating the chair opposite her, she said, "Please, sit."

Emma perched on its edge. She felt as if she were back in high school and had been summoned to the principal's office.

"My nephew," Lady Selby began, "has always had a soft spot for strays. When he was a child, he would bring home a lost kitten, or an abandoned bunny, or a baby bird that had fallen from its nest. I thought he had outgrown that. Evidently, he has not."

Emma was very grateful he hadn't. She should have added that characteristic to the hero in her novel. Well, she could do that with her revisions when she returned to her own time. If she returned.

Lady Selby's gaze landed on her again. "Brandon believes you are Quality. Are you?"

Quality? Didn't he think she was someone's discarded mistress? She floundered for an answer. "Um, we don't actually have that in America."

The lady's eyes narrowed. "Are you certain? Or is that something else you don't remember?"

Emma straightened her spine. "I remember quite well."

"Hm." Lady Selby took another sip of tea. "Tell me about your family."

"I have two sisters. My mother died when I was very

young and I don't really remember her. My father was English, but we moved to America after my mother died. He died six months ago in an accident." Her voice wavered on the last bit.

"That must have been quite a shock. I am so sorry for your loss." For once, Lady Selby sounded sympathetic, instead of suspicious. "Why have you come to London?"

Emma folded her hands in her lap. She couldn't tell the woman she was from the future, but she could reveal some truth. "I think I came to get away from Boston, where my father..." She couldn't say the word again. "I feel close to my parents here." After saying the words, she realized that was the truth. She did feel closer to them in London, as if she belonged in the city.

Lady Selby raised a quizzing glass hanging from a ribbon around her neck. After she had examined Emma for a moment, she said, "You do remind me of someone. Hmm, Blake...Blake. That name sounds quite familiar." She dropped the quizzing glass and shook her head. "I'm sure it will come to me." Her laser gaze landed on Emma again and traveled from her head to her feet and back up. "If we are taking you out in public to discover who is missing you, you are going to need a wardrobe."

Emma opened her mouth to tell her Brandon had already ordered a few dresses for her.

Lady Selby waved away her silent protest. "My nephew told me about Madame Fanchon, but what he ordered just won't do. You will need more than two frocks and a ball gown. We will visit her this morning."

The lady tore a tiny piece from a scone on the plate before her, spread a bit of jam on it and popped it in her mouth. When Emma did not move, she waved her hand. "That is all. You may go."

Dismissed, Emma wasted no time leaving the lady's presence. As she closed the door behind her and stood in the hall, she remembered that she was supposed to go for a ride with Brandon. Going to the modiste's with Lady Selby was the perfect excuse to decline Brandon's invitation. She went in search of him.

She found him in his study and frowning over a document on his desk. He stood as soon as she entered and smiled.

"Miss Blake, have you completed your interview with my aunt?"

Emma sank into a chair before his desk and blew out a breath. "Yes. She's quite formidable."

His lips twitched. "I'm sure you will grow to like her."

She sent him a dubious look.

Glancing down, he thoughtfully straightened the papers on the desk before meeting her gaze. "My aunt is an Irish lady who wed an English baron, and was not well-received by London society because of her ancestry. She shows one side to the people she does not know, and another to her family and those she trusts."

Emma knew at that time the English generally thought the Irish people were below them, so his aunt most likely learned how to deal with those who snubbed her. "That must have been hard for her."

His mouth curled up at one corner. "As you saw, she does not easily trust."

Nodding her understanding, she said, "She wants me to go to Madame Fanchon's with her this morning. I'm afraid I can't go riding with you." Both relief and disappointment tangled in that statement.

"Of course, you can. My aunt wouldn't think of shopping before noon." He glanced beyond her to the clock on the mantle. "We have hours before she'll demand your presence."

"Oh, perfect." Emma tried to force some enthusiasm into her words. She was afraid to go on a ride with him. They'd be alone again, and all she could think of was that kiss from the night before.

A line appeared between his brows. "Don't you want to go on a ride, Miss Blake?"

"Of course, I do. It's just—" She decided the only way to clear the air was to be blunt. "Look, about last night...."

"What about last night?" That line between his brows deepened.

"I don't want you to get the wrong idea." He already had the wrong idea, thinking she was somebody's thrown-over mistress. But he had told his aunt he thought she was *Quality*. What did he really think?

"The wrong idea?" He propped a hip on his desk right next to her. "About what, Miss Blake?" He took up her hand and kissed the tips of her fingers. "Was it about this?" He shook his head. "I don't believe it could be that." Turning her hand over, he placed a kiss on her palm. Frowning in confusion, he said, "No, that couldn't be what worries you. I don't recall doing that." Resting an elbow on his knee, he leaned close. "Perhaps, Miss Blake," he murmured, "you think I might do this again."

Before Emma had recovered from the caress on the palm of her hand that made her insides all gooey, he placed his lips against hers. The spicy lime scent of him filled her nostrils, and the touch of his mouth made every thought in her head vanish. She remained perfectly still, afraid that if she moved just the tiniest bit, he might back off. Or worse, he might continue on. Because if he did that, she wasn't sure she could stop him. She couldn't go down that road. No way was she going to fall for a ghost, who was not a ghost any longer, who was very alive and kissing her. Besides, she had decided she was there to save him, not have an affair with him.

He ended with a swipe of his tongue across her lips, a reminder of the kiss the night before, a promise of what might come. When he straightened, she opened her eyes and blinked, trying to adjust from the fantasy of *him*, to the real world.

His lips curved in a teasing smile, but his eyes held a hint of confusion. "Not quite what I remembered, but rather satisfactory all the same."

Satisfactory? It was way more than satisfactory. It was wonderful, stupendous.

Whoa.

She put the brakes on that train of thought. She had to discourage him, not want more of the same.

Sitting up straight, she said coolly, "It was, as you say, satisfactory. But I believe that in the interest of good behavior and because your aunt is in residence, we should refrain from any further — um — *that*." She waved her hand vaguely, at a loss for what to call what just happened in nineteenth century parlance.

He stared at her for a heartbeat, then threw his head back and laughed. It was a full-throated guffaw that made her cheeks heat, at the same time falling like well-tuned bells on her ears. How could he embarrass her and make her want him at the same time?

When he sobered, he grinned at her. "*That*, Miss Blake, was a kiss, and I am very sure you know exactly what to call it. But we will refrain from doing *that*, if you wish." The look in his eyes challenged, as if silently daring her to abstain from kissing. Standing, he walked around his desk and sat, putting it between them. "I am looking forward to our ride this morning. Will a half of an hour be enough for you to ready yourself?"

"Of course." She was a bit insulted he should think it would take that long to collect a hat and a wrap. But maybe ladies took much longer to ready themselves for an outing in this century. "Excuse me while I go ready myself."

She stood and left the room with as much dignity as she could muster, disgruntled that he knew her protests about kissing were as insubstantial as the air.

She was both looking forward to their ride and dreading it.

EMMA SAT HIGH ON THE CURRICLE'S SEAT BESIDE BRANDON. She loved it. The sense of freedom with just a hint of danger felt like riding in a sporty convertible. The streets were mostly empty, except for those that were close to the shops and markets, so Brandon kept the horses at a brisk trot. They passed down roads familiar to Emma, but looking different than what she was used to seeing. Trees were not as large, or hadn't been planted yet, and some houses hadn't been built. The large townhouses still belonged to a single family, and had not been broken up into smaller flats. Then he turned down the street where she lived in the twenty-first century. As they passed the building where her flat was located, she asked him to slow down.

"Does that house look familiar to you?" he asked.

"Yes." Of course it did. Her father had owned it, had occupied one of the flats in it. Now, it belonged to her and her two sisters, but when he had acquired it was a mystery, the details lost in a jumble of documents.

"What do you remember?" He pounced on her answer, as if he had suddenly found the key to unlocking her memory.

Emma shook her head, pretending forgetfulness. "Not much, I'm afraid. Perhaps I am mistaken."

She turned back to the house. While the front of the building was bare brick in Emma's time, now ivy covered most of the façade of the house and nearly obscured several windows, one of which was in her bedroom. A pair of trees guarded the front door, which were missing in the twenty-first century. The house had the feel of abandonment, yet an open window with filmy curtains on an upper floor indicated someone lived there.

Brandon slowed the horses to a walk. "The house belongs to a reclusive widow," he said. "I understand she was the catch of the season when she made her coming out, and had offers from several titled gentlemen. She chose an untitled second son of an earl instead. He died tragically after only a few years of marriage. She retired from society after that and now hardly ever leaves her house." He gave her a speculative glance. "Odd that the house should seem familiar to you."

"Yes, it is quite odd." Emma was fascinated by the story. Her father had never told her any of the history of the house.

Of course, it most likely had several owners over the centuries. "Perhaps someone else told me the story about the poor woman and I have forgotten," she suggested.

"Of course," he agreed, but she felt his curious gaze.

Seeing the house and hearing the story of its owner unsettled her, as if something was out of kilter. She felt unbalanced, and blamed it on the difference between the centuries. Yet, she couldn't drag her gaze away. That open window with the filmy curtains fascinated her, because it seemed to contradict the atmosphere of abandonment. Compassion for the sad widow who lived there closed up her throat, and she had to swallow several times to push away the tears. She was glad when they had passed the house, and Brandon snapped the reins to get the horses trotting again.

After a moment, he said, "I've had a chat with my aunt. She has a theory about why I found you in such a state in Hyde Park."

"Yes?" Both anxious to hear it and dreading what the lady might have said, Emma clasped her hands tightly in her lap.

"She believes that you are a genteel lady and might have been robbed, or perhaps kidnapped for ransom and then escaped. The bump on your head has made you forget the terrible event." He glanced at her. "Do you remember anything before we ran into each other?"

Brandon still wasn't taking responsibility for nearly running her down, but she ignored that. Instead, she jumped on the opportunity to explain her existence in his time and the change in his opinion of her.

"All I remember is running through Hyde Park, and then I saw you in your curricle," she said, which was the absolute truth.

"Well, then, that supports what my aunt believes." He gave a confirming nod. "I have Runners out trying to gather information, but there are so many cutthroats and scallywags in the city, they may not find anything."

"Thank you," she said, but she knew those Runners wouldn't find one bit of evidence.

They entered Hyde Park not long after. As they drove along the deserted lanes, one rider approached. Emma cringed when she saw it was Stephen, but realized if she were going to help Brandon, she needed to be friendly to his half-brother to discover more about him. He was the villain in her book, a sneaky spy working for the French. Was he the same in reality in the nineteenth century?

Stephen fell in beside them and tipped his hat. "Good morning! What a pleasant surprise to see you, Mrs. Blake," he said, ignoring Brandon.

Emma smiled and offered her hand to force Brandon to stop. "Good morning, m'lord."

Brandon scowled in her direction, but halted the curricle. She hadn't yet come up with a plan to help him, but meeting Stephen like this certainly provided an opening.

"You are out early this morning," he observed.

"Oh, I love the early morning air," she gushed. "And Cousin Brandon was kind enough to indulge me. But you are out early as well." She sensed Brandon's annoyance at her flirtation.

"I enjoy the early morning air, as well." Stephen's gaze was warm and he still held her hand. "Perhaps you would do me the honor of accompanying me on a ride early tomorrow?"

She panicked for a moment, because she couldn't ride a horse. "Oh! That would be delightful, but I'm afraid I must decline your lovely invitation." Emma looked as downcast as she could. "Brandon's aunt has requested my attention for most of the day." Then she brightened. "Perhaps another time?"

Stephen gave her fingers an intimate squeeze. "Of course. I will send 'round a note."

"That's settled then," Brandon said as he snapped the reins. "Good day, Pemberton."

As the curricle began to roll away, Stephen was forced to release Emma's fingers. He tipped his hat.

"Until our next meeting, Mrs. Blake," he said.

Emma waved. "Goodbye!"

Brandon scowled at the horses. "How can you have any liking for that sorry churl?"

"I don't, but I think he might be involved in something he shouldn't be."

His gaze cut to her. "Why would you think that? He

already has everything he could possibly want — my father's approval and inheritance. He has no need to be involved in anything underhanded."

"I saw some strange communication between him and Lord Farley during dinner. If I can charm him, then he might confide in me."

"I don't want you anywhere near him," he grumbled.

Emma placed her hand on his arm. "Brandon, what if I could help you get your birthright?"

He looked down at her hand, then glanced at her. His muscles bunched beneath her fingers, and he turned back to the path before them.

"That's impossible," he muttered.

"But what if it isn't?" she persisted. "What if I could prove that he was involved in something so terrible that your father would disown him?"

He flashed a curious look at her. "What makes you believe that he's involved in something he shouldn't be?"

"Last night, Sir Dotson mentioned a horse that had been smuggled out of France. He seemed very anxious for Stephen to see it, and then Stephen told me an outrageous story about how the horse came to England. After that, he and Lord Farley exchanged this strange look between them."

He shook his head and turned his attention back to the horses. "A smuggled horse and a glance? Hardly enough to prove anything except that you have a vivid imagination."

"But what if I'm right? What if he is involved in something horrible? Your father would have to disown him."

His lips twisted in disgust. "That would never happen. My father thinks my brother is the perfect son."

"I would like to try." She placed her hand on his arm. "Please."

He glanced down at her hand again, then those gray eyes speared her. "Why are you willing to do this?"

"Because you took me in when I had nowhere to go. You took care of me." She left off the part about meeting his ghost. And trying to save him from being shot. And liking his kisses very much.

Something softened in his gaze, then he quickly looked away and shook his head. "I don't like the idea of your being with him."

His protective statement warmed her insides, but the only way she could discover if Stephen was up to something was to pretend to like him.

"What can he do? I have Lady Selby as my companion. And you." She added on that last bit hoping she did have him as a shield.

"You don't know what he's capable of," he said, his tone dark.

She did know. She had seen the hole in Brandon's back. But she wasn't going to think about that, so she kept her tone light. "I can protect myself. I know karate," she fibbed and had to swallow a giggle, remembering how she had threatened his ghost.

His eyes narrowed. "What is karate?"

"It's a form of self-defense. All American ladies know it. That's one of the things we do when we gather in the parks." Thank goodness she wasn't Pinocchio, because her nose would be a mile long.

"Someday, I'm going to have to sail to America to see these sights for myself," he mused.

Emma just smiled.

Nine

Two nights later, Emma found herself walking into Vauxhall Gardens on Brandon's arm. Lady Selby, on his other arm, had declared it was the perfect place to start making inquiries about Emma's traveling companions. Despite feeling guilty about lying, Emma felt a thrill of excitement to see the famous gathering spot of the ton. The research she'd done for her books couldn't match the experience of a visit. Thousands of lamps lit the gardens, with torches stuck in the ground and lanterns strung between the trees. She felt she was entering a fairyland.

Lady Selby had been able to acquire a supper-box, where they dined on ham and salad, and sipped arrack punch. Unfamiliar with the drink, she learned that arrack was made from fermented palm sugar and rice. Lady Selby warned her about its potency.

Emma watched the dancing from their supper-box. Young men claimed the young ladies for partners, and she observed the couples bow and curtsey, circle around each other, move together and apart, all in a dignified cadence. She had seen videos of recreated Regency balls, very formal and proper, but this seemed more relaxed and freer.

Brandon excused himself after the supper to speak with acquaintances. Watching him make his way around the edge of the dancing, she wished he would claim her for a dance, but she doubted he would ask her. They had come on the pretense of discovering clues to Emma's traveling companions, not for an evening of dancing. Beside her, Brandon's aunt was chatting with the lady in the next box.

As Emma kept her gaze on Brandon, she began to wonder how close her book had been to the truth. He was nearly the same man she had described. Stephen seemed to be just as unscrupulous as her villain. In her book, the heroine had discovered evidence that proved the villain was dishonorable. If her time in the past mirrored her story, then maybe she could do the same. Did that mean she was the heroine in this story?

The thought both excited and terrified her.

BRANDON ESCAPED FROM THE SUPPER-BOX, FROM THE beguiling Miss Blake, as soon as supper was over. Emma had looked entrancing when she had descended the stairs in his house, and he had stared, despite his best efforts not to do so. In the coach ride to Vauxhall Gardens, he had purposely sat on the seat opposite, so he wouldn't be close to her, so he wouldn't be able to breathe in her scent of warm vanilla. But her vague outline in the dark coach drew his gaze more than once, in fact, many times.

During their supper, he had distracted himself with making the arrak punch, serving his aunt, and attempting conversation, but all he wanted to do was kiss her. As soon as was proper, he excused himself, intending to distract himself with the conversation of acquaintances. But his gaze kept returning to the supper-box and the lovely, mysterious woman who sat there.

Who was she? Why would she want to help him gain his title? Most importantly, why did he want to kiss her, explore her, make her cry out in passion?

DEEP IN THOUGHT, EMMA WAS STARTLED WHEN STEPHEN rapped on the entrance to the box and asked for entrance.

"Only if you behave yourself, Pemberton," Lady Selby said sternly.

With a charming smile, he said, "I never misbehave, Lady Selby."

She turned away. "Hmph."

Stephen bowed before Emma. "Mrs. Blake, what a delightful surprise to find you here this evening."

Emma glanced up at him. What was he doing here? Had he come to look over the debutantes in search of another wife? Or had he somehow learned that she and Brandon would attend? No, that was impossible.

"If you are not otherwise engaged, I would be honored if you would allow me the honor of this next dance," he said, as he held out his hand.

Emma's mind raced. She thought she would have time to plan how to proceed to get him to spill his secrets before she saw him again. If she refused him now, he might be so insulted that she would lose her chance. This would be a perfect time to charm him into thinking she was in awe of him.

She smiled. "Thank you, Lord Pemberton. You honor me." She placed her hand in his and allowed him to lead her onto the dance floor.

When the music began, she was relieved to hear the notes of a country dance, because she sort of knew the steps. The couples made two lines facing each other, and then each couple moved down between the two rows, eventually

166

ending up last and moving each couple closer to the top. Stephen had placed them second to the end, so she would be able to observe the other couples as they performed the steps. As they waited for their turn, Emma and Stephen had time to converse.

"You are looking quite lovely, this evening, Mrs. Blake," Stephen began.

"Thank you, my lord." She tried to look properly demure.

"Please, call me Pemberton." As the dance called for them to step closer, he whispered, "Or Stephen, if you prefer."

Emma smiled sweetly and tried not to grind her teeth at his arrogant condescension. Since they were still waiting for their turn to get to the top of the line, she said, "I heard you speaking about Tattersall's the other night at dinner. Isn't that the horse auction house?"

"Have you never been?" he asked. At her negative response, he said, "Then you must allow me to take you tomorrow. It's quite a spectacle."

"I would enjoy that." This time, her smile was real, for she was getting closer to Stephen and discovering what he might be plotting. "Will we see the magnificent horse that was smuggled from Napoleon?" They stepped forward and back.

Annoyance flashed through his eyes, and he glanced right and left, as if to see if anyone heard. "That is not a subject to discuss here."

Looking properly chastised, she said, "I'm so sorry. I had no idea it was a secret."

As they came together and stepped around each other, he appeared even more annoyed. "It is not *that*, exactly, but I do wish to keep it quiet."

"Of course," she agreed, but knew he wanted it kept very secret. She couldn't understand why he would have mentioned the horse at the dinner party, and then told her the outrageous story about it. Unless he was trying to impress her. But why? To make Brandon jealous?

They were at the front of the line now, and so she had to concentrate on her steps. This way, and that way, and around, and curtsey. She made it through the dance, only stepping on Stephen's toes once.

Relieved when he returned her to the supper-box, she immediately excused herself from Lady Selby and made her way back to the edge of the dance floor. As she watched the next several dances, she wondered where Brandon was. She couldn't see him anywhere in the vicinity. Then the opening strains of a waltz drifted through the air.

Brandon suddenly stood in front of her.

Bowing, he held out his hand. "May I have the pleasure, Mrs. Blake?" His lips twitched when he said her name.

Emma placed her hand in his, and he swept her out into the middle of the couples. She didn't care that she had never danced the waltz of the Regency, different than the one that was popular several decades later when Johann Strauss became famous. Instead of dancing face to face and whirling around the floor, the dance was more like a quadrille, where couples created circles, occasionally performing twirls and other intricate steps. All that mattered was that she was dancing with Brandon.

Occasionally during the dance, his arm circled her waist and held her close as he spun her around. The feel of him pressed against her side felt perfect, and the hard muscles in his thigh brushed against her leg every time they took a step. She itched to squeeze closer. His scent of spicy lime filled her nostrils, and she wanted to sniff him in.

They danced in perfect unison, and Emma didn't stumble once. The music and Brandon's expert lead made her feel as if she were floating. She had to think about something else besides his well-toned muscles beneath his evening clothes, or the way his hand guided her firmly around the floor. But she kept thinking of the kiss they had shared and the way he felt so solid against her. Naughty things ran through her brain.

"I have been invited to Tattersall's tomorrow," she said, trying to distract herself.

"My brother, I suppose," he grumbled.

"Yes. I plan to find out what he's up to."

Thunder clouds began to form in his eyes. "I don't like your spending so much time with him."

The dance forced them apart so she could twirl beneath Brandon's arm. When they came together again, she said slyly, "I will need a chaperone. Perhaps your aunt might suffer from the mulligrubs."

His brows went up and he cast a considering glance up at Lady Selby sitting with a few other ladies in her supper-box. When his gaze landed on Emma again, humor twisted his lips. "I think I might persuade her to feign some illness."

She smiled, satisfied and happy. Not only would she have the chance to get Stephen to reveal something, she would also have Brandon's company the next day. What could be better?

LATER THAT EVENING, EMMA FOUND A QUIET SPOT TO WATCH the dancers. She caught a glimpse of Brandon chatting with a few other men. Would he ask her to dance again? That memory would stay with her forever.

She felt like she was in a dream. Being in the past was every historical writer's wish, but she missed the twenty-first century. Her sisters were probably frantic. She had to find some way to communicate with them to let them know she was safe. But how could she do that?

"Are you enjoying your stay in London, Mrs. Blake?" a man asked from beside her.

She startled, so caught up in her thoughts that she hadn't

heard him. "Oh, my goodness, sir, you mustn't sneak up on a lady like that."

"My apologies," he said smoothly. "I did not mean to startle you."

Emma had the distinct impression that he had intended just that. He was not as tall as either Brandon or Stephen, and everything about him seemed bland and nondescript—pale brown hair and eyes, pale lips, pale complexion, even his dark evening clothes seemed pale. In his hand was a strange watch, larger than a pocket watch, with many hands and odd symbols on its face. Emma felt vaguely uncomfortable standing next to him. She edged away, as if wanting to get a better view of the dancers.

"You did not answer my question, Mrs. Blake," he said, watching the dancers as well.

"I am enjoying London very much," she said.

He nodded as if he approved of her answer. "A pity you are staying with Connaught. London has so many interesting sights that he will never show you."

She wondered what those sights were. Something about the way he spoke about them made her think she wouldn't want to see them at all. He made her nervous.

Edging away another step, she said, "I'm sorry, sir, have we met?"

He smiled, a thin-lipped curve of his mouth, and bowed. "Forgive me, Mrs. Blake. I am Roger Bowker. I was at school with your cousin, but in a higher form."

His emphasis on the word *cousin* made Emma think he didn't believe the charade, and that maybe he and Brandon weren't friends.

"But how do you know my name, sir?" she asked.

His thin lips smiled. "Everyone has heard of Connaught's beautiful cousin from America."

Emma ducked her head, not sure whether she was pleased or not. The gossip had certainly spread quickly.

"There you are, dear cousin!" Brandon stepped up beside her. "I've come to collect you. Aunt Morrin wishes to leave." He glanced at the man standing next to Emma and nodded abruptly. "Bowker."

"Connaught," Mr. Bowker answered.

Brandon held out his arm to Emma. "Shall we?"

Emma gratefully slipped her hand into the curve of Brandon's arm and tossed a polite smile in the other man's direction. "It was very nice to meet you, Mr. Bowker." Then she let Brandon lead her away.

"He shouldn't have been speaking with you," he said. "You haven't been introduced."

Emma wondered what had caused the enmity between the two men. "He just started chatting with me. Should I have ignored him?"

Instead of answering, a muscle jumped in his jaw. "He was ahead of me at Eton."

"I take it you weren't friends."

He stopped and tugged her aside, away from anyone's hearing. "Stay away from him. He's a bounder, a blackguard."

Emma's eyes widened at his vehement tone. "Of course. Just so you know, I didn't encourage him."

He grunted something and stalked through the crowd. Emma was pulled along after. With a jerk on his arm, she planted her feet.

"Do you mind?" she said, as he turned to glare at her. "I'm wearing skirts. I can't keep up."

His expression softened. "Sorry," he muttered. "We were never mates at school."

"I gathered." Her tone was so dry it could have sucked up a gallon of water.

"Will you promise not to encourage him?" His gray eyes pinned her.

"He gives me the creeps." A tiny shudder ran through her. "I would be very happy if I never met him again."

The corner of his mouth deepened. "Thank you." Raising her hand to his lips, he placed a gentle kiss on her palm. "I very much enjoy how you speak."

"Um-hm."

The touch of his mouth against her skin made every word fly from her brain. When she met his gaze, his gray eyes smiled, and her breath fled as well. How could this man turn her into a speechless, witless ninny with just one tiny peck and a smile? She had no answer as he tucked her hand into the crook of his arm and guided her to where his aunt waited.

"I found her with Bowker," he told his aunt.

Lady Selby's eyes narrowed. "The father was an unscrupulous jeweler and I have no liking for the son." She sniffed in disapproval and turned toward the exit. "Come along. *Mrs.* Blake has created enough of a stir with her appearance. We must keep society guessing about her. The gossip should bring forth information about her people."

Emma was happy to follow. She'd had enough of dancing and smiling and trying not to step on toes. But she doubted the gossip would reveal anything about *her people.*

ROGER BOWKER WATCHED THEM LEAVE. SEVERAL DAYS AGO, HIS instruments had indicated a disturbance in the fabric of time and he'd wondered at its cause. The gears and wheels had been whirring ever since. Now he knew the reason — the woman. Glancing at the time indicator he held, he studied the hands, each moving at a different rate around the dial. Something had brought her to this time. Something momentous. He puzzled over that for a moment.

The first time he had felt such a disturbance he had been very young. His father had explained that someone had traveled through time. The woman—the *witch*—had caused it to happen. She knew what would unlock the portal at the ancient oak tree in Hyde Park. His father had craved that knowledge and had attempted to get the woman to share the secret, but to no avail. Not even dire threats to her family would make her reveal what she knew.

While his father became obsessed with trying to create a mechanism that would allow him the same freedom to pass from decade to decade, from century to century, their financial circumstances grew worse and worse. But Roger didn't care, because he had become as obsessed as his father, and continued his father's work after the old man passed away. He had finally created a device that transported him through small jumps of time, but they were insignificant. He wanted more, to see the future and the past. Possibly to tinker with events to see the outcome.

Emma Blake had not accomplished the travel back in time by herself. He had ascertained that when he had first stepped up beside her, when she had been unaware of his presence. Two of the hands on his indicator had changed direction when he stepped nearer to Mrs. Blake. They told him she was definitely from the future. But which future? And he suspected the witch was involved.

His device had taken him to Mrs. Blake, but told him nothing else. He had to get her to reveal how she had arrived in 1814. That was something to ponder. With another dismissive glance at the couples dancing before him, he turned to leave. He wouldn't have come if he had not been drawn by that fluctuation of time. He needed to examine his instruments again, and more closely this time.

Anxious to return to his laboratory and his notebooks, he made his way to the entrance of the gardens. His father had left copious notes about traveling through time, although he had never been able to accomplish such a feat. He had been jealous of that woman who had been able to time travel using magic. But she had disappeared, and his father was dead.

Roger was certain something was in those notebooks that would help him decipher the strange readings of his instruments, something that might give a hint about what had brought Emma Blake to London in 1814. As he exited the gardens, he hailed a hackney coach and gave the driver an address in Southwark, not a fashionable area, but quite safe from prying eyes.

Ten

After arriving home from Vauxhall Gardens, Lady Selby had immediately retired and Brandon had gone into his library. But Emma wasn't ready for sleep. The echo of his lips against her palm and the memory of his touch during their dance made the blood race through her veins. After pacing in her room for several minutes, she decided to take action, so she descended the stairs and knocked on the door to the library.

At his call to enter, she stepped into the room. He rose from a chair by the fire, a glass in his hand.

"Miss Blake," he greeted, surprise in his voice. Then his lips twitched up teasingly. "Cousin Emma."

She sauntered closer. "I hope I'm not disturbing you."

"Not at all." He turned to place his glass on a nearby

table. When he turned back to her, his gaze held warmth. "I am always interested in conversation before I retire."

"I was wondering, that is, if you're not too tired, would you like to play cards? I'm not ready for sleep." She clasped her hands behind her back and crossed her fingers, hoping he would agree.

"Of course. That's a delightful suggestion. A private game." He gestured to a small table with two chairs against the wall. "I often play chess here, but it will do perfectly for a card game."

A man who played chess and had two walls of books. Emma's heart fluttered. After they were seated, he pulled a deck of cards from a small drawer and began to shuffle. "What game would you like to play?"

"Vingt-et-un," she said.

Interest glinted in his eyes. "A fascinating choice. What will you use to wager?"

"I only have these." She held out her open palm, showing him the four buttons she had found, left from Madame Fachon's visit.

"A king's ransom," he murmured. "I have few coins on me." He fished in his pocket and produced a pence and a loose thread. "Not a very large ante."

She grinned. "It will do. For now."

He dealt the cards, and she won the first two hands, taking both the thread and the pence. He won them back on the next two. And then she won the next three, but he had nothing left to wager with his third loss.

"Bad luck," she said, although she wondered if luck had anything to do with his losing. He was a very shrewd card player.

"I concede," he said, sitting back in his chair. "You have won the game."

"But you still owe me," she said.

He spread his hands. "I have nothing left. May I offer you my vowels?"

"No." She shook her head as a wild idea came to her. She wanted to flirt with him, pretend that he wasn't going to be killed by his half-brother, pretend that they had all the time in the world. Just for now. For the moment. "I don't want your IOU. Suppose I choose what you should pay?" Casually, she shuffled the cards.

Silence came from across the table, as if he were trying to decide if she was going to cost him his fortune.

Smiling, she said, "I want your cravat."

He barked a laugh. With nimble fingers, he untied the piece, pulled it from around his neck, and then dangled it over the table. As she reached for it, he drew it away with a challenge in his eyes. "You may have it as long as the odds are even. I also get to choose if I win the hand."

The thought of undressing before him made her cheeks heat and moisture gather between her thighs. "Of course. Within reason."

He held out the cravat. "Definitely within reason."

But reason had nothing to do with their agreement. And everything to do with folly. Because she was a twenty-first-century woman and he was a nineteenth-century man. A relationship with him was impossible. But she really, really wanted him to kiss her again.

As she slipped the cloth from his fingers, she realized it still held the heat from his body, an intimate bit of him. She spread it carefully across her lap, and that made her throb. When she looked up again, she saw he had undone the top few buttons of his shirt, revealing the hollow of his throat. She had a very strong urge to lick that spot.

"It is your deal, Miss Blake."

Realizing she had been staring, she blinked and met his gaze. His eyes gave away nothing, but a corner of his mouth deepened. He knew exactly what she was thinking. Ducking her head, she quickly concentrated on dealing the next hand.

She lost. What would he demand of her?

Thoughtfully, his gaze ran over her. Anticipation made goosebumps pop on her arms.

"I would like the pins in your hair," he said, as if he had merely asked her to pass the butter.

Letting down her hair was an intimate gesture, so she would use it to her advantage. Slowly, one by one, she pulled out each hairpin and let it drop with a plink in the middle of the table. He watched with the attention of a hawk on its prey. When she was done, she shook out her waves, then fluffed her hair with her fingers.

"That feels marvelous," she sighed. Peeking at him from beneath her lashes, she saw his eyes had darkened. She hid her smile. "I believe it's your deal."

He lost that hand, as well as the next one. She took his coat and vest, leaving him in his shirt, a thin, linen covering over his muscular chest. Her fingers itched to touch.

Then she lost.

"What shall I take as my winnings?" he mused, as he studied her.

Wanting to shift beneath those smoky eyes, she forced herself to remain still.

A triumphant smile curved his lips. "A kiss," he said.

Before she could respond, he leaned over the table and kissed her gently first on one cheek, then the other. She was both surprised at the innocence of the gesture and frustrated, despite enjoying the touch of his lips on her skin. The kiss they had shared after Arlene's dinner party had been staggering. Even the one they had shared in his library the next day had been marvelous. She wanted another.

When he leaned back, a line of discontent appeared between his brows. "I'm not sure that was payment enough." He shook his head. "No, definitely not."

"What would satisfy you?" she asked.

His glance turned sly. "What would satisfy you, Cousin

Emma?" He swept up the cards and dealt. "Another hand to decide."

Frustrated, Emma concentrated on the play. And she won. But she suspected he had let her win.

He spread his arms wide, offering himself. "What will you demand?" His eyes teased.

She ran her gaze over him, as if the decision was difficult, but in her head, she was ruminating the different ways she could kiss him. Should she be direct and demand the kiss? Or should she be more subtle?

Leaning back in her chair, not looking at him, she pushed her cards around on the table. "I would like a dance with you." Glancing up, she caught the surprise in his eyes.

"A dance?" Then he smiled. "A delightful suggestion." His smile fled. "But we have no music."

"I wish to teach you a dance we do in America. It is called the waltz, but very different than the one that is danced here." She stood and held out her hand. "Will you concede to my request?"

"I have never had a lady ask for a dance," he said, "so this is a new experience." He placed his hand in hers and stood. "I am your servant, madam."

Emma led him to the middle of the room and turned to face him. "You put your hand on my back, and hold my hand like this." She held out her arm to show him, then she placed her hand on his shoulder.

"This is quite fascinating," he murmured, taking up the position she described. "And now what do we do?"

Looking up at him, she slipped into his dark gaze. It held her transfixed. The warmth of his hand at her back, the support of his strong hand beneath hers, the proximity of his body at her front made every inch of her tingle. Her glance dropped to his mouth, where she wanted to press her lips.

"Perhaps the dance requires this," he whispered.

With gentle pressure, he brought her closer, closing the small distance between them. And then he lowered his head and kissed her.

A hum of delicious satisfaction escaped her. This was what she had been craving. The pressure of him against her. The flame of his body. The taste of him. The scent of him. She parted her lips and invited him in. Wherever he wanted to lead, she would follow.

His arms crushed her against him, but she couldn't get close enough. Her hands slipped down to his buttocks and held him tight against her. The bulge in his pants fit perfectly between her thighs. A rumble came from his throat. Their tongues dueled. She lost awareness of where she was, for every sense focused on him.

And then he abandoned her mouth and rained tiny kisses along her jaw, down her throat to her shoulder, where he pushed her dress away. His fingers trailed down from her shoulder to her breast that was suddenly free. Somehow, when she was thoroughly engaged with his mouth, he had undone the back of her dress and her stays, but she didn't protest. Instead she leaned back, giving him access.

"Emma," he whispered.

That was all. Just her name. She melted. His thumb flicked across her nipple. A shiver ran through her.

She met his gaze, dark, smoky, hungry. Time halted. And then with just the smallest tip up of his lips, he ducked his head and claimed her nipple.

HER MOAN RAN THROUGH BRANDON LIKE A CURRENT. HE hadn't been this aroused since... He had never been this aroused. She bedeviled him with her innocent sapphire eyes and her mane of dark hair. With her perky walk and bewitching backside. With her pouty lips and dimpled chin. With her intelligence and spirit.

And he knew very well she had beguiled him into playing Vingt-et-un.

As soon as her soft curves pressed against him, he felt his body unwind, as if something had been binding him, holding him in a deep chasm. He had wanted her in his arms ever since he had first seen her in Hyde Park. The mind-shattering kiss he'd shared with her after Arlene's dinner party had only whetted his appetite. She was delicious. Supple and soft. And he couldn't get enough. Her breast fit perfectly in his hand, the tip a hard bud that he sucked and flicked with his tongue. Her breath came and went in tiny gasps, indicating her pleasure. He very much wanted to give her pleasure, to make her moan, to cry out in passion.

His erection throbbed against his pantaloons, demanding release. Soon, he promised himself. But not now. Instead, he would give her release. He pushed her dress off her other shoulder and turned to the other breast. She whimpered. Wriggled closer. Easing her skirt up her leg, his fingers traced up the silky skin to her thigh. His thumb dipped to where she was wet and hot and pulsing. Then he found her nub.

As soon as he touched her, Emma started to tremble. She was a swirling storm of need. This had never happened before, wanting a man so badly. His touch was magical, as if his fingers held some secret wizardry. As if her name on his lips held a charm of summoning. His sorcery tugged at her, engulfed her, overwhelmed her. Intense pleasure flooded her. Gripping his arms, she felt compressed, bound, squeezed. Reaching.

And then she came. In a burst of pleasure. Crying out his name.

She dragged in a breath. Slowly, she opened her eyes. He was watching her, his eyes dark, his expression unreadable. And then a tiny smile curved his lips.

Suddenly dismayed, she stumbled back on wobbly knees, out of his hold. She immediately missed his embrace, but she needed the space to process what had just happened. That little smile indicated he had enjoyed making her come, making her vulnerable, watching her fly apart because of his touch. What had she done? She wasn't going to get this close. She wasn't going to fall for him. Because they lived centuries apart. Except they didn't. Not at the moment.

When she had written her book, she had envisioned this, wanting what her heroine had, but never imagining it could happen to her. And now it had. It had been stupendous. *He* had been stupendous. What would he be like if she slept with him?

She wanted to touch him, place her hand on his chest and feel his heartbeat, wrap her fingers around his erection and watch the heat in his eyes. She nearly reached out. Instead, she curled her fingers into a fist at her side. She needed to process this, think it through. Because now that she had experienced his touch, she wanted more. Much, much more. But was that wise?

As soon as she had backed away, his little smile faded. His gaze was solemn, maybe just a bit concerned. She had to say something.

"That was ..." Her words ended in a croak, because her brain was still swimming in euphoria.

His mouth twitched. "I am very glad you enjoyed it."

With an inner sigh, she realized she had to admit the truth. Meeting his gaze, she smiled. "I did. Thank you."

"My pleasure."

She sputtered a laugh. "I think it was mine." And she wanted more of it. Stepping close again, she whispered, "Next time, it's your turn."

His eyes widened, then crinkled at the corners, his focus intense. Before he could respond, she turned and skipped out of the room.

Eleven

The next afternoon, Brandon watched his brother arrive in his elegant landau to collect Emma for a visit to Tattersall's. The carriage was actually their father's vehicle, but Stephen took every opportunity to exploit the wealth of the family. Brandon strode from the corner of the house and waylaid his brother as he stepped down from the landau.

"Brother!" Stephen said when he caught sight of Brandon bearing down on him. "I had not expected such a personal welcome."

Brandon ignored the hearty greeting. "I've come to warn you, Pemberton. Mrs. Blake is not to be trifled with." The memory of trifling with her the night before flitted through his mind, and he nearly lost track of his purpose, but he chased it away with a frown at his brother. He would never let Stephen touch her like that.

"Trifled with?" Confusion wrinkled Stephen's brow. "I assure you, my intentions are honorable."

"You do not have an honorable bone in your body," Brandon snapped.

Stephen blinked, then a nasty smile curved his lips. "I understand. You have aspirations to keep her for yourself. But not quite the done thing, is it, for she is your cousin, is she not? A relationship that I still do not quite understand."

His brother had hit too closely to the truth, that he did want Emma for himself, especially after their rousing game of Vingt-et-un and what came after. "Through my mother," he ground out, perpetuating the lie she had begun. "And which has no connection to you. Beware, Pemberton. I am watching."

With narrowed eyes, his brother said, "You cannot watch every minute, Connaught. Like this afternoon, when I will be taking Mrs. Blake to Tattersall's."

Brandon hid his satisfaction as he replied, "I will be Mrs. Blake's companion on this outing. My aunt is indisposed."

Just as he finished speaking, as if on cue, a groom led his horse from the mews. He turned to take the reins and smothered his grin at the anger that flashed through Stephen's eyes. His brother had coveted everything that Brandon had — his toys, the love of his life, and now Emma. Stephen might have appropriated most of his toys and he might have convinced Elizabeth to marry him, but Brandon was determined that Emma would not fall to him.

After he mounted, he waited while Stephen went to fetch her. When she finally emerged from the house on Stephen's arm, she looked like a ray of sunshine in her pale yellow frock, far different than the bedraggled and bewildered woman he had encountered in Hyde Park that first day he had seen her. Just before she stepped up into the landau, she sent him a cheeky grin and an audacious wink that sent heat from his chest to his privates. Shifting in the saddle to relieve the pressure, he huffed in amused exasperation. The woman was a she-devil, bright, cunning, and much too beautiful for her own good.

She was determined, it seemed, to help him. Perhaps this outing would reap something he could use against his brother. But he would have to watch Stephen closely, because despite her bravado, Emma had no true knowledge of his brother's knavish nature.

EMMA SAT BESIDE STEPHEN IN HIS ELEGANT LANDAU AND TRIED to concentrate on his conversation, but she was distracted by Brandon, who rode beside the vehicle on a beautiful, dappled gray stallion. When she had emerged from the house and seen him sitting tall and elegant on his horse, her breath caught in her throat. She wanted him, more than ever after last night. He was the epitome of a Regency gentleman, but with a streak of heated passion. Just like she had written him.

His coat was a dark, rich blue that turned his eyes steel gray, and his buckskin breeches, tucked into highly polished riding boots, hugged his muscular legs. An ivory waistcoat was buttoned over a white linen shirt with a simple knotted cravat around his neck. A dark gray top hat and matching gloves completed his ensemble. Emma was so dazzled she nearly stumbled. Fortunately, she held Stephen's arm.

While Stephen looked quite handsome in his maroon coat, gray trousers, pale blue waistcoat and white neckcloth tied in intricate folds, she felt no attraction. Any young woman would be dazed by his looks, if they did not know the man. But she knew the twenty-first century version, and Brandon's opinion of his half-brother was less than commendable, two factors that colored her opinion of him. Besides, she doubted the man beside her could bring her to ecstasy the way the man on the horse had the night before.

Stephen made small talk as they rolled through the streets. She smiled and nodded and pretended to be fascinated, but when she wasn't distracted by the pull of Brandon's presence, she was having fun with a parasol that had been delivered that morning along with a few of her new frocks. It was a dainty thing of white dotted muslin edged in two rows of ruffles. Holding it just so above her head, she created a tiny bit of shade. It made her feel very elegant and very Regency-ish. Another detail she could add to her books. She would make a note of it in the journal she had begun that first day in Brandon's house.

Along the way, Stephen spotted a flower seller, and he had his driver stop so he could buy her a tussie-mussie. She watched him make the transaction, then he disappeared for a few moments behind a hay wagon. When he emerged again and handed her the posies, his smile seemed smug, but Emma decided he was merely satisfied he had been able to purchase something for her in front of his half-brother.

Brandon dropped behind them because the road had become crowded. She wanted to keep turning around to include him in the conversation, but of course, she was supposed to be riveted by Stephen's words. They had just passed through an intersection when a crash and raised voices behind them made her swing around to look.

"Oh, my goodness!" she said. "A wagon full of hay has just overturned. And a hackney has become all tangled in the hay bales. Oh, my goodness! Cousin Brandon is caught on the other side and his horse is rearing!" Frightened, her hand flew to her mouth. She turned back to Stephen. "We must stop and help him."

Stephen glanced over his shoulder, then turned a patronizing smile on her. "I'm sure he'll catch up."

"But —"

Interrupting, Stephen took her hand. "Don't worry about my brother. I'm sure he can handle that beast of his. Besides, this gives us a few moments to be alone." He raised her hand to his lips and kissed her fingers. "I very much wanted to be alone with you, dear Mrs. Blake." Turning over her hand, he kissed the inside of her wrist, just above the edge of her glove.

She wanted to pull away, only remembering at the last moment that she was pretending to be charmed by him. Allowing him to keep her hand, she cast another glance over her shoulder. "But—," she said again. She could see Brandon's horse in the middle of the confusion, but it was riderless. Where was he? A trickle of fear ran through her. Was this when Brandon would be killed, not when he was trying to escape from the false accusation of murder?

Stephen's grip on her fingers tightened, reclaiming her attention. "These accidents happen frequently in London. Connaught has dealt with them before. Do not worry yourself." His tone dropped to an intimate murmur. "Besides, the reprieve gives us a few moments to be alone."

Emma gently disengaged from his grip. Anxiety over Brandon's safety made her glance back once more, and she was relieved when she spotted the top of his head among the confusion. Suspicious that somehow Stephen had arranged the accident with the hay wagon—Had it been when he was out of sight for those few moments?—she wanted to punch him.

Instead, she said, "I hardly know you, m'lord —"

"Pemberton," he corrected.

"— and I think perhaps you have the wrong idea."

His brow wrinkled in confusion. "Wrong idea?"

"Yes. I came to London..." Why had she come to London? She had told Brandon she had come for research, but she didn't think Stephen would understand that concept. Maybe her excuse of "amnesia" would work.

"You came to London...?" he prompted.

She stared at him blankly. "I don't know why I came to London. I seem to have forgotten. The unfortunate accident upon my arrival has mixed me up. I have forgotten a great many things. Perhaps I came here to get over the death of my dear, departed husband. But I am quite sure I did not come to be swept off my feet by such a handsome man." She nearly gagged over those words. Instead, she sent him a shy smile.

He relaxed against the seat and rested his arm along its back. His return smile was conceited and self-satisfied. "And I did not expect to discover such a beautiful and entertaining woman from America hiding in my brother's house."

Emma should have blushed as the next step in this exchange. Instead, she was distracted by all the men coming and going through a wide-open door, and the more than ordinary numbers of horses and their riders clogging the street.

"I believe we have arrived," she said, as the landau slowed and she hid her sigh of relief.

Exasperation flitted across Stephen's face as he glanced around. "So, we have."

After his driver had stopped the vehicle, Stephen stepped down and turned to offer her a hand. His expression had returned to pleasant and benign as Emma accepted his help, but she wondered what he hid behind that amiable façade. Before she stepped down, she glanced back down the road, but Brandon was not to be seen. A niggling finger of fear wriggled inside her chest. She hoped he wasn't hurt, and wished she could go back for him, but the farce with Stephen had to be played out.

As he held out his arm for her, she fiddled with her parasol to give Brandon time to arrive. First, she put it over one shoulder, then pretending that wasn't quite the right position to block the sun, she switched sides. Stephen stood by with patient forbearance, careful not to get poked in the eye. Grinning to herself, she decided she liked the tricks that Regency ladies had at their disposal. But she could only play with her parasol for a short time.

"I do believe you will not need that parasol once we are inside," he said.

"Oh, of course. How silly of me." She settled her parasol on her left side and deigned to take his arm. With a last glance down the road, she allowed him to escort her into the auction house. But still there was no sign of Brandon.

They entered through the wide door into an anteroom with paintings of beautiful horses adorning the walls, and then out into a courtyard surrounded on three sides by a columned portico. The fourth side was open with wide paths leading to stables and barns. Horses were led around the perimeter of the courtyard, while gentlemen and a few ladies observed and chatted in the middle.

Stephen guided her to a spot where they could easily see the horses passing by, and he commented on each one. She barely listened as she waited for Brandon to appear. Surely, the accident with the hay wagon couldn't have delayed him that long. Sir Dotson approached and the two men exchanged greetings.

Stephen said, "Mrs. Blake, you remember Sir Dotson from Lady Farley's dinner party?"

Emma smiled and bobbed a curtsey. "Of course. How nice to see you again, sir." A tingle of excitement ran through her. Maybe this was their appointed meeting and she could figure out what he and Stephen were up to.

Sir Dotson bowed. "Please, call me Doddy. Everyone else does." His wide smile looked a bit goofy, as if he couldn't rub two thoughts together in his head. But looks could be deceiving. He turned to Stephen. "I've looked over that cattle you spoke of. He's a rum prancer."

Emma had done enough research that she knew he was talking about a beautiful horse. She wondered if that horse actually existed or was just a code. "Oh, I'd love to see him. Please, Pemberton, may we go see him?"

Something resembling panic flashed through Stephen's

eyes before he said smoothly, "I'm afraid that's impossible. The public isn't allowed into the barns."

Emma opened her mouth to argue the point, for she had seen several gentlemen being escorted into one of the barns by an employee. Obviously, Stephen was hiding something, so she decided to play the naïve woman. "How disappointing. I do so enjoy admiring a fine horse." She let out a spoiled sigh.

Stephen patted her hand resting in the crook of his arm. "We'll get you some fine cattle to gaze on, Mrs. Blake. Let us walk this way, so you may see the parade better."

He led her past Doddy, nearly brushing against the man. While Doddy tipped his hat with one hand, his other seemed to graze Stephen's coat. She saw a speck of white paper appear between his fingers. Had a note been passed between them? She dearly wanted to read it. What would it say? Would it reveal that the two men were involved in illegal investments? Or something far more sinister, like information between spies? And was the conversation they'd had about the horse an exchange of code words? Or maybe it was just a banal exchange of information about which horse was the best purchase.

She tried to look interested as Stephen pointed out the good and bad points about the horses that passed before them. Her mind wasn't on horseflesh, but how she could get that message out of Stephen's pocket. And where was Brandon? Why hadn't he arrived?

As if her thought had conjured him, he appeared in the courtyard, but he didn't look as put together as he had when they'd left his house. His cravat was slightly askew, a few dark smudges marred his beautiful coat, and the brim of his hat was dented. Those gray eyes were stormy.

She waved to attract his attention. "Cousin Brandon! Over here!"

Stephen grimaced at her enthusiastic call and looked unhappy when he glanced in his brother's direction.

Brandon came up beside them, and ignoring Stephen, nodded a greeting to Emma.

"Are you okay?" she asked, her concern making her drop into twenty-first century slang.

Brandon's mouth twitched. "Yes, dear cousin, I'm okay."

"Okay?" Puzzled lines appeared on Stephen's brow. "That is a term I'm unfamiliar with."

Brandon ignored him again. "I apologize for my delayed arrival. An overturned hay wagon in the middle of the road." While his words dismissed the accident as trivial, his glance to Stephen held murder.

Stephen blinked, then said with a dismissive wave of his hand, "These things happen. I'm glad you arrived unharmed."

"I'm sure you are," Brandon muttered with a glare.

He appeared to suspect Stephen of arranging the accident. Emma wondered the same thing. Not wanting a fight to erupt in the middle of Tattersall's, she slipped her hand from

Stephen's arm, hooked it around Brandon's elbow, and indicated one of the animals parading past. "Cousin Brandon, you must tell me about this brownish horse. He is so pretty, don't you think?" Out of the corner of her eye, she caught Stephen's sour expression at switching her attention to Brandon.

"He is a she, and is a very pretty piece of horseflesh," Brandon agreed with a smile. "A filly, and she's a chestnut with a white star between her eyes and one white sock."

Emma fell in love with the horse. It was a beautiful animal and pranced with lively grace. If she owned it, she would name it Cassiopeia, in honor of the star in the sky and the Greek queen it was named for. But whyever would she own a horse? She didn't belong in the century, and she certainly couldn't take a horse with her back to the twenty-first. She watched the animal as it was led around the courtyard, then remembered she needed to tell Brandon about the message that had passed between Stephen and Sir Dotson.

"I believe I've acquired quite the headache," she said. "Pemberton, I am sorry to cut our outing short, but could you please return me home?" She fanned herself with her hand and hoped she looked pathetic and ill.

Stephen stepped up beside her. "Of course, Mrs. Blake." He took her by the elbow. "It's quite stifling here." His proprietary glance to Brandon staked his claim on her attention.

Feigning weakness, Emma leaned ever-so-slightly against him, despite her aversion. But she wanted to smile, because she was beginning to learn Stephen's secrets. She had been correct to assume the conversation between him and Sir Dotson at Arlene's dinner party had been code for meeting at the horse auction to exchange information, because she had seen the note exchanged between them. And she suspected that the strange glance between Lord Farley and Stephen at the dinner table had held secrets as well. Stephen was deeply involved in something sinister, so similar to what she had written in her book.

Now she had to plan the next step to "fix things," as Ghost Brandon had suggested.

BRANDON MADE A DISCREET GESTURE TO THE AUCTIONEER AND followed Emma and his insufferable half-brother out to the street, where he waited with them for the landau to be brought around. A groom handed the reins of his horse to him and he mounted, hiding the grimace of pain in his hip, caused from falling from his horse when it reared in fright. He wanted to throttle his half-brother for that arranged accident with the hay wagon. Just as Emma was about to step up into the landau, another groom led out the filly that she had admired. It pranced and tossed its head as if showing off.

"Oh, look," she said. "There's that beautiful horse."

As the groom handed the reins to him, her mouth dropped open.

"You bought it!" She stood up in the landau.

Brandon grinned. "For you."

She gasped. "For me?!" Her hands covered her heart. "Thank you! How generous!" Then a line appeared between her brows. "But that's such a precious gift."

"It's the least I could do for my cousin from America." While he was quite pleased with her reaction, what pleased him even more was the sour look on Stephen's face.

"Mrs. Blake, please take a seat," Stephen urged. "You'll startle the horses." He put his hand on her arm and sent Brandon a dark look.

Emma disengaged her arm. "The horses don't seem startled at all." She flashed a smile in Stephen's direction. "Oh, please help me down so I can admire her."

Brandon bit the inside of his cheek so he wouldn't chuckle at his brother's disgruntled expression, which Stephen quickly hid when Emma glanced at him. Stephen climbed out of the landau and handed Emma down.

"I've never had a pet before," she murmured to the filly as she stroked the horse's soft nose. "You are Cassiopeia."

The filly seemed to approve, because she blew into Emma's hand.

Emma's eyes shone when she glanced up at Brandon. "Thank you. This is a wonderful present."

A warm sensation bloomed in Brandon's chest at making her happy. And he had outdone his brother, despite that sneaking cur's efforts to waylay him with the hay wagon. The outing had not been a complete disaster.

He watched as Emma allowed Stephen to guide her back to the landau and help her step into it. When she was seated, she glanced over her shoulder and sent him a huge smile. That warm sensation in his chest grew larger. He had given Emma something that pleased her very much, and that pleased him as well.

But the journey back to his house wasn't as pleasant. Stephen had his driver take them on a roundabout route that took twice as long.

Brandon ground his teeth as his brother took every opportunity to touch Emma, straightening her shawl, fixing a ribbon that had blown awry, brushing a hair back from her cheek. She smiled at his brother and chatted with him, seeming to enjoy the blackguard's company. The joy he'd felt upon gifting her the horse melted away with every warm look his brother bestowed on her, and his wrath sizzled.

The cur barely knew her. Each of his attempts to charm her raised Brandon's ire. But he was the one who had nearly run her over and he was the one who had rescued her. He was the one who was responsible for her. And he was the one who had given her pleasure the night before.

When they finally arrived at his house, he had ground his

teeth so hard, he was surprised they hadn't turned into stubs. Stephen helped her step down from the landau. Bowing over her hand, he placed a lingering kiss on her fingers. Brandon's hands tightened on the reins as if he had them around his brother's neck.

"I would very much like to call on you, Mrs. Blake," Stephen said in his most persuasive tone.

Brandon watched Emma lower her eyes demurely. "That would be very pleasant," she murmured, then sent Stephen a dazzling smile.

Even from the back of his horse, Brandon could see that his brother was smitten. No, he was not going to allow that sniveling blackguard to get his talons into Emma. Not another woman he cared about. Not again. Dismounting, he handed off the reins of both his own horse and the new filly to his groom.

"Cousin Emma," he snapped, then cleared his throat as he forced down his ire. "I believe we have a dinner engagement."

Emma turned to him with wide, questioning eyes. They had no dinner engagement. But his statement accomplished what he wanted, to get his brother out of his sight and away from Emma. Stephen bowed again and stepped up into his landau. Silently fuming, Brandon didn't wait for him to leave before he took hold of Emma's elbow and rushed her into his house.

When they stepped through the door, Emma heaved a

sigh and took off her bonnet. "Well, that was quite an afternoon."

Her comment fanned his anger, tightened the knot of emotions in his chest, and he felt the need to lash out. "Are you referring to the way you beguiled my brother, or the way you charmed me into purchasing a horse for you?" he drawled, both satisfied and ashamed at the shock that crossed her face.

STUNG BY HIS ACCUSATION, EMMA GASPED. "I NEVER CHARMED you into buying the horse. She's a beautiful animal, and I am grateful for the gift of her, but I would never do that."

He raised a cool, disbelieving brow. "No? I suppose you also didn't charm my brother into buying those foolish posies." He flicked the offending flowers with his finger. "What sort of favors and gifts did you charm out of your former protector?"

Emma fell back a step, bewildered and hurt by his antagonism, and rankled that he brought up the fictitious protector again. Her temper heated. "I never had a protector. Why don't you believe me?"

"Because I found you in Hyde Park, alone, and wearing garments that were hardly decent." He scowled. "What am I supposed to believe, *Cousin Emma?* You are quite talented at charm and seduction, like last evening and our game of Vingt-et-un, like this afternoon's outing to Tattersall's with my brother. He is bewitched by you. Only a woman who has experience with men is able to beguile with such ease, like a woman who is from the demi-monde."

Emma's chin went up. "The intent of the afternoon was to beguile your brother so he might become comfortable enough to reveal that he is involved in something unlawful. I told you that."

"And I told you that I want you nowhere near him." His lips thinned, his jaw hardened, and his eyes burned into her. "You will not accept any more invitations from him, for what-ever reason you might fabricate. In fact, you will remain in this house until I learn who you are."

Emma blinked at his dictatorial declaration. Her temper was near to boiling for many reasons. She had only accepted Stephen's invitation to help Brandon. She was an adult and used to coming and going as she pleased. His assumption that she was a kept woman no longer mattered in her century. Besides that, she was perfectly capable of taking care of herself and not relying on a man to take care of her, at least in her own time.

On one level, she understood that as a nineteenth-century man, he didn't understand how customs had changed in her time, and she knew he was distrustful of his brother. But he had lashed out at her, and his assumptions and orders stung deeply.

She drew a breath, fighting down her anger. "I went with your brother to help *you*." He opened his mouth, but before he could respond, she said, "Don't. Don't say a word. I'm going out before either of us says something we're going to regret."

Swinging around, she walked out the door. She needed to be away from him, from his suspicions, from his protection. From his jealousy. Blindly, needing to think and let her temper cool, she stalked down the road, not caring where—or when—she ended up.

ANGRY AND HURT, EMMA'S BRAIN WHIRLED. HOW COULD HE BE so charming one minute and such an ogre the next? He apparently still thought she was someone's cast off mistress, someone with few morals, despite his aunt's opinion.

"Emma!"

She heard his call, but she ignored him. Didn't want to talk to him. Didn't want to look at him.

Needing some distance from him, she ran.

People stared. Horses shied. Carriage drivers yelled. She ignored them. All she could hear was his cold accusation and dictatorial command. He was so different than what she expected. His ghost had been charming, vulnerable and sad. When she arrived in this century, she saw he was so much more, a complete, complex man. He was engaging and caring and generous and sexy. Hot. He made her forget everything when he was near. He made her crazy.

But he was also a man who had been hurt in the past, who had been displaced by a younger sibling in his father's affection. A man who had lost his birthright. Who had lost the love of his life.

But she was trying to help him gain his rightful inheritance. She was trying to prove that his brother was involved in something illegal. She was trying to save him. Tears gathered in her eyes.

She ran until she couldn't run any more. Finally, out of breath, her lovely frock frayed and dirty at the hem, she found herself in Hyde Park. She bent and braced her hands on her knees, drew in great, gulping breaths, and blinked away her tears.

"What would make a young woman run until she was exhausted?"

The woman's voice came from a bit farther down the path. Emma jerked upright. A woman, dressed in black with her head draped in a heavy veil, sat beneath a very small pavilion not far away. Beside her was a table spread with a tea service.

"I'm sorry to disturb you," Emma said and backed away.

"You have not disturbed me at all. Not many people pass this way." She indicated a chair on the other side of the table. "Please join me. I find a cup of tea does wonders for settling the nerves."

Emma was hesitant at accepting an invitation from a stranger, especially one who seemed to want to hide her identity. The veil covering the woman's head and face was so thick that Emma could only see the bright glint of her eyes. But something about the woman's manner calmed Emma. What did she have to lose? She didn't want to go back to Brandon's house. His low opinion of her was like a weight in her chest. Accepting the woman's invitation, she sat.

The woman poured her a cup of tea and pushed a plate of tiny cakes and biscuits closer. "Please, help yourself. A bit of indulgence always makes me feel better."

Emma took a biscuit to please the woman, but she didn't think anything would take away the pain of Brandon's insulting low opinion of her. Besides, she felt if she ate anything, she would vomit. But the tea might help. As she took a sip, she glanced around. The woman was alone, with no servants nearby. How did she set up this wonderful little picnic under the pavilion by herself?

As if the woman could read her mind, she said with an airy wave of her hand, "I sent my servants away." Her voice lowered conspiratorially, "Sometimes, I like to sit here by myself and commune with this old oak."

To Emma's left was the gnarly trunk of a huge old tree.

PATRICIA BARLETTA

Glancing at her surroundings, she realized this was the ancient oak tree near the place where Brandon had nearly run her over when she had first arrived in this century.

"There is a legend," the veiled woman said, "that this oak tree is enchanted. It is said that it will bring you to your true love."

Emma couldn't hold back a rueful laugh. "My true love? I don't think so." She took another sip of tea and remembered her ghost had also mentioned a legend about the Druids and the tree.

"Don't you believe in legends and enchanted trees?" the woman asked.

As Emma fiddled with her bracelet—not hot or tingling at all—she shook her head. "I think the legend is made up." Or was it? She had ended up in another century.

Instead of pursuing her story, the woman said, "That is a lovely bracelet. My husband used to give me such beautiful things."

"Doesn't he give you gifts anymore?" Emma asked.

The woman straightened the spoon on her saucer. "I am alone now."

Emma felt terrible for asking. The lady was a widow. Of course. That was why she was dressed in black. "I'm so sorry. I didn't mean to bring up bad memories."

"My memories are wonderful," she said. "I learned quite early that we must grab the good that life has to offer so that when the bad comes, we have memories to see us through.

Finish your tea, dear, and then tell me why you were so distraught."

After taking another sip, Emma said, "I have met a gentleman, but he has a very low opinion of me."

The lady tipped her head. "Perhaps his low opinion concerns someone else. Gentlemen do not always share what they are truly thinking."

Emma thought back over the afternoon. Of course, he suspected his brother of arranging the accident with the hay wagon. She had suspected the same thing. But did he think she'd been complicit in the deed? Maybe. He had accused her of favoring Stephen. Was he jealous? Hurt? Maybe that's why he had been so angry.

The lady said, "Perhaps you might want to share something with him, something you would only share with those who are very close to you. I have found that is quite disarming."

Emma blinked as she realized that was exactly what she had to do. "Thank you. I think I'll try that."

"I'm sure everything will work out in the end," the lady said with a gentle nod.

After thanking the woman, Emma thoughtfully made her way through the park. She knew what she had to do—tell Brandon the truth, that she was from the future. It was a huge risk. Would he believe her, or would he think she was deranged? Or maybe he would suspect that she was making up the story, that she was untrustworthy and in league with his brother. No matter what he thought, she knew that revealing the truth was the right thing to do. Because she cared for him. Because she had decided the reason she had been sent back in time was to prove his brother was involved in something dishonorable and to help him gain his birthright. And to save him from being murdered.

She had seen the note passed surreptitiously between Stephen and Sir Dotson. What was it? What did it mean? Her writer's brain began coming up with all sorts of answers. Was Stephen planning a scam to get people to invest in a fake gold mining expedition in South America? Was he trying to subvert a bill in Parliament? Was he a smuggler passing along information about the next delivery of contraband goods? Was he a spy?

In her book, he was a spy. And her heroine had discovered the proof hidden in his room. Somehow, she had to get into Stephen's house so she could search. Somehow, she had to convince Brandon that she was trying to help him at the same time she was charming Stephen. But when—if—she found proof of Stephen's illegal activities, she would have to stop him from murdering his father and shooting Brandon in the back. How could she do that?

Needing to think, she wandered through Hyde Park and then out onto the road. With no hat or gloves and bedraggled from her dash through the streets, she received dour and disapproving looks from the ladies she passed. She didn't care. Deep in thought, she drifted down one street and up another, paying no attention to where she was going.

Then it began to rain.

The first raindrops plonked on her head and dragged her whirling thoughts back to her surroundings. Glancing around, she realized that the sun had set and twilight had fallen on the city, made darker by the rain clouds.

And she was lost.

Twelve

B randon ran after Emma as she dodged between pedestrians and horses, around carriages and wagons, but when he followed her into a crossroads, he lost her. Where had she gone? He looked right, then left. Starting down one road, he realized she hadn't gone that way. Back-tracking, he went down another. He searched side streets and alleys. No Emma.

The sun had begun to set, but he refused to give up his search. He had to find her before dark when scallywags and cutthroats roamed the shadows. Reaching the entrance to Hyde Park, he brightened. She had no doubt gone to the park. That was where he'd first found her.

But after he had trodden every path, searched every inch of grass, and looked behind every bush and every tree, she was nowhere to be seen. He had even gone back to the ancient oak where he had first seen her. No one was there.

Discouraged, he stood in the middle of Rotten Row and turned in a circle, searching, hoping he'd catch a glimpse of her. Those few members of the ton who were still in the park at this hour gave him curious stares. He didn't care. He just wanted to find her and explain. Apologize. Beg her to forgive him.

But she was gone.

Perhaps her memory had returned and she had gone back to her companions, those who had accompanied her to England. But who were they and where did they live? The men he had hired to make inquiries had found no trace of them. Why hadn't he heard of any inquiries about her or seen anything in any of the newspapers about a missing woman? That was quite curious.

She had told him she had come to London alone, but he didn't quite believe her. No woman traveled such a distance alone. Perhaps her friends embarrassed her, and so she wouldn't admit to them. When he found her, he would disabuse her of that notion. He would accept her companions, whoever they were. He just wanted to make sure she was safe.

With a last look into the vista of grass and trees and flowers of Hyde Park, he accepted that she wasn't there, heaved a sigh, turned, and trudged back the way he had come.

Why had he said those hateful words to her? Even though he didn't know her family or anything about her, he knew in some deep part of him that she was honorable and virtuous, that she wasn't a Cyprian. But he had watched his cur of a brother charm her all afternoon. Each minute had made him more furious. He suspected that the accident with the hay wagon had been arranged so that Stephen would have Emma all to himself. He had been frantic to untangle himself from that mess and rejoin her. Who knew what lies Stephen was murmuring into her ear? And so he had laid down the command that she was not to leave the house.

That had been a mistake. She was not a woman content to remain behind closed doors, secluded from the world. Even when she was recovering from a twisted ankle, she had managed to hobble to the stairs so she might reach his library.

Her joy at learning that he had bought the filly for her made him nearly burst with happiness. But watching Stephen try to woo her on the trip home tripped his temper.

His chest was tight with worry and regret. He needed to tell Emma he didn't mean what he had said. He needed to tell her that he was grateful that she wanted to help him. More than that, he wanted to kiss her again. Truthfully, he wanted to do more than kiss her, more than bring her release as he had done after their card game. He wanted to run his hands over her exquisite body. He wanted to discover all her sensitive spots, the ones that made her shiver. Perhaps the back of her knee. Or the inside of her elbow. The base of her spine. The sole of her foot. He wanted to lick each spot until she moaned. And then... No, he had to stop thinking about that. He would drive himself mad.

First, he would find her. Then he would learn all there was to know about the mysterious, beautiful, sensuous, maddening woman who had suddenly appeared before him that day in Hyde Park.

And tell her that he was as dumb as an ox.

EMMA TRIPPED AS SHE CROSSED A STREET AND LANDED IN A puddle hiding a pile of horse manure. Climbing to her feet with a groan, she started to wipe herself off, then wrinkled her nose in disgust. The scent of manure drifted up from her frock in a pungent cloud. Her dress was sodden and stained, ruined.

As she brushed herself off and tried to wring the water out of her skirt, something glinted in the puddle. Peering at it, she saw it was her pendant, and her wrist was bare. Her bracelet! She quickly scooped it out of the water. Relief at seeing it before it was lost forever, stranding her in the past, flooded her. But when she tried to put it back on, she realized the clasp was broken. Clutching it tightly, she trudged on.

Miserable, wet, cold, she tried to find a building, a street, something that looked familiar. Footpads and cracksmen and cutpurses might be lurking in the dark alleys and waiting for a victim like her to wander past. Every little noise made her jump. Sometimes it was a rat, sometimes only the wind. Frightened that she would never find her way back to Brandon's house, she plodded on.

Finally, she found herself in familiar surroundings. The dark expanse of Hyde Park spread before her. Skirting the shadowy, spooky space, she arrived on Brandon's street. The night was beginning to lift, and she could hear the calls of the milkmen and chimney sweeps and costermongers selling their wares or services from nearby streets. She ran the rest of way, suddenly afraid of what might be behind her, drawn by the beacon of safety that was Brandon's home.

When she stopped in front of his door, she took a breath. For a fleeting instant, she considered their argument. Would he still be angry? Should she still be angry? A noise behind her — maybe it was just the wind banging a shutter — decided for her. She was too frightened and too cold and too miserable to care. She lifted the doorknocker and banged it against the door. And kept banging it until she heard someone coming, complaining all the way.

The door opened a crack, and Mrs. Porter's face appeared.

"Please, Mrs. Porter," Emma said, trying to hold back tears of relief at seeing a familiar face. "Let me in."

The woman's nose wrinkled in distaste. "You stink. Have you been rolling in the mews with some seedy cove?"

Emma gripped her composure with two fists. "No, I slipped and fell. Please, Mrs. Porter."

"Let her in, Mrs. Porter." Brandon's voice came from the dark hall beyond the housekeeper. "And bring some towels, if you please."

With an unintelligible grumble, Mrs. Porter swung the door wide and retreated to the back of the house. Brandon stepped into the open doorway. At the sight of him, his hair wet and mussed, his dark blue, brocade banyan fitting his frame perfectly and highlighting those incredible smoky eyes, Emma's composure broke. He was her beacon, her homing signal. Despite their differences, despite the centuries between them, he was her hero and she would save him in spite of himself.

Without a word, he pulled her into his arms and hugged her close.

"I'm soaking wet," she sniffled.

"Hush." He pushed the door shut with his foot.

"I see you have found your way back," Lady Selby said from the top of the stairs.

Emma quickly stepped back from Brandon. "Yes, I got lost."

"Hm, and caught in the rain," the lady observed. "Do not keep her in the entry hall, Brandon, or she'll catch her death." She nodded at Emma. "You may tell me the tale of your adventure when the sun is up. I am for returning to bed." Turning, she disappeared back down the hall.

As soon as she was out of sight, Brandon's fingers closed around Emma's wrist. He tugged her close, swept her up into his arms, and carried her into his library. Emma didn't care where he took her as long as he took her back. He was warm and solid. The feel of his strong arms made her feel safe, something she realized she hadn't truly felt since she had arrived in the nineteenth century. She felt like she was home.

BRANDON SAT HER ON HIS LAP, STROKED HER BACK AND murmured soothing words while she shivered and clung to him. Holding her close despite her dripping clothes and the scent of horse manure that surrounded her like a noxious cloud, he sent up a prayer of thanks that she had returned. She'd been gone for hours. Hours of torture and worry. He had scoured the city searching for her. He'd sent out his groom and stableboy and footman. Twice, he had visited the spot in Hyde Park where he'd nearly run her down. Where he'd first met her. When she had appeared out of nowhere in front of his curricle. The only reason he had been home was to change into dry clothing.

But here she was. In his arms. Soft and warm and

distraught and shivering. He had despaired of ever seeing her again, because all sorts of dire things had run through his brain.

She had been set upon by hooligans.

She had been kidnapped by villains and forced into a brothel.

She had tripped, fallen into the river and drowned.

Worst of all, she never wanted to see him again and had hidden away so he would never find her.

"You're safe, Emma," he murmured as he rubbed her back. "No one will harm you here."

She shivered and her fingers clutched his banyan so tightly her knuckles were white. In the short time he'd known her, she had always seemed fearless. He did not like that she had been lost and frightened. Tightening his hug, he tried to warm her.

She sniffled and sat up. "I'm being a ninny, crying all over you," she said, swiping at her eyes and nose. "I've ruined your banyan."

He had no handkerchief to give her, and he was not about to dislodge her to retrieve one. "It does not matter. I'll have it repaired." A ruined banyan was a small price to pay for Emma's return. The house had felt empty without her. He used his thumb to catch a tear that was about to slip down her cheek. "Where have you been, Emma? I looked all over the city for you."

Her eyes widened. "You did?"

"Of course. I wanted to apologize. I never should have said what I did." He shook his head in self-recrimination. "But watching my brother with you —"

"You were jealous," she said, as if she had known all along, as if she could read his thoughts.

His glance slid away. "I wanted to keep you safe. Because you had lost some of your memory. I felt responsible. For your injuries, you see. And Pemberton just didn't understand."

"Thank you for your kindness," she said, her tone solemn, and placed her cold palm against his cheek. "I am truly grateful for everything you have done — giving me a place to stay and the lovely frocks. But I can't—I won't—stay locked up in the house because you are jealous."

He opened his mouth to rebut her statement, then closed it again because he had been jealous.

"Your brother means nothing to me," she said. "I want to help you, and the only way I know how to do that is to pretend that I am interested in him."

Humbled by her generosity, he fumbled for words. "I... He shook his head. "You don't have to do that."

"But I want to." A violent shiver ran through her.

"You're cold," he said, relieved he could interrupt their discussion, because he felt as if a bandage had been ripped from his heart and new, tender skin had been revealed. "We must get you into a warm bed."

Mrs. Porter knocked on the door. "Towels for you, sir," she said.

"Upstairs, please, Mrs. Porter," he instructed as he stood, clutching Emma close, trying to warm her. "Miss Blake needs to be abed. Rouse one of the maids to help her."

He didn't know how to deal with that new skin on his heart, so he ignored it and focused on getting Emma warm and dry.

EMMA CLUNG TO BRANDON AS HE CARRIED HER UP TO HER room. Despite the heat from his body, she couldn't stop shivering. He set her down in front of the hearth and stirred up the coals, which had been lit because of the chill in the air. The heat felt wonderful, but it did little to dispel her shivering. Mrs. Porter arrived soon after with the towels and a yawning maid in tow.

"I'll let you get settled, and then if I may, come back to wish you sweet dreams," he said.

"I would like that," Emma said, reluctant to see him leave, but at the same time, yearning for bed. Had she made him understand why she had been angry? Why she had acted as if she had been charmed by his brother?

Mrs. Porter and Daisy, the maid, distracted her from her

thoughts by stripping off her wet clothes, scrubbing her dry, and tucking her under the covers. She was warmer, but still shivery. Brandon returned as soon as Mrs. Porter and Daisy left. He had changed out of his wet banyan and into another, this time a deep red velvet.

Standing next to the bed, he asked, "Are you feeling better?"

"S-still cold." She huddled farther down into the covers.

He studied her a moment, and then, to her surprise, he climbed onto the bed and lay down on top of the covers next to her. "Come here," he murmured. "Let me warm you."

Wrapping his arms around her, he pulled her close, her back against his broad chest. The heat from his body, even through the covers, felt like heaven. Slowly, her shivers subsided. She was back where she belonged. With him. In his arms. Her muscles relaxed. Their discussion could be continued later when she wasn't exhausted. She slipped into sleep.

And dreamed of him.

SUNLIGHT POKED ITS FINGER THROUGH A CRACK IN THE DRAPES, into Emma's eye, and woke her. She'd had the most wonderful, erotic dreams. She was warm and dry and thoroughly comfortable, cozily bundled against a hard body.

She blinked, trying to focus.

A muscular arm wrapped around her. A chiseled chest supported her back. Strong legs curled beneath her bottom.

No wonder she'd had erotic dreams. Brandon had slipped beneath the covers and slept with her. Cautiously, she felt the arm draped over her. The velvet of his banyan was soft beneath her fingers. He was still clothed. So the erotic dreams had been just that, only her brain making up things. But wonderful things. Things she wanted to explore. But first, she needed to know if he understood that she was only trying to help him.

"Good morning," he murmured, his voice raspy from sleep.

She smiled. "Good morning. Thank you for keeping me warm."

"It was the least I could do."

He started to pull back his arm, but she stopped him with her hand.

"Don't go," she whispered, and rolled over to face him. "I want you to understand why I walked out yesterday."

He lifted an ironic brow. "Because I was being a cad?"

Huffing a laugh, she nodded. "Yes. But a very protective, caring cad."

"I don't trust my brother," he said. "If he ever—"

"Sh," she interrupted. "I won't let him."

Then she cupped his cheek, rough with overnight stubble, and pressed a gentle kiss against his lips. As soon as her mouth touched his, her world seemed to shift, as if the earth shook in order to rearrange itself in its correct order. His lips felt perfect against hers. He hadn't moved, hadn't caressed her. In fact, he lay perfectly still. But she knew, with every tiny molecule, that she wanted to make love with him. This went deeper than anything she had experienced with any other man.

His hands framed her face and he pulled back the tiniest bit. "Emma," he murmured. "What are you doing?"

She gazed into those smoky eyes only inches from hers. And fell into them. Deep. Infinite. Beautiful beyond measure.

"I want you to make love to me," she said.

Heat flared in those gray eyes, followed swiftly by doubt. "Are you certain? Because—"

She placed her finger across his lips before he could say any more. "Yes. I'm certain. More certain than anything I've ever felt."

Before he could argue, she kissed his lips, and his jaw, and with her tongue, drew a circle on the vein pounding below his ear. And then claimed his mouth again.

His arms came around her and pulled her close. She felt every inch of him, the hard plane of his chest, his muscular thighs, and in between, his erection pressing against her belly. The gentle kiss ratcheted up into a wild exploration, with tongues tangling, teeth nipping. Did she breathe? She wasn't sure. But she didn't need breath if Brandon kissed her like she was his life.

She wanted to rub against his skin like a sensuous cat, but his banyan and her nightgown prevented that. Breaking away, she went up on her knees and pulled the offending garment over her head.

His eyes widened. "God's tears," he whispered. "You are beautiful."

His words were as much of an aphrodisiac as his touch. She had never thought of herself as beautiful. But he thought she was. She smiled.

"I want to see how beautiful you are," she said.

"Hardly that," he said, his words wry.

He remained perfectly still, as, slowly, one by one, she undid the buttons holding his banyan closed and pushed it open. His broad chest lay exposed with its muscles and flat male nipples. And lower, his magnificent erection.

She met his gaze. "You are very beautiful."

Before he could protest, bending close, she kissed the hollow of his throat, then trailed kisses down to his breastbone, where soft hairs grew. Her fingers explored, circling his nipples, running down over his ribs, skimming over his flat belly. Wrapping around his erection.

His fingers curled around her wrist, halting her hand from moving. "Keep that up and you'll be my undoing," he warned.

She grinned. She wanted to be his undoing very much.

AT THAT CHEEKY GRIN, BRANDON SWARMED TO HIS KNEES AND stripped off his banyan. He'd had no plan to make love with her when he had crawled beneath the covers to warm her. His only thought had been to stop her shivers. But her sensuous onslaught was the most delicious thing he had ever experienced. When she flung off her nightrail, revealing her pearly skin, he knew he was blessed. She was a goddess, a Venus, an enticement to Heaven, an invitation to sin.

Kneeling before her, he skimmed his fingers over the perfect roundness of her shoulder, the delicacy of her collar bone, the inviting hollow of her throat. At each touch, a tiny shiver ran through her, so he warmed her by following each touch with a kiss. He saved the elegant curve of her neck for last.

She arched back, and her pert breasts beckoned. Taking his right hand, she placed it on one of her breasts. "This is yours," she whispered. Then she placed his left hand on her other breast. "And this one, too."

Her breasts fit perfectly in his hands. He could find no words. Always, he had been able to whisper endearments and encouragements with the women he bedded, but not now. Now, he was speechless with wonder. She had him in thrall.

Framing his face with her hands, she drew him down and placed a kiss at each corner of his mouth. As if a restraint had been loosened, he wanted to taste every inch of her.

He rained kisses across her delicate jaw, down her throat, to one breast, where he teased the tip with his teeth. She moaned her pleasure. He gave the other breast equal attention. She sucked in a breath.

In awe at her trust, he wanted to touch all her secret places, the ones that made her giggle, the ones that made her sigh. He wanted to explore the thatch between her thighs, to see if it wept with pleasure. He wanted to hear her moan again.

EMMA WATCHED THE PLAY OF EMOTIONS ACROSS BRANDON'S face. Fascinated, intrigued. Aroused. Very aroused from the look of his engorged erection. That made her happy. She was about to wrap her hand around it when his fingers trailed up her leg and distracted her. His fingers spiraled up the inside of her thigh. She opened her legs in invitation.

He sucked on her breast. She throbbed. And then his thumb landed with precision against her nub. The perfect spot. Exactly what she wanted. She moaned, and cut it off. Maybe she shouldn't do that. Maybe women in the nineteenth century remained completely quiet when they made love.

"I want to hear you moan," he whispered in her ear as his thumb did wonderful things between her legs. "I want to hear your pleasure."

With his free hand, he pinched and rolled her nipple. His touch was exquisite. She arched up into his hand. Then his fingers slipped inside her. She throbbed. Her muscles clenched. She gripped his shoulders as if he was the only thing that held her to the earth. He sent her higher, higher. Until she climaxed in a burst of light and stars. And a cry that was much louder than a moan.

BRANDON COULDN'T KEEP THE SMILE FROM HIS FACE AS HE watched her come apart. She was exquisite, this woman who had fallen into his life. He wanted very much to be inside her, but he would refrain. Later, he would take his own pleasure.

He slipped from the bed.

"Where are you going?" she asked. "I want to make love with you."

Was she so naïve that she did not realize that he was protecting her from conceiving?

"No," he said. "I'll not plant a seed in your womb and lose another child. Or you."

His concern warmed her. Grabbing his hand, she kissed each finger, then gazed up at him. "I won't conceive, if that's what worries you. Please. No commitments."

The touch of her soft lips against his hand nearly convinced him, but her announcement riveted his attention. "Why? How do you know you won't conceive?" Sorrow that she would never be a mother twisted his heart. "I am very sorry."

"It's okay." A tiny grin curved her lips. "I'll explain later. Trust me. Please."

And then she wrapped her fingers around his erection.

That nearly undid him.

"I want to give you pleasure," she whispered. "Just like you gave me."

Her hand slid up and down his shaft.

He was convinced.

EMMA WELCOMED HIM INTO HER ARMS AS THEY FELL BACK ONTO the bed. His body was warm, hard planes against her. She pushed him to his back, then straddled him. His eyes widened, but before he could question, she shook her head.

"Sh. Just enjoy," she said.

One corner of his mouth quirked up. "If that's what you wish."

She smiled. "That's what I wish."

She twirled her tongue around each of his flat nipples, then traced down across his chest to the dark line of hair that arrowed toward his erection, standing proud. It beckoned. Swirling her tongue around its silky length, she heard his indrawn breath. Then she lapped up the salty drop that appeared at its tip.

"God's tears," he croaked.

She huffed a laugh. "Shall I go on?"

"No. Yes." He blew out a breath. "Whatever you would like."

Emma took him into her mouth. He was silk over steel, satin over iron. She tasted the salty leak from his tip. A throb deep in her core answered.

He hissed in a breath. "Stop. Come here, vixen." He pulled her up across his body, then flipped her to her back. Holding himself above her, he said, "Enough torture."

As he inched into her, she wriggled, then lifted her hips, pushing herself completely onto his shaft. His groan echoed her own sigh as he filled her completely. They fit together like two puzzle pieces. Like needle and thread. Like yin and yang.

"Perfection," he whispered, moving within her.

Emma felt as if she had been waiting for this moment her

whole life. As if she had been waiting for *him*. She floated on the pleasure and held onto his arms, his muscles bunching beneath her hands, while he drove her higher and higher. Then he came with a roar. And stars, planets, galaxies, nebula exploded as her climax crashed through her.

Thirteen

E mma sprawled across Brandon's chest. Their lovemaking had been extraordinary. How could she have guessed that she would find her hero, a magnificent lover, in the nineteenth century? He was everything she had written about him. And so much more. Because he was real, a living, breathing, human man, with strengths and faults, just like any other. But they could never have a relationship. They were from two different centuries, and she might find herself flung forward to her own time at any moment. She had to tell him the truth.

Even with the drapes closed, the room had brightened, since the sun was now high in the sky. She could clearly see Brandon's face, handsome in repose, for he dozed as well. She traced small circles on his chest and watched the tiny hairs spring back into place as she moved them around. Feeling his gaze on her, she glanced up.

She cleared her throat. "Hi."

A corner of his mouth deepened. "You use the most intriguing words. Another word from America, I presume?"

"Yes." She sent him a fleeting smile, then turned serious. "I need to tell you something."

"Yes? Did I not pay attention to some bit of you?" He cupped her bottom. "Here, perhaps?" His fingers traced up her spine and made her shiver. "Ah, still cold, are you?" He flipped her to her back, braced on his elbows, and rose above her. "I believe I found the exact spot that might warm you." Ducking his head, he tickled her nipple with his tongue.

Emma laughed and pushed him off, despite the pleasure that streaked through her. "Please, I'm serious." She sat up.

A faint line appeared between his brows. "Did I hurt you in some way?"

She shook her head. "No. You were perfect." Taking a breath, she blurted, "I'm not from here."

"From America, you said." His brow wrinkled. "Are you not from America, Cousin Emma?"

His teasing name for her indicated he still felt playful. She was glad he was in such a good mood, because she was about to blow apart everything he ever believed.

She placed her hand on his chest over his heart. "Yes, I am from America, but there's more."

He sat up. "Have you regained your memory?"

"Yes. No. Not really." She took another breath, glanced away, then peeked at him. "I never lost it."

Thunder clouds gathered in his eyes.

"Wait, please, before you get upset." She chewed on her bottom lip as she tried to decide how to tell him. But there was no easy way. "I'm from the future," she blurted.

He stared, not moving, not blinking. She wondered if he even breathed. Then a line appeared between his brows.

"Did you bump your head again?" he asked. "Perhaps I should call Dr. Beech."

"No." She shook her head. "I didn't bump my head. I'm from the twenty-first century."

"The twenty-first century?" His tone rose in disbelief.

"Yes. Remember the clothes you found me in when you nearly ran me down?"

"They were certainly...interesting." Warmth entered his eyes.

She huffed. "They were more than interesting. You know that. You'd never seen anything like those. Or my sneakers—"

His brows rose in a question.

"My shoes," she explained.

He stared at her blankly.

Scrambling out of bed, she dug in her wardrobe until she found one, along with her leggings, then brought both back to show him. He took the running shoe and turned it over and over as he examined it.

"It is extraordinary," he agreed with a nod.

She showed him the leggings, stretching them, then crunching them into a ball and letting them fall open, back to their original shape with no wrinkles. "Have you ever seen material like that?"

Taking them, he held them up, then repeated her actions. He stared down at the garment in his hands. Emma waited nervously as he assimilated what she had told him. How would he react? Would he believe her? Or would he think she was deranged?

His glance slid away for a moment, then came back to rest on her. "Yes, I see. From the future. How did you get here?" Doubt lingered in his gaze.

"I think it had something to do with the ancient oak tree in Hyde Park, and a hole in the middle of the path."

His eyes narrowed with skepticism. "I have passed by there many times, and have encountered several holes, one which broke a wheel on my curricle. Never once have I been transported to another time."

"I can't explain it," she said with a shrug. "But isn't there a legend about the Druids using it to travel through time?"

"Probably made up by some drunken sailor who passed out beneath its branches." Humor twitched his lips.

She retrieved her charm from the table where she had put it the night before. "And my bracelet might have been involved."

Something flashed through his eyes when he focused on the charm. Was it recognition? Or more doubt?

She had to make him believe her, so he'd let her stay with him. So she could save him. But how could she do that?

BRANDON DIDN'T KNOW WHAT TO THINK. HE HAD JUST MADE glorious, staggering love with this woman, who just told him she was from the future. Was she lying? Had the bump on her head made her delusional? Or was she telling the truth?

When he had first encountered her in Hyde Park, she had seemed to appear out of thin air. Certainly, her strange clothing was unlike anything he had ever encountered. He stared down at the pantaloons in his hands. Crushing the garment in his fists again, he let them fall open and watched as the material returned to its unwrinkled state. Then he stretched it, marveling that it didn't tear and was not misshapen when he released it. He picked up the shoe, once again surprised by its light weight, despite the fact it looked as heavy as a boulder. Where did these pieces come from if not from the future?

"Brandon." She covered his hand with her smaller one. "There's more." She ducked her head and was silent a moment, then met his gaze. "I saw a portrait of Elizabeth, the woman who wed your half-brother."

He flinched as if she had hit him. "That is impossible." Suspicion curled in his chest like a serpent. "Unless you have been to Cranleigh Manor. With Stephen." He spat out the name.

"No!" She shook her head vigorously. "No. I've never been to Cranleigh Manor. I saw the portrait in my father's antique shop in the future. By the time I saw it, the painting was very old."

"In a shop? Are you saying the portrait was for sale?"

At her nod, he bolted from the bed and strode across the room. How could the portrait be for sale? It was part of the family legacy. Stephen had wed Elizabeth and made her his viscountess. Even though she had given him no heirs and died young, she should have been honored as his wife. Had his brother thought so little of her that he would discard her portrait? Fury turned his blood hot. But then a tiny sliver of logic made him pause. Emma said she saw the painting far in the future. *If* she was from the future, as she said.

"How do you know that the painting you saw was of Elizabeth?" he asked.

Her lips curled in, turning that luscious mouth into a line, as if she needed to hold in a secret. Then she picked up his banyan where he had flung it and handed it to him.

"I need to tell you more," she said, as she indicated the chairs before the hearth.

Curious and wary, he donned the garment and sat in one of the chairs. He watched as she pulled on her nightrail again, then wrapped herself in one of the blankets from the bed. Disappointment flitted through him as she covered up her lovely curves, but he was anxious to hear the rest of her story.

She stood before him and took a breath. "Your ghost told me about Elizabeth, how she wed Stephen instead of you."

"My—?" Dumbfounded, he stared up at her.

A tiny smile curved her lips. "Aren't you glad I had you sit down?"

He was very glad. Shock, doubt, and confusion churned through him. Of course, if she was from the future, he would be dead in her time. Why wouldn't his ghost visit her? She was the most entrancing, delightful, intelligent woman he had ever met. He was attracted to her in this time, so obviously, his ghost would be attracted to her in the future. And his ghost would know if he had succeeded in gaining his birthright.

But before he could ask her, she pulled a footstool close to him, sat and took his hand. "There's something else I need to tell you."

Warily, he waited for her next revelation.

She glanced down at their clasped hands resting on his knee, as if reluctant to speak. Then she raised those beautiful blue eyes and said, "I met the Viscount Pemberton in the future. His given name is Stephen, and he looks very much like your half-brother. He could be his twin. That's why I said his name when I first saw him."

He blinked, then as her meaning became clear, sharp disappointment knifed through him. Unable to remain still, he swarmed from the chair and stalked across the room. His brother had won. Their father had never recognized him as his first born.

Yanking open the drapes, he stared out the window, but he didn't see the small, disheveled garden behind his townhouse. Instead, in his mind's eye, he saw the rolling lawns of Cranleigh Manor, the duck pond, the stables to one side, and the woods beyond. All that was supposed to be his. But it never came to be. It was Stephen's. And Stephen's descendants.

He had lost everything. His birthright. The woman he'd loved. His son. Despair gripped him hard.

EMMA WATCHED BRANDON AS HE STARED OUT THE WINDOW. Defeat showed in his slumped shoulders. She wanted to wipe away his disappointment. Standing, she crossed to him and placed her hand on his back.

"Your ghost told me something else," she said.

He grunted, as if what she had to say would make no difference.

Forging on, she said, "He—You—told me I could help fix things."

He swung to face her. "Fix things? How can you fix things? From what you have told me, my half-brother gains our father's title, weds again, and leaves progeny for generations. While I..." He waved his hand in a vague motion of defeat. Narrowing his gaze on her, he asked, "What does my ghost say about that? About what happens to me?"

Emma was not about to tell him how he met his demise. She was going to try to prevent that from happening. Instead, she scowled. "Are you going to give up? You're not a ghost yet."

He scoffed and turned back to the window.

Annoyed at his attitude, she stepped between him and his view out the window. "I think your brother is involved in something suspicious. If it's illegal, your father would have to name you his heir."

He glanced at her. "Do you understand the scandal that would cause? Besides, we've already discussed this. I doubt we could do it."

His skepticism made her more determined to help him. "I didn't have a chance to tell you before, but I saw Sir Dotson pass a message to him at Tattersall's."

Interest sparked in his eyes. "Yes?" Then the spark died. "No doubt it was a note about betting on the turf."

"Horse racing?" She shook her head. "I don't think so. Aren't bets written down in a book at his club or something? No, this was different. Stephen said something to him at Lady Farley's dinner party that made me think they had a plan to meet at the horse auction. I think Stephen is involved in something. Maybe he's a spy."

In her historical romance, Brandon's half-brother was a sneaky French spy. She thought she had made that up. But what if Ghost Brandon, her "muse," had put that idea in her head when she was writing? What if Stephen really was a traitor? What if what she had written mirrored what actually happened? More than ever, she was determined to give Brandon a happy ending.

"A spy?" He huffed a laughed. "I think you are imagining things that aren't there. Didn't you tell me you write stories, like Maria Edgeworth?"

Emma swung away and stalked to the middle of the room. "I'm not imagining things. I know what I saw. What if I'm right? What if we could catch him doing something wicked and against the law?"

Becoming serious, he asked, "If I agree to this, how do you plan to catch him?"

Excited that he might consent, she began to pace as she laid out her plan.

When she finished, he scowled. "Absolutely not. We already tried this, and he nearly had me killed in that collision with the hay wagon. God knows what he had planned for you. You will not befriend my brother. He has already stolen one woman from me. I'll not allow him to steal another."

Brandon's possessive words warmed her insides. Approaching him, she placed her hand over his heart. "He can't steal me away. I'm not some innocent miss who must do her father's bidding. I can choose the man I want to be with." Cupping his face, she placed a soft kiss on one corner of his mouth. "Please, believe me." Then she kissed the other corner. "I want to be with you."

"You are very persuasive, Emma Blake," he murmured.

"I know."

Then she persuaded him back to bed.

Fourteen

Later, after they had made love once more, Brandon had returned to his own room and Daisy had come knocking on Emma's door to help her dress for the day. When she was presentable, Emma entered the dining room in search of breakfast. His aunt was the only one at the table. Hesitating at the doorway, she wished he was there for back up. She had to pretend that nothing had changed in their relationship. But everything had changed.

As Lady Selby spread marmalade on her toast, she raised a brow at Emma. "So, you have returned. We were quite concerned."

Emma slid onto her chair and became very busy pouring herself some tea. "I'm sorry I caused you worry. I got lost." She pulled her broken bracelet out of her pocket and placed it on the table. "Do you know where I could get this repaired?"

Lady Selby held it up to the sunlight streaking through the window. Then she turned to Emma. "Where did you get this?"

"It belonged to my mother. My two sisters both have a pendant just like it."

"I know I have seen it before," Lady Selby mused. "An unusual piece."

How could the woman have seen the pendant that came from a necklace owned by her mother? Emma decided she must be mistaken. Lady Selby would have been long dead by the time Emma's father gave it to her mother.

"Hmm." The lady examined it again and murmured, "Yes, I know I have seen this before. On a necklace, I believe. A famous piece. A chain of diamonds with three charms, designed to look like flower buds, of a sapphire surrounded by diamonds." Her gaze fastened on Emma. "It was the center of a scandal. The gossip and innuendo went on for weeks before dying down. Strange that it should end up in America."

"Yes," Emma agreed, "very strange." Since her father made frequent trips to London, he could have easily purchased the antique necklace in England and brought it back as a gift to her mother. "Would you tell me about the scandal?"

Lady Selby laid the bracelet on the table, then poured

herself more tea. "It was quite some time ago, and I was quite young. I had just had my coming out, and the diamond of the first water that Season was Miss Sophie Floyd. She was beautiful and the granddaughter of a duke, and would bring a large dowry to her marriage. All the young men were besotted. All the mamas wanted her as a match for their sons. But the jealous girls, who were not as sought-after, spread rumors that her grandmother on her mother's side was a witch. Of course, she laughed at them, and the young swains did not care. They still swarmed around her like bees to honey. Everyone thought she would wed the handsome Earl of Baer, who had just gained his title and was the catch of the Season."

Intrigued by the story, Emma said, "But she didn't marry him, did she?"

"No, she did not." A tiny smile curved the lady's lips as she shook her head.

"Whom did she marry?" Emma thought she might use the tale as the plot for her next historical romance.

Lady Selby straightened the knife on her plate. "The most sought-after invitation that Season was to a masquerade ball hosted by Mrs. White. I was lucky enough to get one. The ball was a magnificent, extravagant affair, with jugglers and acrobats and all sorts of exotic creatures in cages throughout the gardens. Festoons of flowers draped the ballroom, and fairy lights glowed in the shrubbery and trees. Everyone wore a mask or domino, dressed as ancient kings or queens, or gods or goddesses, or wild animals, or other fantastical creatures, but of course, everyone knew who everyone was. Except for one gentleman, whom no one knew. He came dressed as a highwayman in black cape and slouch hat and half mask."

"Ooh, very dashing and mysterious," Emma said. She couldn't wait to hear what happened.

"Yes, quite." A thoughtful expression crossed Lady Selby's face. "The curious whispers flew through the ballroom as everyone wondered who he was. He danced with a few of the debutantes, and then he danced with Miss Sophie, who had dressed as a shepherdess. One could see that they were immediately smitten with each other. He danced with her four times, an unheard of thing to do, unless the couple were betrothed. After the last dance of the ball, he pulled the necklace out of his pocket and placed it around Sophie's neck."

Emma gasped. "That's so romantic! Did you ever discover his name, who he was? Did Sophie and the stranger marry?"

Lady Selby merely smiled. "Of course, the gossip spread like the plague. Miss Sophie's reputation was ruined. Her parents searched everywhere for the stranger, thinking they could force him to marry her, but he had disappeared, just like the highwayman he had impersonated at the ball. Two weeks went by. The Season was over, and families began to travel to their country estates. The day before Miss Sophie was to leave the city with her family, she disappeared. The only thing she took with her was the necklace. A month after that, her parents received a letter from her, telling them she was well, and to make no attempt to find her. The man she had run away with and wed was the second son of a marquis. Because he wouldn't inherit anything from his father, he had become an adventurer, traveling through Indies, Africa and India, acquiring gemstones, and had become quite wealthy. That was the last time anyone heard from her." Lady Selby's gaze speared her. "So you see, it is very odd that you have a piece of the necklace."

Emma opened her mouth to respond and closed it again. What could she tell this woman? How could she explain?

"You must be Miss Sophie's daughter," Lady Selby said.

Emma shook her head. "No, I couldn't be."

"Why is that?" Lady Selby's chilly question demanded an answer.

"Because..." Emma took a breath. If she agreed to the lady's assumption, she'd be caught in a web of more lies. But could she tell her the truth?

"Because she is a Traveler."

Emma's gaze swung to Brandon's voice coming from the doorway, where he stood looking coolly debonair and thoroughly put together, just the opposite of how she felt.

"A Traveler?" she managed to say, glad she sounded normal.

A jumble of emotions washed through her — relief, arousal, apprehension. She had trusted Brandon with the truth, but his aunt might have a very different reaction if the lady learned she was from a different century. She glanced at Lady Selby to gauge her response to his statement. Only a tiny pursing of the woman's lips revealed it had any effect.

As Brandon took his seat, he said, "My aunt believes that fairies are real and they have many abilities not available to ordinary folk." He smiled. "Like helping people travel through time."

"Are you a Traveler of Time?" Lady Selby demanded.

Emma froze, opened her mouth, then closed it, not sure what to say. She hadn't expected to admit to being a time traveler to anyone besides Brandon.

When Emma didn't respond, Lady Selby said, "Do not deny it. I knew there was something different about you from our first meeting."

Despite Lady Selby's relationship to Brandon and despite her apparent knowledge of time travel, Emma wasn't sure she could trust her. She needed time to decide what to do.

"Excuse me," Emma said. "I'm not feeling well."

She started to rise, but Lady Selby caught her by the arm.

"I'm trying to help you. Don't run away." The woman's gaze softened. "I believe there are many things in this world and beyond it that we cannot explain, like traveling through time."

Emma sank back to her seat.

Lady Selby held the pendant up to the light again, then handed it back to Emma. "I know someone who might be able to help. I will send round a note and ask if it is convenient to call."

"Who is it?" Emma asked.

"A lady of my acquaintance. She will explain everything." Lady Selby spooned sugar into her tea, then stirred it, indicating she would say no more.

Emma's curiosity spiked. Who was this person? What could she tell her about time traveling? She wanted to know more about how that worked. If she happened to pass the oak tree, would she be flung back to her own time? If she traveled back to her own time, would she ever see Brandon again? The thought made her heart wrench, despite having his ghost in the twenty-first century.

She glanced at him, seated across the table. She didn't want his ghost. She wanted *him*. Alive. Not accused of murder. Not shot in the back by his deceitful brother.

Before she traveled back to her own time, she needed to be sure that he was safe. That his brother was dishonored and disowned. That he could have his happily-ever-after with a woman from his own century whom he loved. Her heart twisted at that last thought, but her goal was more important than regretting she could never be that woman.

LATER THAT AFTERNOON, EMMA SET OUT IN A CARRIAGE BESIDE Lady Selby, who had remained quite secretive about the woman they were visiting. Brandon had remained behind at the request of Lady Selby, because his presence might make this woman more reticent to share information. When they stopped, she couldn't believe they were in front of the house where the reclusive widow lived, the same building where her father's flat was located in the twenty-first century.

The door was opened by a very proper butler who showed them to a drawing room. Although not large, it was very elegant with silk-covered chairs and matching sofa in pale yellow, and lovely pastoral paintings on the ivory-colored walls. Lady Selby settled on the sofa, and Emma glanced around as she sat in one of the chairs. In the twenty-first century, this room was part of the superintendent's flat. She doubted it looked as elegant as it did now.

Footsteps echoed across the entrance hall and then a woman swept into the room — the same woman who had been sitting beside the ancient oak in Hyde Park, the kindly woman who'd offered her tea and comfort when she'd run from Brandon. Emma rose and curtsied.

"Please." The woman indicated Emma should sit, then sat herself.

She was still heavily veiled, but her frock was gray instead of black. Emma tried to see her features, but only the pale oval of her face was visible through her veil.

"Lady Selby." The lady nodded a greeting. "How may I help you?"

"My apologies for calling on you, Mrs. Edwards," Lady Selby said. "But I believe we have a Traveler in our midst." She indicated Emma. "This is Emma Blake."

"Yes?" Mrs. Edwards' response was cool as she turned in Emma's direction. "Are you a Traveler?"

"I — ah —" Emma wasn't sure she wanted to reveal that, even to this woman who had comforted her when she was so upset. Instead, she said, "Thank you for being kind when we met."

Mrs. Edwards nodded her acknowledgment.

"Show her the bracelet," Lady Selby directed.

Emma pulled it out of her reticule and held it up. The single, tear-drop shaped sapphire and the tiny diamonds that cupped it caught a beam of sunlight and created rainbows on the walls and ceiling. Mrs. Edwards seemed captivated.

After a moment, she said, "You wore that lovely piece when we met in Hyde Park. May I examine it?" She held out her hand.

A tiny tug of trepidation made Emma hesitate, but after a moment, she placed it in the woman's palm. Mrs. Edwards stared at it, then lightly traced the piece with her finger. Even though Emma couldn't see her face, she sensed that the woman was quite moved. Why would a piece of jewelry that had belonged to Emma's mother cause such a reaction? Or did she recognize it from the scandal that Lady Selby had described?

When Mrs. Edwards handed it back, she said, "The pendant is quite valuable, beyond the value of the precious stones. It is a time key. The piece will transport someone through the centuries. But that person must be near the door into time for it to work." Her words were straight-forward and her tone unemotional, the opposite of what Emma expected after seeing her reaction.

Surprised that her mother had owned such a piece, Emma looked down at the bracelet. How had her father acquired it? Had he known the charm was magical? Would her sisters be able to travel through time as well with their charms? If she could somehow communicate with them, then they could be with her in the nineteenth century. She just had to tell them how to get here.

She looked back at Mrs. Edwards. "Is the door into time at the ancient oak tree in Hyde Park?"

"I believe you know the answer to that already." She glanced at Lady Selby. "This is a dangerous object to own, and it must be kept safe. Where were you going to have it repaired?"

"Rundell and Bridge," Lady Selby said.

Mrs. Edwards shook her head. "They are fine jewelers, but I think the fewer people who know about this, the better. A man named Roger Bowker would like nothing more than to take possession of it. If he hears that it exists, well..." She shook her head again. "He has tinkered with mechanisms that he believes allow him to travel through time. I'm not sure he has been successful. Even if he has not, he is a dangerous man."

A chill ran down Emma's spine. "He spoke to me at Vauxhall Gardens."

"Then we certainly must not let him get his hands on it," Mrs. Edwards said. "He must suspect something about you. Leave the bracelet with me, and I will have it repaired. I know someone who is very discreet."

Emma hesitated. If what Mrs. Edwards said was true, she needed that pendant to get back to her own time. Could she trust this woman? Mystery hung about her like a haze.

"I see you are unsure about me," Mrs. Edwards said.

Emma didn't want to insult this woman, but she needed to make her understand. "It's the only way I can get home."

Mrs. Edwards nodded. "Of course. I wouldn't want you to do anything that makes you uncomfortable. But since the bracelet is broken, you may lose the time key." She gave a tiny shrug, as if to say that result was out of her hands.

Emma weighed her choices. Keep the bracelet and possibly lose it? Or hand it over and have it repaired to keep it safe? Either way, being without the pendant that had been her mother's opened a tiny hole in her heart.

"I think Mrs. Edwards is trustworthy, Emma," Lady Selby said.

If only Emma could see the woman's eyes, she might be

able to discern that herself. But that was impossible through the veil. Taking a chance, Emma held out the bracelet.

"Do you know how long the repair might take?" she asked.

Mrs. Edwards scooped the piece into her hand. "That I can't tell you. I must contact the person and wait for a response. And there is the time it will take him to repair it, of course."

"Of course," Emma murmured, wondering whether that might take a few days, a week, months, or longer.

Lady Selby stood, signaling the end of the visit.

Emma rose as well. "Thank you, Mrs. Edwards. You were very kind when I was so upset."

Mrs. Edwards touched Emma's cheek. "I could never abide seeing a young woman in distress. You are quite welcome, my dear."

Her touch brought tears to Emma's eyes, which she quickly blinked away. But something about Mrs. Edwards gave her a warm feeling, like a comforting hug.

As she and Lady Selby drove away, Emma turned back to take another look at the house. The coincidence of Mrs. Edwards living in the same building where she lived in the future made her head spin. But more than that connection, Emma liked the woman, despite her reserve.

She only had vague memories of her mother who had died when Emma was very young. Her father, who had never remarried, had been a wonderful father to her and her sisters, but sometimes during her childhood, she yearned for a mom. But the idea of Mrs. Edwards becoming a friend was absurd. She was a recluse and seemed to want to be left alone.

Emma wrapped her fingers around her empty wrist. She felt bereft without her bracelet and pendant, for she had worn it nearly all her life. Her father had given it to her on her tenth birthday, with the pendant already attached to the silver chain. As she had grown, he'd had links added to make the chain larger, so she could always wear it.

What would happen if Mrs. Edwards kept the piece? Or it was lost? Or whoever repaired it somehow destroyed it? What would she do if she were stuck in the nineteenth century? How would she live? For now, she had Brandon, who had given her a place to stay, but she couldn't rely on him forever. Despite liking him very, very much, she was not going to become a kept woman. She could probably still be an author, but that would take time. She would have to figure out something in the meantime.

But that was for later, because the carriage had just stopped before Brandon's door. And tiny bubbles of anticipation popped in her middle.

Brandon stood at the window and gazed out at the street. He should have gone to his club to get out of the house. Or written letters checking on his investment in the tin mine or the sheep farm. Instead, his mind was on Emma.

She intrigued him, confused him, entranced him. Caused the blood to race through his veins. Annoyed him with her independent ways. Awed him with her audacity. Made him laugh. Drew him like a bee to nectar. He wanted to touch her, kiss her. Take her to bed. Again. He shook his head, as if he could rid her from his mind.

She was from another century.

She did not belong here.

She could disappear at any moment.

He had to stop thinking about her.

That was impossible now. After Elizabeth's marriage to Stephen, Brandon had vowed he would never love another woman. Even though Elizabeth had been married to his half-brother, he had always felt as if just being in the world with her was enough. When she died, a light inside him died, as well. He had been living in twilight. Until he had nearly run over Emma in Hyde Park. Suddenly, his world had brightened and come alive.

No. He was not going to become enthralled by another woman. He had loved Elizabeth, and his heart had been shredded when she rejected him, even though it was forced upon her by her father. He would enjoy the time he had with

Emma, and then let her go, back to her own century where she belonged.

In the meantime, they could romp in bed. That thought curved his lips in a smile. She made love with abandon. And she was definitely not a virgin. She had told him she couldn't conceive. Had something happened to her? An accident? An illness? While that relieved him when they made love, it also bothered him. She would never be able to have a child, never be a mother. He had a sense that she would be a wonderful mother.

Emma distracted him from the pain of losing both Elizabeth and his son. The gnawing emptiness had dwindled since she had arrived in his life. If—when—she returned to her own century, he would miss her very much.

The carriage that had taken his aunt and Emma on their call stopped before his front door and distracted him from his thoughts. Aunt Morrin stepped down, followed by Emma. His aunt swept up the stairs, but for a moment, Emma stood with a pensive expression on the walkway. He wanted to wipe away any worries she had and make her smile. He very much enjoyed seeing her smile.

When she finally climbed the stairs, he turned away from the window. He would greet her and ask about her visit to the reclusive Mrs. Edwards. And then, perhaps, he would take her on a ride through Hyde Park in his curricle. Or perhaps a riding lesson on her horse, Cassiopeia. Whatever would make her smile.

MRS. EDWARDS WAITED UNTIL HER GUESTS HAD LEFT, THEN SHE gazed at the bracelet in her hand and poked at the sapphire and diamond pendant with a finger. She hadn't seen it in a very long time. It was finally in her possession. What to do with it? The answer came immediately. Keep it. But for how long?

While it was in her possession, Emma Blake would have to remain in the nineteenth century, because she could not access the door into time without it. Having her here was something she had dreamed about for a long time. She thought it might never happen. But when she had sensed the shimmering in time, she had started to visit the ancient oak every day. She had no idea what she would do if someone actually popped through the door into time. Her reaction depended on who appeared.

When she had seen Emma in Hyde Park, she nearly jumped from her seat. Fortunately, Emma was so distraught that she had not immediately noticed a woman sitting beneath the tree. She'd had time to control her emotions, a combination of tears and laughter, of fear and excitement. Emma must never know the danger that lurked in this world.

Mrs. Edwards closed her fingers around the bracelet and climbed the stairs to her dressing room. Opening a wardrobe, she knelt down, reached to the back behind frocks in shades of black, gray, and mauve, and felt for the clasp hidden in the floor. It popped open with a muted click. She pulled out a small, painted, wooden jewelry box about the size of a book. Except for a thin strand of diamonds, the box was empty. She dropped the bracelet with its sapphire and diamond pendant into the box, closed it, then secreted it away in the compartment at the back of the wardrobe. With a click, she shut the panel, stood, and closed up the wardrobe. No one would ever guess the secret compartment existed.

She pulled off her veil, and with a tiny smile, decided she would have a glass of port instead of tea. To celebrate.

Fifteen

Later that day, Emma stepped through the door into the foyer and sniffed the daisies Brandon had bought her. They were returning from her first riding lesson, which had gone very well. She loved riding Cassiopeia. While a maid took her hat and gloves, Brandon stepped to a small side table, where a letter sat on a silver tray.

He held it out to her. "It's addressed to you," he said, a frown drawing his brows together. "From my brother."

Unsure what to expect, she opened the note and read. "It's an invitation." She met Brandon's annoyed gaze. "He's invited me on a visit to the country at Cranleigh Manor."

"Obviously, you will decline." As if the matter were settled, he headed toward the stairs. "I'll ring for tea."

Exasperated at his cavalier assumption, Emma said nothing and watched him go. But the matter wasn't settled.

As soon as she read the invitation, trepidation filled her chest. In her novel, the heroine had been invited to the hero's estate, where she had discovered the proof that revealed the villainous half-brother was a spy. The similarities that were occurring between her historical romance and reality made her head spin.

What if she could find the proof at Cranleigh Manor that Stephen was a spy? And if reality mirrored her novel, then the proof would be secreted in his bedchamber. She had to accept Stephen's invitation so she could search. But Ghost Brandon told her he had been shot soon after discovering proof of his brother's treason, after a lunar eclipse had occurred. Somehow, she had to prevent Stephen from killing him. How could she do that?

Then she remembered he'd told her that his father had come to London, so both Brandon's murder and his father's had occurred in the city, not on the estate. She could find the proof at Cranleigh Manor, have Stephen arrested, and save them both.

But a feeling of dread still sat heavily in her chest. Maybe she should decline the invitation. No, she had to accept, despite her misgivings.

While Stephen appeared to be nothing more than a nobleman's son, wealthy and affable, knowing what Ghost Brandon had told her about him made her uneasy. If she accepted Stephen's invitation, she would be with him for several days and able to learn more about him, maybe discover what he was involved in. Maybe search his room. Was this what Ghost Brandon meant when he told her she could "fix things?"

If she could stop Stephen before he murdered the earl, then Brandon would have no need to prove his innocence. He wouldn't need to escape. He would be safe. And alive. Able to live out his life.

What should she do? Accept the invitation and try to prevent two murders? Or decline and avoid Stephen as Brandon wanted.

She couldn't avoid Stephen. She had already decided she had been sent back in time to save Brandon. Going on this visit to Cranleigh Manor might be the only way to do that. Having made up her mind, she started up the stairs to have tea with Brandon and convince him to change his mind.

LATE THAT NIGHT, EMMA ARGUED IN A WHISPER, "BUT I THINK it would be the perfect opportunity to watch Stephen and see what he's up to."

She was laying sprawled across Brandon's chest and running her fingers up and down his arm. He was doing the same up and down her back. They had just engaged in a breathtaking bout of lovemaking and were whispering so they wouldn't disturb his aunt.

Lady Selby had retired to her room after the visit to Mrs. Edwards, so Emma and Brandon had shared an intimate dinner for two in his sitting room. Which led to small caresses. And gentle kisses. And baring an ankle here, a shoulder there. Until their heat exploded into flames. Clothes had been pulled off with abandon and were strewn in a path to the bed.

"I don't care how perfect the opportunity is," Brandon whispered back. "I don't like that you will be spending time at Cranleigh Manor with him."

"What can I do to make you change your mind?" Her hand slipped down to his hip and she made circles in the hollow there.

"What can I do to convince you that you should not try to change my mind?" He flipped her onto her back.

"I'll be perfectly safe." She nipped his shoulder, then eased the sting with her tongue. "Your aunt will be with me."

"My aunt..." He kissed one corner of her mouth. "...cannot protect you..." He kissed the other corner. "...if Stephen decides to spirit you away."

"Where would he spirit me away to?" She spread her thighs and allowed him to settle between them. The pressure of him against her felt so good she nearly lost the logic of the argument. "He won't need to spirit me away. I'll already be at his estate with all his people."

"People?" Dipping his head, he sucked on a breast.

Emma drew in a breath as a frisson of pleasure shot straight to her core. Good lord, he was good. "Mm." That came out as half moan, half affirmation. "People. Like servants and his friends and all the other guests."

"That is the problem." He gave close attention to the other breast. "They are *his* friends and *his* servants and *his* guests."

"But you will be there, too." She had suggested that he follow the coach so he could watch over her, but stay out of sight, the only way she could think to convince him that she should accept the invitation. If Stephen didn't know he was there, then he couldn't shoot Brandon. Cupping his buttocks, she squeezed, enjoying the hard tensing of his muscles.

"But not as a guest. In hiding. Watching from afar." He slid out of her grasp and down the length of her, kissing, swirling circles with his tongue as he went.

"We can decide on some signals I can send. Oh!" This last exclamation came as his mouth fastened on her nub.

"What signals am I sending now?" he asked, his tone playful.

She wriggled her hips. "Am I sending the right one back?"

"Mm. Quite the right one." He continued to lick and suck.

This time, Emma completely lost the thread of the conversation as Brandon paid very close attention to what he was doing. His touch was perfection. At that moment, she didn't care that he had distracted her from their discussion. The delicious tension he created fired every single nerve ending. Until she thought she might burst into flames. And then she did, shuddering in another glorious climax with fireworks and bells, maybe even a trumpet.

As Brandon slid up beside her and cuddled her close, she decided they could continue their discussion later, when he hadn't befuddled her brain and couldn't distract her with his sly diversions.

THE NEXT MORNING AT THE BREAKFAST TABLE, AS LADY SELBY cut her slice of ham, she said, "Brandon, dear, I do believe you have mice."

Brandon stopped chewing and swallowed. "Mice, Aunt Morrin?"

"Yes. I heard all sorts of rustlings last night. They are quite noisy." Lady Selby forked up the piece of ham. "You should speak to Mrs. Porter about it."

Emma sniggered, then immediately turned it into a cough. Brandon sent a warning look her way.

"Emma has been invited to my half-brother's country estate," he said, changing the subject. "I think she should decline the invitation."

Emma cast an irritated glance in his direction, because she thought he had agreed to her accepting the invitation.

Lady Selby's piercing gaze fell on Emma. "How do you feel about the invitation, Miss Blake?"

Emma blinked, surprised the lady was interested in her opinion. "I think it's a perfect opportunity to discover if Stephen is up to no good."

"Yes?" The lady took a thoughtful sip of tea. "I do not like my nephew's half-brother, but I always thought he upheld the family's good name. What makes you believe that he is involved in something unscrupulous?"

"I saw him pass a note to Sir Dotson at Tattersall's." Emma debated whether to reveal that Stephen had murdered his father and shot Brandon in the back, then decided against it. She was going to prevent that, so Lady Selby, and especially Brandon, didn't have to know.

Lady Selby carefully placed her cup back on its saucer and centered it before she spoke. "My sister never trusted Stephen, even when he was a boy. She thought him a sly boots." She paused a moment, then glanced to Brandon. "But that does not mean he has done anything to warrant your father disowning him. That would be the only way you could gain the title."

"But what if he is involved in something?" Emma argued. "Like spying?"

"Treason!" Shocked horror crossed Lady Selby's face.

"You will have to produce irrefutable proof of that," she said sternly.

"I think I can." Emma crossed her fingers beneath the table.

"Goodness," the lady said as she dabbed at the corner of her mouth with her napkin. Placing the napkin carefully across her lap once more, she smoothed it, took a breath, then turned to Emma with a wily smile. "Well, that is another cup of tea entirely, isn't it?" She turned back to Brandon. "I believe the country air will be good for all of us."

And just like that, Emma won the argument. She sent Brandon a cheeky grin, hoped everything turned out the way she wanted, and crossed the fingers on her other hand.

Sixteen

◦⁓◦

Four days later, Emma sat with Lady Selby in a coach as it made its approach to Cranleigh Manor. Something about this excursion into the country made her uneasy, but she couldn't decide whether she was uncomfortable pretending to be flattered by Stephen's attention or concerned about Brandon's safety. He rode alongside, accompanying them as their companion and protector. She had tried to dissuade him from joining them, but he was adamant. She worried because she knew what had happened to him. But Ghost Brandon told her his father's murder had occurred in London, so maybe he was safe for now.

Cassiopeia was tied to the back of the coach, but Emma didn't feel confident enough to ride her for such a long distance. While she loved the horse, and it had seemed quite tame during her riding lesson, she was still a bit intimidated sitting on her back. So she sat inside the coach and fretted, while Lady Selby, who sat opposite, worked on needlepoint. Emma wished she had not packed her journal in her trunk, because she could have been writing down her impressions of the journey.

After watching Lady Selby work on her stitching, Emma was surprised that the bumpy ride over dirt roads didn't make her needle waver, but each stitch was true. "That's a beautiful piece you're working on," she said.

Lady Selby glanced up. "Don't you have any needlework? A woman's hands must never be idle."

Emma shook her head. "I didn't bring any with me. To be truthful, I don't know how."

"What do they teach young ladies in the future?" Lady Selby muttered. Then she swept aside her skirt and said, "Sit here beside me. I will teach you."

As Emma scooted to the other seat, Lady Selby reached into her bag and brought out a small piece of canvas with an open weave. A tree had been lightly sketched on it. Then she pulled out a skein of thin wool thread and a needle.

"It is quite simple, really," the lady said. "This is what you do." She proceeded to show Emma the simple stitch that filled up the space within the outline on the canvas.

Emma took a few stitches and realized the process was soothing, besides giving her something to do and forcing her thoughts away from Brandon's terrible future. Sitting side by side with Brandon's aunt, she felt the woman's chilly reserve begin to melt.

After riding in silence for some time, Lady Selby said, "Brandon's mother was my favorite younger sister. She died when Brandon was only twelve."

Surprised at the revelation, Emma said, "He must have been devastated." Her heart twisted in sympathy for him.

"He was," Lady Selby said with a nod. "He was at Eton by that time, but during session breaks, he would stay with me. After his father had a legitimate son, the earl had little to do with Brandon."

Emma was intrigued by the family history. "Forgive me for asking, but why didn't Brandon's father marry his mother?"

Lady Selby was silent as she took a few stitches. Then she let her needlework fall to her lap. "She was too headstrong for her own good. She fell in love with Cranleigh. I suppose he held some affection for her as well. But his father didn't approve of the match because she was Irish."

"I never understood why the British looked down on the Irish," Emma said.

The lady sighed. "The mistrust goes back for centuries, because the Irish follow the Pope, and the English believe their King is head of the Church. That fear has lessened somewhat, since Ireland now has members in Parliament, but many are still suspicious, like the old earl was when he heard his son wanted to wed the daughter of an Irish marquess. He forced Brandon's father to wed someone else. Then Brandon's mother, my sister, discovered she was *enceinte* and she ran away."

"Like Miss Sophie," Emma interjected.

"Yes, quite similar, except by that time, Brandon's father was already wed to another. The old earl had died suddenly in the meantime, so Brandon's father was the new earl. He set up my sister in the Ivy House on the grounds of Cranleigh Manor. The new Countess of Cranleigh ignored the situation for several years because she was barren, and then she suddenly conceived. By the time Pemberton was old enough to understand he would inherit his father's title, she couldn't abide having her husband's mistress and son, a possible challenger to the earldom, living on the grounds, so she forced them out. My da wouldn't take them in, so they eventually came to live with me." Lady Selby fell silent and gazed out at the passing scenery. Picking up her needlework again, she said briskly, "That's enough of that." She glanced at Emma's canvas. "You missed a stitch."

As Emma corrected her mistake, she thought about the boy who had been forced out of his home, and then lost his mother at such a vulnerable age. But despite that, he had grown into a generous, honorable man, no doubt because he had the woman sitting beside her to guide him.

She felt Lady Selby's gaze on her, and she glanced up.

"My nephew's melancholy seems to have left him since you arrived," Lady Selby said thoughtfully. "I believe you are a good influence on him." She returned her focus to her needlework.

Emma smiled as she stitched. Brandon was a good influence on her, too. Glancing out the window, she could see him riding alongside, tall and handsome in the saddle. Then her smile faded as she became more determined than ever to save him.

WHEN THEIR COACH PULLED UP BEFORE THE IMPOSING entrance of Cranleigh Manor, Stephen came down the stairs to greet them. He bowed graciously to Lady Selby and lingered over Emma's hand. She forced herself not to pull away. Then his glance took in Brandon dismounting from his horse. The corners of Stephen's mouth turned down.

"You did not need to bring your cousin, Mrs. Blake," he said. "You will be perfectly safe."

"Will she?" Brandon drawled. "Can you vouch for all your guests and their principles?"

Stephen's mouth tightened.

With a delicate sniff, Lady Selby said, "One never knows if highwaymen will jump out of the woods. I felt much safer with my nephew accompanying us."

"Of course." Stephen's smile seemed forced. "We will find a spot for him."

"I do want him close by me," Lady Selby said. "I find him a great comfort."

Emma ducked her head to hide her grin. Brandon's aunt had successfully acquired a pleasant room for Brandon, rather than having him delegated to the attic or even the stables, where she suspected Stephen might have put him.

Stephen offered his arm to Lady Selby, as was proper, but his smile was directed at Emma. "Please come inside. My father very much wishes to greet you."

Lady Selby gave another sniff, this one not so delicate. "I'm quite worn out from the journey. Your father will have to extend his greetings later. And I do wish Mrs. Blake to be with me. I find her presence cheering."

Relieved she didn't have to deal with Stephen for the rest of the time until dinner, Emma exchanged a glance with Brandon, who didn't bother to hide his smirk. His aunt had quite nicely taken over the arrangements and had snubbed his father besides.

"Of course." Disappointment flashed across Stephen's face before he replaced it with a placid smile. Without another word, he led them inside.

Emma craned her neck as she stepped into the entry hall. It was cavernous, rising two stories, with a grand staircase descending along one wall from a gallery that ringed the second floor. Stephen's butler directed footmen with the luggage, and Emma, Brandon, and Lady Selby were shown to their rooms. Emma was relieved to escape meeting the earl. She wasn't looking forward to that tense moment.

The room Emma was given was expansive, dominated by a massive four-poster bed. The hangings and coverlet were heavily embroidered in pink and gold, complimenting the huge Chinese rug. A fainting couch sat before the windows which looked out over the back gardens, and through a side door was a dressing room with a large hip tub. While a maid unpacked and placed her frocks in the wardrobe, Emma stood at the window and gazed out at the gardens. Gravel walkways meandered between flower beds and small fruit trees. Beyond, the acreage of the rolling lawn was dotted with small groves of trees before it dissolved into heavy woods. The estate was beautiful, majestic. This was what Brandon wanted, what should be his inheritance. A knock came at the door, and when she opened it, he was standing there, all hunky male.

He walked in and closed the door behind him. "I shouldn't be here in your room," he said as he cupped her face with his hands. "But I needed to do this." He kissed her.

Emma wrapped her arms around his waist and gave herself up to him. Even though he had been with her on the journey there, they had been very proper out of respect for Lady Selby. She felt as if they had been separated for months instead of only hours. How could she have become so attached to him in only a few weeks? She wanted, needed, to be as close to him as possible. She felt as if he was her breath.

She loved him.

Emma jerked back and stared up at him. Oh, no! No, no, no. She couldn't be in love with this man. She was from the twenty-first century. She needed to help him get his birthright, make sure he didn't get shot in the back, and go back to her own life — her sisters, her writing career. Cell phones and showers and cars.

But she realized she had first started to fall in love with him when she was writing her romance and he was her hero. When his ghost had shown up, she had fallen even more. And then meeting him in the flesh had cemented her feelings. She just hadn't realized that until now.

"Emma, what is wrong?" A line of confusion appeared between his brows.

"I — Nothing. Nothing's wrong." She couldn't tell him. Not now. Not ever. Because he still loved his Elizabeth, and when she least expected, she would get flung back to her own time. She'd deal with the pain later. "I'm just worried that Stephen's going to knock on my door. And, you know, I'm supposed to be your cousin, and I'm supposed to be charmed by him and everything, so I can find out what he's up to."

He studied her a moment, then with a nod, he stepped back. "Yes. Of course. Stephen and his nefarious deeds."

His cool tone hurt. But better that than his finding out how she really felt.

Her brow crinkled. "Don't you want to find out what he's up to? Don't you want him disinherited so you can have your rightful title?"

He wandered into the middle of the room. "I don't know. I thought so, but...." As his words trailed off, he turned to face her. "Perhaps I'm trying to gain something that I shouldn't have. That I should never have wanted in the first place."

"Of course, you should have it. Stephen's descendant in the twenty-first century is a jerk. More than a jerk." She followed him and put her hand on his chest. "You are an honorable man. Your descendants should be, too."

He covered her hand and smiled. "You are quite convincing, Emma Blake."

She grinned. "Of course, I am. Now, go away so your brother can come and shower me with compliments and charm."

He placed a gentle kiss on her lips. "I'll miss you," he murmured.

"Until dinner," she confirmed.

"I'll not be at dinner." His eyes turned cool. "I cannot abide sitting at the same table with my step-brother and father." Trailing his fingers along her jaw, he said, "Be careful."

"I will. I promise." She walked him to the door. Just before he stepped out, she grabbed his lapel, drew him down to her level, and placed a hot kiss on his mouth. "Just so you don't forget me." Then she pushed him out into the hallway.

His low chuckle made her smile as she closed the door behind him, but the smile faded quickly. How was she going to get through the next days and weeks, knowing that her true love lived in the nineteenth century? Knowing that when Mrs. Edwards returned her bracelet, her time here could be over at any moment? The legend of the ancient oak had come true, but what was she supposed to do about that? Having her true love living centuries in the past while she lived in the future was heartbreaking, besides being inconvenient. She wondered if the legend said anything about that.

A soft knock came at the door, but instead of Brandon or Stephen, it was a maid, who had come to help her change for dinner. Resigned to the plan she had laid out for herself, to find the evidence of Stephen's treason and save Brandon and his father, she let the maid in. She couldn't think about loving Brandon. Instead, she had to focus on charming and distracting Stephen while she was at Cranleigh Manor.

Because if she thought about what would happen after Stephen was caught, that she would return to her own century and never see Brandon again, she might hide away in her room and cry.

282

DINNER WAS FINALLY OVER, AND EMMA PLEADED FATIGUE FROM the long trip as her excuse for not joining Stephen and the other guests in the salon for an impromptu evening of entertainment provided by those who could play an instrument or sing. She was surprised to discover that Roger Bowker was also a guest, and wondered how he had managed to work his way into Stephen's circle of friends. Fortunately, he had been seated in the middle of the table, too far away to converse with her. But she often felt his pale brown gaze on her. He frightened her, especially after what Mrs. Edwards had told her about him. How desperate was he to get her pendant? Fortunately, it was safely with that lady, but she sensed she should be wary of him.

Two other guests whom she was not happy to see were Lord and Lady Farley. She disliked Lady Farley and Lord Farley made her uncomfortable. Besides, she suspected he was somehow involved with whatever Stephen was up to. Smiling politely in their direction, she avoided contact with them.

As the beginning notes on the pianoforte played, she headed in the opposite direction, because she had no intention of going to bed. She had decided this would be the perfect time to do some snooping while everyone was distracted by the entertainment. And she wanted to find Brandon. Passing through another small dining room, a library, a sitting room, and a few rooms that she couldn't name, she came to a door that was slightly ajar. Voices came from inside. She was about to turn away when one of those voices arrested her.

"The only reason I am here, Cranleigh, is because I am Mrs. Blake's companion," Lady Selby said. "I did not come to reconcile with you. I have never forgiven you for destroying my sister."

"I am sorry you feel that way," Lord Cranleigh said. "I never wanted to hurt her."

"You never—! You made her your mistress, got her with child, then threw her over to wed another!" Lady Selby's words seared the air.

"I couldn't marry her," Cranleigh argued. "She was Irish. My father would have disowned me."

"Rubbish!" Lady Selby's walking stick whacked the floor. "You were an only son. Who else would have inherited the title?"

"He threatened to turn it over to a distant cousin," the earl said.

Lady Selby's response was uttered too low for Emma to hear.

"Morrin, I loved your sister." The earl's tone pleaded.

Emma covered her gasp of surprise and edged closer to the door.

"What of her son?" Lady Selby demanded. "Your first born?"

"I am very fond of him. He is my son as well." He sounded insulted. "You know I did everything I could for him. I had tutors for him, and I sent him to Eton. I gave his mother the Ivy Cottage, so she and Brandon would have a comfortable home."

"Until your countess threw them out. And you denied him his birthright," Brandon's aunt accused.

A pause ballooned.

"He's a by-blow, Morrin. I couldn't..." Regret filled the earl's words.

Lady Selby's walking stick rapped the floor again. "He's your first-born, and the grandson of an Irish marquess."

Silence came from the earl.

Lady Selby hissed, and her steps approached the door.

Emma hurried away, not wanting to be caught eavesdropping. But what she had heard had her brain reeling.

She ran up the stairs, grabbed up a candle from one of the side tables and wandered the halls to think. Brandon's mother wasn't merely his father's mistress, but his true love. And the earl admitted that he loved Brandon. How did the man feel about Stephen, his legitimate son? Should she tell Brandon what she had heard?

She was walking down a hallway on the third floor when a dark shape approached, seeming to appear out of nowhere. Holding her candle high, she saw it was Roger Bowker, the man she was told to avoid by Mrs. Edwards, the man who gave her the creeps. He wasn't holding a light. But she was, and so was very visible to him.

Glancing around, she saw she had no place to hide. She

couldn't duck into one of the rooms off the hall, because all the doors were locked. She had already tried to peep into them to see what was inside.

Bowker stopped several feet away. "Mrs. Blake," he said with a small bow. "How lovely to meet you again."

What was he doing on the third floor? In the dark? Emma decided to play along as if nothing were strange. She nodded a greeting. "Mr. Bowker. I see you have forgone the evening entertainment. Isn't the pianoforte and singing to your liking?"

He shrugged. "I am ambivalent. But neither are you availing yourself of the entertainment. Perhaps you are looking for it elsewhere?"

What was he implying? That she was on her way to a clandestine meeting with a man? Or was it something else? She took a step back and decided to ignore his implication. "I was merely looking for a way back to my room when I became turned around and found myself hopelessly lost."

"I think you are very lost, Mrs. Blake," he said, "if that is your real name. I believe you don't belong here at all."

Emma wondered if he suspected she was from another time, but she wasn't going to let him intimidate her nor tell him anything. Raising her nose in the air as if insulted, she said, "I am the guest of Viscount Pemberton. Perhaps you are the one who doesn't belong." She turned, intending to retreat the way she had come.

"Don't go, Mrs. Blake. I think we might be of use to each

other." His words caught her as surely as if he had grabbed her arm.

"I have no idea what that might be, sir. I am merely in England visiting my cousin," she said with a dismissive wave of her hand. "Perhaps you should speak to him. I believe he mentioned you were acquainted."

"We were." His eyes glinted in the candlelight, an odd effect, considering they were so pale. "He never mentioned that he had an American relation." He took a step closer and lowered his voice. "I don't believe you are a relation at all, Mrs. Blake. And I don't believe you are who you say you are." He smiled, a benign smile that held more menace than she had ever encountered. "I believe —" His words cut off when a door opened farther down the hall.

"Cousin Emma, are you lost?" Brandon asked.

Relief poured through her. "I believe I am." She stepped around Bowker. "Cousin Brandon, would you be kind enough to show me the way back to my room?"

Bowker's eyes narrowed with ugly speculation. "How convenient for your cousin to be here to rescue you. Until we meet again, Mrs. Blake," Bowker murmured as she passed him.

While his tone was mild, his words sounded like a threat. She didn't feel completely safe until she reached Brandon and looped her arm through his. Glancing over her shoulder, she saw that Bowker had disappeared. Where had he gone so quickly? A chill slipped down her spine.

"Are you cold?" Brandon pulled her close. "Come in here. I'll warm you."

He led her into the room, took her candle and placed it on a nearby table, closed the door, and wrapped his arms around her. She snuggled against him, absorbing his strength.

Bowker frightened her. His quick disappearance made her suspicious. Had he ducked into one of the rooms? But they had all been locked. Where had he gone? People did not just disappear. Unless...

Could he travel through time? Was Mrs. Edwards' assumption correct? The answer to that question made her shiver again. She didn't know him, but she trusted Brandon's opinion, as well as that of Lady Selby. And they both disliked the man. If Bowker could time travel, what would he do? Would he merely observe the changes in history? Or would he create havoc? The possibilities were infinite. What could she do to stop him?

"Emma, what is wrong?" Brandon murmured. "What did Bowker say to you?"

"I think he suspects I've traveled through time, and I think he wants my pendant." She shook her head and pushed her fears away. "It doesn't matter. I don't have the pendant with me. He's just a disagreeable man."

Brandon held her away and said, "If he bothers you again, you must tell me. I'll not have him harassing you."

Emma smiled and touched his cheek. "Thank you." Then she turned to look at the room they were in.

It was a schoolroom and nursery, with a dusty, unused smell. A child-sized table with four chairs tucked in around it sat in the middle of the floor. A cradle with flouncy lace draping it was in one corner, and a narrow bed was against the opposite wall. Shelves held various toys — wooden boats, a tiny wagon pulled by a carved horse, blocks, puzzles, a toy theater, and sitting in front, a rocking horse. One shelf held several books. A map of England and a map of the world, both looking rather faded, were tacked up on the wall.

"I have not been up here for a long time," Brandon said, as he wandered to the table and ran his hand along the back of one of the chairs.

"Is this where you were tutored?" she asked, watching him silently reminisce.

"Yes, my brother and I, even though he was years younger. Until my mother and I were forced out." Resentment deepened a corner of his mouth.

"I overheard your aunt and your father arguing," she said. "He is very fond of you."

Brandon shook his head. "He can't stand the sight of me. He sent me to Eton to be rid of me."

She stepped to the other side of the table. "I don't think so. Perhaps he had other reasons for sending you away." Like he wanted Brandon to have an education. Or the earl's wife instigated the removal of her husband's mistress and son. But those questions needed to be answered by his father.

He turned his back and stalked to the window. "I was seven years when he made my mother and I leave Ivy House." His words came out strangled with emotion.

Her heart wrenched at his turmoil. "Have you ever asked him why?"

He swung to face her. "I know why. I don't have to ask him."

Even in the dim light of the candle, she could see the pain in his eyes. She decided to let the matter drop, but he needed to have a conversation with the earl. Maybe she'd be able to bring it up again at another time and convince Brandon his father cared about him.

As if turning his back on the memories, he turned to the window.

Understanding his distress, she stepped up beside him and tangled her fingers with his. Out the window, the moon was a bright disc in the sky, but at its lower edge, a small, shadowy smudge ruined the perfect circle.

"There will be a lunar eclipse tonight," he said. "It's supposed to be a bad omen. Perhaps my brother's luck will finally change." Dark humor threaded his words.

Emma's breath caught in her throat. This lunar eclipse was a bad omen, but it wasn't his brother's luck that would change. Ghost Brandon had told her that only a day after a lunar eclipse, his father had been murdered and he had been shot. But that had happened in London. Since they were at Cranleigh Manor, maybe those events wouldn't happen. Even so, her fingers tightened convulsively around his hand.

"What is it?" he asked, glancing down at her. "Does a lunar eclipse frighten you?"

"No, of course not," she lied and forced a smile. "I'm just excited to see one because they don't happen very often."

He seemed to accept her answer because he turned back to the window. Wrapping his arm around her shoulders, he pulled her back against his chest so they could watch the eclipse together. Two stories below them, she heard voices exclaim as the other guests tumbled out onto the veranda to watch the phenomenon.

This would be a perfect time to snoop, to see if she could discover anything incriminating against Stephen, while everyone was focused on the moon. But the weight of Brandon's arm around her and his broad chest at her back made her reluctant to move. How many more moments would she have with him like this? Before everything went wrong? Before he was killed?

Swallowing back the pain, she gave herself a bit of time to enjoy being with him and tucked away the memory. She was more determined than ever to save him. But in a few minutes. Because Brandon was not going to like what she planned to do one bit.

Seventeen

"**A**bsolutely not!"

Appalled at what Emma had just suggested, Brandon's hand gripped the windowsill so he wouldn't be tempted to shake some sense into her.

She had slipped from beneath his arm and told him about a plan to sneak into Stephen's room to search for proof that would indicate he was involved in spying.

"You are not going into his room and risk discovery. If he finds you there, you will be ruined." He scowled and clenched his teeth.

"I could say I got turned around and was looking for my room," she argued.

The thought of Stephen finding her in his bed chamber made his blood curdle. "I do not trust my sneaking cur of a half-brother. He is not a gentleman. The next time he is at his club, he might brag about having you in his bed." Brandon peered at her. "You're not thinking of being in his bed, are you?"

"Of course not!" She shuddered in revulsion. "How can you even ask that?"

Her affront did nothing to calm his fears. The blackguard might even make up a fanciful tale about what they had done in that bed, just to brag he'd had his step-brother's cousin. The idea turned his stomach and lit his temper.

"Your reputation is a fragile thing," he said. "One mistake and it's ruined."

Emma waved away his words. "I don't care about my reputation. If I can prove he's doing something wrong, then whatever he says won't matter."

"Even if you are not concerned about your reputation, at least be aware of the danger. What if he takes advantage of you and hurts you?"

"I won't let him." She stepped closer and placed her hand on his chest. "Please. I want to help you."

The light pressure of her hand and the pleading in those lovely blue eyes broke through his anger. He wanted to go along with her plan, just because she had asked. But every instinct screamed that he shouldn't. If she was discovered, even if her excuse was as innocent as getting lost, the gossip would fly through society faster than a pistol shot. She would be termed a ladybird and shunned, especially because she was an American.

He knew what being an outsider meant, because he had been one all his life as the bastard son, the one set aside for the legitimate heir. At Eton, he had been ostracized by most of the students. Only a couple of boys had befriended him, like his doctor friend, Jonathan Beech. He didn't want that for Emma, even though she might return to the future at any moment.

She might be able to find that Stephen was involved in something underhanded, but even he couldn't believe his half-brother was a spy. Emma was most likely mistaken.

"Please," she said again. "I promise not to do anything hare-brained."

Brandon thought stealing into Stephen's room was the most hare-brained thing she could do. But according to her plan, he would be watching to make sure Stephen was with the other guests. And against his better judgment, he wanted to please her.

He sighed. "Yes. You have convinced me. But you must promise to be very quick."

"Thank you." She smiled. "I'm sure I'm going to find something. And then..." She cupped his face. "...we'll show it to your father and convince him Stephen isn't fit to be his heir."

She placed a gentle kiss on his lips. Which turned into something much more delightful. As Brandon wrapped his arms around her and indulged in her soft heat, he decided that even though nothing would come of this adventure, having Emma's kisses was worth whatever aggravation he had to endure from his half-brother.

EMMA STOLE INTO STEPHEN'S ROOM AND CLOSED THE DOOR behind her. Oil lamps and candles had been lit, and the bed had been turned down. The maid had already been here. It was a dark, masculine room, with a large tester bed dominating the space and sporting red brocade hangings that matched the walls. Glancing around, she wondered where Stephen might hide something. Of course, that was assuming he had something to hide. But she knew from Ghost Brandon that he was involved in something very shady, and had become desperate enough to murder the earl. And in her book, he had been a spy. She suspected that note she had seen passed between him and Sir Dotson was evidence of his treachery. Now, she just had to find the note or something else to prove it.

Brandon had joined the other guests on the veranda to watch the lunar eclipse, and would delay Stephen if he showed any inclination to leave the gathering, so she had some time. After surveying the room, she started her search at the wardrobe, but found nothing except shirts and coats and pants and waistcoats. She moved on to the washstand

and the small tables with drawers. Nothing suspicious in those. Then she spied the chamber pot cupboard. A perfect place to hide something, for who would want to rummage around in that odorous spot?

The cupboard resembled a decorative cabinet, about waist-high, but when the top and front were lifted, it opened into a chair with the commode in the seat. The chamber pot had been cleaned, so only a faint tang remained. She pulled the pot out of its seat and felt around in the space underneath. A small, folded piece of parchment lay secured to the side of the cabinet with wax, out of sight of anyone who might use the pot or take it out for cleaning. Scooping it up, she replaced the pot and closed the cupboard.

When she unfolded the parchment, a smaller piece fluttered out. She took them closer to one of the lamps to read. A single, nonsensical sentence had been hand printed on the larger parchment, with the numbers one to twenty-six underneath corresponding to each letter. Duplicate letters had been crossed out. She frowned at the strange note, then realized what it was — a decryption key for a code. The smaller piece revealed only a single line of numbers with random spaces between. Why did Stephen have such a thing? The only answer she could think of was that he was using it to pass secret messages. To another spy?

At the top of the larger page was a family coat of arms. It wasn't the heraldic device of the Earl of Cranleigh. She had seen that engraved on the forks and knives and spoons at dinner, and it didn't look anything like what was at the top of the page. But it did look familiar. Where had she seen it before?

She tucked both down the bodice of her dress. All she had to do was figure out what the message said. As she turned to leave, she saw a book laying on a bedside table. She couldn't resist a peek. Flipping through it, she saw it was a journal, listing names and dates, with various amounts of sovereigns, guineas and pounds after each entry. Money owed to Stephen? Or money he owed? She wanted to take it to show to Brandon, but she needed to focus on the hidden note. Replacing the book, she took her candle and let herself out after checking the hall to make sure no one was around.

Her mind raced as she strolled down the hall and acted as if she was rejoining the other guests on the veranda after a visit to her room. Where had she seen that heraldic device? On the side of a coach passing in the street? Above the door of a town mansion? Neither of those were right. But where? She sighed in frustration. She could have seen it anywhere.

Just as she started down the stairs, Lord Farley put his foot on the bottom step and glanced up. His chilly gaze took her in from her head to her toes and back up, as if searching for secrets. She wanted to turn and run the other way, but that would be suspicious, not to mention impolite. Pasting a smile on her lips, she started slowly down the staircase. She hadn't gone two steps when the memory of where she had seen that coat of arms flashed into her head. It had been at Arlene's dinner party.

The coat of arms at the top of the decryption key belonged to Lord Farley. She wanted to race down the stairs and tell Brandon what she had discovered. Instead, she kept her slow pace and smiled coolly at the man ascending the stairs. They met about halfway.

"Mrs. Blake," he said with a nod of greeting. "I thought you had retired for the evening."

"My lord," she returned. "I found I did not wish to do so after all. The phenomenon of the lunar eclipse has drawn me out. But you are leaving the excitement."

"Not the best quality entertainment. I find the slow progression quite tedious." Disdain twitched his mouth.

She sighed dramatically in understanding. "Yes, but when one is in the country and a guest, one must avail oneself of what is available."

"Perhaps we could have a chat and you could tell me about America," he suggested.

Emma blinked. Was that an innocent request? Or was he looking for information? She remembered the strange, silent communication between him and Stephen that occurred at his wife's dinner party. And his coat of arms was at the top of the code key in Stephen's possession. Was he the master spy controlling Stephen?

Smiling, she said, "You honor me, my lord. Perhaps some other time, for I wish to see the eclipse."

With a small bow, he stepped aside. "Of course. My apologies for detaining you." His gaze made her think of a snake contemplating its prey.

Making her way to where the other guests had gathered, she didn't feel safe until she stood next to Brandon. His fingers brushed hers as she stopped beside him. After sending him a smile, she turned her attention to the sky. Half the moon was in shadow.

Anxiety swept through her. The earl's murder and Brandon's death were getting closer. Somehow, she had to thwart Stephen from his murderous path. Somehow, she had to make Brandon's father see that his heir was not an honorable man. Somehow, she had to save Brandon.

As soon as Emma stood beside him, Brandon stopped grinding his teeth. When he had lost sight of Farley amongst the guests, he had eased off the veranda in search of the man. He didn't want him discovering Emma as she exited Stephen's room. When he saw the two of them speaking on the stairs, his blood turned to ice.

Was Farley suspicious of where Emma had been? The man was dangerous in many ways. Arlene had revealed to Brandon that her husband kept a journal, recording all his interactions and observations, anything that he might be able to use as leverage for his own gain. The man was cruel and vindictive, and Brandon tried to avoid him.

He wanted Emma nowhere near the man. And he wanted to pummel Stephen's handsome face to a pulp for inviting the couple. As Emma continued down the stairs, apparently ending the conversation, and Farley headed up, Brandon returned to the veranda and ground his teeth some more.

When she stepped up beside him, the touch of her fingers made the ice in his veins thaw, but it did nothing to make his desire to throttle Farley go away. In fact, he also wanted to shake some sense into Emma until her teeth rattled.

He wanted her to himself. And he wanted to protect her, despite her brave declaration that she could take care of herself. Clearly, she could not.

"I found something," she whispered.

He glanced down at her with the intention of warning her against Farley. The excitement in her blue eyes made the words on his tongue dissipate like smoke in the wind. He felt an odd, warm flutter in his heart.

She grinned. "Stephen is going down."

"Going down?" He raised a cool brow and fought the urge to smile at her strange wording.

"He's in very deep trouble," she said with a nod.

An errant curl bounced at her neck. He felt another flutter. Dismay rocked him. He knew exactly what that flutter meant.

He was in love with this woman.

No, that couldn't be. Not with her. She was from the future. Once the Universe was done with whatever it wanted her to do, it would send her back. He would never see her again. After losing Elizabeth, he had vowed he would never love again. It hurt too much. No. He couldn't acknowledge the feeling. It would go away.

He would help her with whatever she wanted to do and then help her return to her own time. He would never see her again. And that was fine. Because if she wasn't around, then that silly flutter would just go away. That tender skin on his heart would harden into scar tissue.

"I have to tell you what I found." Her whisper sounded urgent.

"Perhaps in the morning," he suggested, wanting to give himself some time to get his heart under control. "We can go for a ride."

Her face scrunched up in disappointment. "Can't we meet sooner?"

Yes, they could. In her room. Or his. And what would follow would be earth-shaking. But that was not going to occur. He would guard his heart.

He indicated the guests standing around on the veranda, some of them chatting, some staring raptly up at the moon. "Someone might see. We're supposed to be cousins, not lovers. We can't be sneaking about in the middle of the night."

A sly gleam entered her eyes. "We could be kissing cousins."

He held back a snicker. Despite never having heard the phrase before, he understood exactly what it meant. The impertinent wench never failed to amuse him. He nodded solemnly. "We could, but no one should suspect that."

One of the guests turned in their direction, most likely curious about why they were whispering.

Emma made a discontented moue with those sexy lips, but she lapsed into silence.

Brandon smiled, his anger melting away. Determined he would not love her, he would enjoy the time he had with her. He would protect her from his brother and Farley. And when she was back in her own time, he would have delightful memories to last the rest of his life.

Leaning close, he whispered, "Meet me tomorrow morning in the stables at sunrise."

At her nod, he savored the anticipation of their meeting. Because he planned to do much more than listen to what she had discovered. Something much more enjoyable.

THE NEXT MORNING, BRANDON STEPPED INTO THE STABLES JUST before sunrise. The world had begun to awaken, hazy gray but light enough to see, with birds beginning to chirp and the horses stirring in their stalls. It was his favorite time of day. He would often steal from his bed in the Ivy House and race here to be with the animals. The horses would stick their heads out of their stalls and nicker. The cats would wind between his legs. The dogs would yawn and stretch, then come greet him with tails wagging. Nothing had changed.

A sleepy stable boy, rubbing his eyes, stumbled out of the tack room. "Can I saddle yer horse for yer, sir?"

"No, thank you, go back to bed for a while longer," Brandon said.

"You may saddle mine, Jacky."

Brandon swung around at his father's voice. He had forgotten the earl also enjoyed this time of day. When he was growing up, they would often meet in the stables as the sun rose.

"Good morning, sir," he said with a stiff nod.

He had assumed that his father would be in London. When he had discovered the earl was in residence, he had been trying to avoid him.

"Going for an early ride?" the earl asked.

"No, I wanted to see the horses." Brandon started to step past him. He was not about to reveal he was meeting Emma, nor did he want to converse with his father.

"Don't go. I wish to speak with you."

Brandon halted. "I'm not sure I want to speak with you."

"Then just listen. You owe me that."

At his father's authoritarian words, Brandon's fists clenched. "I don't owe you anything."

The earl's eyes snapped in anger. Then he sighed. "Perhaps not. But please, hear me out."

Brandon could not remember ever hearing his father say *please* to him. Arrested by the word, he nodded agreement. As he did, he saw Emma framed in the open stable door. Wanting to protect her from the sparring with his father, he made a surreptitious movement with his hand to warn her. She backed away and disappeared.

"What do you know of this woman whom Stephen has invited here?" the earl asked.

Disappointment and anger shot through him. Of course, he should have known his father was only concerned with Stephen.

"I'm sure my brother has told you all there is to know," Brandon said.

"All he has told me is that he met her at a dinner party. She is American, a widow, and supposed to be related to your mother. How did you meet her?" Suspicion narrowed his eyes.

"Quite by chance in Hyde Park." Brandon's tone dared his father to challenge him.

The earl challenged anyway. "How do you know she is

whom she says she is? I do not remember your mother ever mentioning any relatives in America."

"Aunt Morrin believes her." Surely, if his mother's sister accepted Emma, his father would.

"Morrin—" His father shook his head. "The only thing I believe from your aunt is that she despises me."

Brandon stiffened. Just as he was about to defend his aunt, Emma stepped into the open doorway and halted, as if just arriving and flustered to find others in the stable. She looked lovely in a maroon riding outfit. An adorable hat with a black feather that curled down around one ear perched jauntily on her head.

"Oh! I'm so sorry," she said. "I didn't expect anyone else to be here." As the earl turned to her, she bobbed a curtsy and murmured, "Good morning, my lord."

"Good morning, Mrs. Blake," the earl said, then cast a glance from her to Brandon and back again. "The stables seem to be quite popular this morning. Curious, since the hour is so early."

"Cousin Brandon offered to show me the stables and the horses," she said. "He has been so kind since my accident."

"Accident?" the earl asked.

"Oh, yes." Emma nodded. "You see, I was nearly run over by someone driving a curricle through Hyde Park. I bumped my head and couldn't remember where I was staying or even who I was with. Cousin Brandon was so kind to open his home to me so I could recuperate."

Brandon appreciated that she didn't mention that he was the one who nearly ran her down. His father threw him a speculative glance, then turned back to Emma.

"How disturbing for you to lose your memory," the earl said. "Have your memories returned?"

Emma's mouth turned down. "No, unfortunately not."

"Yet you remembered that my son is a cousin." The earl raised a brow, both inquisitive and suspicious.

Emma sent Brandon a quick, warning glance before he could defend her.

"That discovery was quite by chance," she said. "After we chatted, we discovered the connection." She gave a helpless shrug. "The memory is a very strange thing, my lord. Sometimes we can't remember what we did only days ago, yet sometimes we can vividly remember an experience from our childhood."

"I certainly hope that your memory returns soon, Mrs. Blake, since my son Stephen seems quite interested in courting you," the earl said.

Brandon bit his cheek so he wouldn't blurt that Stephen was never going to have any relationship with Emma.

"Thank you, my lord," Emma said.

"It wouldn't do for the next earl to become involved with an imposter," his father added, the implied warning carelessly tossed out as if merely a comment on the weather. He motioned to the stableboy to bring his horse forward and he mounted.

Shock flashed through Emma's eyes, but her lashes swept down and she curtsied as his father rode out.

Brandon kept his anger in check as he waited for him to ride out. Emma was magnificent. "I'm sorry he said that."

Emma waved away his apology. "He's right. I am an imposter."

"You are merely protecting yourself," he said. "Thank you for interceding."

She bobbed a saucy curtsy. "Just playing my part, sir." Stepping forward, she wound her fingers through his. "I think he cares for you."

Brandon shook his head. "He is only concerned with Stephen and his good name. He doesn't truly believe you lost your memory. He thinks you are after my half-brother's title."

With a grin, she said, "Well, he's right. I'm after it so it will go to you." She touched him gently on his chest. "And I don't think Stephen's going to have a title. Let me tell you what I found."

Brandon listened to her description of the decryption key with Farley's coat of arms at the top of the page, and the note that was all numbers. Shocked at what she was saying, he pulled her out of the stables and around the back, where they could neither be seen nor heard.

"Are you saying that Stephen is a spy?" he whispered urgently.

"Why else would he have a code key hidden away?"

He thought about that a moment. "Perhaps he's spying for the King."

"Or maybe he's spying for the French," Emma countered. "I didn't have time to decode the note. How well do you know Farley?"

"Not that well, except I know he is an artful manipulator." He stared off into space while he tried to marshal his thoughts.

"I have to search Farley's room," Emma declared.

That caught Brandon's attention. "You will not!" He nearly shouted, but remembered at the last moment that no one was to hear them. "You will not go near that man."

"Uh-huh," was all she said.

"What does that mean?" he demanded.

"It means that I'm agreeing to what you said."

She smiled, but something made Brandon think she wasn't agreeing at all.

"Do I have your promise that you'll stay away from Farley?" he asked.

"Of course, I'll stay away. He scares me." She shivered, then stepped very close and ran her finger down the front of his shirt.

The slight pressure of her touch sent warmth to his groin, but he refused to be distracted. Although her words agreed with him, something made him doubt she would comply. He captured that wandering finger.

"Emma," he said, his tone earnest, "I know him, and he is a ruthless man."

Her gaze turned solemn. "I promise not to do anything foolish." Then a wicked gleam entered her eyes and she glanced at their surroundings. "You know, I would hate to lose the opportunity of seclusion behind the stables." Her tongue flicked out and wet her lips.

The invitation to kiss her was too much to deny. With a groan of defeat, he pulled her into his arms and took possession of her mouth. And in a tiny corner of his head, he decided that if he saw Farley glancing in her direction, he would whisk her back to London as fast as he could.

BREATHLESS FROM THE KISS, EMMA LEANED BACK IN Brandon's arms. "If we keep this up, we may wind up in the hayloft," she said with a grin.

"Since you are dressed for riding, you might as well ride," he murmured, nipping her ear.

Laughing, she wriggled from his embrace. "The only riding I'm going to do right now is on a horse."

He released an exaggerated, aggrieved sigh. "Very well. I'll get the horses saddled. But you are missing out on an extraordinary experience." To prove his point, he captured her again and planted a swift kiss on her mouth.

She pushed him away with a laugh. He grinned, winked, then strode around the corner of the building. Following more slowly, she sobered. If the opportunity arose when she could safely search Farley's rooms, she would do it, because her intuition told her he was involved in whatever Stephen was doing. Somehow, she would incriminate Stephen, get him arrested, and save Brandon. If he won his birthright, then that would be a bonus.

Not long after, they rode out of the stable yard. She was still a bit nervous on the back of a horse, but Cassiopeia seemed to understand she was a novice rider. Brandon led her across the lawns and into the woods where a path cut between the trees. It was a lovely morning. Birds chirped above her head, and wildflowers popped up through the dead leaves. After some time, the path opened into a large clearing. At the far side sat a large, two-story cottage with a central entrance. Double windows bracketed the central door, and windows on the second floor matched the openings on the first. Ivy covered part of the front and one side.

As they approached, she asked, "Is this Ivy House?"

He threw her a grin. "How did you guess? Would you like to see inside?"

"Very much."

The house looked like it had been closed up for some

time. Some of the ivy had grown over two of the windows, and it threatened to close off the door. After they dismounted, Brandon pulled the vine away from the entrance, then pushed the door open. Emma followed him inside.

She stepped into a rustic cottage. Before her was a narrow staircase leading up. To her right was a kitchen with a large fireplace in the end wall. A plain wooden table and chairs sat in the middle of the room. In front of a window at the back was a rocking chair, waiting for someone to sit and quietly contemplate the scene out the back. Or rock a child to sleep.

The room to her left was a drawing room. Well-worn, comfortable chairs were scattered about. On the floor was a thin carpet. Another fireplace echoed the one in the kitchen. The ceilings in both rooms were plank and beam.

Brandon wandered into the drawing room and gazed around. "I spent the first years of my life here."

Emma followed him into the room. "The house feels very cozy."

She could imagine him as a boy sprawled on the floor before the fire. A bit of something red in a corner caught her eye. Retrieving it, she discovered a toy soldier that matched the set in his house in London. She held it out to him.

Brandon took it and turned it over and over. "My mother bought these for my eighth birthday, just before we were forced to leave. My father's wife had finally got her way. She had always been disapproving of having his mistress live on the property. When Stephen was five, old enough to be aware he would inherit the title, she wanted me gone, as well as my mother." He shook his head and glanced around the room. "I never realized how happy I was here until we were forced to leave."

Sympathy for the boy and his mother clutched at Emma's heart. "Where did you go?"

He kept his gaze on the soldier in his hand. "We traveled to Ireland, back to my mother's home, but my grandfather wanted no part of me or my mother. She had disgraced him."

"What did you do?" Emma asked, riveted by his sad tale.

"We turned around and returned to England," he said with a sad smile. "By that time, my Aunt Morrin had wed an English baron, and she prevailed upon him to let us occupy one of the empty tenant cottages on their estate. I was only there a few years before my father's agent arrived to inform me that I was going to Eton. I didn't want to go. My mother's health had begun to decline and I wanted to care for her."

"You must have still been quite young," she surmised.

"I had turned eleven years." He looked down at the soldier in his hand. "I found out much later that my mother had somehow forced my father to provide a living and education for me until I reached majority."

"You aunt told me that your mother died when you were twelve," she said. "That must have been so difficult."

His gaze traveled around the room. "I was away at school. I couldn't get back in time to say goodbye."

Emma went to him and took his hand. "I'm so sorry."

He turned to her with a smile. "Thank you. It seems quite a long time ago."

"Losing a parent is hard," she said, knowing how he felt.

"It is, and I am sorry for your loss." He raised her hand to his lips and kissed her palm.

Emma fought back the tears that threatened. Her own grief at her father's death was still raw, but her heart went out to the boy who had lost his mother at such a vulnerable age. They were silent together for a moment, each mourning the loss of a loved one. Brandon slipped the toy soldier into his pocket.

"I think we have visited the past long enough," he said, then turned towards the door.

Emma was glad to leave. Having seen Brandon's childhood home and hearing his story, she came to appreciate the man. Despite the sadness he had endured, or perhaps because of it, he had grown into a wise, caring man.

And that made her love him even more.

Eighteen

That evening, Emma collected Lady Selby from her room and together they headed down the stairs. Stephen was hosting a ball. Neighbors from the nearby estates had been invited, so the hum of greetings and conversation, the creak of arriving carriages, and the orchestra's tuning of instruments filled the manor house with noise.

In the main hall, Stephen was greeting his guests, and he glanced up as Emma neared the bottom of the stairs. He quickly sent the couple who had just arrived on to the ballroom, and hurried to help Emma off the last step. He lifted her hand to his lips and placed a kiss on her fingers.

"You are looking radiant tonight, Mrs. Blake," he said. When Lady Selby sniffed at being ignored, he bestowed a bow and a smile on her. "And you are a vision, Lady Selby."

"I am not," Lady Selby snapped. "See to your other

guests, Pemberton, and don't make a fool of yourself. You'll have plenty of time to converse with Mrs. Blake later."

"Of course." Stephen's cheeks heated at the reprimand as he bowed again, then turned to do as he was told.

Emma ducked her head to hide her grin.

Lady Selby tsked. "He is too used to doing as he wishes and getting what he wants."

"Perhaps that will end soon," Emma murmured.

"What do you mean by that?" Lady Selby asked sharply.

Emma sent her an innocent look. "Only that we never know what the future holds."

With a narrow look, Lady Selby asked, "Are you planning something?"

Emma shook her head. "Not planning. It's already done," she whispered quickly, for she saw Brandon approach. "I found something, but I'll tell you about it later."

After greeting them and sending Emma an appreciative glance, Brandon offered an arm to each of them and escorted them into the ballroom. He looked magnificently male and handsome in his black evening clothes. Emma had to force herself not to stare. All she wanted was to drink him in. She hadn't seen him since their early morning conversation behind the stables and that marvelous kiss that had turned her boneless.

Just the thought made her toes curl and a throb pulse deep within her. How did he do that to her? No other man had ever come close to making her feel like that. She had never wanted to be with a man so much. Why did the Universe decide that the man she loved should live centuries in her past?

She had no time to dwell on the question, because the music was beginning and Stephen claimed her for the first dance, a quadrille, and then for the second. She smiled and chatted about the sights they had seen on their afternoon stroll to the village with some of the other guests, complimented him on the musicians he'd hired, and made other small talk, all the while plotting how she could prove he was a French spy. When the dance came to an end, she was relieved that he escorted her back to Lady Selby, then excused himself to go dance with one of the other guests.

Brandon appeared beside her. "I am claiming the first waltz as mine," he said.

Emma checked her dance card. "I regret that dance has already been claimed by another." She heaved a great sigh of mock disappointment. "I'm very sorry, Cousin Brandon."

"It had better not have my brother's name on it," he grumbled.

"I'm afraid so." No one had claimed the first waltz, and she bit her cheek to keep from grinning.

Brandon plucked up the card dangling from her wrist. When he saw it was completely empty, his lips twisted wryly. "Vixen," he murmured.

"Brandon, dear," Lady Selby said. "Would you be kind

enough to fetch me a cup of lemonade? I find I am quite parched."

Exasperation flashed through his eyes and then he quickly tamped it down. "Of course, Aunt Morrin," he acceded in a level tone, then went in search of the refreshment table.

Lady Selby watched him go, then said mildly, "Watch yourself, young lady. I'm sure others can see the attraction between you and my nephew as well as I. You do not want gossip to fly about you."

Emma bit back her sigh. She couldn't stop the attraction she felt for Brandon. Every time she was near him, each of her nerve endings stood at attention. She craved him and wanted to be close to him, to touch him, breathe him in. But she couldn't, not pretending to be his cousin. The point of the ruse was to give her an air of respectability while she remained in his house. If anyone suspected she wasn't who she said she was, the gossip would be ruinous. For both of them.

She would most likely get flung back to her own time when Mrs. Edwards returned her charm and bracelet. The centuries between would make the gossip inconsequential. But what if she never returned to her own time? What if she were stuck in the nineteenth century? Her gaze sought out Brandon, chatting with one of the guests. What if she could prevent his murder and spend the rest of her life with him? The thought made her insides tingle.

She was saved from further introspection by Lord Farley claiming her for the next dance. His hand was cold as he clasped her fingers. Forcing a smile as they came together and parted in the dance, she couldn't wait for the music to end, having agreed to partner him only to be polite.

During a lull, when they were forced to wait for the other couples to promenade, he said, "We never had a chance to have our conversation about America. I am curious why you decided to come to England when our two countries are at war."

It was their turn to promenade, so she was saved from answering, but she suspected his curiosity was more than casual. With another glissade one way, then the other, the dance ended. He bowed. She curtsied, nearly limp with relief. When he escorted her off the dance floor, instead of returning her to Lady Selby's side, he guided her to the dining room, where refreshments had been laid out. Dismay had her muscles tightening.

"My lord," she said, "Lady Selby will be waiting for me."

"I'm sure she won't mind if I fetch you a glass of lemon-ade." As he led her to a corner of the room, his smile made her think of a predator contemplating its next meal.

Only one other couple stood at the far side of the buffet table, and after accepting a cup of lemonade from the servant, they moved off. Emma wanted to escape. She glanced around, wondering if Brandon had seen her leave the ballroom. While Lord Farley acted with the utmost courtesy, something about him threatened.

"Mrs. Blake," he said, blocking her in, "I understand you met Sir Dotson at Tattersall's not long ago."

Surprised at his comment, she nodded. "Yes, he wanted to show Pemberton a horse."

"Is that all?" His mild question held a barely noticeable edge.

"Why else would he have made arrangements to meet Pemberton at the horse auction house except to confer with him about an animal?" Emma's suspicions about him rose. Why was he questioning her about the event? The event where she had seen a note passed?

"Why else, indeed?" He sadly shook his head. "As someone older and wiser, I must warn you about him."

"Warn me? He was a perfect gentleman," Emma said, playing along.

"Of course he was, but you see, he indulges in fantasies." Concern wrinkled his brow.

"Fantasies?" She suspected that Lord Farley was weaving his own fantasy.

With a heavy sigh, he nodded. "He is a delightful gentleman, but he believes himself involved in a conspiracy of spies."

Emma's eyes widened, appearing to be shocked, but in reality, impressed with Farley's misdirection. What better way to keep her from being suspicious than to make her believe that any secretive action she might have seen was merely Doddy playacting.

"Oh, my goodness," she said. "Do all his friends indulge him and play along?"

"Yes, I'm afraid we do." He placed his hand over his heart. "My apologies, Mrs. Blake. I have shocked you. You need not fear the man. He is quite harmless, I assure you, but I felt it was my duty to forewarn you if you happen to see or hear anything unusual."

To show her appreciation, Emma forced herself to touch her fingers to his arm. "I am grateful for the information, m'lord. If I happen to see him acting oddly, I'll be sure to turn a blind eye."

His thin smile appeared to be more of a grimace. "I knew you would understand. Now, may I get you that lemonade?"

The last thing she wanted was to spend any more time with him while she sipped tepid lemonade. "Thank you, but no. I must find Lady Selby, for she will be missing me."

"Of course. I am grateful for your sympathetic ear," he said with a bow.

After bobbing a curtsey, Emma left as quickly as she could. The tale Farley had spun could be plausible, for Sir Dotson appeared to be a ninny. But the conversation about Tattersall's at Lady Farley's dinner table and the passing of the note at the horse auction were both done with finesse. What better way to cover espionage than with misdirection?

Farley had just practiced that on her, so why not Doddy as well?

Was Farley the master spy? Had he somehow convinced Stephen to gather information for him? In her book, the evil half-brother hadn't been working alone. Another man, manipulative and powerful, had urged him on. If Farley was that man, then her historical romance had been closer to the truth than she ever realized.

Now all she had to do was prove it. Along with proving Stephen was deeply involved. If Stephen had the code key, then Farley had some sort of secret communication. At least, that's what she had put in her book. She wondered how soon she could safely search Farley's room. After all, she was gathering evidence to save Brandon.

BRANDON SAW EMMA EMERGE FROM THE DINING ROOM. THEN Farley appeared after her. Had the two of them been together? He had specifically warned her away from the man. As he wended his way through the guests to meet up with her, he saw Stephen waylay her. With a smarmy smile and a bow, his step-brother held out his arm to her. He watched Emma smile and accept his brother's invitation, then the two stepped to the dance floor.

Jealousy hunkered down in Brandon's chest. While his rational mind argued that she was only being polite and was perhaps on her quest to discover Stephen's wrongdoings, the irrational side blazed with fury that his brother had been quicker to intercept her, that she was being courteous when she should have ignored Stephen's invitation and given him the cut direct, and that he, as her *cousin*, should have been the one escorting her onto the dance floor.

Aunt Morrin poked him hard in the arm. "You look like you are about to bite off Pemberton's head. Stop it this very instant. She is supposed to be your cousin."

As he rubbed his arm, he glanced down at her. "She is being much too pleasant to him."

"She is trying to help you. Stop being such a mutton-headed numbskull." Aunt Morrin smiled and nodded to an acquaintance who wandered past, as if she were just passing the time with him.

"I think she was with Farley at the refreshment table," he grumbled.

His aunt poked him again, although with lesser force. "Do you truly believe she has an interest in that profligate weasel?"

He said nothing as he watched Emma disappear with Stephen among the other dancers. While the hard knot in his chest loosened just the tiniest bit at his aunt's words, he still wanted to punch his brother.

"I saw them in the dining room," his aunt said. "They were merely conversing. All very proper."

"I don't like her with him." His teeth clenched.

Aunt Morrin heaved a sigh of forbearance. "Have you asked her to stay?"

"Stay?" he parroted, his brain still focused on warning off Farley and beating his brother to a pulp.

Patiently, in a low voice, his aunt explained. "In this time."

The idea burst in his brain like fireworks, only not beautiful and ethereal, high up in the sky, but hot and painful, searing into him like tiny, sharp pokers. He wanted her to stay. But he couldn't ask her to stay. She didn't belong in his time. Besides, why would she want to remain? After seeing her twenty-first century clothing and those miraculous shoes, he suspected her time held many more advances that made her life in the future much more comfortable. And he had nothing to offer her. He was not the heir to his father's title. And his heart still belonged to Elizabeth.

His thoughts stuttered at that last. He hadn't thought of her since... He couldn't remember the last time. All his focus had been on the woman who had appeared suddenly in front of his curricle that day in Hyde Park. Angry at himself, he resolved to be better at keeping Elizabeth's memory alive.

So he was not going to ask Emma to stay, despite knowing that a part of his heart would always have an empty spot with her gone.

"No," he finally answered.

Aunt Morrin hummed something ambiguous but dire at the same time and wrapped her hand around his arm. "I have quite a craving for lemonade. Be a dear and escort me to the refreshments." In a low tone, she added, "Pemberton is merely dancing with her. He cannot do anything in the middle of a quadrille."

Knowing his aunt spoke the truth, he nevertheless couldn't resist a last glance to assure himself Emma was safe before he took his aunt in the opposite direction.

EMMA ALLOWED STEPHEN TO ESCORT HER ONTO THE DANCE floor. She really wanted to dance with Brandon and tell him about the conversation she'd just had with Farley and her suspicions. But maybe she could extract some information from Stephen about the note she had found.

He led her to the back of the ballroom near the open doors that led to the veranda. As the music began, he murmured, "I asked you to call me Stephen."

Emma sent him a flirty smile. "Of course. Silly of me to forget. You might have to remind me each time we meet."

"Will we meet often?" he asked as the other couples milled about and formed two lines.

"Oh, I'm sure we will." She glanced at him from beneath her lashes.

His gaze intensified. "I would like to meet often. Very, very much."

Emma evaded that intense gaze, for she had no intention of meeting him often.

Before the couples had completely settled into the formation for the dance, stepping closer, he took her hand and whispered, "I've done with dancing. Come with me." Placing a finger across his lips to indicate silence, he pulled her the three steps through the doors to the veranda. His grip didn't allow her to wriggle away.

"My lord! Stephen. Where are you taking me?" A twinge of apprehension made her steps drag. With a quick glance around, she saw the veranda was deserted.

"Hush," he said. "I don't believe anyone noticed our leaving."

She hoped someone might have seen their escape through the doors, because she was apprehensive about being alone with him.

"The moon is still quite full," he said. "Quite a change from the other night during the eclipse. You can see it better from here." He guided her to a shadowy corner, then murmured, "Your skin is like silk in the moonlight."

She felt his fingers trail down her bare arm and she edged away. "The moon is lovely, but I do wish to dance, my lord."

"Yes, yes, of course."

Something in his tone told her he had no intention of dancing. "I think we've been out here long enough. We'll be missed." She took a step away.

Grabbing her shoulder, he stopped her. "I've wanted to do this all evening."

Without warning, he pulled her tight against him and smashed his lips on her mouth. His kiss was rough and invasive, taking what she had no intention of giving.

Shock stiffened her. Then her instinct for flight took over. As she pulled away from his mouth, she pushed against his chest. But his arms were a vise around her.

"Let me go," she said as she tried to wrest from his embrace.

"Why? I'm sure my brother has done more than kiss you," Stephen growled. "How many times has he humped you?"

Emma gasped at his crude question and stomped on his foot, not particularly effective in her dancing slippers, but enough to surprise him. Taking advantage of his shock, she shoved him away, finally breaking free, then fled back into the ballroom.

"Emma!" he called from behind.

Ignoring him, she hurried around the edge of the ballroom and tried to hide among the crowd. As a few of the guests turned to look at her hasty return, she slowed her steps and smiled. Embarrassed because she had been stupid, all she wanted was to hide away. Stephen was more a threat than she ever realized. She had been lulled into thinking he was a gentleman because of his charm and good manners, but she should have known better. The twenty-first century version was a cad, and the character in her book was even worse.

Slipping around the edges of the ballroom, she evaded guests, and particularly Stephen, who had entered behind her. The last thing she wanted was a conversation with him. Besides, she was sure that speculation about their return from the veranda, one right after the other, was making its way around the ballroom. She wasn't in the mood to face the curious glances or gossipy whispers. After finally escaping into the entry hall, she quickly made her way up the staircase and to her room where she closed the door firmly behind her.

Why had she thought she could lead Stephen on? Because he was supposed to be a Regency gentleman? He wasn't a character in one of her books. And not all the men in her books were gentlemen. She should have been wiser and more wary. Angry with herself, she paced across the room and back. She became even more determined to prove that Stephen was doing something heinous.

Taking a deep breath, she blew it out. She had to search Farley's room. Now. While everyone was still at the ball. Before Brandon came looking for her. Checking her appearance in the glass, she pushed an errant strand of hair into place and straightened her dress. No sign of Stephen's unwanted advances showed. Raising her chin, she opened her door and stepped into the hallway.

Right into Brandon.

His fist was raised as if he had been about to knock on her door. He had come looking for her. Warmth erupted in the vicinity of her heart.

They stared at each other in surprise. Brandon was the first to recover. He took her by the shoulders, steered her backwards into her room and pushed the door shut with his foot. Before she had a chance to ask him where he'd been, his arms circled her and his mouth claimed her lips. The kiss seared away Stephen's aggression and the faint sense of slime left from her conversation with Farley. By the time he let her up for air, her knees were the consistency of warm Jello, and other parts were decidedly hot and tingly.

"You came after me," she said, dazed and concentrating on not collapsing into a pile of mush.

OF COURSE HE CAME AFTER HER. BRANDON DIDN'T LIKE HER having a conversation with Farley, and he liked even less that she accepted another invitation to dance with his brother. As soon as she opened the door, all he wanted was to taste her mouth and feel her soft curves crushed against him. Despite his resolve not to ask her to stay in his time, or perhaps because of it, he wanted, needed to touch her.

He glowered. "Watching you have a tête à tête with Farley and accept a dance with my brother was torture."

"Oh, Brandon," she murmured, stepped close, and placed her hand against his cheek, her thumb resting on his bottom lip.

He couldn't help himself. He sucked that digit into his mouth.

An indistinct noise escaped her, halfway between a moan and a whimper. Her lashes swept down and her lips parted. Just as he was about to swirl his tongue around her thumb, she pulled free. Excitement, and not from his seduction, made her eyes sparkle.

"Let me tell you what I discovered," she said. "When Farley and I spoke, he tried to convince me that Sir Dotson engaged in fantasies."

"Fantasies?" His brow crinkled, then lowered ominously "What sort of fantasies?"

Emma grinned. "Not *those* types of fantasies, so get your mind out of the gutter. Fantasies of spying, and all his friends play along."

He huffed a breath. "So he was trying to make you think that anything you saw at Tattersall's meant nothing."

"Exactly. Why go to the trouble of explaining something like that unless he was trying to cover it up?" Her eyes lit with determination. "We have to search his room."

The thought of her anywhere near an intimate space that belonged to the man made his skin crawl. "You will not."

Her brows snapped together. "Why? This is the perfect time, while he's still at the ball."

"Because I already have."

Her eyes widened and her cheeks glowed pink. "You did? Perfect! Thank you!" She grabbed his face and smacked a kiss on his mouth. Before he had a chance to catch her and keep her softness pressed against him, she skipped away. "Did you find anything?"

He pulled a half-burned scrap of paper from his pocket and showed it to her. "I found this on the hearth, but I'm not sure what it means." A few random numbers were written on it. "It looks like a row of figures. Perhaps from a ledger."

"No, not from a ledger. This is so exciting!" She bounced on her toes as if bubbles popped beneath her feet. "This looks like what I found in Stephen's room."

Taking him by the hand, she dragged him to her wardrobe, where she rummaged around a bit. After digging into one of her shoes, she came up with a parchment and unfolded it, revealing a smaller piece inside. She handed him the smaller one. A double row of numbers with random spaces between ran across the foolscap.

"This is Stephen's handwriting," she said. "I recognize it from the invitation to this gathering." Then she indicated the one he'd pulled from his pocket. "This is his handwriting, too. I recognize that little swirl on the end of several of the numbers."

Brandon studied them, noting Farley's coat of arms at the top of the larger sheet. A single sentence was written near the top with a number from one to twenty-six beneath each individual letter, with duplicates crossed out. He realized he held a code key that would unlock the meaning of the two lists of numbers. Obviously, his brother and Farley were involved in something. But what?

A feeling of impending doom settled heavily on his shoulders. Pushing it away, he asked, "Have you deciphered the note you found?"

"Yes, but it makes no sense." Picking up a journal from her dressing table, she flipped it open and showed him. "I've played around with the numbers and letters. All I get is, *The bee can sting the raven and snatch his coronet as he flies past the rock.* I have no idea what that means. Why would a raven have a coronet? And why would a bee sting it?"

He thought for a moment. "Perhaps we're being too literal. What if the message itself is in code?" Silently, he read it again, then mused, "A raven with a coronet. Part of the royal robes of state for a marquis would include a coronet. But I don't understand why a marquis— Bollocks! The estate of the Marquis of Wildford is not far from here. I've known him since we were boys. He is a privateer for the Royal Navy now. I believe his ship is called the *Sea Raven.*"

"Do you think this could be about him?"

Brandon shook his head. "I don't know. But Stephen might be aware of Wildford's activities, since the estates are so close."

Emma looked back at the sentence. "I don't understand the reference to a bee."

"Napoleon's symbol is the bee," he said. "And the rock could mean Gibraltar."

"*The bee can sting the raven*," she read. Concern made her frown. "Do you think the French are planning to capture your friend?"

Staring at the three pieces of parchment, he said, "If this is truly a message to the French... If an English marquis were captured..." His words trailed off, not needing to explain what a blow that would be to England, not to mention the danger that threatened Wildford.

"Well, Stephen still had the note, so he hasn't passed it along yet," she said. "The man who is the crow is still safe." She took a moment to decode the partially burned note. "This note is in French. All that's left is *à les chevals*."

"At the horses," he translated.

"Oh," she said, then drew an excited breath. "I saw Sir Dotson pass a note to Stephen at Tattersall's. Maybe that's where the messages are passed along."

Brandon said nothing as he stared down at the bits of parchment. What would make Stephen betray his country? If his brother were caught as a spy, the family would be dishonored. Would his father believe that Stephen was involved? If he did, would he be furious enough to turn in his son to the authorities and disown him?

Emma placed a hand on his arm. "We have to give these to the authorities."

"No," he said with a shake of his head. "We need to show them to my father first. He deserves to know his son is a traitor."

She inched closer and her eyes beseeched him. "But then we have to tell the authorities as soon as possible. To protect your friend."

Her touch and distinctive scent of vanilla calmed the turbulent thoughts in his head and the roiling emotions in his chest. "Yes. Of course." He stared down at the foolscap again. "Tomorrow. We'll present these to the earl tomorrow." He held out the notes. "Hide these. I'll come for you after breakfast."

She took the three pieces, then wrapped her arms around him "Whatever happens," she murmured against his shoulder, "I'm still here."

He absorbed her warmth for a moment before setting her away from him. This revelation about his brother solidified his decision. He would never ask her to stay now that he knew the dishonor his brother would bring to the family. How could he expose her to the scandal and disgrace? His father might not pass along the proof of Stephen's treachery to the authorities. Or his father might blame him for revealing the family's dishonor. Either way, He would still be the bastard son and an outcast. No, she was better off if she returned to the future where she belonged.

"Yes," he said, keeping his tone distant and cool. "Until you go back to your own time."

She jerked back, hurt darkening her eyes. "I can't go back until Mrs. Edwards has my bracelet repaired. I'm here for you at least until then."

"Of course." He stepped away, needing to put distance between them, or he'd do something idiotic, like try to kiss the hurt from those blue eyes. "Until tomorrow."

He strode to the door and walked out without a backward glance. Guilt gnawed at him. He should be happy he had proof of Stephen's deceit that he could lay before his father. Wasn't that what he had wanted? Instead, his heart felt like a heavy stone in his chest as he made his way to his room.

EMMA WATCHED BRANDON CLOSE THE DOOR BEHIND HIM. Astounded and hurt by his sudden coolness, she couldn't move. Although she had thought about returning to her own time, she had become more comfortable in this time. Besides that, she had become quite attached to Brandon. More than attached. In love with him. But he obviously didn't love her.

Ghost Brandon had wanted her to go back to his time to "fix things," but he never said anything about what would happen if or when she did. She had assumed that she would return to her own time, but what if she didn't? What if she decided to remain in the past? Except Real Brandon appeared not to want her.

Despondent, she rang for a maid to help her undress. She had no desire to return to the ball where she would be expected to smile and be charming to people she would most likely never meet again. All she had wanted to do was help Brandon. She hadn't expected to fall in love with the real man.

When the maid knocked on her door, she swiped away the tears that gathered in her eyes. No one would see how much he had hurt her. Especially not Brandon. Because he didn't love her. And he must never know that she had fallen in love with him.

BRANDON STRODE BACK TO HIS ROOM AND SHUT HIMSELF inside. He'd wanted to rejoice with Emma, congratulate her on her cleverness. Instead, the specter of her leaving rose up like black smoke and blocked out everything else. What good would evidence of his brother's perfidy do if Emma was not by his side, even if it might convince his father to disinherit Stephen?

First, Elizabeth had left him by marrying Stephen, and then she had died, snuffing out the light in his world. Now Emma would return to her own time, and he would never see her again. After Elizabeth, he had vowed never to love again. But Emma had wriggled her way into his heart. Losing her would hurt too much. He had to shut her out, protect himself from the pain of losing her.

He had loved Elizabeth with the wild passion of youth. He had thought she was the epitome of everything he wanted in a woman, shy and gentle, always doing the exact right thing. She was stability in his tumultuous life. Perhaps she had been too safe, and that was why she had bowed under her father's pressure to wed his brother.

Emma was different, not only because she was from the future, but because she completed him in a way no other woman had, not even Elizabeth. He had loved Elizabeth, and he mourned her, but she was a demure and quiet soul. Emma was outspoken and a bit rebellious, not shy about disagreeing with him. She fired his blood in more ways than he could count. He would miss her tremendously when she returned to her own time.

He couldn't think about that. Pouring himself a brandy,

he sat before the cold hearth and forced his brain to concentrate on how he would present the evidence of Stephen's treachery to his father. How would the earl react? Disbelief? Anger? It didn't matter. Stephen was a traitor and needed to be punished. His father's honor would demand it. But what form would that punishment take? Arrest? Banishment? Or something much more dire, like execution? Even he, with his dislike of Stephen, didn't want to contemplate that.

How could they deal with this? Stephen's treason impacted more than the family honor. It would cause a scandal that would reverberate throughout the country.

With Stephen gone, he was the only male left in the family to inherit the title. If he became his father's heir, the title of Earl of Cranleigh carried many responsibilities, one of which was producing an heir of his own. Those toy soldiers sitting in his study needed someone to play with them. What would Emma be like as a mother? He smiled. She would most likely get down on the floor with them. His smile faded. But she had told him she couldn't conceive. Besides, she would be gone, back to her own time.

His musings focused on the woman who had appeared out of nowhere before his curricle that day in Hyde Park. He couldn't help himself. She was the light in his darkness. He hadn't realized how bleak his life had become until she stepped into it. She challenged him. She annoyed him. She made him chuckle. She was brave and headstrong. She was beautiful and sensuous and had the most delicious mouth. What would he do once she returned to her own time?

He downed the rest of the brandy in his glass and poured another. His head would pound in the morning, but he needed to shut out the thought that a time would come when Emma would no longer be with him.

Nineteen

Emma was ready when Brandon knocked on her door the next morning, having been up since dawn. She hadn't gone down to breakfast, but instead had hot chocolate in her room. That was all her nervous stomach could handle. The prospect of laying out the incriminating evidence before Brandon's father made her hands tremble. How would he react to learning his heir was a traitor?

Would this be the cause for Stephen murdering him? How could she stop it? In her novel, the evil step-brother had murdered his father a few days after the lunar eclipse. But this was real, and not all the events she had experienced in the past had happened in the same sequence as what she had written in her book. Except she felt a very real sense of impending disaster.

She opened her door to Brandon with a brave smile, but

it faded when she saw his grim expression. Without a word, he held out his arm. She grabbed up her reticule that contained the notes, took his arm, and they set off down the hallway. When they started down the stairs, she could see some of the guests milling about in the entrance hall, for Stephen had organized a morning ride and picnic lunch. He was chatting with Arlene near the door. As Emma and Brandon stepped off the last stair, he saw them and smiled at her as if he hadn't tried to force a kiss on her the night before. Emma turned away, but she caught the chilly glare Brandon sent his way.

They headed to his father's study, where she had overheard the argument between Lady Selby and the earl. Brandon knocked, and the earl bade them enter. Emma glanced around the large room. A wall of windows looked out over terraced lawns, and the other three walls were lined with shelves of books, interspersed here and there with a small bust or valuable vase or other knickknack. A large fireplace interrupted the rows of shelves to her left. Above her head, the coffered ceiling was painted with scenes of gods and goddesses on its panels. Comfortable chairs sat before the fireplace. Directly opposite them in front of the windows was a large desk of dark wood. This is where they found the earl. He stood upon seeing Emma, but his face held thunderclouds when he saw Brandon.

"Good morning, my lord." Emma dipped a curtsy. "I hope we're not disturbing you."

"Good morning, Mrs. Blake," the earl said, perfectly civil. Then he turned to Brandon. "I am not in the mood to listen to your reasons why you should be my heir. This is not the time." His tone dropped the temperature of the room by several degrees.

Brandon stiffened, but instead of responding to his father's dismissal, he said, "We have something that you need to see."

The earl remained silent.

Emma stepped forward as she dug in her reticule. Placing the notes on the earl's desk, she said, "We think it's important that you see these."

"What are they?" The earl sounded testy as he glanced at them.

Emma pointed at the parchment with the coat of arms and the note of numbers. "These two were in Stephen's possession." Then she indicated the one that was partially burned. "This one was in Lord Farley's possession."

"How did they come to be in your possession?" the earl drawled with suspicion dripping from every syllable.

"What does it matter how we found them? That is of no consequence," Brandon snapped. "God's teeth! Stephen had two of them! Why won't you believe me? Am I not also your son?"

The earl's chin jerked up as if he had been slapped, but said nothing.

Emma's hand twisted in her skirt at the tension between father and son. Her heart ached for Brandon.

After a silent stand-off between the two men, the earl heaved an exasperated sigh and examined the notes more closely. "All I see is a nonsensical sentence and some numbers."

"It's a secret message in code and the code key, my lord," Emma said.

An irritated line appeared between his brows. "Did your accident muddle your ability to make sense, Mrs. Blake?"

She blinked at the affront.

Brandon stepped forward and snapped, "Do not insult her. Allow her to explain."

With a narrow-eyed glance at Brandon, his father said with chilly civility, "Please, go on, Mrs. Blake."

Emma tamped down her nerves and explained about the decryption key, what Stephen's note said, and what they thought the meaning might be, then about seeing Sir Dotson pass something to him at Tattersall's and how it related to the burned scrap that belonged to Farley.

When she finished, the earl stared at her, his gaze unfathomable. Then he turned that gaze on Brandon. "What, exactly, are you saying?"

Brandon looked his father in the eye as he said, "The Viscount Pemberton is spying for the French."

At his declaration, the Earl of Cranleigh did not blink, did not move, remaining as still as if he had just looked upon

Medusa. Brandon stood just as stiffly as he stared back, defiant. The atmosphere in the room crackled with tension. Emma was nearly afraid to breathe, afraid that if she did, something terrible would be released.

Finally, in a very low tone, as if holding back a tidal wave of fury, the earl said, "Get out."

With dignity, Brandon executed a bow and said, "Good day to you, sir." Then he held out his arm to Emma.

Emma bobbed a hurried curtsy before she took his arm and accompanied him out of the study. He closed the door carefully behind them and just stood, his head dipped in thought. A loud thud of something heavy slamming against the door, followed by the sound of porcelain shattering, made her flinch.

Shocked at the earl's violent reaction, Emma stared at Brandon with wide eyes.

"I believe my father needs to decide what he is going to do," he said. "Let us retire to Lady Selby's room."

As if nothing out of the ordinary had occurred, they returned to the front hall and started to climb the stairs. Through the open door, Emma was surprised to see Stephen's guests still chatting and milling about outside as they waited for their horses to be brought around, taking their time to start their ride. Hadn't they left yet? She felt as if they had been in the earl's study for hours rather than minutes. She caught a glimpse of Stephen on his horse, his elegant and suave exterior hiding the true man beneath. She wondered what his fate might be, if what she wrote in her novel would actually come to pass. Arrested and hanged for treason. He deserved whatever punishment he might get.

At her side, Brandon was stiff and silent. He didn't seem to be jubilant that he might finally get his inheritance. In fact, he seemed withdrawn and remote, as if he were holding his emotions tightly in check. What thoughts were running through his head? She wanted to ask him, to comfort him, assure him they had done the right thing, but felt he needed to come to terms with what they had done on his own.

When they arrived at Lady Selby's door, she bade them enter at their knock. She was sipping a cup of tea. A small table before her held a tray with a plate of toast points and ham, and a pot of jam. Her glance swept over them, and she replaced her cup in its saucer.

"Where have you both been, and what have you got up to?" she inquired mildly. "Last night, I was left to ask Pemberton to see me to my room."

Despite that mild tone, Lady Selby's comment made Emma squirm. Both she and Brandon had abandoned her at the ball.

He bowed. "My apologies, Aunt Morrin. We have just presented my father with evidence that my half-brother is a spy for the French, along with his friend, Farley."

Lady Selby's expression didn't change as she stared. Then, as if they hadn't announced such astounding news, she asked calmly. "Did you? How did Cranleigh react?"

"He's considering the evidence." A corner of his mouth deepened.

Lady Selby bowed her head thoughtfully. When she looked up again, concern entered her eyes. "This is quite serious. Cranleigh could believe your evidence and disown Stephen. Or he could destroy it and ignore what Stephen has done. He is, after all, the earl. The potential ramifications for the family are enormous."

A chill ran through Emma and she glanced at Brandon. He appeared unperturbed.

She felt his fingers twine with hers.

"I have every confidence my father will do the honorable thing. He'll most likely turn the evidence over to the Foreign Office, since Farley is also incriminated with the evidence," he said stiffly to his aunt, then glanced down at Emma. "You'll be safe until you return to your own time. I'll protect you."

His touch calmed her and she appreciated his protection, but his impassive statement about her leaving sent a splinter into her heart. He had already accepted that she would return to her own time. Maybe that was best. She should accept it, too, and tuck away her feelings for him, because a knife blade hung over their heads.

Brandon's father could say whatever he wanted and would be believed because he was an earl, influential and powerful. He could speak the truth about his legitimate son and have Stephen arrested for treason, or he could destroy the evidence, bury any evidence that his heir was a traitor. What would happen then? Would Stephen still shoot Brandon? She couldn't bear to see him die. To guard her heart, terrified, she slipped her fingers from his grasp, putting some distance between them.

LATE THAT AFTERNOON, EMMA WALKED THROUGH THE GARDEN as she waited to learn what the earl would do with the evidence of Stephen's treachery. She'd gone back to her room after their visit with Lady Selby, while Brandon went for a ride. He had invited her along, but she needed to be alone, so she had declined. After writing about the discovery of the secret notes in her journal, she had paced in her room and worried about what the earl might do. The possibility that the evidence she'd found might be turned back on Brandon scared her, despite his reassurance that his father would do the right thing.

Walking through the gardens cleared her head. She was admiring a beautiful rose when she heard footsteps on the gravel path. Glancing up with a smile, thinking it was Brandon, she saw Stephen bearing down on her.

"Wagtail!" His face twisted in hate. "Biter! Bitch!"

She backed away from his fury. But not far enough.

Lunging, he grabbed her by the arms and shook her. "You lying, thieving biter!"

Emma tried to twist from his grasp. "Stay away from me." Finally wrenching away, she turned to run.

Stephen caught her gown and jerked her back. "You're not running from me. I knew you were nothing but a trull, swiving that sneaksby who is my brother."

"How dare you!" She pulled at his fingers curled into her gown with one hand, made a fist with the other and whacked him on the chin.

His head snapped to the side, but when he turned back, his eyes blazed. "You dirty little hellcat," he snarled and pushed her.

Emma stumbled backwards. Her foot caught on a plant and she lost her balance, tumbling back, falling into the flowers. Stephen jumped on her, straddled her with his knees and pinned her down.

"I'm going to teach you not to meddle in affairs that don't concern you," he snarled, as he clawed at her skirt.

In terror, Emma opened her mouth to scream, but his hand clamped over it. She bit him and tasted blood. With a yelp, he jerked his hand away, his face ugly with rage. Filling her lungs, she screamed.

"Help! Someone, help!"

"Shut up," he snarled, pressing her into the dirt.

Twisting and turning, she fought to push him off and pummeled him any place she could land a punch. The fury in his eyes was vicious, and his anger made him strong. Despite her struggling, she couldn't get free. As she pushed and tried to wriggle away, she glanced back at the house, at all the windows that looked out on the garden. Didn't anyone see what was happening?

A shadow fell over them and Brandon appeared beyond Stephen's shoulder. Emma sobbed in relief. Grabbing his brother, Brandon yanked him to his feet, then cracked his fist against Stephen's jaw, who went flying into a large, thorny rose bush. Before Stephen could regain his feet, Brandon pulled him up with murder in his eyes and pummeled him again. Emma scrambled to her feet and grabbed Brandon's arm.

"Stop! Please!" She was afraid Brandon might kill him.

Brandon glanced at her, his eyes hard with wrath. With a shove at Stephen, he stepped back and turned to her. "Are you hurt?"

She shook her head, ignoring the aches.

Wordlessly, he contradicted her with a gentle touch of his fingertips to the bruise on her cheekbone. Then he swung back to his half-brother. "If you ever touch her again, I will kill you."

Stephen's splotchy face twisted with hate. Bloody snot ran from his nose, and he trembled in fury. "You have ruined everything!" he screamed. "You and your hell cat! I will get my revenge one day!" Pushing past Brandon, he stomped toward the house, but his sleeve had been torn from his coat and dirt clung to his ripped pantaloons, destroying his furious exit.

"Let me look at you," Brandon said after Stephen had left. With gentle fingers, he again traced over the bruise on her cheek. "We need to take care of that. I should have killed him," he muttered.

Emma's eyes closed at his touch, and she shook her head. "No, you shouldn't have. I'm fine. Thank you for coming to help." But even as she spoke her brave words, cold enveloped her and she began to tremble.

"Come here," he murmured as he enclosed her in his warm embrace.

His strength comforted her, and she soaked it in. He was safety when her world turned turbulent. But that sanctuary was fleeting, because he expected her to return to her own time. He didn't want her. And he would be shot. She mourned losing him.

His mouth thinned. "If I hadn't...." He shook his head. "I'm sorry. I just learned that my father has asked all of Stephen's guests to leave. My brother was furious with him. I should have found you sooner."

A gasp escaped her. "Does that mean your father believes us?" A spark of hope kindled in Emma's chest.

"I don't know." He glanced in the direction Stephen had gone. "I think we should leave and return to the city. I don't trust that sniveling cur. He might try to harm you again."

"But shouldn't we stay to hear your father's decision?" she

asked. "If we're gone and Stephen is still here, he might make up some story and blame you as the spy."

He thought a moment. "All right. We'll stay. But promise me you'll remain in your room with the door locked."

"Will you stay with me?" Despite her assertion that she was unharmed, reaction from Stephen's attack made her crave the warmth of his company.

"I would like nothing more," he said, as he brushed back a stray strand of hair from her face. "But I want to be sure Stephen doesn't try to run off. If he is spying for the French, then he needs to pay."

"Please, be careful," she said, thinking of the events in her book and Ghost Brandon's end. She took one of his hands in both of hers. "There is something I need to tell you." Gathering her thoughts, she bowed her head a moment, her gaze falling on his warm, graceful fingers wrapped around her hand. When he died, those fingers would turn cold and lifeless. Rubbing her thumb across his knuckles, she savored the strength of him, the grace of him.

"Emma?" he said at her silence.

She met his silvery gaze. "Your ghost—" She swallowed and started again. "Your ghost told me that Stephen shot you in the back."

He said nothing for a long moment. What was he thinking, feeling? She wanted to comfort him, to tell him everything would work out. Somehow, she'd find a way to prevent his death.

Then he nodded and looked away, across her shoulder, to the expanse of lawn and the trees beyond. Returning his gaze to her, with a tiny lift to the corner of his mouth, he said, "So you came back in time to "fix things?"

"Yes." She was very certain of that now. She would do everything she could to save him, to "fix things."

He nodded again. "I am not surprised that my brother stooped so low." Tucking her hand in the crook of his arm, he started walking her back to the house. "He will not get the upper hand this time. But I promise to be careful."

Despite his confident words, Emma worried. Stephen was desperate. Who knew what dastardly tricks he might try? And remembering that hole in Ghost Brandon's back made her even more anxious.

EMMA PACED, TRYING NOT TO DWELL ON EVENTS THAT HADN'T yet happened. Brandon's murder. The earl's murder. After Brandon had made sure she was safely in her room and had cool cloths to press against her injured cheek, he had left to make sure Stephen didn't leave the estate. She had turned to her journal to write down what had occurred so far. When she finished, she had nothing to do, and the needlepoint Lady Selby had given her to practice on didn't appeal to her.

She was too anxious. Even as she stood at the window and gazed out at the beautiful garden, her thoughts were on Brandon and Stephen and the earl.

Movement at the edge of the garden caught her attention. Stephen quickly wended his way between the plants and headed across the lawn towards the woods beyond. Curious about where he might be going, she watched him stop in the middle of the lawn, circle back to the garden, then sink to one of the stone benches. Bending forward, he dropped his head into his hands. He was no doubt contemplating how he could get out of the mess he was in.

A movement near the house drew her attention. She watched as Brandon slipped behind a very large bush. He was obviously keeping a watch on his brother.

She had no sympathy for Stephen. Turning away from the window, she decided she needed something to distract her from worrying. Since Stephen was safely out of the house, she could sneak down to the earl's study, find a book to read, and return behind her locked door before anyone was the wiser.

Slipping out of her room, she made her way down to the study. The room was empty when she peeked in. Papers were strewn across the top of the desk, and a few had fluttered to the floor, as if someone had been searching for something. She thought the mess was odd, because when she and Brandon had been in the room before, everything had been orderly.

The earl wasn't present, so she stepped inside and went to one of the walls of books to see what might interest her. Books in Latin, books in Greek, ancient illuminated manuscripts that looked like they had been hand-inscribed. Collectors in the twenty-first century would pay thousands, tens of thousands, maybe even millions for some of the books on the shelves before her. But no novels for her to read.

As she strolled to the next wall of shelves, she heard a low groan behind her. Swinging around, she searched the room, but saw no one. Thinking she had imagined the sound, she returned to her perusal of the books.

The groan came again, louder this time. It seemed to come from behind the desk. She tiptoed over to peek behind it.

And gasped.

The earl was on the floor and writhing in pain. His pale face was covered in a sheen of perspiration.

She dropped to her knees beside him. "My lord! What's wrong? Can I help?"

He groaned again. "Pain," he rasped, as his knees jerked up to his chest.

Emma ran to the door of the room. "Help!" she yelled. "Help! Someone, please help!" A bell pull hung beside the doorframe, and she yanked on it frantically. Then she hurried back to the earl and took his hand. His skin was cold and clammy.

"Someone will be here soon," she said, as she tried to soothe him.

He closed his eyes and nodded. His breathing was shallow and quick, as if the pain he endured was unbearable, and his grip on her hand crushed her fingers. She glanced around, looking for something to help him. Not far away on the floor, an empty glass lay on its side with a wet stain around it. The crystal sparkled in the sun shining through the window. Another glass, with two fingers of amber liquid, most likely brandy, sat on a corner of his desk. She didn't dare give him spirits.

What had made the earl so ill? He had seemed perfectly fine when she and Brandon had spoken with him, and before that, she had seen him early in the morning riding out on his horse and looking very healthy. Glancing again at the spilled glass, she wondered if something in the brandy had made him ill. She picked up the glass, warm from the sun, and sniffed. Along with the aroma of the brandy, she smelled garlic. That was strange. But she had no more time to ponder, for several footmen arrived. She directed two of them to help the earl to his bed and told one of them to fetch the doctor. Then she went to find Brandon and bring the news to Lady Selby.

But something disturbed her about the earl's sudden illness.

Twenty

The Earl of Cranleigh was dead.

Brandon couldn't believe it. He paced across the drawing room. And back again, stopping before the windows that looked out on the expanse of lawn before the estate. But he saw nothing, not the decorative duck pond, not the sentinel of trees that lined the drive. His brain seemed to have stopped working. How could this have happened? His father had been healthy and alive only a couple of hours ago.

The doctor had arrived, but had been unable to do anything. The earl had been poisoned.

Emma had told him about the two glasses in the study, one empty and smelling of garlic, the other still holding two fingers of brandy. When he went to investigate, he saw the messy desk, indicating someone had been searching for something. Had it been Stephen looking for the evidence of his treason or some other document that could deprive him of the title and estate?

Brandon had immediately sent for the justice of the peace, Mr. Buxton. Now, he and his constables were searching the house and looking for evidence to reveal who had murdered his father. He doubted they would find anything.

On the other side of the room, Emma and his aunt sat silent. Aunt Morrin appeared stoic and grim. Emma looked as dazed as the day he had nearly run her down with his curricle. Stephen had withdrawn to his room. The servants had been sequestered in the kitchen, and Mr. Buxton had asked that no one leave the house.

As soon as his brother had heard the news, he had become unnerved, wringing his hands and muttering that it couldn't be. Brandon thought his brother's overreaction strange, since he never thought of him as being that close to their father. Was it possible that this show of grief was for their benefit? Could Stephen have become so desperate that he had murdered their father? The suspicion whirled inside his head.

"Murder!" As if his suspicions had a voice, he heard the cry come from the floor above. "He murdered his own father!"

Brandon glanced at Emma and his aunt, who both stared, their eyes wide in astonishment. Had one of the constables found evidence that Stephen was the murderer? Footsteps pounded down the stairs.

"He murdered the earl!" Stephen yelled as he burst into the drawing room and pointed at Brandon.

Brandon turned to face his brother and wondered what the conniving churl was plotting. He was more convinced than ever that Stephen's reactions were all for show, but what evidence could his brother possibly have manufactured? Stephen's wild accusation had no merit.

"You!" Stephen pointed at him. "You murdered him!"

"Are you daft?" Brandon snapped. "I did no such thing. What would prompt me to do that?"

The justice of the peace stepped into the room. "I'm sorry, Mr. Connaught, sir, but I'm going to have to arrest you for the murder of the Earl of Cranleigh. We found this in your room." He held out a container of rat poison.

Brandon stared at it. His sneaky, lying half-brother must have put the murder weapon there, after he had poisoned his father's brandy.

When he said nothing, Mr. Buxton shifted from one foot to the other. "I'm thinking, sir, that you used it to poison the earl."

Lady Selby stood. "He did no such thing. I saw a mouse in my room and asked him to do something about it. The only murder my nephew has committed is on a rodent."

"No!" Stephen yelled. "He did it! He killed my father!"

In confusion, the justice of the peace looked from Stephen to Lady Selby to Brandon.

Emma stood. "He was with me for the entire afternoon," she said. "He had no opportunity to poison the earl."

"You stupid baggage," Stephen snarled. "He could have put the poison in the brandy at any time."

At his brother's slur on Emma, Brandon's temper soared. His hand curled into a fist, but before he could pummel the cur, Mr. Buxton stepped between them.

"Now, now, we'll have none of that," the justice of the peace said. He shook his head. "This is a puzzle. We're going to have to sort this."

"There's nothing to sort," Stephen declared and stomped out of the room.

Mr. Buxton watched him go, then turned back to Brandon. "We'll be asking questions of the servants, sir, to see if anyone saw anything unusual."

"We understand, Buxton," Brandon said. "Do as you must. We have to attend to funeral arrangements for the earl. Would you permit my brother and I to ride out to speak to the vicar?"

"Of course, sir. If you don't mind, one of my constables will accompany you." With a quick bow, the man left.

Brandon stared at the empty doorway as he tried to get his emotions under control. The closeness he'd had with his father when he was a boy had faded away when the earl had wed and produced a legitimate son. His resentment and hurt over being shut out of the earl's life, over being thrown out of the Ivy House, his home, had clouded everything else. Now his father was dead, and he hadn't been able to do anything to mend the breach between them, nor convince his father to legally adopt him and declare him the heir to the title. The sadness he felt upon his father's death surprised him. But not the resentment he felt against Stephen. For that murdering, conniving, black-hearted churl was the new earl.

Emma stepped close and took his hand. "It will be all right," she murmured. She placed her other hand on his chest over his heart. "*You* will be all right."

"Of course," he said, sounding more positive than he felt. How could he be all right? He might be arrested and hanged for murder. Stephen, whom he suspected of being the true murderer, might go free and assume all the privileges of the title. Emma would return to the future where she belonged.

But that was for another day. Right now, he had to make arrangements to bury his father.

EMMA WALKED OUTSIDE WITH BRANDON, SILENT AND withdrawn, to see him off to the vicar's. Frustration and sadness and anxiety were a tight coil in her chest. Her efforts to prove that Stephen was spying for the French had come to nothing. The earl had died before he could disinherit him, before he could send proof to the authorities.

Beyond that, the sense of urgency she'd felt since the eclipse became stronger, especially now that the earl had been murdered. Events were beginning to telescope, getting closer to Brandon's murder. How could she stop it? She didn't like that he and Stephen would be riding together, but a constable would be with them. Surely, Stephen wouldn't try anything with a witness around.

Ghost Brandon had told her he had been shot while trying to escape arrest so he could clear his name. Real Brandon wasn't escaping. He was merely leaving to meet with the vicar. So events didn't match. Despite that, she had an uncomfortable feeling that something was awry.

A groom had brought around two horses, and she watched Brandon mount. Stephen had not yet appeared. Despite Brandon's solemn expression, he looked handsome and dignified in his dark blue coat, buff-colored breeches and polished boots. A black band of mourning was tied around his upper arm.

"I'll be back as soon as I can," he said. "Be careful. If Stephen is telling the truth and he's not the murderer, then the culprit is still about."

"You be careful, too." She rested her hand on his thigh. "I don't want to hear you've been attacked by a highwayman," she teased, but her levity was forced. Despite trying to convince herself that he would be safe, Stephen would be riding through the countryside with him.

His eyes crinkled at the corners. "There have been no reports of any highwaymen in the area for at least the past century. Besides, we have our intrepid constable with us." He indicated the young man who was sitting uncomfortably on a sway-backed nag.

She smiled, hiding her anxiety. "That's good."

With a glance around, he said, "It appears my brother isn't coming. Take care. I'll be back before you miss me."

He wheeled his horse and started down the drive. As she turned to go back inside, out of the corner of her eye, she saw Stephen coming around the corner of the house. He appeared very intent on something. Then she noticed the pistol in his hand.

Her blood turned to ice.

She had to stop him.

She ran.

Stephen raised the pistol.

No! He was not going to kill Brandon.

Just as he pulled the trigger, she knocked him off balance.

The shot exploded.

Brandon toppled from his horse.

"No!" she screamed.

Terrified, Emma ran to him. This wasn't supposed to happen. Didn't she travel back in time for a reason? Wasn't she supposed to stop Brandon's murder?

He was lying face-down when she reached him. A dark, wet stain spread across the back of his coat. Panic tightened her chest. He couldn't die. She wouldn't let him. If he died, even if she went back to her own time, she'd be lost, devastated. Because she loved him.

"Don't be dead. Please don't be dead," she prayed, unconsciously echoing Brandon's words after he ran into her in Hyde Park. Dropping to her knees, she pressed on the wound to stop the bleeding. "Help!" she yelled. "Someone help!"

He hissed in a breath and mumbled something.

Relief poured through her. He wasn't dead. And then she realized the hole in his coat wasn't in the same spot as in his ghost's coat. It was not in the middle of his back, where the shot might have pierced his heart or lung. Instead, it was high on his shoulder.

"Don't die on me," she muttered. "Don't you dare die on me."

"I'll try not to," he said. Then he rolled over onto his back.

"Don't move." Emma slipped her hand beneath him to staunch the blood. "We have to keep pressure on the wound, so you don't bleed out."

"Bleed out?" He blinked up at her, those gray eyes still piercing. "I do believe it's only a flesh wound." He rotated his shoulder, winced, and his face paled. "Well, perhaps a bit more than a flesh wound."

People poured out of the house—servants, Mr. Buxton

and his constables, Lady Selby, the doctor, who was having tea and biscuits in the kitchen to sustain him on his ride back home. Stephen had disappeared. The doctor rushed over, took one look at Brandon's wound and ordered two of the servants to help him to his bed. Another servant retrieved Brandon's horse that had fled down the drive and was calmly nibbling on the grass. Mr. Buxton demanded to know what happened.

As the constable stuttered through an explanation and Emma filled in the blanks, she watched as Brandon, helped by the two servants and followed by the doctor, stumbled his way haltingly into the house. She wanted to follow him, be with him, make sure he was going to be all right. But she needed to tell Mr. Buxton about Stephen's attack.

When she finished relating the events, he said, "Don't you worry, Mrs. Blake, we'll catch the bloke."

Emma nodded, but she doubted the man's assurance. This wasn't the age of cell phones and the internet, where information could be passed along instantly. Stephen could sneak away and hide anywhere. He could escape across the Channel to France.

As Mr. Buxton turned to his constables and began barking orders, Lady Selby approached. "Come inside, Emma, and get cleaned up."

"I need to go to Brandon." Emma tried to follow Brandon into the house, but Lady Selby stopped her. Medical practices in the nineteenth century were slapdash at best, and she

365

wanted to be sure the doctor didn't do anything that would kill him.

"You have blood all over you," Lady Selby said. "Surely, you do not wish to have my nephew see you in that condition. Let the doctor take care of him."

Emma glanced down at herself. Her hands were covered in blood and her dress had splotches of blood and smudges of dirt down the front. She shook her head. "No, I have to see him." Pulling away from Brandon's aunt, she raced into the house.

Breathless and anxious, she arrived at Brandon's room, quite small with only one little window, but it was very close to Lady Selby's room as she had requested. Brandon was lying face-down on the bed with the doctor bent over him. He had been stripped to the waist. Blood smeared one shoulder.

"Don't stand there hovering, young lady" the doctor said. "Come here and make yourself useful."

Emma hurried to the other side of the bed. Brandon's eyes were closed and his pallor nearly matched the color of the white bed linens. Panic tightened her chest. Was he dead? Had Stephen's shot accomplished what he'd set out to do?

The doctor glanced up at her. "He's lost consciousness. Lost a fair amount of blood. And I've dosed him with a large quantity of rum that hasn't been poisoned. Don't worry, young lady, he hasn't expired yet. Now, sop up that blood coming from his wound so I can see to dig out the ball."

Relief rushed through her. Emma quickly washed her hands and did as she was told, cringing as the doctor dug around in the hole in Brandon's back. She hoped his forceps were clean. Within a few moments, the doctor exclaimed in triumph and held up the bloody metal ball.

"Got it," he said. He plopped it into an empty glass on the bedside table and took up a small pitcher. "Only a flesh wound. No vital organs hit. We'll want to clean this out." He poured the clear liquid onto the wound.

Brandon moaned, and Emma smelled vinegar. At least the doctor was using some sort of antiseptic. Then she pressed against the wound to stop the bleeding.

"All we need do is sew him up, and he'll be right as rain," the doctor said. "I'm Philby, by the way. I don't think we've been properly introduced."

"Emma Blake," she replied. "Thank you for taking care of him, Doctor Philby."

"Had to." He cleared his throat. "He might be the next earl."

"Yes, he might." Emma gazed down at Brandon and brushed the hair away from his eyes. She was surprised when he clasped her fingers.

"Is he done yet?" Brandon murmured, then sucked in a breath as the doctor stitched up his shoulder.

The doctor finally finished and left after bandaging the

wound. Emma knelt beside the bed and swallowed the lump in her throat.

"I'm very glad you're okay," she said.

He smiled. "I'm very glad I'm okay, as well."

"I don't know what I would have done if you had—" She couldn't say the word.

"Died?" he supplied, with an ironic lift to his brow.

She nodded and dropped her gaze to his mouth. Her voice was shaky as she continued. "You see, there's something...that is, I wanted to tell you..." Taking a breath, looking into those smoky eyes, she blurted, "I love you."

Quickly, she lowered her gaze. She couldn't look at him, couldn't see the rejection in his eyes, so she focused on the pattern of the counterpane beneath him. A bird on a vine, its beak open and proclaiming its song to a world of leaves and flowers made of colored threads that would never care. That's how she felt. Brandon would never love her. He still loved his Elizabeth and no one would replace her.

He tipped up her chin with a finger. "Is that so?"

Her eyes met his. "Yes. I know that Elizabeth was the love of your life, but I wanted you to know how I feel. I nearly lost you today. I thought my heart would stop when I saw Stephen with that pistol."

He rubbed his thumb across her lips. "I'm very glad your heart didn't stop." He smiled. "Because I love you, too."

Emma sucked in a breath. "You do?"

"Um-hm." He rolled to his good side and patted the

empty space beside him. "Come up here so I can tell you how much."

She climbed up and stretched out beside him. He smelled of rum and vinegar, but she didn't care. Brandon was alive and he loved her.

"How much do you love me?" she asked, giddy with the knowledge.

"I love you as much as the bees love flowers," he said as he kissed her nose. "I love you as much as the ocean waves love the shore." He kissed a corner of her mouth. "I love you as much as horses love hay." He kissed the other corner. "I love you as much as frogs love flies." He nuzzled her neck.

Sputtering a laugh at his silly comparison, she waited for him to go on. Instead, she heard a soft snore. He had fallen asleep, the result of the trauma of being shot and the rum he had consumed. But that was all right.

Because Brandon loved her.

But he had never mentioned anything about wanting her to remain in his time.

Twenty-One

⌒⌒⌒

Three days later, Emma, Brandon and Lady Selby were having tea in a small drawing room. They were going to remain at Cranleigh Manor for several more days, so Brandon could recover from his wound and ensure that the estate continued running smoothly. He was up and about, having had only a slight fever the day after being shot, and grumbled about his arm being in a sling and not able to do anything by himself. Emma merely smiled and reminded him to be patient.

The earl had been buried the day before in the family vault on the estate after a simple service in the small village church. Many of the villagers had attended, and Brandon solemnly thanked them, one by one, for coming. Emma was surprised at their genuine grief. Evidently, the earl had been a popular landlord. Many of the villagers knew Brandon from when he was a boy and seemed fond of him.

Stephen had not been present. He'd been missing since he had shot Brandon. The justice of the peace and his constables, along with several volunteers, had searched the vicinity, but to no avail. Stephen had disappeared without a trace. Emma wondered if he had already made off for France.

Brandon was in the midst of explaining one of the complicated relationships between several families in the area when Halsey, the butler, entered. "Excuse me, sir. You have a visitor." He held out a small silver server to Brandon.

"A visitor? We're in mourning. No visitors for a week." Brandon slipped a small, white calling card from the server. "Good God! The Duke of Dunbary is here! I thought he was still on his wedding trip. Show him in immediately, Halsey." To Emma, he explained, "One of Dunbary's estates is not far from here. His father and my father often shot grouse together. I haven't seen him since we were boys. He must have come to pay his respects."

An elegant, handsome man, about Brandon's age, strode into the room. His dark hair with lighter streaks was tousled fashionably, and his eyes were an arresting topaz color. Brandon bowed and Emma curtsied.

"I am very sorry for the loss of your father, Connaught." Dunbary turned to Lady Selby with a bow. "Very good to see you again, my lady."

Lady Selby's eyes crinkled in pleasure. "You are looking

well, Dunbary. Marriage seems to agree with you. Please, send my regards to your delightful wife."

With a nod and a smile, Dunbary said, "I will relay your message, Lady Selby."

Emma sensed a mystery there, maybe even an adventure. She would have to quiz Lady Selby to see if the story could be turned into a book.

Brandon turned to Emma. "This is—ah—Mrs. Blake, from America."

The duke bowed. "A pleasure to meet you, Mrs. Blake. My wife mentioned an American lady creating a stir in London. Now I can understand why."

Emma blushed. "You are too kind, your grace." She indicated a chair. "Please. May we offer you some tea?"

"No, thank you." As Dunbary sat, his demeanor became solemn. "Forgive me for disturbing your period of mourning, Connaught. I have some sad news to relay, and I felt I must inform you in person. I apologize for bringing it so soon after the death of your father." He paused a moment. "Your half-brother, the Viscount Pemberton, is dead."

Emma and Lady Selby gasped.

Brandon didn't move. He barely breathed.

Finally he said, "Can you tell me what happened?"

Dunbary glanced at Lady Selby and Emma. "Perhaps this isn't the time to reveal that."

Lady Selby sniffed in indignation. "I may be old, Dunbary, but I am not a fragile flower."

The duke ducked his head in a nod, hiding the twitch of his lips. "Of course, Lady Selby. Please, forgive me." He turned to Brandon. "He was shot while trying to escape to France."

"Oh, my." Emma fell back in her chair. Stephen, not Brandon, was the one with the bullet hole. The irony made her head spin. And made her wonder if her trip back in time had changed events. Had she "fixed things?"

The exclamation made the duke turn to her. "This might be too sordid and violent for ladies' ears."

"I won't faint," she said. "I was surprised, that's all. Was he shot in the back?" As soon as she asked, she realized that a proper nineteenth century woman wouldn't have wanted to know such things. But *she* needed to know.

Dunbary looked at her askance. "I believe he was."

"Mrs. Blake is an authoress," Brandon quickly explained. "She uses such details in her adventure stories."

"I see," Dunbary said. "I will have to tell my duchess. I'm sure she'll want to read one of your books."

Emma opened her mouth to explain that nothing she'd written was available. Instead, she graciously thanked him. Would she be writing in this century? Or would she be going back to her own time and her career there? But that decision was for later, because Mrs. Edwards still had her bracelet with the charm. Besides, Brandon might not want her here. She focused on the duke and what he had come to say.

Turning back to Brandon, Dunbary pulled a packet from

inside his coat and laid it on the tea table. As he unfolded the papers, he said, "Because of my connection to the Foreign Office, your father sent these to me and asked me to look into them. He mentioned that you and Mrs. Blake had discovered them." He turned his topaz gaze on Emma. "If you please, could you tell me where you found these?"

She blinked as she concluded that the man before her either spied for the English Crown or knew those who did. Glancing down at what he'd laid out, she saw the coded messages she and Brandon had discovered.

She pointed to the burned scrap. "This one was in Lord Farley's possession. I saw Sir Dotson pass a note to Viscount Pemberton at Tattersall's, so 'at the horses' could refer to that."

His brows rose in surprise. "Sir Dotson? I didn't realize he was involved. We'll have to look into that." He indicated the other two. "What of these?"

"They were in Viscount Pemberton's possession," she said.

"I won't ask how they came into *your* possession," the duke said with a wry twist to his lips.

Emma shifted on her seat. His words echoed the earl's question nearly word for word.

Without waiting for an answer, Dunbary said, "We have been watching Lord and Lady Farley for some time, so this confirms what we suspected. They have been passing information to Napoleon and using their acquaintances to help them. We apprehended Farley, his wife, and Pemberton as they were boarding a boat in Dover. They were attempting an escape across the Channel to Calais. Unfortunately, Pemberton did not surrender and tried to run. One of the young soldiers became over-zealous and shot him. I'm terribly sorry."

"Thank you for your condolences," Brandon said. "My half-brother and I were never close."

"I gathered that," the duke said wryly. "I spoke to the justice of the peace before I came. He told me that your brother shot you, and that your father was poisoned, most likely by Pemberton." He shook his head. "The earl was a good neighbor. We will miss him."

Brandon murmured his thanks.

The duke gathered up the papers and tucked them back inside his coat. When he stood, he said to Brandon, "I will pass along your information in a report to the Foreign Office." Then he smiled. "I have the feeling we'll be seeing more of each other. My duchess is eager to meet the heir to the Cranleigh title." He bowed to Lady Selby and Emma. "Ladies, good day to you both." After shaking hands with Brandon, he left.

Silence settled into the room. Emma stared at Brandon and he stared back as the import of what they had just learned stunned them both. Brandon would be named the Earl of Cranleigh. He had gained the title he had sought for so long. But at a great cost. The tragedy of his father's murder and the dishonor of Stephen's treason would always be with him. How would he deal with such scandal and loss?

"Well, that's settled then," Lady Selby said as she rang for the butler. When he appeared, she said, "Please fetch something stronger than tea, Halsey." Turning to Brandon, she said, "We have a great deal to discuss. There are many official matters to be dealt with."

"I will contact my solicitor in the morning," Brandon said, looking a bit shaken.

Halsey returned with a decanter and three glasses on a tray. "Irish whiskey, sir, ah, my lord," he said. "Your father kept it for special occasions." He poured generous amounts into each glass and left.

Lady Selby picked up her glass. "*Irish* whiskey," she murmured.

"For my mother?" Brandon wondered as he picked up a glass.

"Maybe he cared for her more than you realize," Emma suggested, picking up the third glass. "And he believed you about Stephen, otherwise he wouldn't have sent those notes to the duke."

Brandon shook his head in disbelief.

"I think he cared for you as well," she added. "More than you think."

Lady Selby raised her glass. "To the Earl of Cranleigh!" she exclaimed, her voice thick with emotion.

Emma's eyes filled with tears. "To the Earl of Cranleigh!"

Brandon raised his glass. "To my father!"

EMMA HAD NO TIME TO SPEAK PRIVATELY WITH BRANDON THAT evening, because he shut himself in his father's study and asked that he not be disturbed. She found him asleep the next morning, with his head cradled on his arms and sprawled across the desk, piles of papers scattered around him. They traveled to London that day, and like their trip to the estate, Brandon rode his horse, while Emma and Lady Selby rode in the coach. But that lady dozed for most of the trip, so Emma was left with her own thoughts, which whirled inside her head.

When Mrs. Edwards returned her bracelet, she would be able to travel back to her own time. But did she want to do that? She would miss her sisters if she stayed. And she loved Brandon. But he had indicated that she should return to the future. Stay or go? The question repeated over and over in her head, but she had no answer, and she wasn't sure she was able to make that decision. The oak tree and her pendant seemed to be in charge of her time traveling.

They didn't arrive at Brandon's townhouse until after dark. After partaking of a cold supper, everyone retired early. But Emma couldn't sleep. She tossed and turned as she worried. What was Brandon thinking? Did he truly love her? Had his declaration to her merely been the result of being shot and the rum the doctor had given him?

Should she stay in the past? She felt an affinity to the time. Somehow, she seemed to fit, despite not being able to do needlework or ride a horse, or dance properly. But needlework and horse riding and dancing and fashion had nothing to do with leaving her sisters or Brandon's feelings for her. No answer came to her.

She climbed from bed, lit a taper and headed downstairs to get a book. As she approached the study, the flickering of a fire on the grate and a single lit lamp told her Brandon was awake as well. Not wanting to intrude if he didn't want to be disturbed, she hovered at the threshold. He was mostly hidden by the back of the chair where he sat before the fire, but she could see his bare feet beyond the hem of his banyan as they rested on a stool.

"Your company would be welcome," he said.

Emma entered and sat in the chair across from him. "I didn't want to disturb you." She noticed he had removed his sling, and he held a snifter of brandy.

He smiled. "I believe I need to be disturbed. I've been thinking very hard all day."

"What have you been thinking?" She placed her taper on the table beside her, the light reflecting in his gray eyes, turning them silvery.

His gaze dropped to his glass, and he said, "I discovered a

letter among my father's papers asking his solicitor to begin legal proceedings to adopt me as his legitimate son."

"Then he truly did care for you. And as the elder son, you would inherit everything, disinheriting Stephen." She wanted to cheer at his father's validation, but his reserved manner held her back.

"Yes. I never wanted the title to come to me like this, with Stephen's treachery and death." Turning to stare into the fire, he said, "I wish my father and I had been closer." He took a sip of brandy, then turned those gray eyes on her. "I have been thinking about my new responsibilities."

One of his responsibilities included siring an heir. Emma's gaze wandered to the toy soldiers arrayed on a table across the room. A few more had appeared, including the one she had found in Ivy House, and their formation was different. What sort of woman would he choose as his wife and mother of his child?

He took another sip from his glass. "I will need a countess."

Emma's heart plummeted. As an earl, he would need a proper nineteenth-century lady. That could never be her. She knew this moment was coming. While she had struggled with the decision to stay or return to her own time, in the back of her mind had always been the hope that Brandon would want her to stay, that he wanted something permanent. But of course, he couldn't have that with her. He was an earl. She was from the future. Not a member of the ton.

Unsuitable as the wife of an earl. Besides, that flimsy story of being his cousin from America would surely be discovered as a lie. Scandal would follow. More scandal to pile on the scandal of his father's murder and Stephen's treachery. No, he wouldn't want her as his wife.

Abruptly, she had an answer to her question. All her tossing and turning, all her worrying about the question of stay or go seemed a useless waste of energy. She knew what she wanted to do. Now that she had figured out that Brandon couldn't possibly want her, she wanted to stay. In the past. With Brandon. The irony nearly made her laugh aloud hysterically.

"My countess will need to be proficient in many things," he said.

"Of course." The words strangled in her throat.

"She will need to be gracious and graceful, kind and loving."

"Those are excellent qualities." *She* could be kind and loving. She wasn't so sure about gracious and graceful.

He tipped his head. "I would like her to be beautiful."

"A beautiful countess is a plus," she said dryly.

"She must be able to dance well, and, of course, be able to sit well on a horse."

Emma's mouth turned down. She was disqualified on both those points.

"And obedient," he added. "I cannot have my countess poking into matters that don't concern her."

"That would be shocking," she agreed falsely.

"I believe I've found the perfect woman." He placed his glass on the table beside him.

"Oh. How...wonderful for you." She could barely say the words. Her heart hurt. Of course he had found someone, most likely someone he knew before she had dropped into his life.

A tiny line appeared between his brows. "You seem rather unenthusiastic about my decision."

"I am happy for you, my lord," she said, standing, wanting to escape to her room and cry. "I'm very tired. If you'll excuse me, I think I'll retire."

As she took a step to leave, he rose and grabbed her hand. "Emma. Don't go. Please."

She stopped, but wouldn't look at him. He couldn't see the tears that clouded her eyes.

"Emma, my love, please forgive me," he said. "I was jesting. Do you really think I care if a woman can ride a horse or dance well?" He went down on one knee. "Emma Blake, you are the perfect woman. Will you marry me?"

Her mouth dropped open. She stared at him. "But—but —but all those things you mentioned. I'm not any of those."

"You are all of them, and more." He placed a gentle kiss on her palm. "You are gracious and graceful. You are kind and loving. You are brave and loyal and intelligent. If you had not poked into things that didn't concern you, I never would have become the Earl of Cranleigh. I love you."

She swallowed against the lump in her throat.

He stood and framed her face with his hands. "I know you are not from this time, and I know you wanted to return to your own time. I will understand if that's what you wish." He took a shaky breath. "I will miss you if you go, more than I can express. You have become part of me."

Emma took his hand and placed it over her heart. "You have become part of me, too. I think I belong here, in your time."

Hope blazed in his eyes. "Emma Blake," he repeated, "will you be my wife? Will you be my Countess of Cranleigh?"

Her decision was already made. "Yes! Yes, yes, yes! A thousand times yes!" Happiness bloomed in every molecule. Somehow, she would get word to her sisters and share her news.

He stood, wrapped her in his arms, and kissed her thoroughly.

That kiss, loving, possessive, arousing, made her want to put her hands all over him. When she unbuttoned his banyan, she discovered he was naked beneath. Oh, yes! So she explored. Somehow, she lost her nightrail. Somehow, he maneuvered her to the couch. Somehow, she found herself straddling him as he sprawled across the cushions.

His mouth was all over her, licking, sucking her breasts, worshiping her mouth. His hands were everywhere, touching, arousing, making her moan. He groaned when she slid onto his shaft. And then nothing mattered except the man who pumped into her and brought her to mindless bliss.

When they had finished, when they both were drunk on the sweet aftermath of their lovemaking, Emma was draped across him.

"Brandon?" she said.

"Hmm?"

"I have something to tell you."

"Yes?"

"I can have children. I've had shots of something called a contraceptive."

"Shots?" Worry darkened his eyes. "Have you been shot as well?"

She shook her head. "No, nothing like that. I'll explain that later. But a contraceptive prevents pregnancy for a while, then it wears off. A lot of women from my time use it to prevent having children. But I haven't had any shots since I've been in this century. We might have just made a baby."

He was silent for a very long moment. And then he laughed. Wrapping his arms tighter around her, he said, "I am very much going to enjoy being married to my wily, disobedient countess."

Emma smiled. And she was going to enjoy being married to her honorable, teasing earl with the very talented hands.

Twenty-Two

Two weeks later, Emma sat at her dressing table and unbraided her hair. In a few short hours, she would be wed to Brandon. She would be the Countess of Cranleigh. Unbelievable. She was living in a fairy tale. Her very own romance.

Since they had arrived back in London, Brandon had visits from several solicitors. He was the heir to the title, so legal matters had to be settled. In addition to Cranleigh Manor and his father's London townhouse, Brandon discovered that he also owned two other smaller estates. He was already financially secure, but his inheritance made him extremely wealthy.

He had opened his father's townhouse for her to occupy with Lady Selby, while he stayed at his more modest bachelor's house. Appearances, he had told her, were everything in the world of society. The townhouse was grand, a mansion with an impressive entry, sweeping staircase, and multiple drawing rooms and bedrooms. Getting used to living in such a large house would take some time.

Running a brush through her hair, she could see through a doorway into the dressing room next door, where maids tittered and fussed as they laid out her wedding clothes and prepared her bath. She was sitting in the mistress's bedchamber, a large airy room dominated by a canopy bed with lovely ivory hangings embroidered in a colorful, floral pattern.

Despite the appearance of living apart, she and Brandon still managed to sneak most nights together, making love, snuggling together and whispering about their future. Until Lady Selby put a stop to that. A week ago, she had accosted Brandon very early one morning just before he crept out the front door and castigated him for his "impetuous behavior." Then later at breakfast, Emma had been subjected to a lecture on decorum and the role a countess must play. From that point on, Emma had only seen Brandon for tea, and strolls through Hyde Park, and dinner on two nights, because Lady Selby said that was enough until they were wed. Emma hadn't seen him at all yesterday, because it was bad luck for the groom to see the bride the night before the wedding, one tradition that had been passed down through the centuries. She missed him.

As she stood to go bathe, something in the mirror caught her eye. A small area in the room behind her had turned blurry. She heard a pop, and then a man suddenly appeared near the foot of the bed. With a gasp, she swung around. It was Roger Bowker.

Anxiety made her heart race. She glanced through the doorway into the dressing room, The two maids were still chattering away, but she could call them if she needed. "How did you get here?" she demanded. "Get out!"

"No, I don't think so, my lady," he said. "But you aren't a countess yet, are you? Only a *missus*." He shook his head. "No, no even that. Just a *miss*. Miss Blake. Emma Blake. With no man's name to protect you."

While his tone was mild, his words threatened. Emma edged back and tried to think of something close enough that she could use for a weapon.

"If you don't leave, I'll call the servants." She glanced down at the dressing table. The only thing she saw was a perfume bottle, a hairbrush and a small dish with hairpins. None would make a very effective weapon.

"I don't believe you want to call the servants," he said. "I think you might want to hear what I have to say."

"Why would I listen to anything you say? You have invaded my room. My home." Her chin went up.

"I apologize for that." He motioned to the opening into the dressing room. "Close the door, Emma."

Her caution urged her to call the servants. Her curiosity made her hesitate.

"I won't touch you," he said. "I give you my word."

Emma put as much faith in his word as she would a con artist. But she did as he asked. She suspected he wasn't here to attack her, but for something else entirely. Mrs. Edwards had warned her about his desire to time travel.

When she had closed the door, she asked, "How did you get in here?"

He smirked. "I was wondering when you'd ask about that. I used a little device that my father invented. Unfortunately, it doesn't work quite the way I want."

She remembered how he had seemed to suddenly appear and then disappear at Vauxhall Gardens and again at Cranleigh Manor. "It transports you from place to place?" How had he been able to achieve that, when scientists from the twenty-first century hadn't been able to? This was the stuff of science fiction.

"It only transports me a few minutes forward or back." He took a step forward. "But you have been able to jump through centuries."

Emma shook her head in denial and lied, pretending disbelief. "Jumping through centuries? I don't know where you got that idea. I came by ship from America."

"I don't believe you did. I believe you traveled quite a bit faster."

Despite his apparent mild manner, his threatening step forward made her wary. He seemed dangerous, so she was not about to reveal anything. She gave a skeptical little laugh. "You are very imaginative, Mr. Bowker."

"Yes, I am," he acknowledged. "I can imagine many things. Including how this came to be manufactured." Opening his hand, he showed her the patch that had torn from her leggings when Brandon had nearly run her down in Hyde Park. "I believe this is yours." He stretched it this way and that as he examined it. "This is very advanced science. Or magic." Meeting her gaze, he held it up. "This fabric is magical, returning to its original shape after it is pulled and stretched. I found it near the old oak tree after you drove away. It seemed to match the scandalous pantaloons you wore. Tell me, Emma, when did you acquire such a garment?"

"I don't know what you are talking about." She imitated Lady Selby's sniff.

"You are from the future," he accused. "I'm not sure which century, but I will find out. And you will take me there."

So that's what he wanted—her help to travel forward in time. Emma had a feeling whatever he wanted to do in the future wouldn't be good. The man frightened her, but she couldn't let him know that. Her only recourse was to pretend skepticism. And she could always call the maids in the next room.

She released a light laugh. "Oh, Mr. Bowker, you are quite droll. The future, you say? The only future I know of is the one immediately before me where I am to wed the Earl of Cranleigh. Now if you will excuse me, I must get ready."

As she turned to the door of her dressing room, he grabbed her arm. "Not so fast. You will give me the device that helped you travel through time, Emma Blake, or I will—"

He halted, distracted by Lady Selby's voice coming from the dressing room as she spoke to the maids.

"You will what?" She wrenched out of his grasp.

With an evil smile, he bowed. "I'll leave you to prepare for your wedding. Think very carefully on my request." Pocketing the bit of material, he pulled out a pocket watch. He fiddled with the knob, turning it one way, then another. As his outline became blurry, he said, "We have not finished, Emma Blake." Then he faded away.

Emma heard a pop just as Lady Selby swept into the room.

"Haven't you bathed yet?" she demanded. "Stop mooning about. We must hurry if you are to be ready in time."

"Yes, of course," Emma murmured, shaken by Bowker's visit. She turned to the dressing room, but Lady Selby stopped her with a hand on her arm.

"Are you well?" that lady asked. "You appear quite ashen."

"I —" Emma was about to say that she was fine, but changed her mind. Lady Selby knew about Bowker, and would be a strong ally if he began to spread rumors. "Roger Bowker was here," she said. "He just popped in."

"Here?" Lady Selby exclaimed. "In your bedchamber?"

"He has the ability to jump from place to place," Emma said.

Lady Selby's mouth flattened. "Then you must have someone with you at all times."

Emma opened her mouth to argue, then shut it when she realized that was an argument for later. Besides, she had the feeling Brandon would be her protector. Instead, she told the lady about Bowker's unfinished threat.

"Hmph," Lady Selby snorted. "My nephew will deal with any threat that man might make. Don't concern yourself." She smiled. "Now come along. There is much to do. I wish my new niece to dazzle my nephew."

"Niece?" Emma blurted.

"Yes. You may call me Aunt Morrin." Then she swept into the dressing room.

Bemused and glad that the lady was on her side, Emma followed her into the room where her bath and all the frippery for her wedding waited.

A FEW HOURS LATER, EMMA SAT IN THE COACH AND STARED AT the door to the chapel. It stood open, the entrance to the next phase of her life. On the other side, at the far end of the aisle, Brandon would be waiting for her. She would be making a commitment to him, to become his wife, his countess. And she would be committing herself to remaining in this century.

She might never see her sisters again, because she didn't know if she could travel back to her own time again. An ache clutched at her heart, a shadow over her joy.

Somehow, she would let them know where she was and that she was happy. She swallowed the lump in her throat. Her tears were startled dry when the door to the coach opened. Mrs. Edwards stepped in and sat across from her.

"I'm sorry to intrude in such a manner, but I wanted you to have this." The woman dangled her bracelet.

"Oh, thank you!" Emma wrapped her fingers around the pendant. It would be her something blue, for good luck. Her something borrowed was a creamy string of pearls that Lady Selby had clasped around her neck at the last minute. Her something old was a strip torn from her tee shirt she was wearing when she first landed in the nineteenth century. She had trimmed it with lace and tied it around her thigh as a garter. Her something new was her gown, a sleek column of white satin.

Mrs. Edwards didn't release the bracelet. "You are making a commitment to the man waiting inside the chapel. This brought you to him. You may not use it to break that commitment."

"Oh, I would never..." Her words trailed off at the piercing gaze she saw through the woman's veil.

"Are you sure you wish to remain in this century?" Mrs. Edwards asked.

Emma's hand dropped away from the pendant. She had gone over and over this in her mind.

"It's just that..." Bowing her head, she threaded her fingers together. "My sisters are in the future." Tears threatened as she glanced up at Mrs. Edwards. "I'll never see them again."

The lady was silent for a heartbeat. Then gently, she asked, "Are you sure about that?"

The challenge in Mrs. Edwards' question gave Emma hope. "Well, they each have their own pendant."

"Do they? Then perhaps they will find themselves transported to this century," Mrs. Edwards said.

Hearing the lady state that seemed to make it more possible and eased the pain of separation from them. Brandon was here in this century. And she loved him more than she ever imagined loving anyone.

With a determined nod, she declared, "I wish to stay."

Mrs. Edwards smiled. "Then I return this to you with my blessings." She wrapped the bracelet with its dangling pendant around Emma's wrist and snapped it closed. Then she curled her fingers around Emma's wrist. "My door will always open to you for whatever you might need."

The woman's grasp around her wrist was strong, but soothing. Emma felt she could tell her anything and she would try to help. "Bowker popped into my bedchamber this morning."

Mrs. Edwards released her wrist and sat back. "Did he?" she shook her head. "That man is becoming too bold and dangerous. I will have to think on what can be done. But that is not for today." She cupped Emma's cheek. "Go marry your earl, Emma Blake. I wish you well."

Through the woman's veil, Emma saw tears glitter in the woman's eyes. "Please, come to my wedding."

The woman's hand dropped from Emma's cheek and she shook her head. "That is kind of you. Thank you, but no." Without another word, she climbed out of the coach.

Emma watched her walk away, seeming to fade into the distance. A mysterious woman, to be sure, but somehow, in her presence, Emma felt comfort. She wondered about the odd question the woman had asked about remaining in this time before wrapping the bracelet around her wrist. If she had answered differently, would Mrs. Edward's have returned it? She didn't want to examine the possibility of that. But what motive would the woman have for wanting her to remain in this century? No answer came to mind.

Lifting her wrist, she watched the light catch the sapphire and diamond pendant. It had brought her here, to this point in time. To changing the direction of her life. To Brandon, who waited inside. She glanced at the door to the chapel. It was time to meet her husband-to-be.

OUTWARDLY CALM, BRANDON STOOD ANXIOUSLY BEFORE THE altar as the music of a single violin filled the chapel. He had not seen Emma at all yesterday, and he missed her. What if she had changed her mind about marrying him? What if she had decided to return to her own time?

Panic tightened his chest. How could he go on without her? If she returned to her own time, how would he find her? Would she be lost to him forever?

The pain of losing Elizabeth had been unbearable, but over time, he had begun to heal. While he had loved Elizabeth, he realized that she had not been his true love. Only Emma completed him in a way he never thought possible. If he lost Emma, the pain would be intolerable. He had never expected to love again, and certainly not a woman from the future. She was unique. A gift. Spirited. Intelligent. Courageous. Beautiful. Sensuous. Delicious.

Where was she?

The silhouette of a woman appeared in the open doors of the chapel. Emma. His love.

His panic receded. He watched her approach, her steps measured and graceful. When she reached him, she smiled. He held out his hand, and she placed her slender fingers in his palm.

"I love you," she whispered.

"I adore you," he whispered back.

Then he turned with her to the priest.

To seal their love.

To seal their future.

Epilogue

E mma sat in a sunny corner of the morning room in the Earl of Cranleigh's townhouse. The day before, she had wed Brandon, the Earl of Cranleigh. She was now the Countess of Cranleigh. She still couldn't believe it.

The Earl of Cranleigh and his new countess had retired early from the wedding luncheon apparently because of the recent, tragic events in the family. In reality, Brandon had swept her away. After carrying her over the threshold of the townhouse and up to the earl's suite, he had undressed her slowly, sensuously, until she thought she might burst into flames. They had made love, sometimes hot, sometimes slow and luxurious, through the rest of the afternoon and into the night.

Emma smiled. Her earl was a magnificent, generous lover. She had left him this morning, still asleep, sprawled across most of the bed. Tempted to wake him with a caress, she had decided he needed to regain his strength. She had donned a silky robe and come downstairs to write in her journal. For now, she had a few moments for herself.

The day before had been more than she ever dreamed, like a fairytale. Except for the intrusion of Bowker. When she had told Brandon about him after their wedding luncheon, her new husband had wanted to hire Bow Street Runners immediately to track him down and warn him to stay away. She had convinced him that she was safe because he was with her. Hiring the Bow Street Runners could wait a day or two.

A step behind her alerted her that Brandon was awake. His hand landed on her shoulder and his fingers trailed up her neck. A delicious thrill shot through her.

"You were gone when I awoke," he murmured in her ear. "I missed you. Are you coming back to bed?" His tongue caressed the pulse that beat in her throat.

Emma's head tipped to the side, allowing him better access. "Mm, yes." She reached up and tangled her fingers in his hair. "I'll be there in a few minutes."

His mouth captured her lips. When she was breathless from the kiss, he whispered, "Don't be long. I'm impatient to explore the toes of my new countess. And the backs of her knees. And perhaps the inside of her elbow."

She smiled. "I can't wait."

Trailing his fingers across her breast, he retreated, leaving her throbbing and impatient to finish her journal. She would just write one line.

The memory of the first appearance of Ghost Brandon as she had finished her historical romance came to her. She had just typed "THE END." But this was her romance. So instead of *The End*, in her journal, she wrote...

THE BEGINNING

I hope you enjoyed reading
ENTANGLED WITH THE EARL
Rogues Out of Time Series ~ Book 1

Please consider leaving a review or a rating
on Amazon by clicking or scanning
the following QR Code:

Keep reading for a Free Preview of
MISCHIEF WITH THE MARQUIS
Rogues Out of Time Series ~ Book 2
Sincerely,
Patricia

Mischief
with the Marquis
ROGUES OUT OF TIME BOOK 2
PATRICIA BARLETTA

Free Preview 1

MISCHIEF WITH THE MARQUIS

ROGUES OUT OF TIME ~ BOOK 2

LONDON, PRESENT DAY

After an overnight flight to London, Maggie relished the freedom of a jog through Hyde Park. Directly from Heathrow Airport, she had gone to her dad's flat, the one he had owned so he would have a place to stay on his extended buying trips to England. It was where Emma had been staying, and when Maggie walked in, she half-expected to see Emma sitting at the desk and staring at her computer. But her sister wasn't there.

After a quick search through the rooms, she discovered Emma's clothes and her purse, with her passport and money still inside. The flat looked like her sister might show up any minute and apologize for not being there to welcome Maggie. As she contacted the police and Scotland Yard and the American Embassy to let them know she was in London, she waited for her sister to come sailing in the door. But Emma never appeared. Where was she?

That question ran through Maggie's head in a loop as she jogged, but she had no answer. Distracted by trying to figure out where her sister might be, she slowly became aware that the tiny, delicate gold key hanging on a thin chain around her neck had turned warm, then suddenly scorching hot. Burning where it touched her skin. She stopped short as a hiss of pain whistled through her teeth. Pulling the key from beneath her tee shirt, she let it dangle in the breeze to cool it down and wondered what had caused it to turn so hot.

Hanging next to the key on the chain was the sapphire and diamond pendant, shaped like a flower bud, that had come from a necklace belonging to her mother. She had died when Maggie was barely a toddler. Her other two sisters each had a pendant exactly like it. As it dangled, a ray of sun pierced the deep shade thrown by the huge oak tree next to her and lit up the jeweled pendant, as if some magical element had been triggered. The effect was mesmerizing. Other-worldly. Then it faded. Weird.

Maggie glanced around to see if anyone had noticed, if anyone else seemed as shocked as she was by the phenomenon. But the few people nearby appeared unaffected. Located in the middle of London, Hyde Park looked as it always did in mid-morning in early summer. People ambled along the paths, a few nannies pushed their young charges in strollers, several diplomatic types hurried across the freshly mowed lawn. No one seemed to have noticed anything out of the ordinary. She stepped off the path and flopped onto the grass beneath the enormous old oak tree that looked like it might house a whole colony of elves. Pulling the chain over her head, she checked beneath her tee shirt for signs of a burn on her skin. Nothing was there, not even a red mark. Weird again.

Holding up the chain, she watched the key swing slowly next to the pendant, as if the two were dancing together. The little key was a lovely thing, its head an intricate filigree of gold. She imagined that it fit into the lock on a beautiful, antique, carved wooden box that held a lady's jewels.

For her last birthday, just months before her father's untimely death, he had told her to choose anything she wanted from his antique shop, the one she had inherited and now owned, stocked with only the best antiques, high-end items that sold in the thousands, occasionally in the tens of thousands. The key had lain in a dusty corner of the single display case in the shop for as long as she could remember, an anomaly that contrasted sharply with the other exquisite items for sale. She had always wanted the tiny trinket from the time she had first spied it when she was a little girl.

When he'd given it to her, he told her it was the key to her heart, to be given away to the man of her dreams. She'd laughed because she didn't see any "hero" in her future, despite the fact that her older sister, who made her living writing about romance heroes, kept telling her that everyone should have a happily-ever-after. Maggie's relationships with men had been minimal and brief, either ending in disappointment or fading into nothing, for which she was glad because she couldn't see herself spending the rest of her life with any of the men she'd dated. She hadn't been with a man for over a year.

The key was a cherished reminder of her dad. The sapphire pendant hanging on the chain beside it was a keepsake from the mother she didn't remember, because she had been too young when her mom died. But her dad had always spoken of her as if a part of his heart was missing. For some reason, Maggie felt that the two items, the pendant and the key, needed to be together.

With a sigh, she closed her fingers around the trinkets and leaned back on her elbows. She blinked back tears as that tug of loss assailed her again.

The loss of her mother, whom she never knew, was a void that her dad did his best to try to fill. Then she'd lost him a year ago when the small, two-seater plane he'd been piloting crashed into Cape Cod Bay. Now Emma, who had come to London to finish her historical romance, had gone missing. The last time Maggie had talked with her, Emma had said that she was working furiously on her manuscript because her editor wanted it earlier than the original due date. And then she had mysteriously disappeared.

When Maggie saw that all of Emma's belongings were

still at the flat, as if she had just stepped out for a moment, a chill went through her. Emma had been gone for days. Was she injured and lying in a ditch somewhere? Had she been kidnapped? Maggie didn't want to think about the worst possibility—that she was gone. The police hadn't been able to pick up any clues to her whereabouts, and she'd heard nothing from Scotland Yard or the American Embassy. Maggie missed her sister and worried about her. Something terrible might have happened to her. But wouldn't she know in her heart if Emma was dead?

The key warmed in her palm, then turned very hot again.

Sitting up, she opened her fingers and let the chain swing in the air.

"What the devil...?"

The man's voice came from somewhere nearby. Maggie glanced over her shoulder, but the expanse of grass behind her was empty.

"*What the devil...!*"

The agitated exclamation came again, this time from above. The branches of the oak tree over her head thrashed wildly, as if they were in the middle of a mini storm, but she felt no wind. The sun still shone brightly, and the sky was blue. Something whizzed past her. Ducking, she threw her arms over her head for protection. She heard a thud on the ground and a grunt of pain.

"*WHAT THE DEVIL...?!*"

She peeked between her fingers. A man lay sprawled on

the grass in front of her. Where had he come from? Maybe he had fallen out of the tree. That would explain the thrashing branches. But what had he been doing up there? Spying? He rolled to his hands and knees and shook his head as if to clear it, then climbed to his feet and brushed himself off as he surveyed his surroundings.

Maggie slipped her chain back over her head, scrambled up and backed away a step, just in case she needed to run. Strangers falling out of trees didn't happen every day. He might have been up there for a perfectly innocent reason. Or not.

He was quite tall, probably about six feet, maybe a little more, and he was dressed — Wait. How was he dressed? She blinked, then squinted, trying to decide if her eyes were playing tricks. No, she wasn't seeing things. He was dressed in tight, buckskin breeches tucked into high boots and a soft, white, full-sleeved linen shirt, open at the neck. He looked all decked out for a historical costume drama. Maybe he was an actor and had been hiding from the film crew working on that historical costume drama.

"Hi," she said. "Are you all right?"

He swung around, took one look at her, and immediately turned his back. "I beg your pardon. I did not mean to intrude upon your — your —" He gave a helpless wave of his hand.

"It's okay. You didn't interrupt anything."

"No?" Peeking over his shoulder, he quickly turned away

again. "Then why are you...?" He took a deep breath. "Where are the rest of your clothes?"

Glancing down at her tee shirt and running shorts, she saw nothing was missing. "These are all my clothes."

He swiveled to face her. "Good God, woman, you cannot wander about London like that."

She frowned. "Why not?"

"Why not? *Why not?* Because¼Because¼," he sputtered, then stopped, scowled, and took two steps closer. Then two more. To within arm's reach.

She fell back, but before she could turn and run, his hand whipped out and captured both the pendant and the key. The chain bit into the back of her neck. She was caught.

"Hey! Let go of that!" She took hold of the length of chain that wasn't in his large fist and tugged. Of course, he didn't release it.

"Where did you get this?" he growled.

Alarmed and angry, she tugged on the chain again. "None of your business."

He inched closer, towering over her. "It is very much my business."

She tilted her head back to look up at him. If he didn't look so threatening, he would have been quite handsome, with dark green eyes, straight nose, square chin, and strong jaw that was covered in a thick scruff. Hair, a bit unkempt and too long, the color of mahogany with light streaks, brushed his neck and fell across his brow. His shirt showed signs of hard wear, and dirt smudged one shoulder. He smelled sweaty, as if he'd been working out, with a trace of salty caramel, but, damn, that smelled good. Then she scolded herself for thinking such a thing because he could be a dangerous criminal. If he was involved in making a movie, he must have been playing a fugitive. But that was a fleeting thought amidst all the other thoughts that were flashing through her head, the loudest and most insistent being to get away as fast as possible.

"Why is it your business where I got the key and pendant?" she asked. Maybe if she kept him talking, he would be distracted enough to release his hold on the chain so she could escape.

At that moment, a skateboarder followed by a friend on roller blades sped past. They caught the stranger's attention. As they disappeared down the lane, he stepped off the grass to watch them zoom away and dragged Maggie at the end of her chain along with him.

He turned to her with a suspicious squint. "What manner of conveyance was that?"

Hadn't he ever seen a skateboard or roller blades? Where was he from?

Maggie opened her mouth to answer, but before she had the chance, the sound of a distant police siren pierced the air. He startled and froze, then as the noise faded into the distance, he glared at her.

"What was that confounded noise? A banshee? Are you a

witch?" he growled. "Have you conjured me into a nightmare?"

She stared in disbelief. "What? No! I haven't conjured you into anything!" Although the fact that he seemed to have fallen from the sky might be considered conjuring. But that was just crazy.

"Never mind." He tugged twice on the trinkets in his fist. "Where did you get this?"

"None of your business," she repeated, this time allowing annoyance to color her words, as she tried to pry open his fingers. "Let go of my necklace."

"*Your* necklace," he scoffed. "You have no right to it."

Was he deranged? On drugs? A thief? "I have every right."

"You do not." Anger darkened those green eyes.

"Why not?" Maggie was angry now, too, and her shock began to morph into fear.

"Because the key is mine." With another tug, he brought her up against his body.

Maggie was aware of two very distinct things. The stranger's body was hard and muscular. And she was suddenly and quite dizzyingly falling...spiraling down, as if she had stepped into a very, very deep, dark hole.

SMACK!

Simon Herrington, Marquis of Wildford, sucked air into his lungs and blinked. How in hell had he wound up on his back in the middle of a lane in Hyde Park with a very lovely woman sprawled on top of him? A woman who was wearing little more than his key on a chain around her neck. One minute, he was upright and confronting the young woman, whose curves, he noticed, fit very nicely against him. The next minute, he was falling through space and slamming into the earth on his back. How the devil had that happened?

That was the second time something very, very strange had occurred. The first had happened just moments before, as he had been silently raging against the fates that had put him in a prison cell. Between one blink and the next, he was falling through the air, bouncing through tree limbs, and landing on his face in Hyde Park. His brain was having trouble keeping up.

The woman squirmed and wriggled her way off him, jamming her knee against his privates in the process. He grunted in pain, but she gave no indication she realized what she had done. Instead, she hissed with annoyance.

"Let go," she demanded, as she tried to pry his fingers from his key.

Her face was only inches above his, caught as she was by the length of chain around her neck. He looked into her eyes, the same blue as the sapphire pendant hanging next to his key. Lovely eyes, surrounded by thick lashes, but at this moment, stormy eyes, because she was angry. A tiny beauty mark sat just at the corner of her left eye, as if the artist who created her had left his mark. Her dark hair was scraped back from her face and tied in a manner resembling a horse's tail and just as luxurious. The rest of her was quite delightful as well, for he had seen much, much more than was proper for the middle of Hyde Park. And he had felt her delicious curves when she landed on top of him. But he knew very well that an attractive exterior could hide an ugly, treacherous heart.

"I will not let go," he said quite equitably, considering she was most likely a thief. Or a witch. "You are in possession of a key that belongs to me."

Her eyes widened, then narrowed. "That's impossible. The key is hundreds of years old. It's an antique. My father had it in his shop for years before he gave it to me, just before —" Her words halted on a catch in her throat.

Something about her father upset her, but he put away that tidbit of information for later. Instead, he focused on the rest of her words.

"Hundreds of years old?" he scoffed. "Your father must have been mistaken. How did he gain possession of it? Was he a thief as well?"

Insult made her rear back to the length of the chain. "How dare you! My father was no thief!" She began to pummel his chest. "Let go of me, you weirdo!" Raising her head, she yelled, "Help! Help!"

Simon clapped his hand over her mouth. "Shush. I will not harm you."

Her cries didn't stop, but at least they were muffled. He ignored the blows she rained on his chest and ribs. The last thing he needed was to attract attention, especially from the authorities. He caught sight of a horse and rider far down the path, trotting in their direction. He didn't want to be seen, especially with a woman dressed in odd undergarments, and in their compromising position.

"If I release the chain, will you remain quiet?" he asked.

She stopped hitting him, studied him a moment, then nodded.

"Will you promise not to run away?" he pressed.

Her nod of agreement was much too quick, indicating she had no intention of remaining where she was.

He held back a sigh of exasperation. "I will not harm you. I just wish to straighten out this misunderstanding. Please, don't run away."

Her nod came more slowly.

Carefully, he unclenched his fist from around the key and pendant. She held very still, her eyes — those magnificent eyes — never leaving his face. Still not trusting that she wouldn't run, in a single, fluid motion, he rolled to his feet, wrapped his hand around her arm and pulled her up with him.

She tried to jerk away. "I said I wouldn't run."

"Sh," he warned, glanced down the path at the horse and

rider, then dragged her behind the huge oak. For some reason, he had the impression the tree was much larger and older when he had fallen through its branches and first encountered the woman. But he had just been pulled from his prison cell and tumbled through the air, so maybe he was mistaken.

The rider came abreast of the tree. "Wildford, is that you?"

Simon winced. He knew that voice. Brandon Connaught, a schoolmate, a friend, whom he hadn't seen in several years. If he remained behind the tree and didn't speak to him, the man would think he was giving him the cut. With a warning glance to the woman to remain hidden, he mouthed, *Stay here.* Then he stepped out from behind the tree while keeping a firm grip on the woman's wrist.

"Hello, Connaught," he said.

Connaught's eyes widened a bit at Simon's disheveled appearance, but instead of commenting on that, he said, "It's been years since I've seen you. Where have you been?"

Simon gave a casual shrug. "Doing a bit of the King's business. And you? Still fighting for your birthright?"

His friend's mouth ticked up at the corner. "All settled. A bit of bad business with my half-brother. The old man is dead. The title is mine."

"Congratulations. And condolences on your father's death." Simon suspected that his friend's brief sentences hid a great deal of drama.

"I have also taken a wife." A happy, smug smile creased Connaught's face.

Simon grinned. "I thought you had sworn off marriage."

"When the right woman appears, a man must submit to the inevitable," Connaught — now the Earl of Cranleigh — said with good humor.

At that moment, a large group of riders, both men and women, approached and surrounded the earl. Simon stepped back behind the tree. He had recognized several of the newcomers, but he didn't want to interact with them. One of them, he was sure, perhaps more, had been instrumental in his arrest. He needed to make a plan before he accused anyone of treason.

The woman peeked around the trunk of the tree, then glanced back at him. "Look at all those gorgeous costumes. Are you shooting a movie?" she asked, her eyes lit with excitement. "What's the title?"

"I'm not shooting at anything." He frowned at her very odd words and questions. "What is a moo-vey?"

She frowned back. "You're kidding, right? You don't know what a movie is?"

Simon heard the words, but most of them made no sense. Perhaps the woman was deranged and speaking gibberish. Or perhaps some spell was wound up in her odd way of speaking. Even so, he was not about to let her out of his sight until she turned over his key. Cranleigh and the other riders moved off, so he felt safe to emerge from hiding. Without answering, he pulled the woman in the direction of one of the exits from the park.

"Wait," she said, hanging back. "Where are you taking me?"

"Some place where we can come to an understanding about the ownership of my key," he said and dragged her along.

"It's my key," she argued, as she tried to pull from his grip. "And I'm not going anywhere with you. I have no idea who you are. You could be a rapist or a murderer."

Simon halted so quickly that she ran into him, then she immediately backed away as far as she could with his hand still wrapped around her wrist.

"I am neither a rapist, nor a murderer," he said tightly, deciding that the men he'd killed in the name of his king and country didn't count as murder. "My apologies for not introducing myself earlier. I am Simon Herrington, Marquis of Wildford." He executed an abbreviated bow, since he still had hold of the woman.

"Oh," she said, appearing a bit shocked. Then her eyes narrowed. "Of course you're a marquis. You play your role very well. You must have the lead in the movie."

There was that word again: *movie*. And she said he had the lead. Well, of course he did. He was leading her and they were moving — *movie* was how she pronounced it. Annoyingly, she did not introduce herself in return, nor nod acknowledgment of his introduction, or even extend a hand for him to bow over. Well, he did have hold of her wrist, so maybe extending a hand wasn't possible. But obviously, she was not a woman of quality. He didn't care. All he wanted was his key. If he had to, he would pay her an exorbitant amount for it, then send her on her way.

They came in sight of the road with its carriages and coaches and drays and riders on horses, and ladies shopping with their maids, and gentlemen making their way to their clubs, and delivery boys and messengers — all the usual traffic. The woman's reluctant steps halted abruptly. When he turned to see what the problem was, she was staring at the road.

"That's quite a movie set," she said.

He gazed at the scene before them as he tried to figure out what she was talking about. "Moo-vey set?"

"Yeah, you know, a fake background so the actors look like they're in a real place." She continued to stare at the road and its traffic as if fascinated.

"I assure you, there is nothing fake about the congestion of London," he said.

At that moment, a nightsoil man, out much too late in the morning with his odoriferous wagon, rolled by. The woman gasped and covered her nose and mouth. After watching the wagon a moment, she turned to him. Her cheeks had turned quite pale, her eyes wide with shock.

"Wha-Wha-What year is this?" she asked, her words barely above a whisper.

"1814," he said, curious why she wouldn't know that. And then she collapsed in a dead faint.

Like what you've read so far?
You can get
MISCHIEF WITH THE MARQUIS
Rogues Out of Time ~ Book 2
on Amazon by clicking or scanning the following QR Code:

Author's Note

When I'm writing, my characters feel completely real to me —and each one has their own story to tell, just as Emma mentions in *Entangled with the Earl*.

One such character is the enigmatic **Duke of Dunbary**, who appears in Chapter 21 to inform Brandon of his stepbrother's death. But Dunbary isn't just a messenger—he has his own romantic adventure with the delightful and clever **Jillian St. Clare.**

Of course, true love never runs smooth—especially when spies and secrets are involved.

Here's a little teaser:

Jillian St. Clare is wiggling her aching toes behind a potted fern at a society ball, when a tiny scroll flies into her empty shoe. A spy's secret message! Her troubles only get worse when a dashing gentleman asks her to dance. He's the notorious Duke of Dunbary and he wants the note. Can she trust him? Or will she lose herself to the duke's dangerous kiss?

You can read their story in

THE DUKE'S DANGEROUS KISS
On His Majesty's Secret Service ~ Book 2

Keep reading for a Free Preview...
Happy Reading,
Patricia

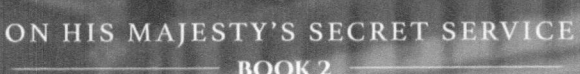

ON HIS MAJESTY'S SECRET SERVICE
BOOK 2

THE DUKE'S
Dangerous Kiss

PATRICIA BARLETTA

Free Preview 2

❧

THE DUKE'S DANGEROUS KISS
ON HIS MAJESTY'S SECRET
SERVICE SERIES ~ BOOK 2

LONDON, EARLY SPRING, 1812

She'd had enough. Enough socializing, enough dancing, enough gossiping. Jillian St. Claire was done. Her cheeks ached from smiling. Her feet hurt from standing. The little chair stuck in a corner of the ballroom behind a tall clump of potted greenery was a welcome sight. With a sigh of pleasure, she sank onto the brocade seat. She pulled at the ribbon ties of her dancing slippers, kicked them off, and wiggled her toes. Long, open windows next to her let in a refreshing breeze and cooled her flushed cheeks.

From where she sat, she could see nearly the whole ballroom without being seen. Before her, the dancers flowed together and apart like the colored designs in a kaleidoscope. The music and conversation washed over her, ebbing and flowing like the ocean waves on a beach. She had not wanted a season in London with the balls, the dinners, the salons, the visiting, but realized it was the only way to free herself from *him*. *He* was her guardian, and *he* had insisted on presenting her to society to find a suitable husband. Besides, it was what her mother had wanted for her, he told her. And so, she obeyed.

Male voices came through the open windows next to her from the veranda. All evening she had seen people escape to it—couples trying for a few secluded moments, gentlemen wanting a quiet conversation or pinch of snuff, ladies needing to revive themselves from the heat and dancing. The voices which came to her now were low, intense, not a conversational tone. Several potted evergreens outside the window screened her from the speakers. She caught the words *secrets* and *smuggle*.

"...little time before the Americans lose their patience," she heard a deep, male voice say. "I'm aware of what a confrontation with them would mean. Parliament seems determined to aggravate them. We cannot afford to fight both the Americans and Napoleon. Tell me about America's naval strength. How many ships? How large? How many guns?" The voice rumbled the questions, deep and demanding. Its tone sent a tiny thrill down Jillian's spine.

"Their navy is small but fearless," another man answered. "You know, of course, of their victory over the Barbary pirates."

"A hollow victory, at best." There was a shrug of dismissal in the first man's voice, as if he might have done better himself, single-handedly. "They were still made to pay ransom for the prisoners and tribute money."

"Not such a hollow victory," the second man disagreed. "The pirates don't harass their shipping any longer. The pirates have no wish to anger them again and receive another whipping. The Americans are arrogant on the sea. They don't follow the orders passed by the Privy Council. They trade with whomever they wish and smuggle where they are legally barred, including with France and her allies. They are angered by the impressment of their sailors into our navy."

Jillian was riveted, both by the information and that first man's voice. Who were these men? The exchange sounded more significant than a casual political discussion between two gentlemen.

"This is an explosive situation. Parliament still thinks of the Americans as our colonies, despite winning their independence. Is there anyone in their government who is against a conflict with England?"

"I intercepted a letter from one of the senators from Massachusetts to a senator who lives in Tennessee. He was urging his colleague to patience. Here is a copy of it."

"Adrian!" a third man exclaimed, interrupting the conversation. "I was just telling Harry about the horse you have running in next week's race."

Jillian saw a hand shoot through the greenery and drop a

tiny, tightly rolled piece of parchment. Instead of landing in the bush, it landed on the windowsill and bounced off into her shoe. It was smaller than her little finger and sealed with a bit of wax. Fascinated, she stared at it.

What secrets did it contain?

"Jillian St. Clare!" a voice hissed.

Wincing, Jillian tore her eyes away from the clandestine note and faced her chaperone.

"What are you doing here hiding by yourself? You should be mingling with the other young ladies and dancing with marriageable young men." The feather stuck in Lady Pennington's turban vibrated with indignation at finding her young charge shirking her social obligations. "Have you no gratitude, girl? Do you think his lordship spent that fortune at the modiste's for your new gowns to have you sit in a corner by yourself? And the time and energy I spent to teach you the proper behavior of a young woman entering society... Well, that is beside the point." Lady Pennington's glance fell on Jillian's unshod, stocking-covered toes. "Put on your shoes!" she gasped.

Jillian hurriedly stuck her feet back into her slippers and tied them. The tight little roll of parchment pressed beneath her toes. Ignoring the pain, she stood to avoid having the older woman's ample, violet-clad bosom in her face. "I'm sorry, Lady Pennington. I meant no harm," she said. "I only wanted to rest a few minutes."

"Hmph. Rest. Young people these days are so weak. Why, when I was your age—"

"Are you giving Lady Pennington trouble again, Jillian?" The hard voice of her guardian, the Earl of Rystoke, broke into the woman's tirade.

Jillian lowered her eyes to avoid looking into the cold, dark gaze of her guardian. "No, my lord, no trouble."

"Then why aren't you dancing? I did not bring you to London to hide behind the floral decorations." He flicked an offending leaf that had the audacity to brush the sleeve of his coat.

Jillian remained silent, wanting to disappear.

"Who is your partner for the next dance?" The earl raised an imperious brow.

Jillian panicked at the brusque request. She had no partner for the next dance.

"Partner?" she parroted to gain time to think. "I...ah... it's..." Rystoke's mouth thinned into an angry line.

Jillian paled before his cruel gaze. She was in trouble now. When they returned to the earl's townhouse, he would berate her for being ungrateful, foolish, stupid, and a host of other terrible things. Lady Pennington would look on without a word, her mouth pursed in the middle of her moon face. Jillian hated the earl. She hated Lady Pennington. Most of all, she hated her season in London.

"Um, it was..." She searched her brain for the name of some young man she had met.

"Don't you remember in that empty head of yours what young blood had asked for the next dance?" Rystoke's eyes narrowed dangerously. "You did have a partner for the next dance, did you not?" The earl did not bother to disguise his sarcasm.

"I believe the next dance is mine," a deep voice said from just beyond the tall group of plants.

Jillian stifled a gasp and peeked around the ferns. *That voice!* The same deep, velvety voice she'd heard through the open window demanding the secret information—the one that had riveted her attention and sent delicious thrills down her spine.

She had imagined the owner of that voice to be handsome, suave, dashing, and perhaps just a bit dangerous. The man who stood on the other side of the plants certainly fulfilled her expectations but seeing him in the flesh left her speechless. He was tall. His dark hair was tousled fashionably. His black evening clothes hung perfectly on his graceful, male frame. But what took her breath away and made her want to duck back behind the potted ferns were his eyes. They were not brown or black, the normal shade to match the man's coloring. They were not even blue, which would have been startling enough. Instead, they were the color of topaz. Jillian was reminded of the eyes of a lion she had seen at the Exeter 'Change in the Strand.

The orchestra was beginning the opening strains of the

next dance. "You cannot dance with Miss St. Clare," her guardian declared.

Jillian was amazed to hear a touch of nervousness in the earl's voice.

"Oh? Why is that?" the dark stranger asked.

"Because it is a waltz and she has not received permission." The earl's tone was smug.

"How delightful," the dark stranger commented. He held out a hand to Jillian. "I do so enjoy the waltz. I'm sure no one will mind if I break the rule just this once."

Jillian knew that he was referring to the rule that young ladies like herself who were just entering society were not supposed to dance the waltz. Before they were allowed to indulge in that scandalous behavior, they were to receive permission from the seven women from Almack's who were the caretakers of social convention. Breaking that rule tarnished the young woman's reputation. She had not yet been to Almack's Assembly Rooms, that temple of the social elite of London. Therefore, she had not been granted permission to dance the waltz, and certainly not with this total stranger.

Rystoke stepped between Jillian and the stranger. "*I* do not give my permission, sir."

The stranger dropped his hand and raised a cool eyebrow. "Really? And who are you, sir, to deny the young lady a dance?"

Veins stood out at the earl's temple. "You know very well who I am, sir. I also happen to be this young lady's guardian."

Amusement lit the stranger's eyes. "I never thought of you as the paternal type, Rystoke. I'm not sure the role suits you. Let us not create a scene. I promise not to abscond with her, and I'm sure the young lady would like to dance the waltz." He held out his hand again and smiled at her over her guardian's shoulder.

Jillian studied his hand. It was large, with long slender fingers. Calluses marked the palm and revealed that its owner practiced often with the sword. She had the feeling that this man broke the rules whenever he felt like it.

Propriety demanded that a proper introduction be made between a gentleman and a young lady before they conversed. To dance with a complete stranger was scandalous, and to dance the waltz... Well, that would shock the members of the ton down to the tips of their well-clad toes.

Jillian wanted to shock them. Most of all, she wanted to defy the Earl of Rystoke and Lady Pennington. Throwing away all caution, Jillian stepped forward and placed her hand into the stranger's, allowing herself to be drawn onto the dance floor. His warmth through her glove was surprisingly comforting. As she slipped past her furious guardian and the scandalized Lady Pennington, she flashed them a quick smile of triumph. Stepping onto the dance floor, she immediately felt her gloating turn to apprehension at what she had done. That little bit of rolled parchment squeezing beneath her toes reminded her why this stranger had invited her to dance.

"If we are to dance, perhaps we should exchange names," she managed to croak.

He smiled. "Isn't it more exciting to be mysterious? We are two strangers who will dance together, then part, never to meet again."

His statement conjured up romantic visions of star-crossed lovers in her head. But this man was not her lover. She did not even know his name. He was involved in something clandestine, maybe even treacherous. Perhaps she had been too eager to escape her guardian. The stranger's arm slipped around her waist, preventing her from fleeing. The heat and flex of his muscles through the sleeve of his coat made her much too aware of how dangerous he might be. Committed now to dance with this man, she placed one hand tentatively in his palm, and with the other she gathered up the small train of her gown. He pulled her closer into the embrace of the waltz, making her breath whoosh from her lungs. Although he held her lightly, as if she were a porcelain doll and quite breakable, his body exuded a restrained strength. As she dragged in a breath, she realized he smelled quite wonderful, like limes underscored by the scent of *him*. Shyly, she peeked up at him from beneath her lashes.

"I have never danced the waltz before, sir," she confessed breathlessly.

"It's quite easy," he said. "Count 1-2-3 in your head and follow my lead."

After a few experimental steps, Jillian found the dance was as easy as the handsome stranger said, even with her toes crowded by the tiny roll.

"I hope you won't think me too forward for agreeing to dance with you," she said.

"Not at all," the stranger reassured her. "If I were a young lady, I would have agreed to do almost anything to get away from Rystoke and that harridan of a chaperone. I despise the idea of parading young women about like race horses to match them up with a profitable husband."

Jillian's eyes flew to his face. "You heard through the windows," she gasped. It had not occurred to her that she could be overheard as well as the other way around. The amused glint in those startling topaz eyes made her lower her gaze. Staring straight at his snowy cravat, she said stiffly, "Thank you for your chivalrous gesture, sir, but you need not feel obligated to finish the dance. You have rescued the damsel in distress. As the knight-errant, you may now continue on your quest."

The stranger chuckled. "This knight-errant never leaves a damsel in the middle of a dance. Too many dangers lurk behind the potted plants."

"Such as conversations that are not supposed to be overheard?" Jillian asked rashly.

The stranger cocked his head in curiosity. "Such as?"

"Nothing," Jillian mumbled as she shook her head. She had said too much. Guessing that what she had heard and what now crowded her toes would somehow get her into trouble, she tried to break away from the man who held her. "Please excuse me," she began. "I must—"

"The dance is not over," the stranger said. His arm tightened about her waist. "Surely you would not embarrass me by leaving me in the middle of the dance floor?"

"I... No, of course not." Confounded and just a little frightened, Jillian fell silent and prayed the music would end quickly. The man's hold on her threatened her equilibrium. Her knees were shaking. Her head felt as though it were floating above the rest of her body. She never should have accepted his invitation to dance. Why was she so impulsive? It always got her into trouble.

"I seem to have lost something that I really must retrieve," the stranger said. "Perhaps you know of its whereabouts?" He gazed down at her with an intent expression.

Unnerved by the question, Jillian stumbled a bit and murmured an apology. Recovering the rhythm of the dance gave her a moment to think. Innocently, she asked, "What exactly did you lose, sir?"

"Nothing of much value to anyone else." He shrugged. "A bit of parchment."

"A note from a lover, perhaps?" she teased, pretending innocence. "Really, sir, if I were that lady, I would be most incensed upon hearing that you lost my gentle sentiments."

As he opened his mouth to respond, she heard the last strains of music. Not allowing the stranger to question her any further, she nimbly pulled free of his embrace, forcing him to escort her from the dance floor. But she could not escape that easily. His fingers curled about her elbow and held her fast.

"Keeping things that do not belong to you could prove to be very dangerous," he murmured.

Without answering, she broke away from him and sought refuge in the crowd. She avoided Pennington who glared at her from the other side of the room, and with relief, saw no sign of Rystoke. She sought out her friend, Phoebe Southwood, another young woman enduring her first season in London. She found the short, curvy brunette at the buffet table, about to select a cream puff from a tray of decadent pastries. Without apology, Jillian snatched the delicacy from Phoebe's fingers, and placed it on a corner of the table.

"What are doing?" Phoebe demanded. "That was to be my one indulgence this evening."

"Sorry," Jillian mumbled, knowing how much Phoebe liked sweets, then grabbed her friend's arm and dragged her toward the sweeping staircase which led to a gallery over-looking the ballroom. Phoebe sputtered her protest, but Jillian threw a pleading glance at her over her shoulder. Her friend tagged along in silence.

When they stood at the balustrade of the gallery, Phoebe

turned to her with a confused frown. "Whatever is the matter with you?"

"I just danced the waltz," Jillian announced breathlessly.

Phoebe's hazel eyes grew wide. "You did? Who was your partner?"

Jillian pointed to the tall, dark man who was leading a strikingly beautiful, pale blonde woman onto the dance floor. "Him."

Phoebe gasped. "*Him*? You danced the *waltz* with *him*?" She glanced from Jillian to the dance floor and back again. "Do you know who that is?"

Jillian shook her head as a hollow feeling opened in her stomach. Phoebe grabbed Jillian and pulled her close. "That," she whispered dramatically, "is the Duke of Dunbary." Jillian stared blankly at her friend.

"Haven't you heard of him?" Phoebe demanded. "He's only *the* most eligible bachelor in England. He's rich as Croesus. He might even be involved in smuggling. I've heard he goes through mistresses like that." Phoebe snapped her fingers to demonstrate. "He's been mentioned in connection with an *actress*." Her eyes widened at the scandalous idea. Then she turned to watch the dancers. "He hardly ever comes to these horribly crowded affairs. I wonder what he's doing here?"

Gathering secrets and being overheard, Jillian thought.

Phoebe gazed speculatively at Jillian. "I wonder why he asked you to dance?"

435

Jillian grinned at the unintended insult. "Why, because I am the most ravishing woman here." She tossed her head and imperiously stuck her nose in the air. She could not tell anyone, even Phoebe, why the duke had really asked her to dance.

Phoebe giggled. "Oh, Jill, I'm sorry. I didn't mean that. You are quite lovely, really. It's just that the duke has a mistress, and he usually takes to older women, like Lady Avingdon." She indicated the spot on the dance floor where the duke was dancing with the platinum blonde.

Jillian watched them. A sense of foreboding surged through her. If what Phoebe said were true, then she had to be careful. The duke had only danced with her to retrieve his secret correspondence. He was involved in something clandestine, and that made him dangerous. She did not think he would give up easily. He would pursue her until he had recovered what he thought was his. But that conversation she had heard through the window made her wary about returning the note to him. What if he was plotting something treacherous? What should she do?

Phoebe nudged her. "There's the Viscomte Pelham," she said, using her fan to point at a young man who was dancing with a lady who appeared to be his mother. "Isn't he just bang up to the mark?"

Distracted from her conundrum, Jillian focused on the dancers below and listened to Phoebe recount the viscomte's qualities. Later, she would decide what to do with the little note that had fallen into her shoe. And the disturbing, handsome man who seemed determined to retrieve it.

ADRIAN BENNETT, DUKE OF DUNBARY, EFFORTLESSLY followed the intricate patterns of the quadrille he was dancing with Diana, his mistress, who also happened to be one of his spies. She had arranged the meeting with his agent on the veranda, who had botched passing him the secret information. Diana usually held his complete attention, but at that moment, his thoughts were on the lovely young woman with whom he had just waltzed.

As the steps in the dance brought him beside Diana, her shrewd blue eyes gleamed. "Your mind is miles away, Adrian," she reproached. "Are you thinking about that bewitching girl you just danced with?"

"How could I think of anyone except you, Diana? You're more than enough woman for me," Adrian answered smoothly.

Diana gave a tiny sniff of disbelief. "I know you are getting bored with our arrangement, just as I am. Besides, it has always been dangerous for us to be intimate. If you wish to break off with me, just say so." The dance forced them apart.

When they came together again, he murmured, "The young lady in question is Rystoke's ward. I'm certain she has the information from my agent in her possession."

Diana drew in a breath as they moved away from each other once more. When they drew together again, she whispered, "Do you think she will pass the note along to Rystoke? He's a very strong supporter of the Orders in Council."

Adrian only had time for a discreet shrug before the dance ended, but he was more concerned than he'd let on. Rystoke had been his adversary for a very long time, and if the older man discovered what was contained in the secret correspondence, England's future could be threatened.

As he led Diana from the dance floor, Rystoke stepped in front of them, as if Adrian's thoughts had beckoned him.

Without even a perfunctory greeting, Rystoke said stiffly, "I will have you know, Dunbary, that I am very displeased with your conduct concerning my ward. I absolutely forbid you to have anything else to do with her. She is an innocent, and should not be subjected to the advances of men like yourself."

Adrian's brow lifted and a dangerous smile played about his lips. "Are you insulting me, Rystoke? If so, I shall have to call you out."

A flash of fear widened the man's eyes before it was replaced with icy disdain. "I have no wish to meet you on the field of honor," he said haughtily, "but be warned that I will make a suitable match for my ward despite any intrusion on your part."

"My dear Rystoke, I would never dream of intruding on your plans of marrying off your ward for whatever gains you are after." Bowing slightly, Adrian murmured his excuses and led Diana in the direction of the dining room.

"What an unpleasant man," she observed as they approached the buffet table.

"He has always been a disagreeable thorn in my side. It's a shame he is guardian to that lovely young lady."

Diana gave a throaty chuckle. "So she *did* make an impression on you."

Adrian smiled down into her twinkling blue eyes. "Mixing business with pleasure is never a hardship."

"I knew you would find someone to amuse you," Diana said with a grin.

As Adrian guided her to a small supper table, he realized that Rystoke's ward more than amused him. Her defiance of both her guardian and society's rules intrigued him. Her quick wit charmed him. Her gray eyes bewitched him. Her golden hair made him want to remove the pins to let it flow across his fingers. And her lithe body made his pulse race. He hoped he could coax her into returning the note. She had no way of knowing just how important the message was— how dangerously crucial to peace. He would have to keep things light the next time he saw her. And once the note was in his possession, he could indulge in the wicked pleasure of dancing with her again. The thought made him smile.

THE EARL OF RYSTOKE WATCHED HIS NEMESIS STROLL AWAY through the crowd with the blonde hussy on his arm. His hands clenched into fists as rage boiled up in him. He would not allow Dunbary to foil his plans. Even if he had to marry Jillian off sooner than he wished, he would not allow that devil near her. What the chit did after she said her vows was her own affair. But for now, her reputation would be as pure as snow. He would see to it, even if he had to lock her up. He sent Pennington off in search of Jillian. It was time they left. The girl was not performing as she should tonight anyway. Annoyance surged through him. How was she going to make an impression on prospective husbands by hiding behind potted ferns? Finally, they were in his coach and rolling down the drive. He turned his attention to his ward, who was huddled in the far corner of the seat across from him.

"Well, girl," he started, keeping his anger in check for the moment. "What have you to say for yourself?"

"I'm sorry, my lord." Jillian ducked her head.

"Yes, yes." He waved away her automatic apology. "But do you understand what you have done?"

Jillian gave a silent shake of her head. "A disaster," Lady Pennington intoned.

With a glance of exasperation at the woman, he turned back to the girl across from him. "There is to be no duplication of tonight's events in the future. Do I make myself clear?" Without waiting for her to respond, he went on, "Besides the fact that you openly defied me, you completely ignored the proper decorum for a young woman by dancing the waltz. I should beat you for your insolence." He leveled a hard gaze on her. To keep her on edge and pondering the error of her ways, he went on more mildly, "We will discuss this further at the house. Pennington will advise you on your mistakes before you retire for the night. That way, you will be able to think about them before you fall asleep and wake up in the morning with a renewed sense of propriety. Tomorrow evening we will be visiting Almack's, and God save you if you should make a *faux pas* there. As it is, I will have to do some very fast maneuvering to get those seven witches who control the place to forget tonight's events."

"Yes, my lord." Jillian's response was barely audible.

Rystoke turned from her and stared out the carriage window. If he had known the girl was going to be this much trouble, he never would have allowed her mother to talk him into becoming her guardian. In all the years that he had supported both the girl and her mother, he had not had very much contact with the chit. Occasional glimpses as she grew up had proved that her looks were acceptable enough, but he had no idea she was so rebellious. Only the promise of a profitable match for her kept him from tossing her into the street. Even that damnable paper her mother had tricked him into signing would not have kept him to the task of finding the girl a husband if he did not think the benefits would be satisfactory. His anger seeped away and a smile played about his lips. The benefits would be more than merely satisfactory. When the Laird of Ayton discovered what he was doing, it would destroy that pesky Scot. And that would be one less enemy he would have to worry about.

JILLIAN LAY IN BED AND STARED UP AT THE DARK CANOPY ABOVE her. The faint lines of the reverse side of the damask swam before her eyes. A sliver of moonlight cut between the drapes, across the small expanse of rug, and reflected in the cheval mirror on the far side of the room, lighting the space to dusk. It was a comfortable room, and she had been surprised when it had been assigned to her upon arriving in London. She had expected to be put in a tiny room under the eaves, although she supposed her guardian had to at least appear to be somewhat generous.

She had escaped another tongue-lashing from him, but had been forced to suffer through Lady Pennington's harangue about how irresponsibly she had acted this evening. The resulting gossip would turn her reputation from a pristine white to gray. Jillian did not care, except that she might have a bit more trouble finding a suitable husband and escaping from the earl. In fact, she had enjoyed dancing the waltz. What had made the experience disconcerting had been her partner.

She squirmed, not sure if her discomfort came from her rash behavior or the man who had guided her in the dance. The relaxed strength of the hand that had supported hers belied the restrained power of the arm about her waist. Instinct told her the Duke of Dunbary could be ruthless in getting what he wanted, that he was not a man to cross. And she had definitely crossed him this evening. Although he had been polite, his last words of warning had sent a chill chasing down her spine.

She lit the candle on the bedside table and pulled the secret message from beneath her pillow. Should she read it? What secrets did it contain?

She rolled the tiny bit of parchment between her fingers. The wax was not stamped with a seal, but marked only by a series of anonymous crosses. She slipped her thumbnail along the edge of the wax. No one would know if she took a peek. She unrolled the secret letter and began to read.

The writing was extremely tiny and filled the paper edge to edge, top to bottom. As she had overheard through the open window, the letter was an appeal to patience concerning the English Orders in Council. That was all it was. Nothing about war, nothing treasonous. Perhaps she had missed something.

She held the parchment closer to the candle flame and reread the letter. She gasped when she saw other writing appear, its lines running perpendicular to those already visible. She quickly pulled the paper away from the flame and waved it in the air to cool. But the parchment had not been damaged and the other writing remained, trailing off into invisibility. She realized the heat from the candle flame had revealed the secret writing. Carefully, she held the paper up to the flame again and passed it slowly back and forth. More writing appeared.

It was a message to the duke from his spy. The Americans were angry about the impressment of their sailors by the British and the Orders in Council, which required neutral ships to stop in an English port before trading with France or her colonies. Some northern Americans wanted to attack Canada to drive the English off the continent. Others in the south thought that taking over Spanish Florida would help because Spain was England's ally. A bargain was being discussed between the northerners and southerners to help each other with the plan.

Jillian's hand shook as she set the note down. This could only mean that America was very close to declaring war on England. The final sentence gave one ray of hope: that immediate concessions by Parliament concerning the Orders in

Council could prevent war and the loss of England's American territories. She held the future of England in her hands. But what was she to do? Should she give the letter to Rystoke, whom she did not trust? Or Dunbary, whom she did not know?

Her mother had taught her to trust few men. As the earl's ward, she had come to value that lesson. Jillian intended to hoard her information until she knew what to do with it. She had little knowledge of politics and less of spies. She'd grown up in relative seclusion on her guardian's estate in Northumberland, far from London where one could become well informed about national and international affairs. Now, she chafed at her ignorance. But she did know that England was already involved in a war with France, and becoming involved in another war would be disastrous.

Rising from her bed, she went to her writing desk and carefully rolled the piece of parchment up as tightly as before, sealed it with her own wax and stuck the original wax on top. She needed to hide the note. Her gaze fell on a rag doll her mother had made for her fourth birthday. Besides her clothes, it had been the only personal possession she had brought to London from the country. If she sewed the secret letter inside, no one would ever suspect its hiding place. She collected her sewing basket and set to work, snipping at the seam down the doll's back, stuffing the note inside, and then skillfully resewing the seam. Turning the doll over, she smoothed back its red-woolen locks.

A tear slipped from her eye. She would turn nineteen tomorrow, her first birthday since her mother's death ten months earlier. She swiped the tear away. The day would be hard to live through with no little birthday surprises from her mother, no special meal or sweetmeats. All she had to look forward to was a visit to a solicitor to receive one last message from her mother. And an evening at Almack's Assembly Rooms with her guardian.

Jillian wondered if the Duke of Dunbary with his wild reputation was accepted by the seven lady patronesses who ruled Almack's invitation list. She fervently hoped he was not. She did not want him asking in that smooth, deep voice what she had heard through the window. She did not want to reveal to him that she had his secret letter. He was dangerous and made her feel strange. Those topaz eyes seemed to bore into her. As much as she wanted to irritate her guardian, even she would not be foolish enough to be seen again with a man such as the Duke of Dunbary. Yet, she had to admit to herself, that one dance had been very exciting.

Like what you've read so far?
You can get
THE DUKE'S DANGEROUS KISS
On His Majesty's Secret Service Series ~ Book 2
on Amazon
by clicking or scanning the following QR Code:

About the Author

Patricia Barletta is an award-winning author of historical and paranormal romance. A former teacher of British Literature at an all-girls high school, Patricia later earned a Master of Fine Arts in Creative Writing from Stonecoast at the University of Southern Maine.

She is the author of *The Auriano Curse*, a four-book "romantasy" series set in late 18th-century Europe, and *On His Majesty's Secret Service*, a three-book historical spy-romance series set in Regency England. In addition, she has written three stand-alone historical romances set across various time periods. Patricia has published both traditionally with Kensington Books, writing under the pen name Amy Christopher, and independently under her own name. She is currently working on an exciting new three-book time-travel historical romance series.

Patricia's work has garnered numerous accolades, including the 2016 Colorado Romance Writers Award of Excellence, the 2016 Gayle Wilson Award of Excellence, and the 2018 New England Reader's Choice Award. A passionate historian, she resides in a century-old house in Mass-achusetts, designed by an architect to resemble a Belgian cottage. Her home was even featured in *Smaller Houses of the 1920s* (Dover Edition) by Ethel B. Power.

Patricia loves to hear from readers. You can contact her at patricia@patriciabarletta.com

Sign up for Patricia's Newsletter for updates on new releases, contests, giveaways, promotions, and more...
by clicking or scanning the following QR Code:

Complete Book List

PATRICIA BARLETTA

THE AURIANO CURSE SERIES

Moon Dark

Moon Shadow

Moon Bright

Moon Gold

ON HIS MAJESTY'S SECRET SERVICE

(Duke Spy Series)

The Duke Who Loved Me

The Duke's Dangerous Kiss

Confessions of a Dangerous Duke

ROGUES OUT OF TIME SERIES

Entangled With the Earl

Mischief with the Marquis

Dallying with the Duke

www.ingramcontent.com/pod-product-compliance
Lightning Source LLC
Chambersburg PA
CBHW020459260626
47156CB00006B/1783